A HANDFUL OF DUST

Recent Titles by Tessa Barclay from Severn House

A BETTER CLASS OF PERSON
FAREWELL PERFORMANCE
A HANDFUL OF DUST
A LOVELY ILLUSION
THE SILVER LINING
STARTING OVER
A TRUE LIKENESS

A HANDFUL OF DUST

Tessa Barclay

This first world edition published in Great Britain 2004 by
SEVERN HOUSE PUBLISHERS LTD of
9–15 High Street, Sutton, Surrey SM1 1DF.
This first world edition published in the USA 2004 by
SEVERN HOUSE PUBLISHERS INC of
595 Madison Avenue, New York, N.Y. 10022.

British Library Cataloguing in Publication Data

Barclay, Tessa
A handful of dust
1. Crowne, Gregory (Fictitious character) - Fiction
2. Missing persons - Investigation - France - Avignon - Fiction
3. Detective and mystery stories
I. Title
823.9'14 [F]

ISBN 0-7278-5919-6

Typeset by Palimpsest Book Production Ltd.,
Polmont, Stirlingshire, Scotland.
Printed and bound in Great Britain by
MPG Books Ltd., Bodmin, Cornwall.

One

Liz Blair gave a little shriek and sat back hard in her chair. 'Thrushes?' she cried. 'The pâté is made from thrushes?'

'So the menu says. *Pâté de grives à la Provençale.*'

She studied the face of her companion to see if it was a joke. The waiter hurried up – any excuse to lean close to the pretty *Anglaise*. '*Problème?*' he enquired.

She looked to the Prince von Hirtenstein for help. He explained that the young lady was concerned about the thrush pâté. 'Oh, I assure you, of the very best,' the waiter gushed. 'From thrushes killed in an October hunting trip. Cooked with champagne – and then kept very cool, not frozen, you may be sure of that, because nothing harms a pâté so much as to be frozen in the glass.'

Greg translated all this for his best beloved, who continued to look appalled. 'I'm not eating thrushes,' she said. 'And if you order it, I'm moving to another table.'

'My angel,' he soothed, 'you know I'm a music lover. How could I eat a songbird?'

The waiter stood by, baffled by the conversation but happy enough to breathe in the perfume the young lady was wearing – L'Air du Temps, if he wasn't mistaken. Good sense when it came to scent even though she seemed to have odd ideas about food. But, of course, the English . . . Monsieur, however, was not English. And though his French was perfect, he wasn't local. Yet it seemed he was to some slight extent familiar. As if perhaps he'd appeared on *le téléjournal*, or had his picture in *Hello!*

If asked his name the gentleman would probably have said he was M Couronne. In England and other English-speaking countries he was Mr Crowne. In Germany he was Herr Krone, in Italy Signor Corona, and so on wherever his work as a concert arranger might take him. To announce himself as the ex-Crown Prince Gregorius von Hirtenstein usually meant one of two responses – either an embarrassing servility or a cross shrug of resentment.

He and his companion had been very late coming in for lunch and the waiter had been on the verge of saying the chef had gone home. But they were a good-looking pair – she slender, chic, fair with long wavy tendrils framing the intelligent face, he tall, spare, his glance rather cool from dark-grey eyes. Altogether quite an ornament to the restaurant should any other passer-by think of coming in. And there was a bottle of red that had breathed but which no one had ordered, and plenty of the *daube* left.

It was hard trying to be a vegetarian in rural France. In Paris, yes – especially among the smart restaurants catering for the model girls of the fashion industry – there it was possible to order a vegi-burger with ease because the restaurant owners understood that these skinny young women were thinking about their figures. And, though only a fashion buyer and not a model, Liz had a care about what she ate.

But in Provence you thought about your appetite, not your figure. Liz was beginning to discover that hereabouts you had to order what the caterers considered only the trimmings of the meal – *aïoli* served over potatoes, or *tian*, which was a casserole of rice and vegetables baked deliciously with cheese. Liz was in fact only a semi-vegetarian, and so would have eaten the restaurant's fish dish, except that it had gone off the menu by this time, but nothing, *nothing* would have tempted her to eat little garden birds. And anyhow it was such a cool day she was happy to accept the *soupe du jour* as a starter.

A January day. Although she was accustomed to very chilly days in Paris for the dress shows, she'd somehow thought that the sunny south would be warm – and so it was, of course, much warmer than London. Greg had warned her to bring a sweater or two for this short break, and she'd partially taken his advice. She was clad in beige Capri pants, black socks and trainers, a knitted silk jersey and a black button-up cotton jacket. The waiter thought she looked delightful.

By contrast, Gregory von Hirtenstein, known during his

travels in France as Grégoire Couronne and to Liz as Gregory Crowne, looked quite citified. He'd come to meet her straight from an office in Avignon where he was, as usual, involved in putting on a concert of classical music for the Winter Festival. Avignon was a city where the businessmen liked to look tidy and expected co-negotiators to look likewise.

On the rare occasions when His Serene Highness figured in the newspapers – at the wedding of some minor royal, perhaps, or awarding prizes at a music academy – readers might take it for granted that he was living a life of ease on some family fortune. Or that a state somewhere gave him a substantial pension. Nothing of the kind.

The Communist Party of Hirtenstein had run his mother, his father and his grandmother out of the country in a belated revolution. Recently it had been replaced by a government of technocrats who seemed to be in process of making Hirtenstein the call centre of the world. But there was no thought of returning the royal family's property. So ex-King Anton continued to make his living by teaching equestrian skills on a little farm just outside Geneva, ex-Queen Mother Nicoletta decorated the homes of rich people in Switzerland and elsewhere, and the heir to the non-existent throne made a happy career out of classical music.

And was in love with a girl his grandmother totally disapproved of. A commoner, a girl who didn't even *design* clothes but copied the designs of others and sold them to chain stores. An absolutely unsuitable girl, declared Grossmutti, though she'd never met Liz.

Hence these stolen days at a distance from ex-Queen Mother Nicoletta. Provence was too far for her to make her disapproval felt.

'So what's she like, this girlfriend you're meeting this evening?' Liz enquired, Very casual. But to tell the truth she was intensely curious and more than a little jealous. She was sure she herself was the woman in Greg's life, yet she didn't relish the thought of a rival.

'She's not a girlfriend. She's not a girl, from my viewpoint. She's just someone I know.'

'Oh, really? Who somehow manages to be in romantic Provence while you're here?'

'She's here on business. She's looking into what she calls "funny business" in the world of music.'

'What, bribes for playing Bach? Cheques for promoting Tchaikovsky?'

He laughed. 'What's on offer for playing Shostokovitch?'

'You got me! Those are the only two composers I know, practically. Oh, there's Beethoven, but I already used Bach. But that's not the point. Funny business usually means money. And I thought there was no money to be made in the classics?'

'Alas, only too true,' he agreed with mock solemnity. 'I was just reading the *Culture* section of *Le Monde*, a page headed Music, and do you know what it was about? Bach? Beethoven? No, it was all about *les raves, les free-parties, musique électronique, le techno hardcore.'*

She was enjoying her soup but swallowed quickly so as to reply. 'Now I could understand if there was "funny business" there. There's a lot of hype in the pop world.'

'Hype! That's the word I was looking for. That's what Barbara is looking into.'

'There's hype in classical music?' She gave him a disbelieving look.

'Of course there is. Your Sir Thomas Allen was speaking about it a little while ago.'

'Sir who?'

'Thomas Allen. Your great baritone. One of the best Dons I ever heard.'

'Are you speaking in tongues?' asked his beloved in bewilderment. 'First it was "*raves*", whatever they are, and now it's Dons, and that's a football team – I think.'

'A football team?' He paused, seeing they were heading for a quagmire, which sometimes happened because, though his English was excellent, he wasn't always clued in about tabloid culture. 'Thomas Allen sang Don Giovanni in the opera of the same name. *Raves* are raves, which I gather are parties where people jump about in a barn or a garage or something, to the accompaniment of sounds I'd find distressing.'

'And where does hype come into it?'

'Some of the advertising for recorded music. Young women

who play as a string quartet, photographed wearing wet T-shirts . . .' His strong, rather long fingers traced shapes in the air.

'What's wrong with that? As long as they have the figure for it.'

'But, Liz, playing music has nothing to do with how you look. Some of the greatest singers in the world are like barrage balloons.'

'Yeah, and that's what's wrong with opera,' she retorted. 'But if you've got the figure, why not flaunt it?'

'Oh, come on. Imagine a symphony orchestra with all the women in wet T-shirts.'

She began to laugh and almost choked on her last spoonful of soup. While the waiter removed their plates she recovered. She said, 'But this sounds a bit thin to me. Coming all the way to Avignon to talk to you about the publicity pix for a few up-market recording stars. I begin to think this woman fancies you.'

'Nonsense.' The thought had never even occurred to him, and it still didn't seem likely. Although, now he came to think of it, it did seem strange that Barbara should come all the way from London to discuss money and music. 'She's a journalist,' he went on, anxious to put the record straight. 'You must know her, surely – Barbara Rallenham, writes for the *Clarion*?'

'What, Rally – "Rally's Round-Up" – that one?'

'That's the one. She told me she thinks there's a story in the cash that's changing hands to get certain performers into the classical top ten.' He paused. It didn't sound altogether convincing, since, from what he knew of her career, she was mostly famous for going after politicians and directors of companies and other big guns.

'So who's here in Provence that she's targeting?'

'Well . . . er . . . I'm not sure, she didn't fill me in on that. But of course there are a lot of people here for the festival.'

Avignon puts on a festival of music every winter, to help stretch the tourist season. It begins in late autumn and runs until spring, with diminishing frequency of events until the influx of the early-summer holidaymakers. There are seasons, too, at Grenoble, Toulouse and Nice. Among the rich and famous who have villas in the South of France there are of course music lovers. Or if they don't love music, they love the idea of showing off their evening clothes, the women adding a few diamonds. And if people from the lower income groups like to come along and listen to the performances too, that always helps to fill the hall.

Gregory Crowne had several recitals and concerts going on. He usually arranged a series every year, minor events but rewarding both financially and morally. They were a chance to present music less often heard, or to introduce a new performer. Among his artistes this current year he had a young baritone from the town where he and his family lived, Geneva. It pleased him to promote a fine new voice and to do something for the prestige of the Swiss, who are usually thought of, alas, as a stodgy lot. But only by those who had not heard Robert Jäger singing love songs . . .

Somewhere among the audiences that came to the events, Barbara Rallenham apparently thought there was a subject for one of her famous exposés. She called the process 'digging the dirt', and she wrote in a racy, easily understood style.

'She asked me to have a drink after the recital tonight and give her some background,' Greg now explained to Liz. He hesitated. 'You can come too, if you like.'

'Nah,' Liz said inelegantly. 'If she's really going to do a column, she won't want an outsider listening in. I see they've got a James Bond film on at one of the cinemas. I'll go to that.'

'It'll be dubbed into French,' he warned. Liz could speak enough to get by, particularly in the fashion world. But whether she would understand the fast-paced jargon of espionage and criminality, he doubted.

'Never mind,' she teased. 'He's just so gorgeous to look at.'

'Hmm. It would be better if you stayed in the hotel room and read a good book.'

'Better for whom?' But she kissed a finger tip and leaned across the table to tap him on the nose.

She did, indeed, stay in their room for part of the evening, but only after a long wander among the fashion boutiques of the city. Fashion was her business and her hobby. She particularly studied the accessories in the shop windows, translating the prices from euro to pound, occasionally making a sketch on the back of an envelope. Part of her job entailed arranging displays of ready-made clothes in fashion departments throughout the country. It was useful to have suggestions for how to enhance them.

She had a snack at a bistro then went to the hotel where she was sharing Greg's room. She found a show on television which seemed to be a French version of *Fame*, and settled down to watch. Greg, she knew, would be back about eleven. The performers he was watching over this evening were a group of young wind players, and their part in the programme was due to end at nine thirty. Give him half an hour to tell them they'd all been great and see them off to their digs, then an hour or so in a bar with the scandal-chaser, and he ought to be coming in looking tired by eleven.

But eleven o'clock came and he didn't turn up. Eleven thirty and she was cross. Eleven forty-five and she was jealous. Midnight and she was worried, wondering whether she should do something about it. She tried calling him on his mobile but there was no response – unsurprisingly, she realized, when she noticed it lying on the dressing-table. Mobiles are unwelcome at performances of classical music.

She looked at the digital clock blinking by the bedside. Twelve ten. She was really going to do something. She'd go to the hall and ask. She put on her jacket and was reaching out for the door handle when the card key whispered in the lock and the door opened.

'Darling!' she exclaimed, and threw herself on him. 'What on earth have you been doing?'

'Waiting,' he said in a vexed tone.

'Waiting? She stood you up?'

He sighed, then went to the little fridge. 'I need a drink.'

'But weren't you meeting her in a bar – you said for a drink?'

'No, she said she'd come to the hall. I explained I had to look after Lucius and his group, and she said great, she'd meet me there, it was easy to find, you know – she doesn't know the town. So I congratulated Lucius and Marcel and so on, and they went off to celebrate their success—'

'Was it a big success?' she asked, to show an interest.

'Oh yes, a full house, but of course they're all local players – well, that doesn't matter, I hung about in the foyer until the concert ended, and then I hung about outside, and then I thought I'd ring her hotel, but realized I didn't bring her card with me.' He went to look for it on the dressing-table. 'Dammit, here it is. Well, I'm not going to ring now, it's too late.'

'If this is the way she goes on, she can't keep many friends.'

'It's unlike her,' he countered. 'She's very well organized as a rule, but then she doesn't speak much French, and in a strange town . . . Perhaps I ought to ring and make sure she's okay—'

'No, no,' soothed Liz. 'You've had enough anxiety for one night. Ring in the morning. What you need is a nice relaxing shower and then a nice relaxing drink.'

So the inconsiderate Ms Rallenham was forgotten until quite late the next day. By the time they'd convinced themselves it was time to get up, she didn't seem very important. They went down to the little hotel restaurant to drink coffee, eat croissants and plan their day. There was no performance for Greg to worry about, although a Hungarian violinist was due to arrive and must be met at Nice airport. They therefore decided to spend the day in Nice.

Greg had brought his car to Avignon, so they drove in the elegant old Mercedes, looking out over the winter landscape as they went. It was bright, clear weather, still not cold by British standards. The vines stood in their forlorn rows, like school children waiting to be called in to their lessons. They passed quiet farms, villages where the house-doors still stood open and where flowering plants still graced the window-sills.

'Glorious,' sighed Liz. 'I don't know why you were so bothered about bringing warm clothes.'

'Just you wait. If the mistral starts to blow, you'll be glad of a sweater. Two sweaters, in fact.'

'Oh, the mistral, I've heard of it, it's a wind that makes you feel poorly or something.'

'And can bring snow, which covers the palm trees along the esplanades.'

She shrugged. She'd heard these yarns about snow-covered palm trees but never really believed them. 'Well, if the mistral blows I'll spend my time in the boutiques. I'm looking forward to some shopping in Nice—'

'If you think I'm going to lurk in the background while you try on dresses, think again, my love.'

'You can go and have a drink. Or perhaps there's an afternoon concert you could go to.'

'Liz, we didn't decide on spending the day—' He broke off. She was teasing. 'Well, all right, there's an organ recital in one of the churches . . .'

Laughing, she put an arm around him to give him a hug. She promised not to go dress hunting.

It was only when they were finishing lunch that he remembered he should have rung Barbara Rallenham at her hotel before setting out.

'Do it now while I pay the bill,' she suggested. It was their habit to share expenses for, truth to tell, her income was greater than that of the ex-Crown Prince.

He had a phone card, so used that rather than his mobile. He came out of the cubicle in the foyer looking irritated. 'She seems to have gone out. Left no message for me, apparently – though the young man on the desk there is hardly a paragon of efficiency.'

'Where is she? At the Angleterre?'

'No, she's in some little place a few miles out of town. Heaven knows why, because I think the newspaper pays all her expenses.'

'Maybe she's the kind that likes a bit of peace and quiet when she gets the chance.'

'I never would have thought so. She's a . . . now what's the expression? A go-getter, is that what I mean?'

'Likes to be in the thick of things.'

'Yes, and full of energy. A little thing, you know, smaller than you in height but plump and rather pink-cheeked and rosy.'

'Do you mean she's cuddly?' she asked with menace in her voice.

'Ah. I've never wanted to embrace her, if that's what you're asking. No, she is not cuddly. And though she's old enough to have decided on her *genre*, she's not good with clothes. You'd want to take her in hand and re-dress her.'

'Well, that's all very satisfactory,' Liz remarked. 'She sounds as if she's no threat to me, and as far as you're concerned she's a dead loss. So let's forget her.'

'*D'accord*.'

They went out for a walk through the streets of Nice, busy even out of season, visited the Musée Dufy because Liz adored his airy style, then spent time on the places that she really wanted to visit – the department stores in the Nice-Étoile. In the evening they collected the Hungarian violinist. And so their day ended, and the next began, and soon it was Monday of the following week.

They were sitting in a popular bar a few doors from their hotel over a cup of coffee and a baguette to see them through in lieu of dinner. A young woman came hurrying straight towards their table.

She was clad in a short skirt of pale-pink suede topped by a little jacket of improbable pink fur. Her legs were by no means slender but they were shown off by tights patterned in light grey and black. Her hair was a mass of tight black ringlets which hung about her face like unravelled wool. Her face was saved from being uninteresting by very clever make-up – eyes enlarged by eye shadow and lashes lengthened by mascara, lips filled out to a pout with lip-enhancer, the rather plump cheeks made more oval by shadowing under the cheek-bones.

Could this be Barbara Rallenham? If so, she'd found a *genre* that made her attractive to men, because those in the bar were entranced by her. As she passed some of them made little kissing sounds to themselves.

But no, she couldn't be Barbara, because Greg was staring at her with no sign of recognition as she approached.

'You're this Gregory Crowne?' she demanded angrily as she reached them

He stood. 'Yes, and you are . . . ?'

'I'm Mandy Rallenham, and what I want to know is, what have you done with my sister?'

Two

The only response to this astonishing question had to be a stunned silence. Then Greg, still standing, twitched a vacant chair from a nearby table and said politely, 'Do sit down.'

This wasn't what the newcomer had expected. She crumpled into the chair. The confrontation she'd been keyed up for melted into a row of tears on the thickened lower lashes. The prince signalled the barman and mouthed, 'Cognac.' Liz took one of Mandy Rallenham's hands in both of hers and murmured a soothing, 'There, there.'

The brandy came. Ms Rallenham was persuaded to sip a little, bit her lip, and returned to the attack in a less aggressive style. 'Where is she? What's happened to her?'

'Nothing, as far as I know,' Greg said. 'What makes you think something's happened?'

'Because she hasn't been in touch, that's why! She rang me to say she'd arrived OK and give me her hotel number and so on, but that was Wednesday and since then, nothing!'

'Perhaps she's been busy,' Liz suggested.

'No, no, you don't understand – we always keep in touch. Almost every day, and certainly she'd have rung on Saturday – Saturday was my *birthday* and she never misses that!'

'You've tried ringing her?'

She gave him a glance that said 'Are you a moron?' 'Of course I've tried! But there's no answer on her mobile, and the hotel says she's moved out. So where is she?'

Greg looked at Liz, and she looked at him. 'I've no idea,' he confessed. 'She was supposed to meet me Friday evening at the Salle Dubois, but she never turned up.'

'So did you ring her?'

'She'd sent me a business card with her hotel phone and

her mobile but I didn't have it with me then.' He couldn't help feeling a bit guilty as he went on 'I rang the hotel next day and they said she was out. I left a message.'

'And did she get back to you?'

'Well . . . no.'

'So what else did you do?'

'Well, nothing.'

Words seemed to tremble on the tip of her tongue but she held them back, taking instead another reviving sip of the brandy.

Greg enquired, 'How did you know where to find me?'

'Oh, God, it's taken me hours! She'd talked about you and said she was meeting you at some little hall, so I got a concert list at the Tourist Office and saw your name as the arranger for a thing at this Salle Dubois, and went there, but there's nothing happening there tonight, but the ticket office told me your hotel, so I went there, and the lady at the desk said you were probably at this café.' She hesitated before adding, 'She said you were tall and wearing a brown jacket. She said you were with a fair-haired lady. I thought . . . I thought it might be Babs.'

Tears flowed again. Liz patted her and made comforting sounds. Greg was silent. After a few minutes the tears stopped and Liz said, 'Come on, let's go to the ladies and mop you up.' The two women rose. Liz gave Greg a half-smile that said, 'We'll sort it out.'

He felt in his jacket pocket for the business card with the telephone number of Barbara Rallenham's hotel. But, confound it, it was on the dressing-table again.

He'd more or less dismissed Barbara from his mind when she failed to contact him with any apology for not turning up. After all, she was a responsible person, a forty-year-old journalist with plenty of character – if she decided not to bother with him, that was up to her.

For himself, he'd had other things to worry about – a temperamental violinist who wanted to change his published programme, and who later got drunk at the airport before being helped aboard his flight home. And a piano tuner who didn't keep his appointment to attend to the piano hired for the baritone's recital. And so on.

But all the same, the sense of duty inculcated in him by his formidable grandmother made him feel he should have done more about Barbara. After all, she was in a strange country, where she didn't speak the language to any great degree. He should have made sure she was all right. Of course she *was* all right. She'd probably changed hotels. Not every establishment suits the guest. She'd checked out and gone elsewhere.

But without leaving word of her whereabouts? Not even a message for her sister?

The sister returned looking more in command of herself. She'd tidied back the woolly ringlets so that her features were more visible, and mopped up the running mascara. Although flushed with the recent tears, she was still attracting favourable attention from the male occupants of the bar. Cuddly – Liz had asked if Barbara Rallenham was cuddly.

No, not Barbara. But the sister had a high cuddle quotient.

'Mandy says it's quite unlike Babs to get out of touch like this,' Liz announced. The diminutive versions of the names were to tell him that they were now on terms of friendship. 'As you'd expect, Babs travels a lot in her job but *never* fails to contact Mandy every day or two.'

'And my birthday especially,' Mandy put in, sounding childishly hurt. 'She never misses my birthday. You know, she's older than me by quite a bit, she sort of helped bring me up when our parents died, and she . . . she . . . Well, it's just not like her.'

'I see.'

'When nothing came in the post on Saturday, not even a card, I was shattered because she never forgets. I had to go out Saturday night – I had a client – but all next day I was trying her mobile and then last night I . . . sort of panicked, I suppose, and I just made up my mind that today I'd be in Avignon and I'd find her.'

'And she needs help now, Greg, because she's just been telling me she doesn't speak French.'

He gave an inward groan at this but said nothing. Liz, who was so attuned to him that she almost heard the groan, ploughed on. There was something she had to clear up, in case he got the wrong impression about the Saturday-night client – particularly considering Mandy's dress style and the way the men were watching her. 'Mandy's a make-up consultant,' she said. 'It sounds absolutely fascinating, she goes out to famous people's houses before a party or something, and does up their faces for them, and she does body painting—'

'Tattoos?' he asked, surprised.

'No, no, it washes off,' Mandy said with something of a superior smile. 'But you see, though we keep in constant touch, Babs and I live entirely different lives, so I don't always know exactly what's she's got going, and to tell the truth I thought you were her latest boyfriend.' She hesitated, and the flush on her rounded cheeks became deeper. 'I apologize for the way I came at you when I got here. I see now I'd . . . well . . . you know.'

He nodded. Liz, looking down at her plate, said, 'These baguettes look a bit frayed. I'm sure Mandy could do with something to eat, she's been travelling practically all day. Let's order, shall we?'

When that was done, Greg returned to the matter in hand. 'Do you plan on staying?' he asked Mandy.

'Oh, of course. Until I find out what's been going on.'

'No problem. We'll get you a room at our hotel, I know there are vacancies. So let's think what else to do.' He paused. 'You thought I was . . . er . . . her latest boyfriend?'

'Well, yes.'

'She has men friends? I mean, she develops new relationships from time to time?'

'From time to time.'

'So might not that be the answer? She's found a new man.'

'No, no!' Mandy cried, shaking her head so that the black ringlets jounced. 'She'd have told me! She's not . . . what I mean is, she doesn't have all that many . . .' She paused then burst out, 'She's – she's quite old-fashioned in a lot of ways. Sort of twin-set and pearls. So when she falls for someone, it's quite important, and she always talks to me about him.'

'But perhaps she's been swept off her feet,' Liz offered. 'Hasn't come up for air yet.'

Mandy looked almost scornful. 'She's not the sweep-off-the-feet kind. You know her, Mr Crowne. She notes every appointment in her organizer and can produce a receipt for every item in her expense account. Does that sound like someone who'd dash off with some stranger?'

He thought it quite possible, but didn't say so. Liz said, 'So what should we do?'

'Tell me the hotel number, Mandy. I'll ring and see what I can find out.'

He thought it wise not to make the call on his mobile within hearing of the sister. Who knew what he was going to be told? So he went out to the entrance of the bar. But the receptionist at the hotel had nothing exciting or abnormal to report.

'Yes, monsieur, Mlle Rallenham checked out on Saturday afternoon.' He could hear her tapping at computer keys. 'There are no special notes, and we have no mail for her or anything of that kind.'

'Did she say where she was going?'

A pause while she tried to be helpful. 'Back to England, I presume, monsieur.'

'But she had business in Avignon. Surely she had booked for a longer stay?'

'Well, yes, but guests often change their minds, after all.'

'Did she say what flight she was taking?'

'Oh, I didn't speak to her, I'm afraid. I'm not on duty at weekends.'

Mandy was turned to watch for him when he came back from the foyer. He shook his head. 'She simply paid her bill and left.'

The food they'd ordered had arrived. Time was getting on. Greg had a rehearsal to go to, a local choral group putting the finishing touches to some songs by Passereau.

'Should we go to the police?' Liz asked, sensing that decisions must be made.

He would have said no, but Mandy seized on it. 'Yes, that's it, if the hotel is keeping something back they can question them. Yes, let's do that.'

'I'll go with you,' said Liz. This was to let Greg off the hook. He gave her a look of gratitude then suggested they should eat up and get out. He walked them to the Place Pie then hurried on past the silent market halls to his rehearsal.

The singers had become discouraged by the rigorous simplicity of the sixteenth-century songs. The next two hours were hard work, a tightrope walk between telling the chorus master he was trying too hard and encouraging the choir to give their voices full throat. He got back to the Hotel Glaneur very tired but cautiously hopeful.

Liz was awaiting him with a glass of wine at the ready. 'How was it?'

'It will be all right on the night,' he said. 'Isn't that what theatre directors say when they've done all they can?'

'As bad as that, eh? Well, Mandy and I didn't do any better.'

'I'm sorry.' He drank half the glass at a gulp.

'We couldn't get them to take us seriously,' she complained. 'They asked how old was Barbara, and when we told them forty-one and divorced, they smiled and said we should just wait and all would be well.'

'They think she's found a lover.'

'Yes. And it made Mandy furious, so in the end they almost threw us out.'

'How is she?'

'Zonked out. She's in a room a couple of doors away, she practically fell into bed before I could get her shoes off.' She shook her head in recollection. 'This business has really shaken her up. She got so angry at the police station she tried to hit the sergeant.'

'I should have gone with you,' he sighed.

'No you shouldn't. The cops are probably right, it's just that the buttoned-up older sister has undone a button or two and the little sister can't bear the thought.'

'Yes.' In his head he was still hearing the opening line of the first Passereau song: '*Il est bel et bon . . .*' He is handsome and good. Perhaps Babs Rallenham had been lucky enough to find someone like that.

But as they were settling down to sleep in each other's arms he said to Liz, 'Tomorrow we'll go to the hotel and see what we can find out. Face to face is always better.'

Once again they were late in setting out, but this time it was because of Mandy Rallenham. Exhausted both emotionally and physically, she slept on and on until the chambermaid roused her with her vacuum cleaner in the passage. She came downstairs looking heavy-eyed and bewildered. Liz, waiting for her in the glassed-over porch, ordered fruit juice to be brought.

'Nothing to eat,' said Mandy. 'I never eat breakfast. I've got a weight problem.'

'Not just a brioche? Or toast? They understand about toast, they have English marmalade.'

But Mandy accepted only the juice. 'Where's Mr Crowne?'

'Talking to his grandma.'

'What, she lives here?'

'No, I meant on the phone. He keeps in touch with her, she's in Geneva.'

'Oh, that accounts for it. I somehow didn't think he was English. He's Swiss then, is he?'

'His passport says he's Swiss.' She explained nothing more. If Greg wanted her to know his background, he'd tell her himself.

'I sort of got the impression that Babs thinks a lot of him,' said Mandy. 'Though it seemed a bit odd, because she's not the least interested in music. Not even pop music.'

'It appears she was going to do some sort of snoop into the recording industry – something about back-handers to get classical stuff into the best-selling list.'

A frown appeared between Mandy's neatly plucked eyebrows. 'That sounds a bit low-key for Babs.'

Liz made no comment, although the sister's view coincided with her own. Greg joined them at that moment, having had a long and peaceful conversation with ex-Queen Mother Nicoletta.

'So how is La belle dame sans merci?' enquired Liz.

'In a good mood. She's going to decorate a new guest house in the grounds of some millionaire's mansion in Lugano.' He gave Mandy a little nod. 'How are you this morning, Mandy?'

'Not bad, I suppose – a bit bleary but I'll recover. I'm wondering what I ought to do next . . .'

'I thought we might go to Ardève.' It was a suggestion waiting for her yes or no. To tell the truth, he'd decided to go on his own if she said no. His conscience was needling him.

'Ardève – that's where she was staying? Is it far?'

'About twenty-five kilometres – twenty miles, give or take. It's a tiny place, I think.'

She frowned again. 'What's she doing out there in the middle of nowhere?'

My question exactly, he said inwardly. He quoted Liz: 'Perhaps she likes some peace and quiet when she can get it?'

'Not Babs. She likes to be where it's at.' She hesitated. 'Perhaps it *is* a man, after all.' She thought about it. 'But even so, if she was moving on, surely she'd let me know?'

'Well, let's go and find out.' Liz got up, stretching. Today she was clad in chinos and a flannel shirt of tan and beige. Mandy in her bright clothes looked like a plump parakeet alongside a linnet; she was wearing a vertically striped sweater under a tapestry waistcoat, trews of rough orange and brown checked cotton, and little cuffed boots of tan suede. The only thing that could be said in her favour, thought Greg, was that her make-up had been toned down, and her assertive hair was tied back in a yellow silk scarf. He himself was the least noticeable of the trio, in his brown jacket and Dockers.

She looked surprised when she saw their transport. 'How old is this?' she demanded.

'It's a ninety-one Mercedes.'

'Good heavens.' But she got in the front so as to sit with the driver, leaving Liz to go in the back.

Just watch it, Liz said silently to the nape of her neck. *He belongs to me*. She'd seen how the men liked to watch her last night. She was probably used to making easy conquests. *Not today, dear*, thought Liz.

Greg, unaware, drove sedately eastward out of Avignon. Liz recognized the route: they'd been this way to admire an underground river that gushed in full force out of a cave at the foot of a wall of rock and had eaten some delicious fresh fish in a nearby restaurant. But soon they were beyond the part she recognized. They turned a little north, ignoring a sign for Pernes and taking a minor road. There was one of those sudden changes that makes the area so challenging – rocky hills speared with evergreens to their left, a leafy plain ahead with a stream running through it, and on their right what looked like cracked limestone pavement chequered with scrub oak.

At a bend in the road, set a little back, there was a low-roofed stone building. A sign on a post announced 'Auberge

Mignard'. It was clearly a *mas*, an old farmhouse restored and extended as accommodation for country-lovers, for hikers, anglers, rock climbers, cyclists and hunters. Geraniums still bloomed in its window boxes, a canary still flitted about in a cage by the door where the sun could warm it.

'Well, this is very nice,' said Mandy.

But a long way from anywhere, thought Greg. Really, why would Barbara Rallenham come here?

He parked in an area shielded by tall cypress. They got out and had a conference. He was thinking that if Mandy was inclined to get emotional, it would be better if she took no part in the questioning. Liz, as if by telepathy, understood.

'What I think would be nice, you know, is to have coffee and a bite to eat. You must be hungry by now,' she said to Mandy. It was just after eleven.

Mandy said she'd like coffee. It so happened there was *tarte aux prunes*. Home-made, of course, and from plums from their own trees. They all sat down outside in the mild January sunshine to enjoy the view. A team of cyclists, preparing perhaps for the Tour de France, whirred past on the road. The canary chirped and fluttered its daffodil wings.

When they'd shown goodwill by buying food and drink, Greg strolled alone into the entrance hall. It was panelled in old unpainted pine, paved in stone, with a bentwood stand for outerwear and racks for rods and guns. No one was about. He rang the bell on the reception desk and after a noticeable pause a young man appeared from a door in the panelling.

Greg sighed inwardly at sight of him. Young, determined not to be a country bumpkin, he'd spiked his dark hair with gel, had two gold rings in one ear, and a James Dean scowl on his face. He wore a black linen jacket with a name badge: Émile.

'Monsieur? *Il y a de quoi?*' This was said with a sullen reluctance and in French that tried not to sound Provençal.

'I'm enquiring for Mlle Barbara Rallenham, who was staying here last week.'

'Ah?'

'I rang yesterday and was told she left on Saturday afternoon. However, the young lady to whom I spoke wasn't on duty that day. Might I speak to someone who was?'

'That'd be me,' said the lad.

'Ah, in that case, you arranged Mlle Rallenham's bill for her?'

'Sure.'

'Did she say why she was leaving?'

He shrugged.

'Did you have any conversation with her? Did she ask for a taxi?'

'Had her own car. At least, a rental, I think.'

'Did you take out her luggage? Notice where she was going?'

Another shrug.

'Well, did you?' This was in a less amiable tone, a tone that said 'mind your manners.'

It had its effect. 'No, I didn't. We were a bit busy, you see – Saturday afternoon, people booking in for the weekend. Desk duty isn't my thing, I only help out at weekends as a rule, but Louise is off sick today, which is why I'm filling in.'

'Do you remember Mlle Rallenham at all?'

He was about to shrug but thought better of it as the tall stranger fixed him with a cool gaze. 'Room eighteen. Quite a lot of wine on the bill.'

'Mlle Rallenham – she's English, of course . . .'

Émile had decided to be obliging. He was picturing the scene at the desk. 'Tall, lots of brown wavy hair, wearing a pale-green padded jacket by one of those classy English firms and carrying a Vuitton handbag.'

'Tall with brown wavy hair?' repeated Greg.

'Oh yes, quite a looker, a bit *tzigane*, that sort, you know, but wearing the wrong kind of clothes if you ask me.'

Greg's mind was racing. 'How did she pay? In cash?'

'No, credit card.' Now Émile was interested enough to go behind the desk and consult the computer. He tapped a few keys. 'Yes, credit card.'

'But surely, if you checked the card, it came back a different name?'

'What?' He stared at the screen. 'No, the card was OK, came back with her card number and everything.'

Then something seemed to click behind his forehead and he coloured up.

The prince's glance changed from cool to icy. 'It wasn't Mlle Rallenham who paid the bill. Mlle Rallenham isn't tall with wavy brown hair. She's a fair-haired Englishwoman.'

Émile said nothing.

Greg said, thinking as he spoke, 'But the card came back okay?'

'Yes.'

'It was Mlle Rallenham's card?'

'Must have been.'

'But you knew that wasn't Mlle Rallenham.'

'No I didn't.'

'You knew it wasn't. You might have been busy at the desk, but you knew Mademoiselle – she'd been staying here since Wednesday. You knew she had a rented car. You remembered a moment ago that there was something odd about the bill.'

'No.'

'I'd like you to call the manager—'

'No, no—'

'Then tell me what happened about paying the bill.'

'Well, this woman . . . she was OK, you know, she had a business card with Mlle Rallenham's name and home address, and it had OK written on the back, and she said mademoiselle had decided to check out but was too busy to come herself.'

'OK on the back? That's all?'

'Yes.' But there was more to the story, and it was easy to guess the rest. He'd been given a handsome tip to accept the card.

Anyone can write OK on the back of a card. Greg went on with his interrogation, but the lad was very much on guard now. He knew he'd done something against the rules. He wasn't going to incriminate himself further. And, in fact, perhaps there was nothing more. Someone to whom Barbara Rallenham had entrusted her credit card had paid her bill. It happened – people let friends and relatives do things like that.

When he rejoined the others they'd finished their coffee and plum tart and were waiting with some impatience for him. 'Well?' said Mandy.

He sat down. 'Someone paid her bill for her. A good-looking

woman – tall, gypsy-like. Does your sister have a friend who looks like that?'

Mandy was staring and shaking her head. 'She may have, for all I know. Are you sure about this?'

'The desk clerk says she had your sister's business card with OK on the back so he went along with it.'

'Went along with it?'

'She paid using Barbara's credit card.'

'Oh . . .' It was an indrawn breath, with something of alarm in it. ' I don't think Babs would . . .' The protest died away. It was clear Mandy was trying to search her mind for some close friend of her sister. 'What was she like again?'

'Tall, dark, wearing a pale-green padded jacket and carrying a Louis Vuitton handbag.'

'Oh!' Now there was more than alarm in the sound. 'That sounds as if – as if—' She broke off, swallowing hard. 'Babs has a Burberry padded jacket. And more than one handbag by Vuitton.' She gave a stifled sob. 'Somebody's wearing Babs's *clothes*!'

Tears began to flow. Liz offered comfort and by and by she was able to persuade her to the car and into the back seat. She sat there with her, murmuring replies to Mandy's moans of distress during their return to Avignon. There, Mandy insisted they must go to the police with this new evidence.

As they drew up in the Place Pie, Liz gave Greg a hard stare in the driving mirror. A return visit by this semi-hysterical young woman wouldn't be at all welcome at the enquiry desk. He nodded agreement. She persuaded Mandy to let him go in alone, while she meanwhile took the wheel and found a legitimate parking place.

The desk sergeant knew M Couronne. Or, he knew *of* him. Monsieur had been a frequent visitor to Avignon and around, looking after concert artistes. Moreover, it was rumoured he was some sort of minor royalty, and though the sergeant was a Communist, anyone even distantly related to the Princess Diana had to have something good in him. So he took him to see one of the detectives.

Aristide Cuzor listened with respect to Greg's tale. 'So . . . you say someone else was using her credit card, eh? Well, the inspector's gone to lunch but I'll just give a little tinkle to the hotel and let them know we want to speak to . . . who was it . . . Émile?' He picked up the instrument, dialled the number Greg gave him, and had a short, unrewarding conversation. He looked up and sighed. 'He's taken off. Knew he'd be in trouble for accepting a forged signature. He's probably off to Marseilles where he'll never be found.'

'But you'll send someone to make enquiries?'

'Well, you know, monsieur, I don't think it would get us anywhere. It sounds as if he acted on the spur of the moment, was probably offered money to accept the card. I doubt he's told anyone else about it. So all I have is your story.'

'You don't believe me?'

'Of course I do. But I still think the lady's gone off with a lover.'

'But this woman had Mlle Rallenham's card and appears to have been wearing her clothes.'

'That makes it all the more likely. Women lend each other dresses and coats. All it means is the lover is a woman, not a man.'

The prince frowned.

'You don't think so? My friend, it happens more often than you'd think. Away from the ties of work and routine, in surroundings she probably would think romantic, she feels a new temptation.' He thought of something. 'Didn't you tell me she is divorced? That's a pointer – she tried a relationship with a man, found it didn't suit her, and for all we know has maybe had other liaisons of this type.'

'But her sister – she's gone out of touch—'

'Very true. Is it possible the sister would be shocked if Mlle Rallenham told her she had gone away with a woman? For the time being she decides not to telephone. Moreover, monsieur, in the throes of a new passion, eh? One forgets mundane responsibilities.'

Greg could see that Cuzor had convinced himself of this Byronic version of events. He stayed some minutes longer, trying to ensure that some enquiries would be made at the auberge and leaving with the feeling the matter wouldn't be pursued with any enthusiasm.

He met Liz and Mandy walking back from the parking area

behind the market. They stopped on the busy pavement while he recounted the police view.

They were less surprised by it than he expected. In the worlds in which they made their living, same-sex relationships raised no eyebrows. But Mandy nevertheless looked dubious. 'It's possible, of course. Anything's possible. But you see, no matter how hard she'd fallen, she wouldn't let anyone use her card. I mean, she's obsessive about finance and accounts and things.' She paused. 'And anyhow, why should she? Why couldn't she go to the hotel and sign out herself? I don't believe that she'd be "too busy" to attend to it herself unless . . . unless perhaps she's ill or something. No, it's not like her.'

In his head Greg heard the policeman: 'In the throes of a new passion . . .' He didn't know Barbara Rallenham well. He'd met her here and there, at opera first nights, at diplomatic parties. She'd never struck him as the sort who'd lose her head over anything or anybody.

However, he'd given enough time and energy to the problems of Barbara's sister. He had work to do. He suggested a decent restaurant where the two women might lunch, while he for his part met his baritone at the train station.

Robert Jäger was in his twenties, with a father who ran a construction firm. Papa had hoped Robert would follow him in that career and in fact the boy had studied engineering at university. But he'd always been a singer, a member of the church choir, a lead voice in the university male chorus. So the father was willing to finance his musical studies now, hoping he'd grow out of this desire to sing obscure songs by dead German composers.

Young Robert had a lot going for him. He was tall, well built, earnest and sincere. He was also a bundle of nerves whenever he appeared in public. Greg was extending his experience by launching him quietly in the South of France in front of a kind-hearted audience, and with a not-too-demanding programme: traditional Swiss songs, a couple by Messager, and Schumann's *Dichterliebe*.

They dropped off his luggage at his hotel – a much more luxurious establishment than the Glaneur, thanks to Papa's money – then had a light meal together. Jäger would hardly taste his food. He was already reaching forward to the afternoon, when he would meet his accompanist and begin rehearsals.

The accompanist was Jacques Troulles, a middle-aged local musician with a decent reputation. He was already at the studio when they got there, trying out the piano, which had at last been tuned to recital standard. They decided to begin with the Messager songs, with which he was already acquainted.

It didn't go well, however. Jäger was tense, Troulles was impatient, they couldn't agree on tempo. The prince soothed and encouraged, they went on to the Swiss songs. It became clear that though Greg had given him the sheet music a week ago Troulles had hardly bothered with them.

'A-major, A-major,' sighed Greg. 'And you see it's marked *vivement* – come, M Troulles, that means something more urgent than your tempo.'

'Anything that's called "Hail, Perfumed Spring!" can't be taken like a march, monsieur.'

'Come on, have a heart, it's a sprightly little song by a nineteenth-century composer in an Alpine village. He wants to cheer everybody up after a long winter. Are we ready? One, two, and – "*Voici le printemps de retour*" . . .' He sang along to help Jäger get started, but it was hard going. It ended in collective disagreement about the songs, so he ruled that they wouldn't go on to the Schumann until next day.

The recital was still three days off. By then, he hoped and prayed, singer and accompanist would have learned to live together.

Weary and rather anxious, he went to meet Liz for dinner. It was her last evening in Avignon. Next day, Wednesday, she must be back in London.

To his dismay, Mandy seemed to have included herself in their arrangements. She seemed not to be aware of the proverb that three is a crowd.

They had dinner together in the bar-bistro down the street. It was inevitable that they talked about Barbara and her disappearance.

'Those stupid policemen can say what they like but Babs

isn't the sort to behave like a kid,' Mandy declared. 'Besides – what everybody seems to have forgotten – she came here for some story she was on, now didn't she? Whatever sort of love life she might get into, Babs is never going to drop a story. So even if she didn't want to confess to me she was off on a jag, there's no reason why she should stand *you* up, Greg.'

This was true enough. Yet journalism was a career where chance played a part. Something better than her hype-and-bribery story might have caught her eye. But then . . . but then . . . why not ring her sister and say so?

'I'll go back with you tomorrow, Liz, if that's all right,' said Mandy. 'I think I ought to have a look at Babs's flat. There might be something there – she'll have her organizer with her, but there might be something in her desk diary, or on her computer . . .'

'That's a good idea,' said Greg.

'Why don't you come too?' Liz suggested. She hated to part from him.

'Well, I've got these two men ready to knock each other on the head. Today's session was disastrous.'

'What two men?'

'My singer, Robert Jäger, and his accompanist. If I tell the truth, I think I made a mistake about the accompanist – but I thought it would help attract an audience if one of the duo came from the locality.'

'Why don't you leave them to it?' Liz said. 'If they're going to play in public on Saturday, they've got to get along, haven't they? Let them fight it out by themselves.'

'No, no.' But as the evening progressed it began to seem more and more attractive. He too didn't want to part, and the nervous Robert Jäger would have to learn to relax, and the testy Jacques Troulles would have to stop sneering at the music, and by Saturday they would have to sink or swim together, confound them both.

Next morning he went to the studio, where Troulles was already making contemptuous stabs at the second of the Swiss songs, 'The Exile'.

'Sentimental nonsense,' he grumbled at the prince.

'So it is. Songs of that period seem to be full of self-pity and home-sickness. Think of Schubert's song cycles. "A stranger I was when I arrived, I leave again as a stranger" – he's very sorry for himself.'

This began a conversation during which Troulles seemed to soften a little. By the time Jäger arrived, the atmosphere was almost cordial. When Greg announced that he was off to London for a few days, something like panic showed on Jäger's face, but after a little he calmed down.

'You can concentrate on getting things right,' Greg urged, 'and I'll be back in good time on Saturday for a final run-through.'

'Well . . . OK . . .'

And with this reluctant agreement, he left to join Liz and Mandy en route to Nice airport.

He was pleased. Not only would it give him a few more days with Liz, it eased his conscience about Barbara Rallenham. He would go with her sister to her flat and there, he told himself, he would find some explanation for her strange behaviour.

Three

Mandy seemed to have elected herself the organizer for the trip. At the airport she summoned a taxi and had them driven straight to her sister's flat. This was on the ground floor of a handsome old house in Maida Vale, standing back from the road behind a garden and an old-fashioned gravel drive. The entrance was guarded by an electronic number pad. Mandy keyed in the code and had the key to the flat. She unlocked, they walked in and dumped their travel bags in the little hall.

Everything was as neat as the proverbial pin. In the study, the big desk was clear of clutter: pens and pencils in a tray, small elegant phone, computer with a plastic dust cover, and an inexpensive ring-bound diary lined up to the right-hand edge. Mandy swooped on it. Her red-tipped fingers flipped it open to a bookmark.

'There,' she said, showing it to Greg and Liz. 'An appointment Tuesday ten a.m. – the day before she left – Mrs Barnell.'

They looked at her for enlightenment. But her answering gaze was puzzled. 'Who on earth is Mrs Barnell?'

'A friend of your sister's?' Liz suggested.

'No, if she was a friend the note would be "Nancy" or "Mary" – you don't write a friend's name with her title.' Greg was looking over Mandy's shoulder. 'Nor do you write in her address.'

'No, of course you don't.'

'Besides, this is her work diary,' Mandy added. 'Her personal diary is in the drawer.' She found it, flipped it open at January, but found nothing noted for the previous week except a dental appointment on the Monday, and this was run through by a pencil mark to show it had been attended to.

All her enthusiasm had evaporated. 'Walthamstow?' she

muttered. 'Nobody important lives in Walthamstow.'

She opened and closed drawers in the desk but all she found was stationery. She looked at the computer, her hand hovering towards the On button. But she sighed, shaking her head. 'She'll be furious if she comes home and finds I pried into her files.' Tears began to gather again on the thickened eyelashes. 'Oh, it's pointless,' she cried. 'When she gets back I'm going to give her a piece of my mind! Going off like that, and if it's for some toy boy she'll get the edge of my tongue!'

It seemed she was accepting the version favoured by the Avignon police.

'Her car?' Greg suggested.

'What?'

'The desk clerk at the auberge mentioned she had a rental car. Sometimes people leave notes or reminders in the glove compartment. Her own car's here?'

'In the garage, I suppose,' said Mandy. 'But it's no help because she's probably taken the keys with her in her handbag and I don't know where she keeps the spares.'

Dejected, she trudged to the hall and picked up her bag. 'Let's go,' she said. They went out, conferred on the drive, and decided to go their separate ways by Tube. Mandy shared a house in Mayfair – where else? Liz and Greg headed for her less glamorous flat near the Archway.

It was afternoon of a dull, chilly London day. Normally when Greg came to London he stayed in a bachelor pad in a somewhat stately home in Surrey, where he was given very favourable terms by the estate agents in view of the cachet supplied by his lineage. Other tenants, who paid a lot more for their flats, were happy to say that they lived in a building alongside an ex-crown prince.

But since this was a very short trip, and he had a little business to conduct in central London – and moreover it meant he'd see more of Liz – he was staying with her in Holloway. Less salubrious surroundings, but the view inside compensated for the view outside.

Liz sat down as soon as she got indoors and, still in her wool coat, began to return the calls announced by the blinking light on her answering machine. Greg, examining the refrigerator, understood there was nothing by way of ingredients for a meal. Since it was well past lunchtime, he began looking up nearby restaurants among the advertisements stuck to the fridge door by magnets.

'I don't want to go out to eat,' she told him in a gap between calls. She was still in her coat. The heating hadn't yet kicked in. 'There's a pizza place that's not bad. I'll ring them in a minute to order something.'

So they ate pizza. The food was quite good but Liz paid very little heed to it. She was making notes with one hand while conveying wedges of pizza to her mouth with the other. 'I have to be in Bristol the day after tomorrow,' she announced. 'And I've got an appointment in town tomorrow morning – where are the sketches I did for Cheep-Cheep?'

'Cheep-Cheep?'

'It's a shop for penniless teenagers. Might do well if they can attract the kids with money.'

'Excuse me, if it's for penniless teenagers, how can it attract ones with money?'

'Oh, duckie, you're *so* clueless. It's all to do with street cred. The shop sells grungie-looking, inexpensive stuff but if it has the right 'attitude' it could attract the goldilocks. They'll buy ten or twelve shirts at a time.'

'I see,' said the prince, though he didn't.

When they'd parcelled up the pizza container for the dustbin, Liz looked as if she needed to return to her own affairs. She had taken up a charcoal stick from a desk, and was tacking paper to a board. Display ideas were in her mind.

'I think I might look up this Mrs Barnell,' Greg suggested.

'Who? Oh, the name in the diary. Yes, why not? Couldn't hurt.' She gestured vaguely. 'Want to give her a ring first? The phone book's on that shelf.'

'No, I think I'll just drop by. Phone calls from strange men don't go down well with women.'

'Depends how strange they are,' she countered, accepting a kiss goodbye while opening the drawers of a document cabinet.

He went by Tube to Walthamstow and, since he didn't know the area, picked up a taxi there to deliver him to Vickleham Street. It proved to be a row of quite substantial houses, Victorian perhaps. Mrs Barnell's door was painted plum, had a handkerchief-sized garden to one side and two bell pushes on the doorjamb. He pressed the one labelled Barnell and was reward by a door chime playing 'Greensleeves'.

After a pause there came the sound of an inner door being opened, and then the outer door. A buxom elderly woman looked out at him from a narrow aperture. 'Yes?'

'Good evening. Mrs Barnell? I wonder if I might have a word with—'

'I'm not changing my electricity supply again,' she interrupted. 'Too much hassle.'

'No, I'm not a salesman. I'm a friend of Miss Rallenham's—'

'Oh, Rally's Round-Up, yes, of course, she was here last week.' Her round face lit up. 'Come in, anything I can do for her . . .'

He stepped into a tiny hall. The house had clearly been divided into two flats, not very expertly but so as to give the upper part a door of its own at the foot of the internal stairs. Mrs Barnell led the way through another door immediately to the right of the staircase, along a passage to the back of the ground floor. There a substantial kitchen opened on to a conservatory, where cane furniture and curtains patterned with castanets and guitars gave the illusion of a Costa Brava setting. A television set was showing one of the afternoon house-improvement shows.

Mrs Barnell found the remote to switch off the TV. 'Such an interesting lady,' she remarked, waving Greg to a chair. 'I read her column regularly. Quite a thrill to have her here in my house.' She settled herself in a cushioned chair, brushing long silver hair back behind her shoulders. She wore an Alice band to keep it in place, pale blue like her hand-knit cardigan. In her youth she'd been a very pretty girl. 'And you're from her newspaper, are you?'

'No, no, I'm just a friend. My name is Crowne, Gregory Crowne.'

'Oh yes? A writer, are you? I do admire what Barbara writes – racy, you know, without being offensive like some of them.'

'You know her well?' he asked.

'No, no, only that one time last week, quite surprised, I

was. But she was so nice! She asked me to call her Barbara. I thought that was sweet of her.'

'So she came to see you last week – on Tuesday, I believe.'

'Right. It was a thrill! I hoped she might find it interesting when I wrote to her – that was three or four weeks previous. She rang about it, but I didn't really expect her to come to see me.'

'You wrote to her?'

'Oh yes, that's on the end of her column, you'll recall. "Tell me about it! I'll clear it up for you!" She's always quick on the uptake about funny goings-on.'

'So what was it you wrote to her about?'

Mrs Barnell gave a frown. 'It's an exclusive,' she said. 'Are you trying to steal her exclusive?'

'No, no, I'm not a journalist, music's my profession. No, it's just that if I knew why she was in France I'd have something to start from.'

Mrs Barnell got up. 'Probably on holiday,' she remarked. 'Would you like a cup of tea?'

'No, thank you, Mrs Barnell—'

'I think I'll put the kettle on.' She moved into the kitchen, calling to him through the open door, 'Coffee?'

'No thanks, Mrs Barnell.' He got up and came to the doorway to make it easier to speak. 'This exclusive, was it about recording companies?'

'Beg your pardon?'

'Recording companies. About how they pay for publicity.'

'What, pop stars and all that? What gave you that idea?' She was running water into the kettle, speaking over the sound. It was an intentional distraction. He'd frightened her off by asking about Barbara's investigation.

'Not pop stars. People who play or sing the classics,' he explained.

'Like Handel's Largo, you mean.' She laughed, set the kettle on the worktop and switched it on. 'You're well off the mark, dear.'

'It's really important, Mrs Barnell.'

'To me and Miss Rall—Barbara, I mean. But I'm not going to tell you, young man, if you're hoping to do her down. So that's an end of it.'

'Look, please don't brush it off. Barbara came to see you last Tuesday and next day she'd taken off for Provence. Now she's vanished and—'

'What?' She was so startled that she dropped the mug she'd just taken from a cupboard. It landed on the worktop, rolled, and Greg caught it before it went over the edge.

Mrs Barnell was leaning back against the cupboard. She'd gone pale. 'Vanished?' she repeated weakly.

'Yes, she was to meet me Friday night but never turned up.'

'Oh!'

'So you see, I need to know what she was working on.'

'No,' she said, shaking her head. 'No!'

'If you could explain why—'

'Oh, what have I done!'

'What did you write to her about?'

'Nothing! Nothing. It was just a silly idea of mine. I shouldn't have bothered her with it.'

'But it seems there must be a connection—'

'No, no, nothing about France, I never said anything about France, if she went there it had nothing to do with me!'

'But Mrs Barnell—'

'I don't want to hear another word! I've been a silly old woman! Oh, why did you come here with this silly scare story?'

'It's because I'm worried, and Barbara's sister—'

'Leave me alone! Just leave me alone! It's nothing to do with me, nothing, and I'll thank you to leave my house!'

'But if you have information that might—'

'No, no, what I said about France was just a suggestion. There was nothing serious in it. I'd like you to go now, coming here and upsetting me like this! What right have you got? Get out, get out, I want you out of my house!'

There was nothing for it but to go. He shook his head at her, worried that she might be working herself up to a faint. She made shooing-away motions with her hands as he turned to leave, and he could hear her heavy footsteps behind him all the way to the inner door. This she closed and locked behind him. He stepped to the outer door, hesitated, but could see nothing else to do.

As he went out, another man came in. Burly, not young,

in a worn anorak. He grunted 'Cheers' as Crowne held the outer door for him, and headed for the inner door that closed off the stairs to the upper floor.

When he recounted the events Liz was astonished. 'She threw you out?'

'Yes.'

'It sounds as if she got in a real old state.'

'But only after I said Barbara had disappeared.'

Liz was giving her attention to the big sheet of paper on which she was working. 'Old ladies get hot and bothered about next to nothing,' she suggested.

'So you say. I just wish she'd let me know a bit more before she got upset.'

'Well, she's spooked now. No good going back and trying again today.' She stood back from her sketch of garments on dummies, the dummies standing on a dais and holding out large sunflowers. 'I'll leave that to cook,' she remarked. 'How about going for another look at Barbara's flat? We didn't look seriously this afternoon.'

'Sounds sensible.'

'We'll get Mandy to come with the keys.'

Mandy had left her telephone numbers with both of them. Liz rang her mobile. It was answered almost at once.

'It's me, Liz Blair. Listen, Mandy, are you free at the moment? Because if you are. . . No, we thought we ought to go back to Barbara's . . . Well, perhaps we really should look at her computer . . . ' She began nodding in silent reply to Mandy's comments at the other end. She put down the receiver. 'She says she'll meet us there.'

It was now early evening. When they got to Barbara's address, they had to wait for Mandy to come with the keys. The first thing that struck Greg as they entered the flat was the scent of lemon kitchen cleaner in the air. Liz, amused, said, 'This is a clue that the cleaning lady's been here.'

'Yes, Mrs Dandry – she's in one of those tower blocks up towards Kilburn. Comes in every day except weekends – Babs has this thing about everything being clean and tidy.'

They went into the living room, where they looked at side-tables and the shelf holding TV and hi-fi equipment – anywhere that might have had a note, a scrap of paper. Mandy went into the bedroom to look at the bedside cupboards. Liz opened the wardrobe, so as to feel in the pockets of coats. Nothing.

Greg called from the study.

The two women stopped what they were doing and went in response.

He pointed. 'Her work diary is gone.'

And so it was. The spot against the edge of the desk where it had lain was empty.

'Mrs Duster has put it in a drawer,' suggested Liz.

'Mrs Dandry would never do any such thing,' said Mandy in a worried voice. 'Babs would cut her head off if she touched her desk.'

They stood looking at each other. Then Mandy began opening and closing the desk drawers. The work diary wasn't there.

'Computer,' urged Greg.

She sat down, switched on, and after it had opened for business she began pressing keys. But the folders she opened were empty. She typed a password and summoned up an address list. It was blank. She tried the Recycle Bin but there was nothing in it.

She turned in the chair to stare at them. Her lips were trembling, but she couldn't summon the words.

'Somebody's been here,' Greg said.

'Mrs Dandry?'

'No, Liz, Mrs Dandry w-wouldn't – wouldn't d-dare . . .'

'She's just down the road, you said? Can we get her here?'

'She's probably g-getting her kid his tea.'

'Mandy, is she on the phone? Can you ring her?'

Mandy made a great effort and pulled herself together. She picked up the desk phone and pressed a memory button. 'Mrs Dandry? This is Mandy Rallenham. Were you here at my sister's place this afternoon. . . ? Well, it's just that her diary is missing and—' An outburst on the other end let them know the result of this apparent accusation. After listening for a moment Mandy said, 'Well, if you could come . . . Yes, all right.' She glanced at them. 'She's on her way.'

They spent the few minutes' wait in looking about the rest of the flat, but there was nothing helpful to be seen. They heard a car stop in the drive, and then Mrs Dandry announced her arrival by ringing and then flouncing in with a mouth already open to reject all accusations.

'I never touched nothing, and if you say I did I'll have the law on you! Six years I been doing for Barbara and she knows I never touch nothing.'

Mr Crowne sighed and decided to stay out of it. Yet another highly emotional woman. He'd had more than his share in the last three days. He turned himself a little aside from the scene, pretending to study a wall calendar.

'It's all right, Mrs Dandry,' said Mandy, 'we just want to clear things up. We were here earlier and Barbara's work diary was—'

'It wasn't me that took it then, it was him. You know very well I never touch—'

'Him? Who do you mean?'

'That man, friend of Barbara's, him. Mr Rivers, I think his name was.'

'Mr Rivers?' Mandy looked baffled. She sat gaping at the cleaning woman in silence.

Liz took it up. 'When were you here, Mrs Dandry?'

'Three o'clock. Always three o'clock of a Wednesday, just the half-hour. Flick around with the duster, wash up any crocks, though Barbara's really good, she never has a dinner party on a Tuesday night so there's only breakfast dishes on a Wednesday. You ask Barbara, only the half-hour on a Wednesday afternoon, got to get Billy from school by four.'

'So while you were here, Mr Rivers rang the bell.'

'No he never. Scared the life out of me. I was in the kitchen wiping the sink and checking the crocks and I heard the front door open. Grabbed a knife from the block, I did. I scared *him*, I can tell you!' She smiled in satisfaction, miming her action, fist in the air like Lady Macbeth.

'He let himself in? With a key?'

She nodded vigorously. 'Here was I with a knife and him holding up the key like it would protect him.' She was still half smiling. 'All the same, he'd no right. I always ring the bell before I use Barbara's key.'

'And he told you his name was Rivers.'

'Yeah, Rivers . . . Ribble? Rivett? No, I think it was Rivers.

But I wouldn't a let him stay in the flat if he hadn't got Barbara's business card.'

Liz gave a gasp. Greg looked round. Mandy put a hand up to her mouth.

'Her card?' Liz said in a low voice.

'With her OK on the back, so I knew it was all right.'

'You recognized her writing?' Greg asked.

'Recognize?' Mrs Dandry turned her lips down at the corners and moved her head from side to side, not exactly in denial but certainly not in assent. 'It was just the letters, OK.'

Mandy began to cry. 'Her card, her key, her clothes! Oh, Babs, Babs, where are you!'

The cleaner stared in consternation. 'What's up, then?' she demanded hoarsely.

'Something's happened to her! I *told* you something was wrong!'

Greg gave Liz a look which she rightly interpreted as a hint to do something about the loud wails. She put a hand under Mandy's elbow, helped her up, and led her out of the study, uttering soothing words.

Greg was sitting on the edge of the desk. He pushed the desk chair out. 'Sit down a minute, Mrs Dandry. We're a bit worried about Barbara.' He was wondering by what somersault of political correctness it came about that the cleaning woman called her employer Barbara whereas they called her Mrs Dandry.

'She's in a right state,' she agreed, jerking her head towards the departed sister. 'Gets in a tizz about nothing, so Barbara often says.'

'Well, I agree, she does seem to give way sometimes. Now about this Mr Rivers. What did he say?'

'Not much.' She shrugged. 'He apologized for giving me a fright, I apologized for the bread knife, he said he'd come from Barbara to collect some of her stuff, and I said right you are. I knew Barbara was off on a story somewhere, she left me a note.'

'And so what did he do?'

'Well, I went back to the kitchen to put the bread knife back and when I came out again he was here in the study. So I didn't interfere because I knew he must be somebody special.

Barbara's strict about this stuff in here. I glanced in, the door was ajar, he was sitting at the computer – you know, you could see the flickers as things changed.'

'Did you see what was on the screen?'

'Not me. No interest in that sort of stuff. I watered the plants' – she jerked her head towards the sitting room where there were some spectacular parlour palms – 'didn't really need it but I didn't want to go until this man left. Not that I suspected anything, like he'd take this diary you mentioned. I just felt I had to lock up like I always do.'

'How long did he stay?'

'Ten minutes? About that. Time was getting on, I had to get to the school, so I says to him, "You finishing soon cos I got to get going." And he says, "All done," and switches off the computer, and came out with me all polite, holding the door for me and all that.'

'And what then?'

'We go out to the front door and out into the drive, and I make sure the door's locked shut and stand waiting, cos his car's blocking mine, and he gets into his car and drives away.'

'What kind of car?'

She groaned. 'Men always ask that. A blue car, not old. And don't ask if I got the number cos why should I?' She frowned at him. 'What are you, some kind of cop?'

'No, no, nothing like that. Just a friend of Barbara's. She's got out of touch, her sister's worried.'

'She would be, never properly grown up if you ask me.' She shrugged about in her jacket, patted her pockets for keys. 'Anything else? I got to get back, Billy's on his own.'

'What did this man look like?'

'Look like? Ordinary. Not as tall as you, brown hair going a bit thin, nice suit, trench coat like Humphrey Bogart.'

'Foreign? A Frenchman?'

She looked taken aback. 'Not that I could tell. Seemed English to me.' Then she held up a finger. 'But there now – the woman with him, she mighta been foreign.'

'A woman?'

'By the car. Didn't get too good a look at her cos she got in as soon as we came out. But she was ever so smart in her way, long dangly earrings with pearls in 'em, big hair – you know, the just-got-out-of-bed look, thick and glossy and dark in a tangle. And she was wearing this super shawl.'

'A shawl?'

'Yeah, bright colours, a big bold pattern, and expensive, I'd say – I think it was a silk and wool mix.'

A Provençal shawl. A gypsy look.

He went to the door to call to Liz. She called back, 'Yes?'

'Can you leave Mandy and come here?'

'Just a minute.' He could hear the clinking of bottles and guessed she was getting Mandy a drink. A moment later she came out of the sitting room and crossed the hall to the study.

'Can you do a sketch if Mrs Dandry describes someone?' he asked. 'I think she's seen the woman from the Auberge Mignard.'

Four

Mrs Dandry was quite pleased with the sketch Liz made from her descriptions. 'That's really quite like her, dear,' she declared in some surprise. 'You're a clever thing, aren't you?'

'And the man?' Greg urged.

'We-ell . . . Yeah, that's sort of like him.'

But the fact was that her description had been poor. Not so tall as Greg, brown hair going a bit thin, roundish face, trench coat . . . The face looking out from the sketch could have been anybody. The woman, however, was not just anybody. She had a narrow face, high cheekbones, eyes that Mrs Dandry had called 'sooty', a tangle of loosely curling dark tresses. Liz studied her and wondered aloud: 'Slav?'

'Could be.'

Mandy had come in during the making of the artwork. She looked at the two pictures and shrugged. 'Nobody I ever met, but then I didn't know all Barbara's friends. Anyhow, what's the point?'

'I thought we might show the sketches to some of her colleagues. If they recognize anybody, they might have names, addresses – it could clear up the whole thing in ten minutes.'

'Not if the French police are right and she's having a passionate fling with a stranger,' Liz said. 'But you don't go along with that theory, Greg?'

Mandy held up a hand in a sudden bid for attention. 'I think we should take these sketches to the police.'

'The British police?'

'Hey, now, wait a minute,' said Mrs Dandry. 'You never said nothing about calling the police!'

'But my sister's missing!'

'Yeah, maybe, but you know, Barbara's sort of picky and

choosy – dunno whether she'd want you dragging in the cops.'

It was clear to Greg that she didn't relish the idea of meeting policemen. Perhaps her earnings as a house cleaner weren't being declared to the authorities so that her family benefits or social security or whatever it was called in this country might be curtailed.

'Let's start with the people who know Barbara socially and at work,' he said, earning a flash of relieved gratitude from Mrs Dandry. 'Can you make out a list, Mandy?'

'Umm . . .' She had already said that she and Barbara lived in separate worlds. But prestige was now involved. She didn't want to admit she couldn't summon up more than three or four names. 'It'd be best to start at the *Clarion*.'

'Her newspaper – yes – but it's evening, would the staff still be there?'

'Sweetie, this is London, not sleepy old Geneva. Of course newspaper staff will be working – there could be late-breaking news.' Liz was rather proud of this phrase. She'd learned it by watching CNN in hotel bedrooms.

They held a discussion. Mrs Dandry wanted to get back to her flat where by now her son would probably be getting up to mischief. Liz had work awaiting her at home. It was agreed that Mandy should go to the newspaper offices, and that Greg should go with her in case she got weepy yet again – although this last was unspoken agreement between Liz and Greg.

The *Clarion* had moved out of Fleet Street long ago with the rest of the press, and was now in an unattractive new building far down the Thames Estuary with Canary Wharf in its view. There was a tight security barrier in the main entrance hall, but Mandy was able to prove her identity with her driving licence. This showed her last name to be Rallenham. Consulting a list assured the receptionist that Rallenham was the name of one of the features staff. He allowed Mandy to use the desk telephone to call the features editor.

The features editor was in fact at home but his deputy agreed at once that he would see Barbara Rallenham's sister. White tags were produced, they wrote their names on them and waited while they were put in plastic covers with pins to attach to their lapels. They were escorted to the lift, the correct button was pushed for them, and they sailed upwards. A young secretary-type awaited them. She led them through an open-plan office to one side where a line of doors gave access to glass-screened rooms.

David Franklin rose to meet them. 'Mandy Rallenham? How d'you do? Mr Crowne, are you—'

'We're here to ask about Barbara,' Greg said in haste, to prevent the enquiry on the other man's lips, which would have been: 'Are you that mini-royal from somewhere in Europe?'

'Yes, Barbara – she's off on one of her toots,' said Franklin. 'France, if I remember rightly. The office makes her travel arrangements, you know.'

'Has she been in touch since she left?'

'Er . . . lemme see . . .' He ferreted around his desk until he found a photocopied sheet. It was clearly from a wall schedule showing assignments and the original was probably on a board in the office of his boss. 'Yes, last Thursday morning, text message from her mobile saying "Tally-ho". Means she's on track with her story.'

'And her story was what?'

'Ah.' He leaned back in his chair, clasped his hands behind his head and looked thoughtful. 'Why are you asking?'

'Because she hasn't been in touch!' exclaimed Mandy. 'It's very worrying.'

'Not at all, not at all,' soothed Franklin. 'Barbara always plays her cards close to her chest. Days can go by and we don't hear from her.'

'But *I* hear from her,' Mandy protested. 'She always rings me wherever she is. And I haven't heard for a whole week now.'

Franklin clearly didn't have the same view of family relationships. 'She's busy,' he said. 'If her story hotted up, she might not have time to ring—'

'But what is her story?' Greg interrupted. 'She told me she wanted to talk to me about bribes for getting records into the top ten, but—'

'She told *you*? But if you're who I think you are, you're not interested in the pop industry.'

'She said it was about greasing palms, and there may be a certain amount of that even in classical music.'

'Oh, fiddle-faddle! Must have been a cover story. Barbara wouldn't waste her time on a thing like that.'

'Then tell us what she was really investigating.'

'None of your business, chum,' said Franklin.

Mandy spoke through rising tears. 'Listen, Mr Franklin, this could be quite serious. People have been to Babs's flat and made off with her notebooks and—'

'What?' It was a cry of alarm. 'Somebody's broken in and snooped on her stuff?'

'Well, they didn't break in. They had her keys and a card giving her permission. But —'

'Oh, then that's all right.'

'No it isn't. She hasn't been in touch! I didn't even get a birthday card,' sobbed Mandy.

Franklin gave her an impatient glare. 'Look here,' he said, speaking over the sound and addressing himself to Greg, 'Barbara's a big girl, she can look after herself. I know enough not to interfere with her projects once she's on a roll. And as far as giving you information, all I can tell you is that she had air tickets to France and she let me know it was going well.'

'But did you get the impression she was into anything dangerous?'

'A scandal follow-up, that's all. That's all I can tell you. And listen, I'm busy, presses have to go with the first edition in a coupla hours and I can't hang around smoothing the wrinkles on your brow. So you'll have to leave.' He wanted to be rid of the sobbing sister. He pressed a button on his desk and the young secretary-type jumped up from a desk in the main office. 'Mary'll show you out. And listen, stop worrying. Barbara will be back when she's got copy.'

There was nothing for it but to go. They were shepherded to the lift. Mandy mopped her eye with a crumpled tissue. 'What a horrible man,' she sighed.

'But he wasn't worried, Mandy. Perhaps you've got into a state about nothing.'

She was just enough impressed by the deputy features editor's confidence to have no reply. They went down to the hall. It was now a fully dark January evening outside, the breeze from the Thames biting cold and raw. She shivered.

They walked out to the main road, where there was a convenient bus stop. A bus came along, they boarded, they wended their slow way back to central London.

Once there, they parted at a Tube station. 'You must be tired. Try to get a good night's sleep,' Greg urged. 'We'll talk again tomorrow.'

'Oh! Wait a minute, tomorrow's Thursday, right? I've got a client tomorrow morning at the salon – don't ring me there.'

'All right. What time would be right?'

'Let's say . . . two o'clockish? Two thirty, that would be better.'

'Very well, that's fixed.'

She gave him an unexpected hug, then hurried off to the Piccadilly Line escalator. He headed for the Northern Line. He had mixed feelings. Firstly, he was glad to be rid of Mandy's company. He found her irritating with her easy tears, yet he felt he ought to be sympathetic in case something really had happened to her sister.

He understood about family ties. He himself kept in touch when he was away. His fearsome grandmother insisted on it because of some deep-seated foolishness about his safety. She was half convinced that anti-monarchists might assassinate him. When he said he was too unimportant to be assassinated she'd say darkly, 'Remember the Archduke Ferdinand? *He* wasn't important.'

If Barbara Rallenham failed to keep in touch with Mandy, was it truly significant? Or was it just Mandy being absurd? Or trying to puff up her sense of her own importance?

He was weary, and hungry, and had concerns of his own. Notably, that Liz would be gone early tomorrow morning on some fashion trip, and he was wasting precious time on fruitless encounters with hard-headed newsmen.

After Liz left the following morning, he himself had an important meeting. He was going to consult Margo Evangelista about his baritone, Robert Jäger. Evangelista had had a short career in opera some twenty years ago before some strange virus had robbed her of her voice, attacking her larynx and reducing her to an angry silence. Her long but unavailing battle to get her career back had taught her almost all there was to know about voice production. Moreover, having to face an audience with only the remains of a once lovely contralto had taught her a lot about stage fright.

Madame Evangelista, now grey haired and with the wrinkles of years of anxiety, listened to the demonstration CD he had brought. She asked him to replay it twice. Then she said: 'It's a young voice.'

'He's twenty-six,' he objected.

'I don't mean it's immature – although of course it *will* ripen as he grows older. I meant that it was blithe, full of happiness . . .'

'Yes?'

'And he's singing sad songs, songs about losing your beloved, about being an outcast.'

'Those are the songs in the repertoire, Margo.'

'Oh yes, I understand your problem. But you say he's nervous. That may be because some instinct is telling him that he's singing the wrong music.'

'You mean he mustn't sing sad songs? He's temperamentally unsuited to Schubert and Mahler? He must never sing Verdi?'

'Of course not. A great voice deserves great songs, and the great songs are, for the most part, about loss and loneliness.' She gave a little cough, trying as ever to clear her throat. Rising from her armchair, she made for the drinks cabinet. 'Come, it's nearly noon, time for a little aperitif, eh? I usually have an Amontillado about now.' She picked up the bottle, showing him the label.

He got up to accept his drink and to carry hers for her to the little tray fixed to the arm of her chair. She spent most of her time in that chair, listening to recordings of singers past and present, still learning from them how to use the voice to its best effect and ready to pass on that knowledge.

She asked questions about Robert Jäger's routine – what did he eat, did he take enough physical exercise, how long did he practise each day? 'His people have money, you say. He's had a happy life, eh?'

'I imagine so. I'm only his mentor, Margo, I'm not his Father Confessor.'

'And what do you plan for him in the long run? Are you going to be his business agent?'

'Good lord, no, that's not on the cards. No, I just want to get him as much public exposure as I can for the moment, in hopes that someone influential will take him on. Ideally I'd like to see him get a season or two with one of the minor opera companies.'

She cocked her head to one side. 'I would be against that. Almost all the baritone roles want him to be sad or wicked – except perhaps for Schaunard in *La Bohème*.' She gave a wicked smile. 'I once fell madly in love with a Schaunard during a season in Prague . . .' She shook her head over her youthful folly then returned to the matter in hand. 'Your boy could sing Schaunard now, I'd say. But Iago . . . Rigoletto . . . the parts with cruelty or bitterness . . . If he ever gets those roles, his voice will be dark enough to suit them when he's turning forty.'

'That's very unencouraging, madame,' Greg sighed.

'Minor opera companies, you said,' she recalled as she sipped. 'Minor opera companies . . . What about minor operas, Gregory?'

'What, Cav and Pag? But he'd have to be with an opera company—'

'No, no, not Cav and Pag. I was thinking of operetta.'

'Not *The Merry Widow*?' groaned Greg. 'Nobody puts that on except Vienna, and it's really a bit of a drag.'

'My dear boy, there are operettas other than *The Merry Widow*. For instance, Lehar – what else did he write?'

'*Frederika? Frasquita?*' He was searching his memory. His grandmother sometimes sang to herself when she was planning new designs for a ballroom, tuneful little sounds that generally seemed to be waltzes with German words.

'Those, yes,' agreed Evangelista. 'But, more importantly, he wrote *The Land of Smiles* – in which the great Richard Tauber had a huge success.'

'Tauber . . . yes . . . He was a great Mozart tenor . . .' He had the singer among his collection of discs at home in Geneva.

'That's my point, Gregory. He was a great operatic tenor, but he was happy to sing the part of Sou Chang, or Ching, I forget which, in an operetta by Lehar. Full of lovely melodies that the voice takes to with pleasure. Your young man could enter into roles like that and make the whole world fall in love with him.'

'But, Margo, the hero of *The Merry Widow* and *The Land of Smiles* has to be a tenor.'

'Oh, rubbish, all you do is take the music down a key or two. And, anyway, there are good baritone heroes. Lawrence Tibbett went on to sing at the New York Met for years, but he started in operetta – I think *The Dollar Princess,* that sort of thing. One of the best baritone voices of the thirties and forties.'

He sighed in amazement. 'Do you know everything, madame?'

'Everything to do with what's good for the human voice. I think it would be a good idea to get your Jäger to study one or two of the operettas—'

'But who's ever going to put them on?' he interrupted. 'They'd cost a fortune to stage.'

'Good gracious, boy, you aren't going to do a full production! Put one on as a concert performance – singers standing on a platform, no costumes, but a full orchestra – at one of the summer festivals, it could be a roaring success.'

'And it could be a desperate failure,' he said. 'The plots are usually nonsense.'

'But you're not going to bother with the plot, only the music. And a good baritone singing, "Oh Maiden, My Maiden!" in an open air performance on a summer night could be very romantic.'

She'd fallen in love with the idea and went on about it until he had to leave. Nobody would ever do it, he thought to himself as he went down in the lift. Getting a cast together would take months – who in their senses would want to sing Lehar in a concert performance?

He was taking the manager of a small concert hall to a wine bar lunch. En route to the bar he thought about Evangelista's concept. He'd need a backer because it would cost a lot: it would call for six or eight good voices and a sizeable orchestra, because you couldn't accompany that lot with three violins and a piano. No, no. But all the same . . .

Downsize the thing. Try it with just Jäger and an accompanist. An Evening with Franz Lehar. Melodies of the Master.

Summer Songs by Lehar. He put the idea aside for the moment. But he'd try at least one of Evangelista's ideas – he'd find some optimistic songs in the classical repertoire for Jäger to sing. Perhaps she was right, perhaps that young voice needed to rejoice, not to grieve.

After an hour with the manager of the hall he went back to Liz's flat so as to put his feet up for an afternoon of phone calls. His first was to Mandy. She picked up at once, her voice unhappy.

'I finished with my client a bit earlier than I expected, Greg, so I dropped in on a couple of Barbara's friends. One of them is in a PR firm just down the street, and Linda is a freelance so she was at home.' She sighed noisily. 'Neither of them recognized the people in the sketches.'

He made commiserating sounds.

She went on. 'Linda said something about deadlines. She said Barbara wanted to complete what she had on hand because she's got an interview lined up with Shaun Winkworth.'

'Who?'

'Winkworth? The stand-up comic whose girlfriend did a kiss-and-tell on him?'

He hadn't a clue what she meant. 'What about him?'

'Babs had persuaded him to tell his side of it. He's in the Seychelles, gets back early next week.'

'You mean Barbara has an interview with him, perhaps Tuesday or Wednesday?'

'Yes, and that's less than a week away. Honestly, Greg, Babs wouldn't disappear into the blue if she might miss a meeting like that.'

'No.'

'I mean, she's a stickler for deadlines. I am too, if it comes to that. I'd never let down a client if I'd promised a consultation. So I know how Babs feels about it.'

He understood that very well. He too was always struggling to meet deadlines – getting musicians with their instruments and their music scores to the right place at the right time.

'I've decided to go to the police,' she resumed. 'I don't care what Mrs Dandry said.' She waited. He felt she wanted him to say he'd go with her, but he had business calls to make and

Liz was due home that evening So he remained silent, and Mandy ended by saying, 'I'll give them your name and phone number, shall I? I expect they'll want to hear your side of it.'

'Of course. Anything I can do.' And with this meaningless offer they disconnected.

Liz got back around eight. He'd booked a table at a nearby restaurant, so they went out again as soon as she'd freshened up. She was full of tales about her trip: the stands she'd asked for hadn't been covered in the correct colour of felt, it was so difficult working in a section of the department closed off only by tarpaulins, in days gone by you could have spent all of Sunday getting it right but now department stores opened on Sundays . . .

Finally she talked herself out. She asked, 'How was your day?'

He knew better than to enter into a discussion about the difficulties of putting on a recital of songs from operetta. Instead he related the news from Mandy.

'Ooh,' she said on an indrawn breath. 'That's not good. If Barbara had a date fixed up with somebody as important as Winkworth she would never miss it.'

'But she could get back in time, you know. Tomorrow's Friday. This interview isn't until Tuesday or Wednesday.'

'I suppose so.'

'Mandy said she was going to the police.'

'Well, that's up to her. But what will they say? There seems very little to go on.'

'They'll say what the *agent municipale* said in Avignon. Barbara's not a flighty teenager, and she's perfectly entitled to give her keys to a friend so as to fetch something from her flat.'

'If they follow it up with you . . . ?'

'I'll tell them what I know. Which, when you come to look at it, is almost nothing.'

'Ah well.' She sighed. 'We've done what we can, haven't we?'

'Yes.' And because their time together was limited they put the problem out of their minds. They had other and more pleasant things to do.

* * *

Friday morning Gregory went to his flat in Surrey to fetch some CDs he'd left there. Liz had an appointment in Bond Street. They agreed to meet for a late lunch at a tapas bar they frequented off Marylebone Road.

They were halfway through a plateful of spicy fish *croquetas* when he felt his mobile vibrate in his pocket. He half decided to ignore it, but then decided it might be the manager of the concert hall with a reasonable hiring fee for next March. He asked permission from Liz, took it out, and answered it.

The voice on the other end belonged to his baritone, but there wasn't any joy in it today. His words were tumbling over themselves, he'd reverted to his childhood and was speaking Génévois French. 'Greg, what are we going to do? That accursed M Troulles has walked out on me!'

'What?'

'Walked out! He just stopped playing in the middle of a bar, got up and walked out.'

'For heaven's sake, Robert, why?'

'He said it was rubbish. The Swiss stuff – he hates it all. We were doing "L'Exile" when he took his hands off the keys and just left.'

'When was this?'

'About an hour ago. I went after him but he'd got in his car and driven off. I rang his home number and eventually I got a reply, but all he'd say was that he wasn't coming back. He says he'll forfeit his fee.'

Greg muttered a few rude words. 'That's very big hearted of him! If I meet up with him when I get back I'll chew him up and spit him out.'

'What am I going to do, Greg? I can't sing without an accompanist.'

'No, of course you can't.'

'Is there someone else I can contact? You know the musical circle of Avignon – but even if we can get someone, the recital's tomorrow evening! How is the accompanist going to learn the music in time? The Schumann, OK, he might know that – but what about the Swiss songs?'

Greg stifled a deep sigh. 'It's all right, Robert. Don't get in a panic. I'll play for you.'

'You will?' Relief rang through the two words. He knew

that his mentor played well, had once had youthful dreams of becoming a concert pianist. And, more to the point, Greg knew the programme already, had played for him back home in Geneva when they were roughing it out. 'Oh, thank heavens! But, Greg, we need to rehearse.'

That was only too true. Greg hadn't sat down at a piano in days, although at home he liked to play as often as he could. He needed to get familiar with the instrument at Avignon, he needed to refresh his memory of the music that went with the Swiss songs. 'I'll catch the next available flight,' he said.

'Oh, thank you, Greg. You don't know what this means to me!'

Right. After the recital, while he was still in that mood of intense gratitude, it would be easier to put to him the idea of singing a programme of Lehar or Offenbach. Look on the bright side, Greg told himself. But the dark side was that he had to say goodbye to Liz almost immediately.

He was lucky enough to get a seat on a mid-afternoon flight. He arrived at Nice in time for cocktails. Jäger was waiting for him at the Hotel Glaneur, striding about with agitation in the old stone-paved hall. Greg took him into the bar for a soothing drink, and there then followed a long discussion about whether Troulles was right, whether they should drop the Swiss songs and substitute something well known.

'He kept on saying they were trash, Greg. Perhaps they're too unsophisticated for a French audience.'

'Look here, the setting of one of those songs is by Mendelssohn, and one's by Weber. If the composers of *Fingal's Cave* and *Der Freischutz* aren't good enough for them, they're hard to please. Stop thinking we're in the wrong, Robert. It's Troulles who's too big for his boots, that's the trouble.'

By dint of running down the high-handed pianist and boosting Jäger's confidence, Greg was able to get them to the rehearsal studio, where he put in some practice alone while Jäger went off in search of dinner. Then, for the remaining hours of the evening, they worked on the programme. The Swiss songs took up most of their time. Jäger's confidence had been very shaken. And, in fact, some of the folk songs weren't the very best material. But they were something different, and simple enough to send the audience home singing to themselves: 'Halleri, i-oup, trahi, falera,' just like a goatherd.

Late though it was, he rang Liz. She answered sleepily. 'Oh, it's you, sweetheart. How's it going?'

'Not bad, not bad. Jäger's calmed down and we did a couple of run-throughs. Tomorrow we're allowed into the hall so we can check on the acoustics.'

'Sounds good.' She paused, then giggled. 'Acoustics – sounds good! How's that for wit at midnight?'

'Very learned. How are you, my angel?'

'I'm OK. And now you've rung, I've got news.'

'Good or bad?'

'Ahem,' she said. 'Point one, Mandy went to the cop shop as promised and got a brush off.'

'Oh, well . . . What did they say?'

'Much the same as you. Perfect right to enter the flat, the visitor had Barbara's keys and her OK. They'll contact the Avignon boys just to be polite – but you know what the Avignon boys thought.'

'Yes. Well, all we can do now is wait.'

'That was only point one, Greg. Point two is that Mandy's flying to Nice first thing in the morning.'

The prince groaned. 'Oh, *sia dannata,*' he muttered.

Five

He said it again – 'Confound the woman!' – as she came in at the door of the breakfast room next day.

He'd gone to bed late, slept badly, crawled out of bed to shower and shave with only one eye open, and had hoped to spend a quiet hour over coffee and croissants to get himself going. He tried to hide behind his copy of *Nice Matin*, but she called his name and hurried towards him. Needs must. He rose to greet her.

'Oh, Greg, I'm so glad you haven't gone out. They told me at the desk you were probably still having breakfast.' She sat down opposite him. He summoned the waiter, who darted forward with eagerness, his eyes fixed on the cleavage she revealed as she peeled off a skinny knitted jacket.

Greg had asked Liz what she thought of Mandy's dress style. He'd thought she'd shrug it off as terrible, but no. 'A bit OTT,' she acknowledged, 'but "funky" is probably right for her. For the kind of customers – no, sorry, clients – she deals with, "ladylike" would hardly be good business.'

Having threaded his way through this Sibylline response, he'd gathered that the bizarre clothes Mandy wore made the right impression somewhere. And certainly men – perhaps particularly Frenchmen – were favourably impressed.

She was clad in stretch blue jeans, red platform shoes, and a T-shirt with a very scooped neckline. The T-shirt was emerald green with a sequined logo across her bosom: Twin Peaks.

She ordered coffee. While they waited for it, she began an account of her activities since they had parted.

'And you know, they hardly bothered to listen after the first few sentences,' she complained. 'So if the London police won't help we'll have to start again in Avignon, see what we can find out—'

'Excuse me,' he intervened at once. Better to get it settled from the outset. 'I'm afraid I can't be of any help, at least for the present.'

'What?'

'I've got work to do this weekend.'

'Work? What work? This music festival stuff?'

'I've got to do a run-through in the hall today and then there's the recital this evening.'

'But you don't really need to be present.'

'I do indeed. I'm having to stand in as accompanist for my singer. And he's repeating the performance tomorrow in Nice.'

She was utterly astounded. He'd been so responsive to her first appeal that she'd taken it for granted he'd still be available. She sat gazing at him helplessly, mouth a little open like a nestling waiting for a titbit from its parent. In her hands she held photocopies of the sketches Liz had made, and now she held them out towards him. 'I'm going to ask around, ask if anyone's seen her,' she faltered. 'B-but, Greg – you see – I don't speak very good French.'

'I'm sorry, Mandy. I really can't go with you.'

The young waiter came bustling up with her coffee. He'd brought everything else he could think of – cream, sugar, little Italian macaroons wrapped in paper, a single rosebud in a narrow holder.

She was naturally flattered. 'Oh, *merci* a lot,' she said.

'It's nothing, mademoiselle,' he replied in English.

In that moment Greg knew Mandy had found another interpreter. She smiled warmly on Jules, and Jules smiled back. But he had to clear tables, so he turned away for the moment. Mandy went back to her quest. 'Take a couple of these, Greg,' she said, holding out the photocopies. 'Ask around.'

He was going to spend most of his day inside a recital hall. But he took the copies, and listened rather guiltily to her plans. She was still sitting over her coffee when he went out to meet Jäger, with young Jules the waiter watching her over his shoulder.

As he hurried along the busy pavements, a thought occurred to him. Mandy regarded him as an on-site interpreter. Perhaps her sister had had the same idea. Everyone seemed to be surprised that Barbara should suddenly become interested in classical music, even if on the track of some underhand action. When he'd tried out the idea about classical records on Mrs Barnell in Walthamstow, she'd been absolutely at a loss.

Yes, she'd agreed that something had taken Barbara Rallenham to France. But now that he thought about it, he began to feel fairly sure it had nothing to do with the record industry.

At a PR event for a well-known charity in London a fortnight ago, they'd had a conversation. The usual social chit-chat: 'What are you doing these days? Oh, I'm only here overnight from Avignon. Really, how interesting, I'm going there in a day or two.' That sort of thing. She'd at once asked him to meet her there, and spun him what he now recognized as quick invention about hype in the world of music. Her real reason might have been to hook him as a kind-hearted interpreter.

Having entertained this train of thought, he at once felt guilty. After all, he should be feeling concern, not suspicion. The poor woman was missing and it was wrong to think badly of her.

All the same, journalists were very opportunistic, as he knew to his cost. From time to time gossip columnists had tried to marry him off in their pages to princesses or countesses he'd only met once, if at all.

He stopped on his way to the Salle Dubois at a local print-shop where he sometimes had publicity material made. He'd ordered some flyers showing a head-and-shoulders of Robert Jäger, only black and white but looking young and quite handsome. The printer had arranged for them to be distributed in Nice today, to tempt an audience for tomorrow afternoon's recital. Greg had approved the proof and now had to pay the bill.

He was putting away his credit card when his hand encountered the folded copies that Mandy had given him. He hesitated, almost didn't bother, but conscience pricked him on. 'Do you by any chance know either of these two people, Arnaud?' he asked, showing the sketches.

Arnaud picked them up, stared at the picture of the man. He shook his head. 'No, never seen him that I know of,' he said. He picked up the other sketch. He looked at it, was about to hand it back, but changed his mind. 'Well now . . .'

'What?'

'It's not a very good resemblance, but it's a bit like . . . what's her name? Grashenko, I think.'

'Grashenko?'

'Émilie? Élise? Something like that. Anyhow it might be her, Grashenko.'

'A Russian?'

'No, no – well, maybe her parents, but she's French. She had a one-man show somewhere down on the shore – Nice or Cannes or St Trop.'

'An artist, then.'

'No, a potter. Mind you, some of her work is almost sculpture, very big' – he was holding his hands apart vertically to demonstrate – 'quite striking. I didn't care for it myself, but you know some people like that rough, earthy stuff.'

'You were at the exhibition?'

'Yes, the wife dragged me there, she was into pottery a couple of years ago.

'Any idea where she has her studio?'

'Thinking of buying some pottery?' Arnaud asked with a grin. 'Or are you more attracted by the potter? She's quite something, isn't she! Well, the address of her studio was on the placard outside and I couldn't tell you now what it said . . . but it wasn't in Cannes or Nice, that's for sure. Some artists' community . . . you know, out in that area north-east of Fontaine de Vaucluse . . . they'd know if you asked around there.'

'Yes . . . Thank you, Arnaud.'

In the countryside north-east of Fontaine de Vaucluse. He certainly didn't have the time to do anything about it at the moment. He'd leave a message at the hotel for Mandy, so that she could follow it up with Jules.

At the Salle Dubois, he and Jäger tried out the acoustics. Not bad. They rehearsed until mid-afternoon, then went off to their hotels to rest, have a meal, and change into evening wear. Then early at the hall to have a final run-through, to ensure that everything was in order.

The recital went well. The opening group were French songs, nothing demanding, Messager, Adam, Gretry. Then the hard part, Schumann's *Eine Dichterliebe*. The audience liked the voice, applauded more than politely. At the back, Greg noticed the abominable M Troulles sitting grim and disapproving with his hands folded in his lap. *You rat*, thought Greg, *you're going to get up and walk out during the Swiss songs.*

Luckily the first of these was a folk song, the one about the goatherd. When it came to the absurd chorus, 'Halleri, i-oup, trahi falera,' Jäger sang it with so much bounce and amusement that the audience actually laughed. From his seat at the piano Greg looked out at Troulles. He was gazing about at the others in astonishment, simply couldn't believe they were enjoying it.

So they went through the five songs playing to people in a responsive mood. The crowd even liked the one about the exile. They held on with their applause at the end and it was clear they wanted an encore. So after a few whispered words Greg launched back into the accompaniment for the goatherd's song. Inspired by the unexpected bonhomie Jäger made conducting movements when they got to the chorus. So there was the well-heeled audience in the Salle Dubois singing, 'Halleri, i-oup, trahi falera, falera-a-a!'

It was so much fun that Greg forgot to look for M Troulles. And then they had to clear the platform for the next set, a pair of guitarists playing difficult stuff by Takemitsu. So it was over, and they hugged each other, and went off to get mildly drunk at Robert Jäger's expense.

'It was a triumph!' cried Gregory to his beloved before he got ready for bed in the wee small hours. 'They really liked him!'

'You've been celebrating, I gather.'

'*Femme sage et de façon, Jamais dit que de raison.*'

'And what on earth does that mean?'

'A wise and good woman speaks only the truth.'

'So you *have* been celebrating?'

'Only a little, darling. I'll celebrate more if he does well tomorrow.'

The performance at the Institut Hervy in Nice next day attracted a reasonable attendance. Greg played rather better but Jäger sang a little less well because he was more scared of an audience in a high-fashion resort. They returned to

Avignon relatively content but with no reason to splurge on a champagne celebration. Jäger was going home to Geneva next day, Monday, and Greg decided not to start on Evangelista's idea about songs from the operettas. Time enough for that when they were both less tired and in their home environment.

He went down next day to find Mandy already at breakfast. Her Monday morning outfit was black tights, a hip-length maroon chenille *blouson* left partly open over a silver fabric corset, and scarlet boots. It took quite an effort of politeness to sit down opposite.

She looked pleased to see him but didn't ask how the recitals had gone. He for his part asked about her enquiries.

'Well, it's not easy, you know,' she informed him. 'Jules is a darling of course, but he doesn't pay attention.'

'So you haven't got anywhere?'

'Not so far.'

'Did you go to Fontaine de Vaucluse?'

'Where?'

'To the artists' place. I left a message for you.'

'You did? When was that?'

'Saturday afternoon.'

'Really? I never got it. But then, of course, we haven't been around the hotel, because Jules took time off by saying he was sick, you know, so that wouldn't have gone down well with the manager. I only got back here late last night – fun and games are lovely but you need a shower and change of clothes in the end, don't you?'

'I see.' He was going to tell her about Mlle Grashenko but checked himself. If he told her, he'd have to take her there, and perhaps the besotted Jules as well. What good would it do? Though Mandy seemed prepared to take a little time off from her quest, she did seem sincerely attached to her sister. She might weep, or get hysterical, if things turned out badly. No, on the whole, since he had nothing needing attention until next day, it would be better if he went on his own.

'Don't bother with my message,' he said, 'it's old news now.' And before he set out he took care to retrieve the message slip from the reception desk.

The road to the romantic old village was well known to

him because he'd taken others besides Liz to see the magnificent gorge. But beyond this tourist attraction the roads were always less busy. To travel north-east he had to move on narrower routes. Stopping at a hamlet to enquire for an artists' settlement he learned that Parady, which seemed to suit the description, was about ten or eleven kilometres further on. He would see a sign saying 'Groupe Lo-Danièle' at a turning off to the right.

He nearly passed it. For, in fact, what it said was 'Groupe Locke Daniels.' It was a board embellished with a scattering of artefacts – framed paintings, copperware, baskets and pottery. An arrow pointed up the track, promising it was only 1200 metres to the settlement. He trundled on, and began to see the first buildings.

It was clearly a *mas*, an old farmhouse that had been developed to make a showroom and restaurant, with outbuildings old and new scattered around. Another board announced that this was the *Groupe Locke Daniels,* offering a painted map with the names of the artists or artisans on their premises. The pottery of Estelle Grashenko was shown to be at the far end, quite a large set-up, somewhat off by itself.

Wide gates of metal mesh stood open at the entrance to the community. He drove in slowly. There was a short well-kept road to a car park alongside the farmhouse, which was now the showroom, café and offices. There were two doors, but each bore a sign saying 'Closed'. He parked and got out.

Most of the workshops seemed closed and deserted. There was someone cleaning windows at the basket shop. He enquired for Mlle Grashenko.

'I think she's here, monsieur. She had something to take out of the kiln today, I believe.' She gestured with her window mop. 'Just keep on along the path.'

He followed her instructions, passing one or two other workshops with slight signs of activity, but clearly the *communards* didn't expect many customers on a chill January morning. The last building, where the path turned to lead round again past other shops to the entrance, had quite a narrow frontage but went back a long way. The door stood open. The sign on it said, 'Estelle Grashenko, *potière*.'

Inside in the little vestibule stood an extraordinary vase,

about forty centimetres tall and with a translucent blue sheen. It was shaped in a fashion that made clear it was never intended to contain anything. A lettered card pinned to the wall above it explained that manganese mixed in the clay accounted for the attractive blotches showing through the glaze. If it was for sale, it had no price tag – which in Gregory's experience usually meant it would cost a lot.

He walked on through the door ahead of him. It opened on to a short passage with windows, on the sills of which stood other pieces of pottery – a sort of display area. Then came a door to the left, standing open; it looked messy inside. Cupboards and shelves housed plastic-wrapped clay. On a table stood a rough piece of work, near which lay a wire that looked very like a cheese cutter from a delicatessen. The floor was studded with little scraps of clay of different colours.

He went on. The next door was closed but through its glass upper half he could see two contraptions rather like washing machines, one square and one round. The round one had a red light glowing, which might mean it was working. But if this was the kiln from which something was to be taken, clearly Mlle Grashenko didn't expect it to happen immediately for she wasn't in attendance.

Through the window in the far wall of that room he could see another building – a shed, rather. It had a stubby chimney at its far end. Another kiln? But to get to it he'd either have to retrace his steps or go on in hopes of a back door. He went on because there was still another glass door to look through.

A woman was standing at a table with her back to him. She had her arm raised, in her hand a jug. As he stood watching she tilted the jug as if to pour, but on to what, he couldn't see because her body masked it.

He waited. From the tension in her back, he could tell this was a vital moment for her. Time passed, perhaps ten seconds. She set down the jug, relaxed, flexed her shoulders and stretched her arms.

He tapped on the glass. She gave a start, then turned. He opened the door enough to put in his head and ask, 'Mlle Grashenko?'

'Yes?'

'May I speak to you a moment?'

'I'm rather busy. If you want to buy something, the showroom will be open at noon.' She had moved a little, so that he could see she'd been pouring green glaze on the shoulders of a narrow brown urn.

'I don't want to buy anything, mademoiselle, I came to speak to you.'

'Really? Do I know you?'

'No, we've never met. My name's Grégoire Couronne. Could we talk?'

'About what?'

'About Barbara Rallenham.'

Her head was half turned towards her work. At his words she turned completely as if to study the result of the glaze application. She leaned over the urn, then turned the stand on which it stood to see the back. She made a sound, perhaps a little grunt of satisfaction. She turned back to him.

'What was that you said?'

'I came to ask about Barbara Rallenham. Is she here?'

'Who is Barbara Rallenham?'

'She's a journalist, a friend of mine. She seems to have dropped out of circulation and I thought she might be here.'

'Rallenham?' She put a folded cloth over the top of the little jug and then stood a capacious wire protector covered in gauze over her urn. She gestured to him to go out. Clearly the surface of her work mustn't be contaminated by dust or threatened by movement.

He went into the passage, she stepped out after him. She led him back to the room with the washing-machine-like equipment. The red light still glowed. She glanced at it but made no move towards it.

'I can give you a few minutes,' she said.

'I was enquiring for Barbara Rallenham.'

'Did she buy something here?'

'Not that I know of. But I thought you might have seen her.'

She shook her head.

She was a fine-looking woman. Her head came to about his shoulder level, and on it she wore a loose net of crocheted cotton that held back her thick dark hair. Her eyes were deep set, a rather sombre brown and thick lashed. Her face was broad, with noticeable cheekbones tinged with a faint flush. Her clothes – worn blue jeans and a grey cotton shirt – were spattered with streaks and spots of colour. Her hands looked strong and were as clean as a surgeon's – presumably for the task of applying glaze.

She seemed quite uninterested in his enquiry. She stood waiting for him to go on. He was trying to think what to ask next when she said, 'I'm really very busy. Is there anything else?'

'Barbara is an Englishwoman, about forty, fairish, rather plump. You might have met her in Avignon?'

'Avignon? I seldom go to Avignon.'

'Do you go to London?'

She seemed to give it some thought. 'I went for the Aztec Exhibition,' she offered.

'More recently? I thought you might recently have been in Maida Vale.'

The conversation had been in French but the mundane English place name seemed to shake her. Her lips pressed together over her teeth as if to dam something back. But then they relaxed into a polite smile of denial. 'Is that a place? I never heard of it, monsieur. I'm sorry.'

Once again he tried to think of something. 'She was staying at the Auberge Mignard, not far from Fontaine de Vaucluse.'

The smiling lips didn't tremble. She glanced pointedly at her watch. 'I have to get back to my work, monsieur. This is a tricky point for the glaze. You'll have to excuse me. I'm sorry I can't be of help.' She shepherded him towards the door, came out behind him, closed it, and with a little gesture of farewell and a murmured 'Good day' went back towards her glazing room.

Gregory made his way out into the chill bright air. He stood studying the outside of the pottery, but it told him nothing. He walked slowly back to the parking area, where he found that the showroom and its little restaurant were about to open. He went in, was given a surprised but smiling welcome, and ordered a Belgian beer. After his first satisfying sip, he felt in his inside jacket pocket. He took out the photocopies, unfolded them, then stared at the face that looked back at him.

It was the woman in the glazing room. Shake her hair out

of the cotton net that held it back, allow for the fact that Liz had made her face a bit too narrow, and there was no doubt. She was the woman who had paid Barbara's bill. She was the woman wearing a bright shawl outside the flat in Maida Vale.

There could be explanations. She might be the recipient of stolen goods, Barbara's Burberry jacket, her handbag with credit cards and house keys. But thieves don't usually pay off the victim's hotel bill. And there was the worrying fact that, if the things had been stolen, Barbara had never reported the theft.

When Grashenko's unknown male friend had entered Barbara's flat using Barbara's keys, he'd proved a strange kind of thief. He'd taken nothing but notebooks and diaries. Mandy had ascertained that her sister's small collection of jewellery was intact, that the supply of ready cash hidden in the drinks cupboard was still there.

What had the man taken? He'd taken *information.* That's to say, he'd *removed* information. Was that because he wanted it for himself, or was he simply preventing others from accessing it?

Although Barbara's sister knew that she'd come to Provence, she didn't know why. It might have been for something a lot more important than the pretended reason, the silly invention about bribery among the string players. The deputy features editor had said it: 'Barbara wouldn't waste her time on a thing like that.'

It seemed undeniable that Estelle Grashenko had been in some contact with Barbara. She'd been wearing her jacket, carrying her handbag. She'd been outside Barbara's flat a few days ago.

Pottery? Barbara Rallenham had been on the track of a scandal to do with *pottery*?

He groaned to himself at the idea. He refolded the sketches and put them in his pocket. Absurd though the theory was, he had to take it to the police. For the sketch from a description by Barbara's cleaner in London resembled Estelle Grashenko almost exactly.

Yet Grashenko was denying she knew anything about Barbara.

Six

Liz listened in startled silence when he rang her. 'So I showed the sketches to the police and they've agreed to take it a bit higher. I mean, higher than a sergeant.'

'So that's good.'

'Yes, but they're still sceptical.'

'How d'you mean, sceptical?'

'Well, in the first place, the witness who gave the description for the sketch is in London. They only have my assurance that she gave it.'

'You can't mean they think you're telling lies?'

'No, not that. But you see, Liz, they're tremendously unwilling to have a missing-tourist case on their hands. Fingers can get burned in cases like that. So they want to have every T crossed and every I dotted.'

He heard a hesitation then she asked: 'You're really sure it's her?'

'Positive. But she says she hasn't been in London since the Aztec Exhibition, which was ages ago, wasn't it?'

She ignored that, because it was a fact, to ask instead: 'So what are you going to do?'

'I wish I knew. This morning I avoided telling Mandy that I'd got a name for the woman in the sketch—'

'Why was that?' she enquired, though pleased to hear it.

'*Ach, je!*' He sighed. 'I find it hard to put up with her. She's been off philandering with one of the waiters this weekend, you know. That's why I held off about Parady and went on my own – she might have insisted on taking lover-boy with her. And I'm still unwilling to tell her, because she might go dashing off there on her own – and the French police would take a very poor view of that now the matter's in their hands.'

'Mm-m.'

'In any case, she's out doing some gum-shoe work at the moment, presumably with the boyfriend, and I've got to go to Nice to collect my *charango* group.'

'Charango?'

'It's a kind of guitar – made from the shell of an armadillo—'

'You're kidding!'

'Not at all. They make their flutes from condor bones.'

'Who are they, bushmen from Africa?'

'Wrong continent. They're from villages up in the Andes, so they don't speak a word of French.'

'Don't tell me you've paid air fares from Argentina! You'll never make a profit—'

'No, no, I'm getting financial backing from a cultural organization in Bolivia – not Argentina, they're nothing to do with Argentina. They've got an escort with them who's seen them through passport desks and so forth but all the same, they'll need a lot of attention.'

'Greg, why do you do such difficult things? Why can't you just handle nice sophisticated people who can look after themselves?'

'But the music's so good, my darling. That's the point – you hear something you never heard before, and it stretches your understanding.'

'Don't get lyrical, now! What we have to decide is, are you going to tell Mandy the latest news once you've settled your South Americans in their hotels? Or do you have to shut yourself up with them while they rehearse in the hall?'

'They play in the open air, that's the big plus on this event—'

'Stop talking about the armadillo players. What about Mandy?'

'I suppose I'll have to tell her,' he sighed.

So late that evening, once Los Aldeanos had been introduced to the manager of the hostel where they were to stay, he sought out Barbara Rallenham's sister. Rather to his surprise, he was told she was on the premises – in the bar, to be exact. He found her there, sitting over a Pernod.

'Had a good day?' he asked, and at once could have kicked himself, because she so obviously had not.

'Absolutely foul,' she replied. 'Jules completely let me down. He had to go back to work, said he'd lose his job if he didn't turn up – although all they do here is breakfast but I think he's on the bar at some other place in the afternoons.'

'So you've been on your own?'

'Yes, and let me tell you, it isn't easy! You know I've been trying to find out if anyone's seen Babs in and around Avignon – the main square, the travel agents – but people seem to get the wrong impression, especially the men – I mean to say, the way they *goggle* at me . . . !'

He could easily imagine. He said: 'Well, I have some news. I don't know whether it's progress, but I thought I ought to let you know.' He related how he had come to make the trip to the artists' settlement at Parady, and his complete lack of success in getting anything helpful there.

'That was this morning? Why didn't you let me know at once?' she demanded, her colour rising in perhaps justified anger.

'You weren't in the hotel,' he said, although he'd never enquired for her earlier. 'And I had to go to Nice this afternoon to fetch some musicians from the airport. But the police are going to look into the Parady connection—'

'I'm going to go there tomorrow.'

'No, Mandy, you mustn't. The French police don't like interference.'

'Good God, it's not interference! I just want to know what's happened to my sister!'

'I understand that. But the system in France is very well defined – they like everything to be official. So until they've been out to the community and made their enquiries, you shouldn't do anything there.'

'But I can't just sit here and do nothing!' Tears began to tremble on the mascara of her lashes. 'Greg, it's over *ten days* since I heard from her. You don't understand – we've n-never g-gone ten days without being in t-touch!'

Seeing her genuine distress, he was ashamed. Just because he found her a bore and didn't like her dress style, that was no reason to belittle her concern for her sister.

'Perhaps tomorrow we could try something,' he ventured.

'You mean you'd come with me?'

'Of course.' *And please wear something less strident*, he added inwardly. 'But not to the ceramics place. What exactly have you done so far, you and Jules?'

'Oh, Jules . . .' She shrugged. 'He kept wanting to go back to his digs and go to bed. But anyhow, we asked at the big hotels, to see if Babs had moved into one after she left that auberge. And we went to travel agents to see if she'd booked tickets to anywhere.'

'Did you go to the car hire firms?'

'Car hire firms?'

'She must have had some means of getting around. She'd booked herself into a hotel right out in the country.' Out towards Parady, he added to himself. Was that significant? 'If I remember right, the hotel clerk said something about her luggage being put in a hired car.'

'We never thought of that,' she said, meaning herself and Jules.

'We could try that tomorrow.'

'And you'll come with me, and do the talking? Because I only know hello and goodbye and things like that.'

'Yes, I'm at your disposal tomorrow.' His South American group were to be entertained by a local goodwill organization, shown the sites and given lunch. After lunch, weather permitting, they'd play in one of the town squares. Although good manners called for his presence, it probably wouldn't matter if he turned up a little late, given the length of time a Provençal lunch could last.

She joined him for breakfast next day. To his relief, she was wearing an outfit that, for her, was quite sedate: the stretch jeans, a Chinese jacket of dark blue embroidered with yellow dragons, and quite ordinary black shoes. The Tuesday morning outside looked a little windy so she carried the skinny knitted jacket and had trapped her hair in a yellow tam-o'-shanter. They set out on foot about nine thirty.

The car rental firms were all in the Boulevard St Ruf. At the first one, Greg's enquiry was met with some hesitation. 'Why are you asking, monsieur?' asked the blazer-clad woman behind the desk.

'Miss Rallenham seems to have gone out of touch,' he replied. 'This is Mlle Mandy Rallenham, her sister.'

Mandy, hearing herself named, summoned up a smile. 'How do you do?' she said in English.

Still some hesitation. 'Show her some identification,' murmured Greg.

'Oh – yes – golly!' After fishing in her handbag she produced a card case and offered a business card. He had a glimpse of it. 'Mandy Rallenham, Cosmetics Consultant.'

Reassured by the title 'consultant', the receptionist relaxed. 'I asked, because the police have already been on the telephone to us about this,' she said to Greg. 'And the answer is no, Mlle Rallenham did not rent a car from us.'

So they were merely following the official line of enquiry. All the same, Greg decided to go on. No luck at the next two offices. In the fourth, the young man went through the formalities but then agreed that Mlle Rallenham had hired one of their cars. 'She had a recent-model Fiat,' he said. 'She hired it at our office at Nice airport.'

'And when did she return it?'

'The police already asked that. She returned it a week ago Saturday.'

'To the airport?' Greg asked, relieved. Everything was becoming clear. Barbara had flown on to some other city, perhaps back to London.

'No, no, she left it at the bus station.'

'The bus station? In Nice?'

'No, here in Avignon. That's quite common, you know, monsieur. She rang us to say she was leaving it there, with the keys inside.'

'She rang you. You didn't see her?'

'She rang this office. The assistant manager took the call. He went out later in the day to retrieve it.'

Greg related a brief version to Mandy. 'That's weird,' she said. 'The bus station?'

'She might gone on to Nice in the bus.'

'Greg, why should she? She had the car, she could have driven on to Nice and returned it there.'

'Yes, of course.' Of course. Her luggage in the car – why should she transfer to a bus when she needn't bother?

He turned back to the desk clerk. 'Did Mlle Rallenham leave her luggage in the car?'

'Oh, certainly not. Nothing valuable, sir. We would have returned it to the address she gave us – London, I believe.'

'Did she leave anything. A guidebook, perhaps?' Because Barbara had said she didn't know the area.

'No, I assure you, monsieur. Just the usual stuff – a couple of sandwich wrappers, old newspapers, scraps of paper – I cleaned it out myself when Leo put it in our garage.'

'Thank you,' sighed Greg. He paused. 'A map? You give clients a complimentary map, perhaps?'

'No, sir, we don't do that.' He too paused, frowning. 'Wait a minute. There was a map, though. Just a sketch. That was one of the pieces of paper – there were one or two, bills from a bar, receipts from restaurants. One of them was a receipt from Isola Bella, you know, that Italian place in the Rue de la République.'

He knew it. His memory conjured up its signboard – a black-on-white silhouette of a little island with tall pine trees. The restaurant's bills had the same logo and were quite large. The back of one of those would be a handy place to make a little map.

'A few roads drawn in pencil, monsieur, with arrows to show where to turn – I think she must have been looking for a disco or something. *Élysée? Éden?*'

'Parady?' Greg suggested.

'That was it, *Paradis*. Outside the city somewhere, I imagine, because I never heard of it.'

'You wouldn't still have the sketch map, I suppose?'

'Oh, no, sir, I put it all in the trash.'

'Did you mention all this to the police when they rang?'

'Why no. They just asked if she'd hired a car and I said yes, and they asked if she'd returned it OK and I said yes.'

'But did you tell them she left it here at the bus station?'

'No, monsieur. Is it important?'

'Who knows?' Greg was not optimistic. A map on a scrap of paper, now gone to the incinerator. It was all so tenuous. Not even definite enough to call circumstantial evidence. The police would sigh and shake their heads.

'Thank you.' He shook hands with the young man, leaving a little currency in his palm in doing so.

Outside, Mandy asked with eagerness, 'I heard him say it – Parady – that's the place you went to, isn't it?'

He recounted the conversation to her. 'So we should go there at once,' she replied, grabbing his elbow as if to steer him back to the Hotel Glaneur and its car park.

'No we shouldn't. The police are on the case now and they've probably been out there already asking questions.'

'But we can tell this Madame Grashenko that Babs had a map—'

'No we can't, because we haven't even seen the map. And even if we had it, it only proves that she intended to go there. It doesn't prove she got there.'

The minute he said it, he was sorry. Mandy went pale under her make-up. 'Oh! Oh, you mean – something happened to her on the road? A car-jacking?'

'No, no, for heaven's sake, Mandy! I only meant . . . well, she could have changed her mind about going.'

'Then why were Grashenko and her friend at the flat? How did they get her keys?'

'It's still possible that she gave her keys to them.' But if she'd never gone to Parady, how could she have handed over the keys? Talk sense, he said to himself.

He paused so that they stood on the pavement with the pedestrians dividing around them as if they were an island. He decided to try to follow the possibilities raised by the car at the bus station.

'She may have got some lead on this big story she came here for, whatever it is. So she's taken off, gone by bus to some other part of Provence – or by train, the bus station is right alongside the train station.' But then, he thought to himself, the woman who paid the bill at the auberge collected the luggage and drove off in the rented car.

The car was left at the bus station by Grashenko. Not by Barbara. And it was probably Grashenko who telephoned the car rental office to say it was left there for retrieval. That seemed the logical conclusion.

They went to the bus station in the Boulevard St Roch to ask at the ticket office if anyone resembling Barbara Rallenham had booked a seat on a bus ten days ago. The enquiry was greeted with disbelief. '*Mon cher monsieur*, there are dozens of *anglaises* in town for the Winter Festival. Impossible to know if your friend was here.'

It would have been even more useless to ask at the ticket desks in the railway station. Then Greg bethought himself that the long-distance buses went from the Avenue Montclar.

But Mandy had had enough. Her shoes were hurting, she was unused to so much walking, she was thirsty, she thought she'd rather go back to the hotel. He put her in a taxi and waved her off.

The Avenue Montclar was no more productive than the other public transport offices. And, moreover, he hadn't really expected any results from them. He was convinced in his heart that Barbara had never driven her rented Fiat to the car park at the bus station. Estelle Grashenko had done that, wearing Barbara's Burberry jacket and carrying her handbag. The luggage she'd collected from the auberge? Easy enough to transfer it to her own car or a taxi and take it safely away. By now it was probably at the bottom of the Rhône, or in a rubbish tip.

But why? Why?

It was now well past noon. He had lunch at the Hotel Sourire in the city centre, where the service was lethargic. Afterwards he went to the Place de l'Horloge in time to greet his South American musicians. They turned up in white shirts and trousers under ponchos of brightly woven llama wool, and straw hats. The cool breeze had died, the afternoon sun was gently warm. Students from the Conservatoire crowded out to listen to the concert, while clients at outdoor restaurant tables looked on while they ate their leisurely dessert or sipped a glass of wine.

His attention was taken up with explaining the musical instruments to idle enquirers. 'The large flute is a *taka* I believe, and the smaller one is an *anata*. I'm afraid I'm no expert. Yes, the little guitar *is* made from the shell of an animal.'

By four it was over, to appreciative applause and the depositing of some euros on the surface of the drum – although this was supposed to be a gratis performance. He congratulated them, thanked their escort Señor Mejanes, saw them into their car and waved them off to the hostel.

Then, by now sharing Mandy's feelings, he headed for his hotel. He plumped up the pillows on the bed, kicked off his shoes, and made himself comfortable with the telephone.

First he rang Bredoux, the little farm where he lived just outside Geneva. His father, the ex-king, picked up. 'Ah, it's you, Grego. Your grandmother is off doing the guest cabin, you remember? How are you? The musicians are behaving, eh?'

They had a comfortable chat. Anton von Hirtenstein gave him news about the horses, which were his hobby, his livelihood and his greatest love. He taught dressage and equitation, which Liz Blair said were words for fancy riding.

Once family duty had been done, he braced himself and rang the police station. Inspector Latouche took the call.

'Ah, M Couronne. I regret I have very little to add to your previous information. My man went out to the artists' encampment and spoke to Mlle Grashenko. She insists she has never met nor heard of Mlle Rallenham, has not been to London recently, and her assistant, a fellow called Coco, verifies that.'

'Barbara Rallenham intended to go to Parady, Inspector. I checked around this morning and was told there was a sketch map in her rented car, showing the route to Parady.'

'Indeed . . .' The inspector didn't sound pleased at being shown up as inefficient. After a moment he said, 'It seems she couldn't find the place. It *is* rather tucked away.'

'Her sister, Mlle Mandy Rallenham, thinks she might have been the victim of a car-jacking.'

The inspector covered scornful sound by coughing. 'A Fiat from a rental firm? Monsieur, we have plenty of thieves who take cars, but they go for vehicles that will fetch a big price. And they mostly take them from car parks or the street. Stopping a moving vehicle – no, that's most unlikely.'

'I agree, but I felt I should mention it.'

'I appreciate your cooperation, of course.'

'Is there any other news?'

'The London police force has been in touch. We asked if mademoiselle's credit card had been used, but no. The last transaction was the payment of her bill at the auberge.'

'Is anything known concerning Mlle Grashenko?'

'Only that she is an artist who makes and sells pottery.' The inspector took in a breath. 'Monsieur, in deference to your standing, we have followed this up as far as we can. There's nothing to say that Mlle Rallenham has come to any harm. She has every right to drop out of sight if she wishes to, particularly since her editor in London tells the local detectives that she does so if she is following up a story.'

'But the man who entered her flat, took all her notes, tampered with her computer—'

'You disregard the business card, giving her permission?'

'Well, Inspector, I'd put more faith in it if it had a word or two, and her signature.'

'Agreed. But, so far as we can tell, she sent someone – a friend, a colleague – to get information that she needed at her new headquarters.'

'But her computer files are gone – normally when one transfers to disk one leaves the original file.'

'What does it matter? If her colleague emptied the files to disk, they can be reinstated at any time.'

'Yes.'

'We feel – both our friends in London and the team here – that Mlle Rallenham will be in touch in her own good time.'

'I see. Thank you.'

As he disconnected he was shaking his head. They were humouring him, because he was who he was. They'd gone through the motions.

To reward himself for having gone through that conversation, he rang Liz. There was no reply at first, but when her machine had answered and he'd announced himself, she picked up the receiver. 'How are you, sweets?' she enquired, a trifle breathless.

'Weary. How are you?'

'Just come back from a run round the park. Now I'm about to have a bath and then go out to a first night.' She drew in some loud breaths for his benefit. She knew he thought her habit of running round city streets in shorts and a sweatshirt was absurd.

'Oho! A first night!'

'I'm not paying for it. One of my shop-owning clients wants some quick sketches of the celebs so they can do rip-offs by the end of the month.'

He translated this mentally as meaning she was to make notes of the dresses of the famous for purposes of copying. When Liz was in what he thought of as model-girl mode, it was often difficult to know what she was talking about.

'So everything's going well with the recitals and things?' she asked.

'Yes, it's the Andean musicians, remember?'

'Oh yes, flutes from eagles' feathers or something. And how about Mandy?' Her voice sharpened a little as she said the name. She still harboured a suspicion that Mandy was out to get Greg.

'We spent all morning trekking . . . what's the other word . . . tramping round . . .'

'Traipsing?'

'Thank you. We went to car rental firms and bus stations and so on and on.' He explained what they'd been doing and what he was thinking Then he told her the official view.

'I suppose they could be right, Greg.'

'I can't quite believe that. I think it's absolutely certain that she was heading for Parady. But why, Liz? She's a journalist who goes for scandal to do with people high up in the world, often people involved in the City. Nobody can make me believe that there's a big financial swindle connected with *pottery*.'

'No-o . . .' She thought about it. 'Picasso? He had a spell when he went in for ceramics, didn't he?'

'Yes, at Vallauris – the main street there is nothing but shops selling bowls and jugs and ornaments, a lot of them in the style of Picasso. But so what?'

'Well, could this Grashenko be making fake Picassos? An art scam?'

'You mean not like the Vallauris product – actually claiming they're real?' Then he said, 'But, sweetheart, would there be much money in it? Because drawings by Picasso are the easiest things in the world to forge and they don't go for vast sums, so would fake pottery do better?'

'Depends what you think of as vast sums. Suppose you got ten thousand euros a go. Suppose you sold . . . say six a year.'

'Well . . . that's not the sort of money that interests Barbara Rallenham. She goes after millions, usually. Or else it's political, she wants the scalp of some minister who's having an affair with his secretary. Or it's a football star taking drugs, or something like that.'

'Oh well, it was just a thought. What are you going to do now?'

'I don't see what to do, except hang around hoping the police will change their minds and poke about a bit more. Otherwise it seems to be a dead end.'

'Perhaps it's time for you to close the file and concentrate on your marimba players.'

'Marimba players? What kind of an education did you have? The marimba is played by Latin Americans who had contact with African slaves. The Andean people never saw a marimba.' He was laughing. He sometimes teased her over her lack of knowledge about what he thought of as 'real' music, but he knew she was always going to be bored by Bach, stupefied by Shostakovitch. Equally, she knew he was never going to know a Chanel from a Schiaparelli. It was a marvel they had ever fallen in love.

'Enough of the one-upmanship,' she riposted. 'Are you going to say *finito*?' Secretly, she wanted him to. Then he wouldn't have to keep seeing Mandy.

'When in doubt, tough it out,' he quoted. 'An American guest instructor said that to me during my military service. There must be *something* we've overlooked.'

'The desk clerk at the Auberge Mignard? He took off, didn't he?'

'Ye-es, but that was just because he knew he'd be in trouble over accepting a forged signature on the credit card. No, from *this* end I don't see what else to do. But . . . Liz? What about Barbara's flat?'

'What about it?'

'The inspector and I had a word about it. The man who let himself in with Barbara's keys took her diary and note-books—'

'Yes, that's what Mrs Dandry said—'

'And emptied her computer files.'

'Yes.'

'Are you a computer expert?'

'Me? No.'

'You couldn't get her files back?'

'No.'

'Well, to quote a well-known English saying, I know a man who can.'

Seven

The man in question was one of the musical mafia, as Liz called the network of friends whom Greg had met at concerts, exchanged CDs and precious vinyl records with, and kept in his address book. His name was Steven Stokes, and he ran a computer programming business. His greatest desire was to produce some meaningful music by means of his computers.

So far no luck in that regard.

But he agreed at once to retrieve the ditched files from Barbara Rallenham's PC. On the following morning, after she'd recovered from her first-night revelling, Liz Blair found Mrs Dandry's address in the phone book, collected her key to Barbara's flat, and went with Stokes and his bag of gadgets to let him in.

She hovered while he switched everything on. Then she went to look around the flat while he addressed the problem. Mrs Dandry was clearly keeping up her housekeeping visits and watering the plants. On Liz's return to the study, Stokes said: 'Um, this might take a while. I thought you said her files had been transferred to disk or something?'

'Well, haven't they?'

'No, sirree. Everything's been wiped.'

'But . . . wait a minute . . . according to the cops the man who came here and fiddled with the computer. . . they're saying he was a friend, collecting information she needed.'

Stokes, in faded jeans, a flannel shirt and outrageous tie, gave a shrug. 'Nothing saved. Whoever he was, he didn't come here to collect stuff, he came to get rid of it.'

'Oh lord.'

'Not to worry, he was only an amateur, ' he said, beaming encouragement at her. 'Not bright enough to defeat Stokes the Strategist. But it'll take a while, you get me? If you've got something to do, I'd take off.'

'Well, in fact . . .' She had an appointment with a department store executive in Guildford. 'Could I leave you to it? Just pull the doors closed when you're finished, I think they both lock by themselves. I have to head out of town but I'll drop the key in with Mrs Dandry and ask her to check later that everything's secure.'

'And when I get the files back?'

'Ah . . . Well, Greg wants those.'

'Everything?'

'Oh no, I'd imagine only her work diary. She up and left for France on Wednesday – actually two weeks ago today, if I've got it right. She was supposedly on the track of a story – for her paper, you know, the *Clarion*. What he wants to know is why she went.'

'Right. Work diary, check. Anything else?'

'Address book?'

'Address book, check. I'll retrieve everything but I'll send on only those two things. How's it to go? Direct link with his computer?'

'He hasn't got a computer with him, only his organizer, and that's an old-fashioned model.'

'Fax? His hotel got a fax machine?'

'I'm afraid I don't know. Look, here's his telephone in Avignon and his mobile. Ring him and arrange something, will you?'

'Whatever you say, babe.'

She was glad to leave him to it. She didn't care for men who called her babe. When she rang Greg on her return from Guildford late that night, he had the information in his hand.

'Steven faxed it through. But you know what? Her work diary's in some sort of code!'

'Good grief!'

'Unless Steven's made a mistake and it's come out all garbled. But that's not likely, he's what you call a whiz where all this IT business is concerned. And he's added 'Good luck' at the end, which I think means he knows there's a problem.'

'Her diary's in code! My word. Her editor said she liked to play things close to her chest, and she does!'

'Well, I can't believe the code is up to the standards of Enigma. It's scattered about with question marks and full stops so it does somehow make sense. I'll have a go at it tomorrow. I'd try it tonight only I've been giving the Aldeanos a tour of the night life so my brain's a little worn down.'

'The night life? There isn't any night life in Avignon.'

'There is, if you compare it with life in a village in the Andes.'

'Oh yes, I forgot about that. Here, just a point that I think I should mention – your pal Stokes said nothing had been saved to disk or tape or anything. He said the intruder just tried to delete everything.'

'What?'

'Stokes said . . . What's the matter? He seems to have got everything back.'

'Yes, but . . . Don't you see . . . If our friend the mysterious Mr Rivers was trying to get rid of information, he was probably trying to make sure nobody else got it.'

'Yes, that sounds reasonable.'

'But, Liz, Barbara wouldn't want all her information lost. Now would she?'

'I don't know. I never met her.'

'She asked to meet me in France. I think now she wanted me to act as her translator. From her secrecy about it, it seems likely it's a really big story. Are you telling me she sent someone to wipe all that out?'

'Well . . .No-o . . . it sounds unlikely.'

'So it seems pretty certain that the man who came to her flat and tried to empty her computer was no friend of hers.'

Liz drew in a long breath. 'Oh, Greg . . . !'

In silence they considered this possibility.

'No friend of hers. Yet he had her keys.'

'Yes,' he took it up, 'and Grashenko had her clothes and her car and her credit card. Which, if our idea is the right one, might have been taken from her against her will.'

'Greg, this is *not* good.'

'No.'

'Do you think you can work out that code? If we could find out why she was really in France it would be a big help, wouldn't it.'

'I'll start first thing in the morning. Let's hope she hasn't bought some awful computer program that transposes what she types as she types it.'

'I don't think so. Mr Stokes would have found that too, wouldn't he?'

'So he would,' he agreed in relief. 'So it's likely to be something approachable. If only I felt a bit more clear in the head . . . I should have said goodbye to those Bolivians a lot earlier.'

'Never mind. Go to bed and wake up tomorrow bright and early. *Buenas noches,* if I've got my Spanish right.'

'Your Spanish, like you, is perfect.'

'Hold that thought,' she said to him, and put down her phone.

At around seven in the morning, when some sound of activity from the hotel staff roused him, he sat up, looked fuzzily around the room, and forced himself out of bed. It took him longer than usual to get showered, shaved and dressed. He had a well-deserved headache. He took the fax sheets and the telephone pad with him to the breakfast room. After a cup of strong coffee he was able to concentrate on groups of letters.

He gave his attention to the most frequently typed letter. In English, the most frequently used letter is 'e'. A brioche and another cup of coffee later, he'd recognized the cipher as a simple letter substitution. For every 'e'. Barbara had substituted 'i'. So you entered the next vowel in the well-known list of five English vowels: 'e' for 'i', 'u' for 'o' and so on. On that principle he entered the next consonant for the existing consonants in the groups.

What he then got was gobbledygook. A not so simple letter substitution.

He worked on, sitting at the breakfast table until other hotel guests appeared and the day began to roll out its routine before him. He had to go to the hostel to see if Los Aldeanos had survived their experiments with pastis and Armagnac and crème de menthe. It appeared they were a hardy bunch. They were in the back garden of the hostel, practising for their afternoon performance.

Just as he'd left them to check their afternoon venue in the

Place St Didier, his mobile rang. It was his Swiss baritone, Robert Jäger.

'Good morning, Grego. Not too early for you, I hope?'

'Not at all. How are you?'

'I'm well. Listen, Grego, I played the tape of my Avignon performance to Papa and he was – well, he was taken aback, I think. The applause, you know? I don't think it had really occurred to him that I could please an audience so much.'

'It's a wise father who knows his own son.'

'What?'

'I think that's an English proverb,' he said, rather doubting it now. 'What I meant was, he didn't know how talented you are.'

'Well, I didn't ring you just to crow about Papa being impressed. The point is, he's offered some money.'

'Really?' Papa Jäger had always been opposed to his son's singing career.

'In a way I think it's sort of a shoot-to-kill offer. He'll give us the cash to promote a short series of recitals. If we make a profit – and that's the touchstone as far as he's concerned – he won't stand in my way any more.'

'That's great. Because, as a matter of fact . . .' He began to describe his visit to the great voice teacher, at which Jäger exclaimed in astonishment. 'Yes, well, I wanted her opinion about how to go forward. And she suggested you should try some of the music from operetta.'

'Operetta?' Jäger gave a moan. 'Not the dreaded *Fledermaus*!'

Greg couldn't help smiling as he went through the arguments he himself had had with Evangelista. After ten minutes of pep talk, Jäger began to bend a little.

'We-ell . . . As a matter of fact, that might please Papa. He always says he likes a tune he can whistle.'

It was agreed that Jäger should think about the project, so that on Greg's return to Geneva they could discuss it at length. He promised to find some operetta scores so that they could have an idea of what the music was actually like.

Now it was getting on for noon, so Greg found himself a snack bar, ordered a pancake made with chickpea flour and filled with grilled tomatoes, and got the fax sheets out of his pocket. He made the mistake of going back to the original groups of letters, but an hour later he was still convinced that what he'd got by transposing at least the vowels was correct. Where it all began to go pear-shaped was when he used the same theory on the consonants.

Now it was time to head for the Place St Didier to marshal his Bolivians. It seemed to him that they played less well, but whether that was due to last night's festivities or to a sudden drop in the surrounding temperature, he couldn't tell. The audience still seemed to like them.

Back in his hotel room he got out his scribbles so as to begin again on Barbara's coded work diary. After about half an hour's bewilderment he was interrupted by a tap on his door. Surprised, he went to answer it.

Mandy Rallenham was outside.

'Greg, so there you are! You'd gone out when I got down to breakfast this morning.'

He agreed this was so. She was stretching up so as to look over his shoulder at his room. 'Busy, busy, busy,' she said, taking in the papers on the bedside table. 'You never seem to take time off to enjoy yourself.'

'But I do, Mandy. It's just that while I've got musicians to look after, I have to give them proper attention.'

'I spent the whole day on my own,' she said in a doleful voice. 'Jules was busy, and since you weren't around it was no use me trying to ask anybody about Babs.'

'I'm sorry. Did you go sightseeing?'

'I did some shopping. There are some quite nice boutiques in the Rue Joseph Vernet, you know. And I had a nice lunch in a place a few doors up from the handbag shop. But you know, Greg, it's no fun on your own.' She edged past him and into the room. The only chair was the one he'd been occupying while he worked on the fax sheets. She sat down, picked up the sheets, and scanned them idly.

'What on earth is this?' she asked.

'It's . . . er . . . it's your sister's work diary, Mandy.'

She threw the sheets back on the table and gave a little snort of laughter. 'I *thought* I recognized the stuff! Babs was always into that even when she was at school. Secret messages! She and her chums sent each other notes about their boyfriends and things.'

'Really?' he said eagerly. 'Do you know the code?'

Picking up the paper, she eyed the typing. 'Never bothered with that kind of kinky twaddle. I mean, if you want to let somebody know something, why not just tell them?'

'But did Barbara ever tell you how she invented her codes?'

'How did you get hold of this?' she asked, waving the paper.

'From her computer.'

'But her computer had been emptied.'

'I got a friend of mine to go into it and sort it out.' He recounted how he'd got his friend Stokes involved, his tone apologetic because he realized now that he should have asked her permission. Luckily Mandy wasn't struck by that aspect. She was shrugging even as he was telling her how he'd spent the day trying to unravel the cipher.

'You're wasting your time,' she muttered. 'She once showed me how to get started on a secret letter she was going to give to Amy Pinford, but when I'd gone to all that bother she said, "Now for stage two", and it just seemed such a waste of time, because anyhow she was fourteen and I was only eight, so I ask you was it likely I'd be able to do it!'

He was going to explain that if they could translate the work diary they might find out why Barbara had come to Provence. But Mandy had lost interest. She rose from the chair, moved to the bed, sat there and kicked off her shoes.

'Gee, I'm tired,' she said. And she looked as if she were about to lie back on the pillows.

Alarm bells rang in his head. He turned so as to look as if he didn't see the move she'd made, and headed for the door. 'What you need is a cup of tea,' he said. 'I know the British like afternoon tea.'

'Tea?' she echoed.

'The great reviver,' he said, from outside in the corridor. 'I know a patisserie where they make it properly. I feel I need a break myself, you know. I've been struggling with that code all day.'

He heard the sound she made feeling about for her shoes, and the little puffs of breath as she put them on. As soon as she was on her feet, he walked off, calling over his shoulder, 'Pull the door closed, will you, Mandy?'

He kept up his usual long-legged stride so that she had to concentrate on keeping up with him. Two streets away they went into the pâtisserie Demarc where, luckily, Mandy found such comfort as she might need in sampling the Florentines.

It couldn't be said that Greg enjoyed his tea. But they whiled away enough time so that any romantic notions had died. 'I have to go to the hostel this evening,' he said. 'The Aldeanos have to get themselves packed up for our early start tomorrow.'

'Early start? Where are they going?'

'They're performing in Marseilles over the weekend.'

'You're *not* going with them?'

'Oh yes, of course. It was OK leaving them with their escort in Avignon. But Marseilles is a big wicked city.'

Her mouth was full of dried fruit and praline, but a sound came from it that might almost have been a sob. After she'd swallowed she complained, 'So I'm going to be on my own again all day tomorrow and Saturday.'

'I'm afraid so, Mandy.'

'But Greg . . .' She looked down into her teacup. 'Could I come to Marseilles with you?'

'Well, if you want to. But the Bolivians and I are going to be in a hostel.'

'A hostel? You're going to stay with them in a hostel?' She sounded appalled, and it comforted him to hear it.

'I feel I owe it to them.' He shrugged.

A long silence. Then she said, 'The truth is, I'm really just a drag.'

'Not at all. We got some useful information, the two of us.'

'But I can't do anything on my own, now can I?'

'Not here. But back in London perhaps you could be more active.'

'Doing what?'

'Well, Steven has put your sister's computer back into action. Why don't you go and have a look at it, see if you can spot anything.'

'Oh, computers . . .'

'Or talk to her friends.'

'Well . . .'

'At least in London you'd feel at home.'

'I suppose so. You think I should go?'

'Why not? Besides, your clients must be wondering where you are. The weekend's coming up – surely there are party-goers who are wanting your talents?'

'We-ell, that's true'

'If anything turns up here, of course I'll let you know at once.'

'But you're not going to be paying any attention to Babs. You'll be off with your folk singers.'

'They don't sing.' But why should she care. He went on: 'I'll take the work diary pages with me, Mandy, and keep going on it.'

He breathed an inward sigh of relief when he saw his suggestion taking root. When they returned to the hotel she lingered by the desk to ask them to ascertain flights home next day. They parted company on leaving the lift, on the grounds that he was going to be up and out early next day for a train to Marseilles. 'Keep in touch,' they murmured. She insisted on giving him a hug and a squelchy kiss on the cheek.

In his room he looked out the printed instructions for next morning to give to his musicians. They were in very simple Spanish, because the Bolivians came from a village that spoke its own dialect. He relied on their escort to translate anything they didn't understand but he'd made it as easy as possible by having times and dates printed very large. Each paragraph was labelled in order, so that a quick glance would tell his protégés what they should now be doing.

Stage one. Stage two. That was what it amounted to.

And in his memory he heard Mandy complaining about her efforts to work out her sister's secret codes. Stage one . . . 'Now for stage two.'

He got out the fax sheets. He'd done stage one, he was sure of that. The only way to deal with the prevalence of the vowel was to identify it as 'e' and then, for the others, substitute the next vowel in the chain of five.

So what was stage two?

If you've dealt with the vowels, he told himself, perhaps you should take the consonants as stage two. He sat down with the phone pad and began trying substitutions. Using the next consonant after the one in the code didn't work, because he'd already tried that. He tried the next obvious step.

Right. For every consonant, enter the consonant two letters on. He applied this system to the last entry.

What he got back was still in a very weird form. His heart sank. Yet it was in English, although in a strange, abbreviated style.

'C.W. to Prov. Cash moved? Names click. How long plan? Check Co's Hse. Mrs B. says addr. L. Daniels, check, check!'

He got himself a soft drink from the little fridge then sat down to consider this.

'C.W.' remained a mystery to him – a person, a place or an organization? 'Prov.' was likely to be Provence. 'Cash moved' spoke for itself. 'Names click' meant, surely, a connection in the names. But which names? Next: whatever Barbara was looking into, she'd wondered how long it had been planned. And next: 'Check Co's Hse' – 'Co' had a house, perhaps, but who was 'Co'?

'Mrs B.' could only be Mrs Barnell; he was almost sure of that. And she said an address – *the* address? – was 'L. Daniels'. Who was L. Daniels? He ought to know that. He was sure he already knew that.

Some forty minutes later, when it was high time to be hurrying to the hostel to talk about next day's journey, it came to him. In his mind's eye he could see it on the signboard as he turned into the track for the artists' community. L. Daniels was shorthand for Locke Daniels.

And that was why Barbara Rallenham had come to Provence, had taken a room in an auberge in the countryside north-east of Avignon: to visit the Groupe Locke Daniels at Parady.

So she'd set out for Parady. But if she'd got there, it seemed she'd never come back.

Perhaps – *perhaps* – loving hands had held her there. Perhaps she was having a secret affair with someone there, idyllic, romantic, revelling in the warmth and passion of it all.

Perhaps – *perhaps* – she'd found some great news story and had gone off in pursuit, clearing away any traces she'd left so that no rival could beat her to it, and was now uncovering something that would make a big splash in her paper. Perhaps she didn't want to be found.

But if either of those conclusions was correct, there remained two questions. Why had she made not the slightest move to reassure the sister who would certainly be worried about her? It would be easy to send a message to Mandy without revealing her whereabouts.

And why had someone come to her home and tried to wipe all the files from her computer? Barbara Rallenham was almost obsessive about keeping everything organized.

To fall head over heels in love and forget about her job seemed very unlike her. To cut off all communication with her sister was extremely strange. To send someone to trash all her notes and research was unbelievable.

The only other conclusion was that harm had come to her.

Having reached this sombre inference, Greg put everything in a drawer and hurried for the lift. The next two hours were spent in painstaking explanations about next day. He spoke in Spanish to Señor Mejanes who then translated his directions into some form of Inca dialect and translated back any queries from the musicians. Their chief query was whether they could go on another pub crawl in Marseilles.

He got back very late. He was tired, and he was going to have a very early wake-up call in the morning. He decided to ring Liz, because she was always up and about early – sometimes even out running.

When he dialled her number, only half awake in the darkness of the January morning, he got her answering machine. Was she out loping round the park? He'd leave a message, but that meant she might call him back while he was at the station trying to get Los Aldeanos and their instruments on the train.

She picked up. 'I'm here, I was just sitting down to the drawing-board to finish those fashion sketches from the first night "do". What's happening?'

'I worked out the puzzle from the fax sheets, Liz. It seems clear Barbara came to Provence so as to investigate something at that confounded pottery.'

'Oh, come on!'

'I mean it. And as far as I can tell, Mrs Barnell seems to have given her the information that sent her here.'

'Mrs Barnell,' she repeated. 'Hmm. I'd almost forgotten about her.'

'Listen, Liz, I can't come to London, I've got to take the Bolivians to Marseilles.

'Oh, this is the Marseilles weekend, is it?'

'They're doing a series of three performances there. Their escort, Mr Mejanes, is having a bit of trouble with them, because they've begun to be tempted by the French way of life. Sunday night, thank heavens, he's taking them north to Paris by train and I don't have to worry about them any more. But I have to see they're all right until they've done their stuff in Marseilles.'

'I understand. So?'

'So . . . Liz . . . Would you go and talk to Mrs Barnell?'

'Aha. I might have known you wouldn't be ringing me so bright and early without a good reason.' For it was well known to her that His Serene Highness was not a morning person.

'Will you do it?'

'What will you give me if I do?'

'Five golden rings and a partridge in a gum tree.'

'A pear tree, you numbskull. So what am I going to talk to her about?'

He thought about the notes he'd scribbled from the decoded fax. 'Ask her what she said to Barbara that sent her to Provence. Ask her about L. Daniels. I'm almost sure that's Locke Daniels.'

'Who's that?'

'It might not be a who, it might be a what. A firm called *Groupe* Locke Daniels seems to be the people who own or manage Parady.'

'But that's an English name, surely?'

'Oh, lots of people have bought property in France and set up businesses, it's not unusual. So ask about them. And then there's a set of initials – C.W. And something or somebody called Co. That's spelled just as it sounds, and he or she has a house, I think. Co's House, it says. Though oddly enough house is spelled with a capital.'

'Wait a minute, wait a minute, I'm trying to write this down. I'm to ask about L. Daniels, about C.W., and about Co's House, House with a capital.' She was scribbling. She stared at what she'd written. 'Greg . . .'

'What?'

'Co's House. I'm looking at it.'
'Yes?'
'You know in English we say Smith and Co?'
'Yes?'
'Meaning Smith and Company.'
'Yes.'
'Could Co's House mean Companies House? In Portland Place?'
'What? What's Companies House?'
'It's where you go to look up and find out if a business has been officially registered.'
He gave a laugh of astonishment. 'You clever, clever girl! There's no way I could ever have known that. Of course, that's what it is. She's telling herself to go to Companies House to check – to check perhaps whether Groupe Locke Daniels is registered in any form in London. So she *is* investigating them.'
'Greg,' she said in alarm, 'I can't go to Companies House, I think you can spend hours there, fossicking around.'
'Fossicking?'
'Never mind. In fact, I can't even go to talk to Mrs Barnell today. I've *got* to finish these sketches and get them to Lionel by this evening – he wants the dresses in his shop windows by the end of the month.'
'Yes, right, absolutely. I understand. I've got my Bolivians, you've got your sketches.'
'Should I ring the police, ask them to see her?'
'Ah-h.' He gave a long sigh as he thought about his encounter with the lady. 'She got scared when I tried to ask questions. I think it would be better if it was you that turned up on her doorstep. You're a nice, friendly looking type. You could take Mandy with you. Get her to play it *molto doloroso*.'
'Mandy? I thought she was still in Avignon.'
'Leaving today.' 'Thank heavens' was implicit in his tone.
She allowed herself a grin at that. Mandy had tried her wiles on Greg and had got the brush-off.
'Well, okay,' she said, 'I'll see what I can set up. You've got Barbara's address book from your computer bloke, haven't you? Let's have Mrs Barnell's whereabouts.'
With a feeling that at last they might be about to learn

something important, he read out the address and phone number.

'Ring me if you get anything useful,' he said. 'In fact, ring me whatever happens. I'll have my mobile.'

'It won't be until tomorrow, Greg. And I don't really want to take Mandy with me.'

'You're the boss.'

'You never spoke a truer word, boyo,' said she.

Eight

All Friday Liz Blair was busy. Saturday morning she went out for a run, but when she got back it was still too early to make phone calls. About twenty minutes to ten she felt even slug-a-beds would have surfaced so she rang Mrs Barnell's number. She got a voice asking her to leave a message, which took her momentarily aback.

Experience in the fashion industry had taught her that immediate impact worked best. So she said: 'Barbara Rallenham' – because that was Mrs Barnell's point of interest – 'er . . . her sister and I would like to drop in on you, Mrs Barnell, when it's convenient.' She left her name and her mobile number.

She had to be at a shop opening in Reading. Her attention was so taken up with meeting and greeting that it wasn't until well after lunch she remembered Mrs Barnell. There had been no call-back. She tried again. The same mechanical voice began to ask her to leave a message. She disconnected.

Saturday, of course. People had things to do on a Saturday. She tried again at tea-time. Same result.

She rang around nine. Time for the big film on television to start, so Mrs Barnell might be making herself a cup of tea before settling down to watch. But the result was the same as ever.

She began to be a little perturbed. She rang Greg, who from the sound of it was in the middle of a large noisy gathering. 'We're at a bistro on the waterfront,' he explained at the top of his voice. 'The Aldeanos are entranced by the sea. It seems they've never seen it at close quarters before.'

'Greg, I can't get Mrs Barnell on the telephone.'

'What?'

'I keep getting a recorded message from Mrs Barnell.'

'Oh. Well . . . presumably she's out.'

'You don't think anything's happened to her?'
'What?'
'. . . Happened to her.'
'Oh, I see. Well . . . How often have you rung?'
'Three times. Should I go there, bang on the door?'
'Er . . . Not at night, Liz. It might scare her.'
'Well, then, what?'
'Try again in the morning. And then if there's no reply, perhaps . . . perhaps you should go there.'
'Right, that's the plan. And if there's no answer at the door, what then?'
'I don't know. Ask her neighbours?'
'Sounds all right. I'll do that.'
There was a diminution of the surrounding noise. It seemed he had moved away from his companions so as to be heard. 'Liz, I'm sure it's OK. But be careful all the same, you know?'
'Got you. Goodnight, lover.'
'Goodnight.'
Once more she left it until a reasonable hour in the morning. She was expecting the same electronic response when the phone was lifted and a creaky elderly voice said: 'Hello?'
She drew a breath of relief. 'Mrs Barnell?'
'No, this is her neighbour, Miss Lessiter. Who is this?'
'My name's Liz Blair, Miss Lessiter. I've been trying to get in touch. Is Mrs Barnell ill?
'No, no . . . She's on one of those coach trips to chocolate factories and TV studios. I'm just bringing in some milk and bread for her.'
'I see. That's good of you—'
'Nothing of the kind, we do it for each other all the time.' A slight coughing fit. 'Do you want to leave a message? She's home this evening. About six.'
'Oh, if you wouldn't mind! As I said, my name's—'
'Just a minute till I find a pen . . . Where's she put it? Oh, right, here it is . . . Just a minute, I'll have to sit down.' Rustling sounds and a protracted clearing of the throat. 'Ready.'
'My name is Blair, and I wanted to know if I could come to see her with Barbara Rallenham's sister.'
'How do you spell that? Glare?'
'No, no, Blair.' She realized she'd have to go a lot slower.

'And Mandy Rallenham.' She spelled it all, enunciating clearly. 'That's Barbara Rallenham's sister. B-A-R—'

'Oh, I've heard of her. Yes, she's in the papers. Right, her sister.' A little cough. 'So what's the rest?'

'Could we come to see her? I'd like Mrs Barnell to ring me and let me know. OK?'

'Just let me read that back,' said the creaky voice, and breathed heavily for some thirty seconds. 'Miss Blair wants to come with Barbara Rallenham and her sister, and would Celia let her know if that's convenient.'

It wasn't accurate, but it was near enough. Liz agreed, thanked her helper, and rang Greg to let him know that there was no problem at the Barnell household.

He told her that he was relieved to hear it. He confessed he'd only just got up and that, besides discovering the sea last night, the Aldeanos had discovered Grenadine. 'And liked it a lot,' he mourned.

'Oh dear,' she said.

Next she rang Mandy Rallenham's mobile. It was switched off. She looked her up in the phone book and tried the house phone. She got her answering machine. She left a message: 'I'm trying to fix up a visit to Mrs Barnell. Please ring me so we can arrange to go together.' She still didn't much want Mandy's company, but she felt she ought to invite her now that she'd mentioned her to the old lady at the house

Somewhere around eight that evening, when she was getting herself a meal, Mandy returned her call. She sounded fragile. 'What's this about visiting Mrs Barnell?'

Liz explained that her sister's work diary confirmed Mrs Barnell as the source of the information taking her to Provence. 'Greg asked me to talk to her and I thought you'd like to go too.'

'Go where? Where is this place?'

'It's an address in Walthamstow—'

'Walthamstow? You're seriously thinking of going to Walthamstow?'

'I haven't fixed it up yet. I'm hoping she'll ring me, but perhaps it won't be until tomorrow now.'

'So when are we supposed to be going?'

'Well . . . tomorrow some time, I imagine.'

'No can do. I've got three consultations tomorrow, one of them a showbiz kid, and they're the *worst*.'

'How about in the evening?' Liz suggested.

'One of the consults is in the evening. I wish now I hadn't taken so many appointments. I don't know if I'll be able to get through them.'

'Under the weather?'

'I was at an all-night party, didn't get home till almost noon and I've only just got up. I haven't really got my eyes open yet . . .'

'I could arrange to see Mrs Barnell on Tuesday, if you like, but really the sooner—'

'You don't need me there, do you?' groaned Mandy. 'I mean, you could tell me all she says, if it's anything important?'

'That's true—'

'OK then, that's it. You do your thing and let me know. I've got to go, Liz, I'm coming over woozy again.'

Liz disconnected. She quoted to herself, 'If you can keep your head when all about you, Are nursing theirs . . .' Everyone else seemed to be suffering the after-effects of festivity. But she was pleased not to be taking Mandy with her when she went to see Mrs Barnell.

She came back from a morning run next day to find her answering machine blinking. Mrs Barnell had left word she'd be pleased to see her and the Rallenhams and give them afternoon tea. No need to respond unless they couldn't make it. Liz debated whether to ring and explain that neither Barbara Rallenham nor her sister would be coming, but decided against it. Remembering Greg's lack of success, she felt perhaps Mrs Barnell would cancel the meeting.

She held a debate with herself about what to wear. Nothing too casual, or Celia Barnell might not take her seriously. She had a business meeting in the morning but her black suit was a trifle too funereal for a social visit. She compromised on aubergine slacks, cream shirt and heavy plum-coloured knitted jacket.

Her arrival was timed for what she thought of as 'afternoon tea-time', a little after three thirty. The January afternoon was cold and cloudy so that it was almost dark. The street lamps provided enough light for her hostess to study her if she wished, but Mrs Barnell opened the door at once, having been watching for her from her bay window.

'Good afternoon. I'm Liz Blair.'

'Yes, and are others coming separately?' enquired Celia Barnell as she ushered her in.

'Mandy couldn't make it. She's a cosmetics consultant and she had clients.'

'A cosmetics consultant! Well, that sounds interesting. And Barbara?'

Liz laid her hand on the arm of her hostess. 'The fact is, Mrs Barnell, Barbara is still missing.'

Mrs Barnell gave a gasp and threw up a hand to her mouth. She seemed to sway. Liz put her arm round her. She steadied in the embrace, and moved rather uncertainly towards her inner door. They went into the flat and down the passage to the bright room at the back. Liz recognized it from Greg's description.

A table was laid with an embroidered cloth and fine china. The scent of newly baked scones was in the air. Liz felt like a traitor.

'I'm sorry,' she muttered. 'I should have let you know . . .'

'I'm . . . I'm a bit . . . taken aback,' panted Mrs Barnell. 'Let me . . . just sit down.'

Liz lowered her into one of the chairs at the tea table. She hovered. 'Can I get you anything? Should I make the tea?'

Mrs Barnell gestured at a cupboard. 'I think I . . . I think I need a drop of something stronger.'

Liz found brandy and a set of flower-decorated wine glasses. She poured in a healthy amount then took it to the other woman, who was leaning with her elbows on the table and her head in her hands.

After a sip or two, she straightened. Her colour was patchy, but she seemed recovered. She had clearly dressed in expectation of her visitors – bright blue jersey skirt and jacket, floral blouse with a big tie bow, a blue Alice band to hold back her silvery hair. It all seemed inappropriate compared with her distress now.

'So,' she said, though unwilling to start the conversation, 'how do you come into it?'

'You remember Mr Crowne? Who came to see you early in the month?'

'What, the tall one I shooed out of the house?'

'That's the one. Well, he and I have been in Provence trying to find Barbara—'

'Oh!' cried Mrs Barnell, and began to sob. 'Oh, I should have told him. It's weeks now, isn't it – weeks!'

'Nearly three,' Liz acknowledged. 'And we can't get word of her.'

'God forgive me. If any harm's come to her . . .' She shook her head so that the silvery locks caught on her shoulder. She pushed away the brandy as if it were wrong to be drinking anything so good.

'Could you let me have some idea of what took her abroad in the first place?' Liz suggested.

'Yes. I think I ought to. But, my dear, you came all this way to see me and I promised you tea—'

'No, no—'

'Yes, it's the least I can do.' It was clear she needed activity to help her through this moment. 'If you'd like to take the cover off that plate, dear, and there's clotted cream and home-made strawberry jam in the fridge in the kitchen . . .' She lumbered to her feet so as to switch on an electric kettle.

It was best to leave her alone to do these comforting tasks. By and by they were settled opposite each other with hot tea, scones, cream and jam. Celia took a bite of scone, swallowed it, sipped tea, then looked at her guest.

'Well, it's a sort of long story,' she said. 'And it's about my tenant.'

'Tenant?'

'Upstairs.' She jerked her head upwards. 'Thomas Shanigan. He rents the upstairs flat. Been there going on five years now. He keeps himself to himself a lot, and that suits me well enough, you know, because I have my own circle of pals for bingo and that. Tommy, he asked me to call him, but we don't have much chat.'

'Yes?'

'About two years ago, he began to have a lot more money. He's got a decent job – runs a lathe or something, down the industrial estate, you know, a company that makes special containers, I think it's quite special work. He always liked a bit of a flutter on the dogs.' She glanced at Liz, sipped tea, and explained in case Liz was at a loss, 'Greyhounds. He's always down Romford or Catford, throwing money away.'

'I see.' Liz sipped her tea also, and sampled the scones. She'd have been ashamed to admit that she was hungry and found the scones irresistible.

'He used to lose a lot, from what I could see. If I happened on him of a weekend he'd often look fed up, and now and again a betting slip would be on the hall floor – and you don't bring those home if you've won, now do you?'

'I suppose not,' Liz said, although she'd no idea. The only gambling she indulged in was a raffle ticket or two at Christmas.

'About two years ago, a bit less maybe, he seemed to hit a winning streak. He said that was what it was, anyhow. But I didn't believe him because you never get a winning streak that goes on for ever, and he's always flush these days.'

'You mean he's been buying expensive clothes, or cars, or—'

'Him? Nah,' Mrs Barnell said scornfully. 'He bought a couple of dogs.'

'Racing dogs?'

'Yes, and let me tell you, it'd surprise you how much they cost! And it's not just the buying, he boards them and has them trained, and one of them got too old so he retired it and bought another, a big-name racer, and I think he may even be trying to breed them, but it's all money flowing out.' Celia nodded for emphasis. 'He has to pay all kinds of expenses, I think – vet's bills, special transport when they race somewhere a long way off. But he's still got plenty. He goes wherever his dogs are going to run – sometimes he's off to Northern Ireland, but all over the country anyhow.'

'So you're saying he spends a lot on this hobby and gets nothing back.'

'He says his dogs win races, but they don't!' declared Mrs Barnell. 'He gets these special racing newspapers and now and again I look at them when he puts them out for recycling, and none of his dogs do much good that I can see.'

After this outburst she sat back, shaking her head in

emphasis. 'So where does all this money keep coming from?' she concluded.

'Is this what you told Barbara?' Liz enquired, somewhat dashed.

'Oh, that's only the beginning.' She put clotted cream on a second scone, dabbed it with jam, then let it sit on her plate. 'One evening last year, I come home from bingo early – I wasn't feeling too good, too much pizza at this take-away place I go to before the programme. Well . . . Someone was coming out of Tommy Shanigan's flat that was a perfect stranger.' She mimed her shock, putting hand on her heart and opening wide the faded blue eyes. 'I can tell you, it gave me a start!' She waited for murmurs of commiseration then went on. 'He could see I was put out so he says, 'I'm a friend of Tommy's, he give me his keys, so I could just fetch something he was going to let me have.' So he holds up a squashy parcel, not a very big thing' – she held up her hands about ten inches apart' – all done up in brown paper and sticky tape.'

'Go on.'

'Well, you know, Tommy Shanigan's a perfect right to lend his keys to anybody, hasn't he? By next morning I'd got over it and didn't give it much heed, but I happened to mention it to Miss Lessiter—'

'Oh yes, she took the message.'

'She's all right,' said Celia Barnell tolerantly. 'We do each other good turns like pushing give-away papers right through the letterbox so people won't know you're out. And I'm sorry for her of course because of her bronchitis. But she's ever so nosy! Nothing passes her by, you can bet on that. So when I just happened to say I'd had a bit of a fright with this man, she says, 'Oh, but Ceelie, he's been coming to your door for weeks and weeks now.' I can tell you, I was flabbergasted.'

'I don't quite see,' Liz began, 'if you agreed that Mr Shanigan had every right—'

'But he only came when I was out at bingo on a Friday,' said Ceelie. 'And Tommy was usually out too, at the dogs. So there was this stranger, coming into my house with a set of keys when no one was home . . . I didn't like it, I can tell you, so I nerved myself to speak to Tommy about it, and he apologized and said it was just to fetch something from his flat, and I said to him, "I wish you'd make some other arrangement if you don't mind, for it's not a nice feeling having him come in, unless you'd like to introduce him to me properly." And he said he'd see about it.'

'And he introduced you?'

'No, he never. And the man never came any more. But instead,' said Celia Barnell, deepening her voice and holding up a finger, 'every Saturday morning first thing Tommy Shanigan goes out to the post office and posts this parcel. His shift ends at about five o'clock of a weekday afternoon, you know, so it'd be a bit of a tight squeeze to get a packet to the post office on the Friday, so he goes on the Saturday morning, instead. And he has this envelope – a padded envelope like you can buy – and that happens every Saturday except when he's on his holidays.'

She sat looking at Liz in expectation.

'So . . . what . . . you think he's posting the thing – whatever it is – that used to be picked up by the visitor.'

'Exactly!'

'But I don't see—'

'Wait,' said Mrs Barnell. 'One Friday he was in a big rush because there was a dog derby in Belfast and one of his dogs was running. So he goes dashing off to catch the plane and I think to myself, "Has he posted his packet?"' She gave Liz a rather shamefaced look. 'I just wanted to . . . you know . . . reassure myself . . . So I went into his flat—'

'You have a key?' Liz exclaimed.

'Of course I have a key!' cried Mrs Barnell with indignation that masked a sense of guilt. 'It's my property!'

All right, said Liz to herself, *let's hear the rest*. 'What did you find?' she asked.

'He'd left the packet on the little table just inside his door. I think in his hurry he'd forgotten to take it with him to post at the airport.'

'Did you open it?'

'Oh no, I couldn't do that.' Scruples at last, thought Liz. But no. 'I didn't know where he kept his sticky tape so I couldn't have stuck it back together if I'd opened it. Of course I've got sticky tape too, but it wasn't the same kind. But I picked it up and I had a feel of it. And it was like I expected – sort of soft and squishy.'

'Like what? Papers?'

'No, no, paper isn't soft. A packet of papers would have edges, corners. No, this gave way under your fingers when you pressed it. It wasn't paper.'

'So what do you think it was.'

Mrs Barnell leaned across to her, touched her on the shoulder with one finger, and said in a dramatic whisper: '*Dr-r-ugs!*'

Nine

When Liz reached this point in her report to Greg, she was greeted with a gurgle of amusement.

'What?'

'Sending drugs from England to a place about a hundred kilometres from Marseilles?'

'Oh.'

'Well, never mind, go on.'

Liz rearranged her approach. Until that moment she'd been quite taken with Mrs Barnell's theory.

'She wrote to Barbara Rallenham saying she thought something funny was going on. She didn't actually mention drugs – I checked that with her. She can't remember exactly what she said and she didn't keep a copy of the letter, hang it! We went over it two or three times and she's certain she explained that the mysterious packets were going to an address in Provence.'

'Does that mean Barbara was already interested in something that she thought was going on here?'

Liz sighed. 'Whatever Mrs Barnell wrote, it made Barbara ring her to make an appointment for a chat, and she was at her door about two weeks later.'

'Ye-es, that's significant. What did she actually say to Barbara? Can she remember?'

'She told her seemingly what she told me. She was so chuffed at having this famous columnist in her house that she has good recall. She said she thought the packet Shanigan was sending contained cannabis. Barbara clearly didn't laugh at her.'

'I'm sorry, I shouldn't have laughed either. But anybody wanting small regular amounts of cannabis could grow it here in a backyard, or get it easily on the streets of Marseilles.'

'Yet Barbara seemed to think there *was* something in the story. Because when Celia repeated the address it was going to, she asked her a lot of questions. And the address, of course, was Groupe Locke Daniels, Parady, Fontaine de Vaucluse, France.'

'*Bizarre!* What can a greyhound-lover send to an artists' colony in Provence?'

'Cash? Celia says she didn't think it was paper in the envelope because documents have corners, they have a definite shape. But banknotes might feel squishy.'

'His winnings? To turn into euros? But explain to me, what is the advantage? And besides, you told me this Shanigan doesn't win money with his dogs.'

'No, she says not.'

'It's perfectly legal to change gambling profits into another currency. It isn't against the law, there's no tax problem because – I think I'm right – what you win on a race or in a casino is not taxable. If he wants euros he could walk into a bureau de change.'

'But in any case he doesn't win – unless it's not profits from the dogs; perhaps he goes to a *casino* and wins. After all, Celia can't know every little thing he does.'

'But why would he send his winnings abroad? And so regularly?'

'I don't know.'

'Perhaps he's being blackmailed? He has to send a sum of money each week or else his dreadful secret is unmasked.' Greg was allowing himself to fantasize a little.

'We know he's acquired a substantial income fairly recently. By doing something criminal? And someone is going to tell on him.'

'That might be the answer. That would interest Barbara. It might tie in with information she already had – some scandal that might make an article for her paper.'

'I suppose a blackmailer might demand his money in cash. But once a week? I mean, if he's asking for, let's say, a hundred a week, wouldn't it make more sense to send four hundred once a month?'

'*Ah, je ne le crois pas!* It's not banknotes. What is the smallest British banknote? Five pounds, yes? And then there is a ten pound note, and twenty – even to make a hundred pounds, that would be a thin packet. You could send that in an ordinary letter envelope.'

'Well, perhaps he's sending a lot more than a hundred a week. Perhaps it five hundred.'

'Even so. Five hundred in twenties is only twenty-five notes if he cares to collect twenties. The packet Mrs Barnell had in her hands was bigger than that. You said a medium-sized padded envelope.'

'About A4 size, I think. A couple of inches thick. And squishy.'

'How much did it weigh?'

'We-ell . . . She said it wasn't heavy. That's why she thought it was cannabis – that's plant leaves, isn't it? – lightweight?'

'Tell me things you think are squishy.'

'Well, from what you say, it *isn't* cannabis and probably not anything in powder or crystal form because you seem to think that's sort of like sending coals to Newcastle.'

'Newcastle? This is one of your obscure English-isms.'

'Yes, it is, but let's not bother with that. Are we any farther forward?'

'We know that Mrs Barnell gave Barbara the address of the settlement. And within days Barbara had come here to Provence.'

'So it made sense to her. It was important. And a couple of days after that, Barbara goes completely out of circulation.'

'And an attempt is made by Grashenko and our friend Mr Rivers to clear up after her.'

'What should we do, Greg?'

'Go to the London police?' He heard her make a muttered sound. 'What does that mean?'

'Mrs Barnell doesn't want to do that. She . . . er . . . went into Mr Shanigan's flat without his knowledge or permission, and interfered with the Royal Mail. That's against the law.'

'Interfered with the Royal Mail? You make it sound as if she held up a stage coach. All she did was look at the address on an envelope.'

'All the same, she shouldn't have done it. And besides, she's a bit scared of Tommy Shanigan.'

'Why? Has he given her cause?'

'She says, and I quote: "He's a big fellow, and he's got keys to let himself in at my front door at any hour of the day or night."'

'I understand.' He pictured to himself the figure of the man who'd come into the little hallway just as he was going out after his single unhappy visit to Mrs Barnell. It was true: he was burly, about twice the weight of his landlady.

'But if the police took him into custody, Liz—'

'On what grounds? I've thought about it, love, and really, what's he guilty of? He sends a package to Parady every week. There's no law against it.'

'And if they question him, he'll guess that Mrs Barnell has been snipping. No, snooping, is that the word?'

'Yes. And he'll say the contents of the packet are – I dunno – Kendal mints, used jigsaw puzzles, knitted squares for a charity afghan . . .'

'A polythene bag of home-made muesli, vitamin supplements . . .'

'That sort of thing.'

'Poor Mrs Barnell. Mr Shanigan might be quite annoyed if he thought she'd caused the police to visit him. So of course she doesn't want to go to the police.'

'On the other hand, she's in a mixed-up state – sort of quite angry with him. If he's caused harm to come to Barbara, she wants him to pay for it. She thinks a lot of Barbara Rallenham, you know. I think it's because Barbara has this everybody's equal manner – asking people to call her by her first name, like her cleaning woman, you remember? And besides that, she's very upset to think that in some way she's responsible for something happening to Barbara—'

'No, no—'

'Exactly, it's not her fault. I promised we'd try everything we could think of to find her, and said it would be better if she didn't get in Shanigan's hair. In the meantime, why didn't she go away for a week or two, I said.'

'That's a good idea.'

'She's got a friend in Brighton who runs a guest house. She was going to ring her and ask to stay with her for a bit.'

'Makes sense.'

'What else should I do?'

He thought about it. 'I don't see what you can do. We don't want to alert Shanigan. And, for heaven's sake, if you tell Mandy about this, don't mention him – Mandy might go rushing to see him, sobbing and demanding to know what he's done with her sister.'

Which was exactly what Mandy had done when she thought Greg was responsible for her sister going out of contact.

'How right you are.'

'I'll think it over, Liz. There might be something I can do at this end. I might go to Fontaine de Vaucluse and chat to people – someone might know something about the artists' colony.'

'Show the photocopy of the sketch – oh, no, you've already established that Grashenko is the woman.'

'Yes but . . . the man?' He considered for a moment then muttered a few bad words under his breath.

'What?'

'The local police are satisfied that Mlle Grashenko couldn't have been outside Barbara's flat because she hasn't left Parady recently.'

'I think you told me that.'

'That fact was verified by her assistant. I think they said his name was Coco.'

'Yes, I remember.'

'But what if Coco is the man in the sketch?'

Liz drew in an agonized breath. 'Oh, *no*! Oh, Greg – why didn't we think of that?'

He couldn't answer that. The problem was, they had other matters to distract them. Their attention was elsewhere on occasions. She had her fashion shops. He had his musicians, and the problem of tracking down scores of ignored operettas.

Liz had collected her thoughts. 'But the police had copies of the sketch—'

'But that was of a man Mrs Dandry saw in a London flat. Someone helping Grashenko with her kiln, in a work shirt and perhaps with some dirt on his face . . . that's quite a different man.'

'And it wasn't a very helpful sketch to start with,' she admitted. 'But listen – we think the man in the flat – the so-called Mr Rivers – Mrs Dandry said he was English. If he answered the detective, wouldn't he sound English?'

'Depends how much he said. *Oui* and *non* and a shrug or two – perhaps that was all he needed.'

'I suppose so.'

'Wait!'

'All right, I'm waiting,' she riposted, surprised at his tone. 'What now?'

'Mr Rivers. An Englishman. Could he be the man Mrs Barnell saw at her house?'

'Him? No, because—'

'Because what?'

'Because we've just been saying that Mr Rivers might be Grashenko's assistant – and he lives in France.'

'But that's *now*. Mrs Barnell saw the stranger months ago. It was after Shanigan started sending his packets from the post office that she went up to his flat and nerved herself to write to Barbara. Our Mr Rivers could have been living in London earlier, collecting the packet from Shanigan's flat every week. And after she got alarmed about him, they started the postal system and Mr Rivers moved to Parady.'

'Now known as Coco. I wonder what his last name is?'

'I'll go to Fontaine de Vaucluse in the morning and ask around.'

'Greg, be careful. He may have friends there, and if they know he's got some little scam going they may not like somebody nosing around.'

He gave a good-humoured sigh. 'I told you to be careful when you went to see Mrs Barnell, and you got cream scones and home-made jam.'

'But Mrs Barnell is a nice old lady. You're more likely to get a mouthful of knuckles.'

'What a phrase! Very descriptive. I feel I'll never complete my study of the English language.' And with that they said a goodbye which, on her side, contained some anxiety.

Greg's intention remained the same next morning, Tuesday. He rose at what for him was an uncivilized hour, after a night made restless by the mass of detail whirling around in his head. He couldn't make sense of it, which made him angry with himself.

He tooled the old Mercedes out of the parking area with the rising sun still struggling to make an impact on the temperature. It was chilly, so he had put on a lightweight windproof jacket. The sky above was an endless sapphire blue, with thin veils of clouds trailed by the high winds.

Traffic was light. He reached the outskirts of Fontaine de Vaucluse at an hour when the shops were just beginning to take down their shutters. He thought to himself that it was pointless to go in with sketches of Mr Rivers when most of the population was still indoors drinking their first cup of coffee.

So he headed north-east for Parady. Few were driving on the country roads. He glimpsed a post van nosing its way down a track to a farmhouse, and a motorized cart bumping along between rows of vines to the left. On the breeze he could just make out the whine of a circular saw as some forester tended his trees before the winter weather caused any branches to fall.

The gate to Parady was, as before, wide open. He drove in, parked by the building that housed the offices and showroom. The showroom door had a 'Closed' sign, but the door to the offices of Groupe Locke Daniels stood ajar. Inside the lights were on, so office staff must have arrived before daylight. He glanced in. It was empty. Someone had switched on a computer, but had left it, because now the screen-saver was melting and re-forming – an Impressionist design of wicker baskets and earthenware jugs on a field of green.

He walked on a few paces, looking for tenants of the shops – just someone to chat to about Coco the potter's assistant. But the dwellers of Parady seemed to share his aversion to early rising. No one seemed to be about in the area next to the showroom.

He turned the corner of the old farmhouse and took a few paces along the side alley. It made its way between this main building and a few of the workshops. It ended in a private parking area, and then there was a copse of bare-branched willow – for basket-making, he supposed – and beyond that the roofs of six or seven houses. This was the accommodation area where the artists and artisans were still perhaps abed.

He stood for a moment in thought. Then he turned back,

looked in at the door of the office, glanced over his shoulder to see if anyone was around and, finding himself unobserved, went in.

It was just an office. Not very big, with only one desk and one chair. Most of the modern accoutrements were visible – computer, printer, scanner, fax, small telephone switchboard. Filing cabinets. He edged towards them, but one tug at a drawer handle told him that though the computer had been started the cabinets were still to be unlocked.

There were papers neatly stacked in a little tower of shelves on the desk. He twitched one of them out. A letter in French enquiring about the terms for hiring premises. The reply to the enquiry was stapled to it. He put that back and tried the little shelf next below. Correspondence in English. *Dear Sirs, With reference to your letter of the 23rd December last . . .*

He tried the next little shelf. Italian, an agreement to open a shop selling flavoured olive oils. The next shelf yielded Spanish. So this was the correspondence system, and no doubt if he tried each shelf he'd find German, Dutch, and so on. He turned away. The computer was still showing the stately dance of the wicker baskets. Should he tap a key to find out whether anything helpful would appear?

Just as he was about to do so, the post van turned into the parking area. Out jumped the postman, a slight elderly man engulfed in his regulation padded jacket. He picked up a collection of mail from the passenger seat, left his van door ajar, and turned towards the office.

Greg was struck motionless.

In bustled the postman. '*B'jour, b'jour,*' he said, '*Fait un peu froid, non?*'

'*Tu dis,*' agreed Greg.

The postman thrust the mail into his hands. '*St Antoine, tu sais. Toujours fait froid après la St Antoine.*'

They nodded assent about weather conditions after the feast of St Antoine, the postman hurried out, and a moment later his van was buzzing back the way it came.

The collection of mail consisted of some twelve or thirteen letters, a catalogue in a polythene cover, and a padded envelope with English stamps. It was addressed to Groupe Locke Daniels. A little label in the left-hand corner bore the obligatory words in block letters, 'SMALL PACKET'. Turning it over, he saw a similar label with a hand-written return address, but the handwriting so bad it was difficult to decipher. It looked like *T. Shilliband, 41 Victoria St, Ldn, England.* Near enough. He was sure it should have read: *T. Shanigan, 41 Vickleham St.*

He had put down the other items. He stood with the packet in his hand. He looked around. No one, nothing.

Without letting himself think about it, he tucked it inside his windcheater and zipped it up. He went quickly back to his car, got in and drove away. He had a hard time not stamping on the accelerator but took the little exit road at a moderate speed.

He glanced in his rear mirror as he went out of the gates. Quite far back on the main pedestrian path a man was standing staring after him. Outdoor clothes – slacks and a thick jersey. Too far off to ascertain his features.

Might have been Coco aka Mr Rivers, for all he knew. But this wasn't the time to be hanging around asking questions.

He got on to the metalled road and drove a few miles. In a quiet spot with a track and a notice-board about fishing, he stopped. He thought about what he'd just done. He'd interfered with the postal system of the République. He was a criminal, more so than Mrs Barnell.

He unzipped his jacket, took out the packet, and studied it.

It had been used and re-used. Several layers of brown sticky tape showed where it had been sealed on at least three occasions. Sticky tape was so applied as to cover previous stamps.

A very economical correspondent. And so *ordinary*. Uncle Jim sending a collection of used postage stamps to little Pierre. Grandma sending hand-knitted socks to Guillaume.

He let his fingers pry at the sealing tape. Then he made himself stop. He couldn't open it here on the highway. In the first place he'd no idea what he might find – Pandora's box, he reminded himself.

He resumed his journey. No thought now of going to Fontaine de Vaucluse, he wanted a place where he could open this packet in privacy and safety. Because having stolen it he ought to get something useful out of his crime.

He drove back to Avignon, parked at the Glaneur, went up to his room. The maid was making the bed. He hesitated, glancing around. Murmuring an apology for interrupting her work, he put the packet in his briefcase, locked it, and put the briefcase in the wardrobe.

The maid said, 'You want to use the room? I'll be gone in a moment, monsieur.'

'Thank you.'

He went out. Avignon had woken for the day's work. He went into an office supply shop. He bought scissors and a roll of sticky tape of the same appearance as that on the packet.

Thus equipped he went back to the hotel. As promised, the maid had finished and gone. For safety while he undertook this unlawful act, he clicked the internal lock on his door, got out the briefcase, and sat down on the only chair at the dressing-table. He cleared it of the imitation leather folder that held information about local attractions, and the decorative lamp with its parchment shade. Plenty of space to deal with whatever was to come.

The packet still looked innocent. He pressed it with his fingers. Squishy.

Painstakingly he cut the sticky tape along the line that marked the edge of the envelope flap, using one blade of the scissors. He peeled the flap away. The top of the contents could be seen – the folds of a transparent polythene bag.

He took a deep breath and gently teased it out. Something dark blue was revealed. An inch more, than another, then the contents came out easily.

He was looking at a set of dark blue industrial overalls, neatly folded into the polythene bag so as to take up as little room as possible.

Industrial overalls?

Ten

He was embarrassed. So much so that he didn't look up, for fear of seeing himself in the dressing-table mirror.

He was very, very glad that Liz wasn't with him, to witness this absurdity. The great criminal, the highwayman holding up the stage-coach at gunpoint for the satchel of gold . . .

For quite a while he sat with his hands resting on the dressing-table, head turned so that he was looking out of the window. He thought of an old German proverb: *Hochmut kommt vor dem Fall,* which he thought Liz would translate as 'Pride goes before a fall'. He had to admit to himself that he'd been rather proud of himself for snatching the packet – the famous packet – from the very jaws of the enemy.

And what did he get for it? Overalls. And the word made him grin all at once, because it brought to his mind another word for which the contents of the packet could be cockney rhyming slang.

Well, so much for that. Rousing, he took up the polythene bag, the squishy polythene bag, and squeezed it so that it would go back into the padded envelope. He sealed the package with the newly bought sticky tape. He studied it. Looked just the same as before he'd opened it.

He put it in his jacket, hurried out, and posted it in the nearest wide-mouthed letter box. There. No one would ever know it had been tampered with. No one need ever know what a fool he'd made of himself.

He went out in search of a drink. Early in the day though it was, he felt the need of something restorative. He'd given himself a fright by stealing the packet, and a slap in the face when he saw its contents. Time to get everything back to normal.

He spent the rest of the afternoon browsing in some of the old shops behind the Place des Carmes, and was rewarded by finding a copy of the score of *Friederike*, the operetta about the poet Goethe by Franz Lehar. He felt he had been led to it as a consolation for his mistakes of the morning. He took it with him to study over lunch.

He was interested to see that one of Goethe's songs was a version of 'Rose Among the Heather', much better known in the version composed by Schubert. When he got to the last page, he found that the plot ended unhappily, and for a moment was dashed. But then he recalled that he and his baritone weren't thinking of putting on the operetta, they were merely going to give a recital of its songs. He counted four solos that would do very nicely as a beginning.

Heartened, he rang Robert Jäger to give him news of this find, the first of many, he hoped. He even sang some of the tunes to Jäger over the phone, and was greeted with laughter but some enthusiasm.

Next he rang his family in Geneva. His father picked up. 'Rousseau is pining for you, Grego,' he reported. Rousseau was Greg's red setter. 'When are you coming home?'

'End of the month, when my list of performers have done their shows.'

'But can't you come home for a little break?'

'What's the matter? Not getting proper food?' The ex-Queen Mother Nicoletta was away doing some work on some millionaire's guest cabin so the catering at Bredoux consisted of an occasional stew concocted by the daily help, or frozen dishes from the supermarket.

'Well, you're good at handling Mme Valors. I don't like to tell her what to cook – she gets offended.' Ex-King Anton was too shy to deal with the bustling Mme Valors. How he had ever managed during his short reign as King of Hirtenstein, his son couldn't imagine.

'I don't think I'll be home for a while, Papa. There are things here . . .' He let the words die away. Why couldn't he go home? None of his performers was due to appear until the coming weekend. He could fly back for a couple of days, hand the score of *Friederike* to Jäger, take Rousseau out for a few runs on the snowy hillside, and generally relax.

'Oh, well, all right,' sighed his father. 'I hope everything's going well for you.'

'Oh yes, fine,' said Greg, keeping the irony out of his voice. 'Give my love to Grossmutti.'

A glance at his watch told him that Liz would probably be in the midst of some meeting or project or event. He'd ring her in the evening. Meanwhile he busied himself with inspecting the church where his organist was to give a trio of programmes over the weekend: Bach, Buxtehude and Messiaen. He knew the organist would only have attracted a small audience but for the fact that a local trumpeter was to accompany some of the items.

Around seven in the evening, when the stars were bright overhead, he rang Liz. She was eager to speak first. 'I had a thought, Greg. I should have taken that sketch of Mr Rivers and shown it to Mrs Barnell.'

'Ah! Well, perhaps there's no point, Liz.'

'What's that?'

'I'm beginning to think it's a . . . *Sturm in Wasserglas* . . . wait a minute . . . storm in a teacup.'

'Good grief, what brought this on?'

'When you hear what happened, you'll see what I mean. It's like that famous film, where the men go on a river trip and think the local people are trying to kill them . . . And when one of them gets back, he sees the locals are quite ordinary.'

'You mean *Deliverance*. What's the matter, precious?'

Bracing himself, he confessed his misdeeds. She listened in silence, and had the grace not to giggle. There was rather a long pause when he ended, which may have been because she was trying to get her voice steady. But when she spoke she only said, 'Overalls? You mean, white painter's overalls? Bib and brace?'

'No, dark blue, the kind that zip up the front, I think. More the sort that men would wear in a factory. I suppose he's sending them for someone to use while they do some of their arts and crafts at Parady. Perhaps they're for the man who tends the big kiln. There's one by itself outside the pottery workshop, a big old one that I think would need special work – with bricks and things, perhaps. The overalls might be for that.'

'For our friend Coco.'

'Perhaps.'

'Oh dear.' After a pause she went on in a worried tone: 'But all the same – where's Barbara?'

'It seems the police here may have been right. She's gone off after a big story, or on a romantic adventure. She certainly wouldn't be in Provence to inspect overalls.'

'I suppose not.'

'So it's just as well you didn't build the thing up by showing Mrs Barnell the sketch.'

'Yes, you're right.'

'I ought to contact her to say we think it was all a mistake—'

'No, don't telephone from a long way off,' she broke in. 'Not with a message like that. I'll drop by and break it to her gently.'

'Would you? You are an angel.'

'Of course I am.'

True to her word, she rang Mrs Barnell but got the answering machine. She left a message, asking if she could drop by some time next day. There had been no response by lunch-time Wednesday, so she left another message. She rang Greg to let him know she was still trying.

'Perhaps she's gone off to the friend in Brighton,' he replied. 'Didn't you say she was arranging something like that?'

'Of course, that's probably what's happened. Well, what should we do? Leave it till she comes back? I suppose that would be all right . . . But, Greg, it will be on her mind all the time, wondering what happened to Barbara.'

'Yes.'

'I'll tell you what. I'll try to get the number of the Brighton place, and ring her there.'

'I thought we'd agreed we couldn't tell her this on the telephone?'

'Oh . . . well, I could drop by. It's not very far, and I've got a business contact in Brighton who'd be pleased to see me.'

She could tell he was smiling. 'You really are a very nice person,' he said.

'Oh, well known for it,' she agreed.

'But how will you get the address of the Brighton friend?'

'I'll make a bet with you. That nosy neighbour, Miss Lessiter – I bet she knows it.'

'Ha! Not only nice, but clever.'

Next day when she had a pause in her work she found Miss Lessiter in the phone book and rang her. The creaky old voice she'd heard before came on the line.

'Miss Lessiter?'

'Y-yes?'

'This is Liz Blair. Remember, we spoke when I was trying to get in touch with Mrs Barnell and you were bringing in the milk.'

'Oh yes, Miss Blair, I remember.'

'Miss Lessiter, I've been trying to get Mrs Barnell and I keep getting that message service. Has she gone to Brighton?'

A little fit of coughing. 'I gather she has, dear.'

'You gather? But I thought you looked after each other's affairs when you go away?'

'Mm-h-mm. Mostly it's Ceelie who goes away. I'm too old for it these days, dear.'

'Well, does that mean she hasn't gone yet? Or what?'

'If she's gone, she didn't let me know.' A silence. 'Miss Blair, I wonder if you'd do me a kindness. Would you come to see me?'

'I beg your pardon?'

'Come to my house. I'd like to have a talk. I don't quite know what to do.'

'How do you mean?'

Miss Lessiter coughed and got out of breath. 'I'm just . . . not up to this sort of thing, that's what it is. I'd like someone young and active to come with me.'

'Come with you where?'

'Ceelie's flat.'

'Why? What's the matter?'

'I don't know, dear. That's why I'd like you to come.' There was desperation in the old voice.

'I'll be there as soon as I can,' said Liz.

She threw on a raincoat and hurried out. She had to battle the home-going rush hour but was at Miss Lessiter's door in a little over an hour. She'd been told the house was opposite Mrs Barnell's. The old lady, leaning on a stick, was opening up for her as she raised her hand to ring the bell.

'Come in, dear.' She was led into a room furnished with good quality Art Deco that looked like a handsome inheritance from parents. The windows were veiled with fine voile curtains. A pleasant warmth was sent out by the imitation coals of an electric fire that fitted neatly into the twenties fireplace. 'Please sit down.' She sat in a cushioned chair with wooden arms. Miss Lessiter had a chromium coffee percolator plugged in and, without asking, switched it on. 'Biscuit?' she offered, nodding at a plate on a little walnut table.

She was clearly a woman of character. Old now, and not in good health judging by her pallor and the weary lines of her face. Her dress was an out-of-date but well-tailored striped gabardine with a silk collar.

'I'm so grateful to you for coming, Miss Blair—'

'Liz.'

'Liz. That's for Elizabeth? I have a great-niece called Elizabeth.' She sighed. 'Married and in Singapore now, gone out in search of a good career like most of my family. And I think Ceelie told me you did something interesting – cosmetics consultant, was it?'

'No, that was an acquaintance of mine.' The coffee began to gurgle, causing the old lady to prepare for the effort of rising. 'Let me,' said Liz, and poured hot strong coffee into two fine china beakers.

'Thank you, dear. This is very kind of you.' She sipped, and the heat of the coffee brought on a little coughing fit. 'Oh, bother this bronchitis!' she exclaimed. 'Can't go five minutes without a hacking fit.'

'Is there something you take for it? Can I fetch it?'

'No, thank you, it just goes when it's ready. Listen, Miss Blair dear, I want to ask you what I should do. I'm worried about Ceelie.'

'Why's that?'

'As you said, when she goes away she always lets me know. Yet this time she's gone off without giving me a knock beforehand.'

'She's gone?'

'Yes.'

'To Brighton?'

'Well, I suppose so. She was talking of going to her friend Peggy. But I understood Peggy couldn't take her until the weekend because she had the painters in. Guesthouse, you know – refurbishes in the winter.'

'Yes, of course. So she was going at the weekend – Saturday?'

'Yes, Saturday morning, she said.'

'But you think she's gone already?'

'Dear, she went in a minicab yesterday just before noon. And I don't understand it, because she never said a word to me about it.'

Liz wondered how to ask the next question. She didn't want to sound as if she was implying criticism of her habitual curiosity. 'You saw her leave?'

'Well, yes, I did. I heard the minicab pull up and the driver knocked on her door. I was a bit surprised, it being only Wednesday, but there you are. So he went in, and I thought, "He's gone to bring out her bag," and he did, and she was with him.'

'Yes. And then you expected her to come over and . . . what? Give you her key?'

'Oh, I've got her key, dear. And she's got mine. We look after each other. I just expected her to nip across and explain why she was leaving on the Wednesday instead of Saturday. But she just got in the car, the driver put her bag in beside her, and they drove away.'

'Perhaps her friend in Brighton let her know the painters had finished?'

'Yes.'

'You don't sound very happy about it.'

'No. To tell the truth, Miss Blair, Liz, I'm . . . I'm not easy in my mind.' She coughed, cleared her throat, and took a gulp of coffee. 'You think I'm a silly old woman,' she sighed.

'Not at all. If you're worried . . .' She tried to think of some action. 'Would you like us to ring her friend in Brighton and ask her if she's all right?'

'Well, that's *it*, you see. When she goes away she generally gives me a telephone number so I can ring her if anything goes wrong. Some silly lads scrawled graffiti all over her front door one time, very rude words . . . But though she's gone to

Peggy fairly often, I don't have the phone number. She gives me one of those yellow labels, and I stick it on the mirror above the telephone. And then when she comes back I pull it off and throw it away. So she always gives me a fresh label, whenever she takes off and wherever she's going. And she didn't, this time.' Miss Lessiter turned anxious eyes on her visitor.

'You know the friend's last name?'

'Kersley, I think. And the guesthouse is The Garden House because it backs on to a park.'

'Shall I ring and see if I can get the number?'

'Would you?'

She got out her mobile and enquired. Within thirty seconds she had the number. With a smile at her hostess she pressed the buttons. The phone at the other end rang for a moment then a businesslike voice said, 'The Garden House, may I help you?'

Liz handed her Nokia to the old lady. 'Hello?' she quavered. 'Is that you, Mrs Kersley? This is Mary Lessiter. Hello, yes, nice to speak. Yes, and she's spoken of you. No, she's not ill. No, that's why I'm ringing. She's not with you? No . . .Yes . . . Yes, I thought . . . Yesterday around lunch-time.' A long pause while she listened. 'Yes, I knew it was to be Saturday. I know, I'm puzzled too.' Another pause. 'I will, I'll let you know at once.' She handed the mobile back to Liz, who switched it off.

The message was only too clear. Celia Barnell had not gone to her friend in Brighton.

'This is what you suspected?' Liz asked.

'Well, I . . . It seemed so strange. But you know, if you make a fuss and everything turns out to be all right, they think you're going gaga at my age. So I . . . well, I . . . I didn't know what to do. I was so glad when you rang me! It felt as if I had someone to turn to.'

Liz tried to think of something encouraging. 'Perhaps she decided to go somewhere else for a couple of days before going on to Brighton.'

'It's . . . I suppose it's possible. She seemed very eager to get off to Brighton, even though she'd just come back from that chocolate factory trip.'

'Has she any relatives she might have dropped in on?'

'Her husband's sister, but she doesn't get on with her. That's up in Preston. I haven't got her telephone or address, Ceelie never goes there.'

'So we shouldn't bother trying to track her down there.'

Miss Lessiter shook her head. 'If everything's all right and she comes back as usual, she wouldn't thank me for dragging her sister-in-law into it.'

'Does she have favourite holiday places?'

'Costa Brava. She wouldn't go there for two days before going on to Brighton, now would she?'

Liz smiled. 'I'd hardly think so. But in this country – does she go to stay with friends – in London, perhaps?'

'I've never heard her say so.' She hesitated then said, 'I've had the feeling this last couple of weeks that Ceelie's had something on her mind. She's seemed different. Keyed up, if you know what I mean.'

'Did she give you an idea what it was?'

Mary Lessiter smiled with some regret. 'She doesn't tell me everything, dear. We're not bosom pals. Besides, she thinks I'm a wobbly old thing that mustn't be told anything sad or depressing. But I got the impression something was nagging at her. And I wondered . . . but it seems so unlike her. . .'

'What?'

'If she went away suddenly to . . . you know . . . ' The thin old hand went up to her lips as if to hush the despairing thought . . . 'find a way out of some trouble.'

Suicide? 'No, no,' protested Liz. 'She struck me as being quite a strong person. Besides, would she have taken her suitcase with her?'

'Oh,' cried the old lady in relief, 'of course you're right! What a fool I am!' But then she became anxious again. 'But it's *so* unlike her to take off without letting me know.'

'I understand how you feel.' She did indeed. She was worried too.

'So I thought, since I had her key, I ought to go over and just . . . you know . . . see that everything's all right.'

'And you'd like me to go with you?'

'Would you, dear?'

'Of course.'

She helped her on with her coat whose label, she noted, named Debenham and Freebody as the maker. The department store had been gone from its London premises for about fifty years, but it said much for Miss Lessiter that the coat still fitted and looked good

They crossed the street to Mrs Barnell's house. Miss Lessiter opened the main door and then the inner one. They entered the passage of the ground floor flat, Liz feeling for and finding a light switch. At the end of the passage was the extension room, which Liz already knew.

On the table where she'd had the scones and jam there was a plate, a knife and fork, and a coffee mug. A folded puzzle magazine lay alongside, showing a pencil track round a circular maze of words.

In the kitchen adjoining the living room they found a saucepan on the draining board, with the remains of some pasta dish. A few vegetable peelings were wrapped in paper towel, ready for disposal.

'No,' whispered Mary Lessiter. She went slowly back into the living room to sink on to a chair. She let her walking stick clatter to the floor.

'What's the matter?'

'Ceelie would never have gone away and left her flat in this condition! She'd have done the washing-up!'

'But if she'd ordered a minicab and he came early?'

'She'd have made him wait. No, no, she never would leave her kitchen with rubbish waiting to be taken out. No matter what she was planning. That's not Ceelie Barnell.'

After waiting for Miss Lessiter to recover, Liz suggested, 'Should we look in the other rooms?'

'Her bedroom's next to the kitchen, it looks out on the back garden.' They went there, once again switching on lights.

It was a pretty room if somewhat too girlish for Liz's taste. Pink walls, pink patterned duvet cover, white furniture decorated with flower transfers, frilled lampshades. Going to the wardrobe, Miss Lessiter slid open the doors. Plenty of clothes on hangers, including the blue jersey two-piece Liz had seen Mrs Barnell wearing.

'Can you tell what she packed?' Because that might give some clue where she was headed.

'I'm afraid not. But . . . but . . .' The old lady pushed the hangers aside one by one. Agitation was in her jerky movements.

'What is it, Miss Lessiter?'

'Her winter coat is here!'

'Yes?'

'That's why I felt something was wrong! Of course! When she came out of the house with the minicab driver, she wasn't wearing a coat!'

'But . . . if she was going somewhere by car – to stay with a friend in London, perhaps – she wouldn't need a coat.'

'My dear Miss Blair, yesterday was a cold January day. And Ceelie isn't young any more. Of course she'd be wearing her coat! And as to staying with a friend in London, even if that was the case, why didn't she come over and tell me?'

Liz could offer no explanation.

'I knew there was something wrong!' lamented Miss Lessiter. 'My eyesight's not perfect but there was something about it – I knew it wasn't the way I'd have expected. And then she didn't come across to say bye-bye and leave the telephone number.'

'But, Miss Lessiter, you say she had her travel bag – she was packed and ready to go, expecting the minicab—'

'That doesn't prove anything! Ceelie always begins her packing days ahead. She's very fashion conscious, you know. She'd put her bag on a chair and put things in and take things out—'

'But she picked it up and came out to the car—'

'No, *he* had it. He had it in one hand and he sort of had her by the elbow—'

'Are you saying she was unwilling?' Liz broke in in alarm.

'We-ell . . . No . . . I can't exactly say . . . My eyesight isn't what it was, after all.' Liz looked doubtful and Miss Lessiter exclaimed, 'I knew you'd think I was a silly old halfwit! I'm not making it up! I tell you, now I look back on it, now I realize that she didn't have her coat on, I know, I *know* there was something worrying about it.'

She sank down on the pink duvet, tears beginning to trickle down among the wrinkles on her cheeks. 'Oh, Ceelie! Why did I dither so long?'

Liz found a box of tissues on the dressing-table and brought her one. When Miss Lessiter had recovered she said, 'Can you describe the cab man?'

'Describe him? Well, he wasn't an Asian, that I do know. She and I use the same minicab firm, though of course I generally only go to the supermarket or the arthritis clinic. Most of the drivers are Asians. Lovely young men – they respect their elders.'

'But was it anyone you'd seen before?' She was thinking of Tommy Shanigan's visitor, the man who had frightened Mrs Barnell, the man who might be the mysterious Mr Rivers.

Miss Lessiter was shaking her head. 'I can't say, dear. I didn't have my glasses on.'

They went back to the bright living room, where they sat going over the story and wondering what to do. Miss Lessiter was loath to inform the authorities. 'They'll just think I'm another senile old nuisance,' she faltered.

'Then I'll ring them, shall I? They can't say *I'm* senile.'

'Are you sure it's worth it? They never did anything about the graffiti on Ceelie's front door.'

'This is different,' said Liz as she picked up Mrs Barnell's telephone.

The local police invited them to come to the station and make a report. She called a taxi – a black London taxi – to get them there. Miss Lessiter was looking more frail and coughing more by the time they got back, nearly an hour and a half later.

Liz then rang Greg. 'Greg, Mrs Barnell's gone missing.'

'I'll be on the next plane,' he said.

Eleven

He scrambled to Nice-Côte-d'Azur in time for a late flight. Liz was waiting to drive him into London. Once she'd manoeuvred through the exit roads she felt at liberty to talk.

'What's happening to your weekend "do"?' was her first topic. 'It was something in a church, wasn't it?'

'Lucius Kremer is the regular church organist, he'll look after things. How is the old lady?'

'Deep in dreamland, I hope. We had a bite to eat when we got back from the police station and she was really hyped up, trying to work out the change she'd seen in Celia Barnell in the last few days, wondering what it had to do with this sudden exit.'

'And what conclusion did she come to?'

'None, really. Mrs Barnell had mentioned having a visit from Barbara, and Miss Lessiter said she was "making too much of it". But then I gather Miss Lessiter has a low opinion of scandal sheets.' Liz chuckled. 'She takes the *Financial Times*. As far as I can gather, Celia didn't tell her why Barbara had been to see her. Miss Lessiter looked down her nose and said she wasn't interested in knowing other people's business. After a bit it all drained out of her and she took a prescription that gets her through the night without coughing. While she got ready for bed, I made sure everything was locked up – back door, windows, everything. Then all she had to do was lock the front door behind me and totter off upstairs.'

'What happened with the police?'

She sighed. 'They were polite and tried to be very reassuring. They said elderly people sometimes took this notion to go off on a jaunt but usually came back in their own good time.'

'Ah.' It was more or less what he expected. 'Tell me about Mrs Barnell.'

She recounted what Mary Lessiter had told her. 'No coat?' Greg murmured.

'So she says, and in fact Mrs Barnell's wardrobe had two coats hanging in it, a wool winter coat and a hip-length jacket. There was a raincoat hanging on a wall frame just inside the flat door – a pine thing with pegs. Miss Lessiter said those made up her usual winter things. Her summer coat was put away, she said.'

'And she couldn't describe the car driver?'

She shook her head.

'What about Mr Shanigan?'

'Miss Lessiter didn't bring him into it because it seems pretty clear the guy she saw was smaller than him. Besides, it was midday, and Shanigan would be at his factory.'

'Do we know that?'

'I mentioned it to the police constable when I managed to get a bit of a word with him in private. He said they'd check on it.' She hesitated and added, 'They weren't treating it with any urgency. And I can see why. Mrs Barnell went off in a car with some luggage. She'd said she wanted to get away for a few days.'

'But she didn't tell her neighbour she was going on Wednesday.'

'No, but the constable seemed to think that perhaps the two of them had had a bit of a tiff. They *are* very different, Greg.'

'I see. And you didn't tell them about Barbara and Mr Rivers?'

They'd stopped at a traffic light so that she was able to turn her head to give him a look of exasperated uncertainty. 'Miss Lessiter was sitting right there. She was shook up enough! I didn't want to start giving her nightmares about a man who'd already been able to disappear Barbara and might have disappeared her neighbour as well. Although she'd heard something about Barbara from Celia Barnell, I'm certain from the way she spoke that she didn't know Barbara had already gone missing. And I thought Celia Barnell was enough for her to worry about.'

'I understand.'

'Besides, it would have meant them getting in touch with the police at the station that Mandy went to. And that would have meant getting in touch with Mandy to ask. It all seemed such a fuss when it was getting later and later. I wanted to get her home to bed, poor darling. I thought you could do all that when you got here.'

'All right, I can do that. But if they get interested and want to look at Mrs Barnell's place tonight, it means waking Miss Lessiter for the key.'

'No, I've got it. She was almost desperate to get rid of it.'

He had no hesitation in ringing Mandy. He was sure she was a night owl. Her mobile number brought him a response from a lively gathering, but not a club or a disco. 'I'm having dinner with friends,' she explained. Dinner? It was past one in the morning.

He asked her to go to a quieter spot and, when she'd done so, enquired which police station she'd contacted. 'Maida Vale,' she said. 'Why, 's something happening?'

There was just enough slur in her speech to warn him not to try long explanations. 'Something's come up about Mrs Barnell—'

'Who? Oh, her. Where are you then? Thought you were in Avignon.'

'No, I'm in London. I won't keep you, Mandy, since you're—'

''S all right. My friends are talking 'bout wind-surfing. Never done it, never wanted to. You ever done wind-surfing, Greg?'

'No, never.'

'Well don't you bother cos it sounds like you spend a-a-all your time picking yourself up outa the water.' She giggled.

'I'll take your advice. Goodnight, Mandy.'

'Goo'night.'

She hadn't even asked for any news of his activities in Avignon. Just as well, because he could never have brought himself to relate to her the fiasco of the postal packet.

The police at Maida Vale, reminded of Mandy's visit and informed of Mrs Barnell's unexplained departure, were disinclined to come rushing to Liz's flat to take a statement or fetch the key. It was agreed that they would meet Liz at Mrs Barnell's home at nine next day.

After spending the scant remains of the night fast asleep in each other's arms, Friday found Greg waking with great unwillingness to the sound of Liz coming in at the front door. He staggered out of bed, and, after groping bleary-eyed for his dressing-gown in her wardrobe, went out to find her in pink sweatshirt and joggers, making coffee.

'Morning.'

'Morning, sleepy-head. You'll have to get a wiggle on if we're to be in Walthamstow by nine.'

'Agh . . .' He yawned. 'We should just not turn up, and then they'll send a police car for us.' He subsided on a kitchen chair. 'You've been running?'

'Yes, and don't start telling me I look a mess or I won't give you a croissant.' She brandished a paper bag from a local bakery, the grease already beginning to penetrate. 'Ten minutes while I warm them, and if you're not back awake and aware by then, I'll eat them all by myself.'

As he took a hasty shower and shaved, he reflected that he ought to take her cross-country skiing one winter. That would cure her of the absurd notion that trotting round a London park was serious physical exercise. He thought now of the snow-clad slopes of Taninges, experiencing something that was almost a pang of longing for the cold purity of the air, the silence, the sense of being alone with a power greater than mankind's highest endeavour. And at night, stepping out from the travellers' huts, to see the stars in their majestic course . . .

But coffee and croissants were calling, he reminded himself ruefully. Only a little later than the deadline, he presented himself at the breakfast table.

She inspected him. He was clad in grey suit and pale-yellow tie. His think-of-me-as-a-business-executive mode. She nodded approval and poured coffee. She left him to eat, while she herself showered and put on beige slacks, camel hair sweater, and a loosely knotted scarf of striped green silk. Her think-of me-as-businesslike-but-not-power-mad look.

'Now,' she said, picking up a tailored brown jacket, 'let's be off.'

They were, in fact, going to be late. They found a plain clothes constable on the doorstep looking irritated. They went inside, where Liz once again viewed the remains of Mrs Barnell's lunch and the vegetable peelings by the sink. The central heating in the flat was still in action. The peelings were developing mould.

With Greg at her side, she showed Detective Constable Derring the steps she and Miss Lessiter had taken last night. She gave him a careful account of what Miss Lessiter said about the arrangement between the two neighbours. She produced yet another copy of the sketch she'd made according to Mrs Dandry's description.

'So you're saying what?' asked the constable, who seemed to be a dependable mid-thirties type. 'That this man here is in some way concerned in the disappearance of Ms Rallenham, and also in the departure of Mrs Barnell.'

'Yes.'

'But, as I understand it, Miss Lessiter couldn't describe the man that Mrs Barnell left with.'

'That's right. But she said he was smaller than Mr Shanigan.'

'Now Shanigan's her upstairs tenant, right? North Walthamstow checked on him, and he was in the factory canteen around the time she left. So you're right, it wasn't *him* that drove her away.'

'No. She wouldn't have gone with him anyway. As far as we know, they weren't on friendly terms.'

'So this Mr Rivers is your suggestion, but you say she'd never met him.'

'Well, she might have come across him.' She told him of Mrs Barnell's encounter with a stranger in her hallway.

'But in that case, would she have let him in the house? If she'd already had a scare?'

'He probably showed her a business card with Barbara Rallenham's OK on the back. Mrs Barnell was a great fan of hers.'

'Oh well in that case . . .' Constable Derring looked vexed.

'No, no, we think Barbara's belongings were stolen in Provence.'

'In Provence?'

'Yes, that's where Barbara went missing. That was in the report her sister Mandy Rallenham made to you, about ten days ago.'

The constable blew out a breath. 'Yes, of course I looked it up, but . . . I think we'd better nip back to the station and try to join up the dots. Can't deny it's hard trying to match up what might have happened here with this story about happenings in France.'

Liz asked for a few minutes to drop in on Miss Lessiter. Up and about at her usual hour and wearing her glasses, Miss Lessiter had been observing the goings-on at her neighbour's. She welcomed Liz in. After enquiring after her health Liz explained that they were now about to go the police station to take things a stage further.

'You mean you've had some news?' asked Miss Lessiter with faltering eagerness.

'No, but there are formalities—'

'Oh, I had enough of those last night! They don't want me to go, do they?'

'No, at the moment they're just content with me,' joked Liz. 'But they might have to come back to you later, Miss Lessiter.'

'I suppose if they must . . .Well, thank you, dear. I don't know what I'd have done without you. If you get any news of Ceelie, you will ring me, won't you?'

'Of course.' She gave the old lady a hug, a careful one because of her arthritis. She was still standing looking after her when Liz closed the front gate and joined Greg in the constable's car.

The constable had been in communication with Maida Vale police station. When they reached it, after a frustrating battle with traffic, the constable showed them to a room furnished with decent furniture – a pine table, several chairs, a bookcase on which stood a potted fern. He invite them to sit and disappeared. After a short wait, a strapping young man entered bringing with him a breath of Imperial Leather soap and a dark-red folder.

'How do you do. I'm Detective Sergeant Orlan. You're Ms Blair and you're . . . er . . . ?'

'Gregory Crowne.'

'Yes, thank you, sir.' It was clear the sergeant had been briefed as to Greg's identity. 'Can I get you anything? Tea? Coffee? Soft drink?'

'No thank you,' chorused his guests. They knew it would be from a machine.

'Well now, I've been in touch with our colleagues in Avignon and so let me run through the story-so-far from their side. Ms Mandy Rallenham came to you there to ask what had happened to her sister. You were supposed to have a meeting with her? Right? Right. You went to her hotel and learned that someone with her bank card paid her bill. Paid on the first Saturday in January.'

'Yes.'

'So now let me come to the London end. A cleaning woman at Ms Rallenham's flat gave you a description of a man and a woman, and a sketch was made by Ms Blair here.' He produced copies of the sketches and held them out for verification. Liz nodded. 'Later you, sir, went to a location not far from Avignon and believe that you met the lady shown in this sketch.' He tapped the one of Estelle Grashenko.

'Yes.'

'Ms Blair paid a visit to Mrs Barnell, who provided information about a package regularly sent to the address near Avignon.'

'Parady – yes.'

'Two days after Ms Blair's visit, Mrs Barnell leaves her home unexpectedly and has not been in touch since.'

'Exactly.'

'That's to say, two women are missing – the first is the one who visited Mrs Barnell in search of information, and the second is the woman she visited.'

'Yes.'

'You are suggesting that the two events may have some connection with the postal packages to Parady.'

'Well,' said Liz, 'Barbara Rallenham set off for France within a couple of days of talking to Mrs Barnell. Mrs Barnell had written to her because she thought the packets contained drugs, but it seems they only contained clothing.'

'Clothing?'

'Working clothes – overalls.'

Thus spared the tricky business of confessing he'd stolen a mail packet and opened it, His Serene Highness Gregorius von Hirtenstein breathed an inward sigh of relief.

Detective Sergeant Orlan, shrugging, made a note. 'We weren't aware of the contents of the packet,' he remarked. 'I

. . . er . . . I gather from the statement you gave to North Walthamstow that Mrs Barnell had been into Mr Shanigan's flat to examine the packet.'

'Yes.'

'And are you suggesting that Mr Shanigan has been in some way motivated to get Mrs Barnell out of the way because she made an illegal entry to his flat?'

Liz said, 'The description of the man who drove away with Mrs Barnell is nothing like Mr Shanigan. Greg says Shanigan is a big burly fellow.'

'That's correct. He was interviewed first thing this morning and it's clear he was at the factory when Mrs Barnell left.'

'What we're suggesting is that the car driver might have been the man in this sketch,' Greg said, touching the sketch of the unknown Mr Rivers.

'Who entered Ms Rallenham's flat in Maida Vale and was seen outside speaking to the lady in the other sketch.'

'Her name is Estelle Grashenko—'

'But I'm informed by the Avignon *sûreté* that she was at her workshop on the day she was supposedly seen outside Barbara Rallenham's flat.'

Greg spoke in apologetic disagreement. 'Let me point out that her presence there is verified by an employee at Parady. We think that employee is *that* man,' with a nod at the sketch. The sergeant was about to speak, but Greg surged on. 'I think if you enquired at the airlines, you'd find she and that man flew to London around the date Mrs Dandry saw the people Liz sketched.'

'Ha,' said Sergeant Orlan with cynical joviality, 'we're not so slow as you seem to think, sir. We've checked. No one called Grashenko flew to London at the specified period.'

Greg and Liz were reduced to silence.

In a kinder tone the sergeant went on. 'I'm not saying there isn't something very odd about all this. You can rely on it, we'll be trying to find out where Mrs Barnell's got to, because a missing pensioner is always a cause for concern. And our colleagues across the Channel have said they'll give more time to the Rallenham case because we have to note that it's almost a month now since she's dropped out of sight.'

'It's very worrying.'

'Yes, sir, I can see it worries you. But as far as we can tell, Mrs Barnell left of her own free will, and Ms Rallenham might have taken off on the track of some attractive scandal. Her editor at the *Clarion* assures us she's done this sort of thing before. Then there's the aspect that no actual illegality seems to have occurred on our turf, if we make allowances for Mrs Barnell intruding into Mr Shanigan's home. And with manpower being a bit short, we have to think of priorities. If the French police come up with anything, or you think of anything you can add, we'd of course get going on it.' He waited with raised eyebrows for any facts they might produce.

They could think of nothing.

After some chit-chat to smooth any rough edges, the detective sergeant saw them out. It was now past noon of a raw, damp London day, and Liz was depressed. 'Let's go somewhere and have a good lunch,' she said. 'I'm starved.'

They caught a bus and hopped off when they came to a likely area. They found a capacious fish restaurant nearby, settled in with an aperitif while they studied the menu. Over North Atlantic sea bass and a good Chablis they skirted round the subject of the police interview, feeling that they should somehow have done better, somehow conveyed their apprehension and forced a more active investigation.

'We have to see it from their point of view,' Greg said. 'They did in fact check the airlines. Grashenko didn't make the flight.'

'She could have gone by sea.'

'It's not likely. To go to London by the Channel ferry or Eurostar means getting to Calais, which is quite a long way even by train. If, as we're supposing, they were clearing up after a crime, I'd think they'd go by the quickest route.'

'Mmm.' She ate some fish, sipped some wine, then suggested, 'Perhaps she travelled under another name?'

'Quite likely. But that doesn't help us, because we don't know what name, and that would mean trying to get airline staff to remember her from a description.'

'Well, she was wearing a very colourful shawl.'

'Liz, that was in London in a car. Would she board a flight to England with only a shawl? She'd have a top-coat, surely.

And the sketch is black and white, after all!' Having let his irritation get the better of him he was sorry and added in a more agreeable tone, 'Well, we'll tell the police about the shawl. She might have been wearing it even with a top-coat.'

Liz broke into a rueful grin. 'What's Mandy going to say to all this?'

'Lord knows. Last night when I spoke to her she was more concerned about her dinner friends than about Mrs Barnell. In fact, she could hardly remember who she was.'

'Poor Mrs Barnell!' Liz groaned. She'd taken to her when she paid her visit. Where was she, what was happening to her? 'She was so thrilled at having been contacted by Barbara Rallenham. Miss Lessiter told me it had made her "a bit above herself". Whereas Miss Lessiter's a bit scared, and I don't blame her.'

'But it's the unknown car driver she's scared of, isn't it. Mrs Barnell, on the other hand, was scared of Tommy Shanigan.'

'Because she thought he was involved in drug smuggling. If only she'd known it was just work clothes.'

Greg pushed his plate aside in irritation and turned his attention to the remains of the wine in his glass. After a moment he said, 'I thought they were probably for one of the craftsmen at the colony.'

'Quite likely.'

'No.'

Liz, chasing a piece of fennel round her plate, said, 'Beg pardon?'

'Every week? Shanigan sends a set of overalls to someone in Parady every week? Is that 'quite likely'?'

'Well . . .' Her face clouded, she stared out of the restaurant window.

'New ones?' he insisted.

'I don't know.'

'How much does a set of overalls cost?'

'No idea.'

'Nor have I. Why does anyone need a new set of overalls every week?'

'Don't ask me.'

'It's really strange.'

'Yes, it is. But, as Sergeant Orlan pointed out, it's not illegal.'

'No, not at all, you'd think. Yet two women have vanished.'

'Oh, Greg . . . I can't . . . I can't go on thinking about it. My head reels with trying to sort things out.'

'You're not the only one.' He sighed. 'I'll tell you one thing that has struck me. Whoever is the instigator of all this, it's not some big-time criminal. Do you think? I mean, it seems as if something happens that takes them by surprise, they react, then they try to clear up after themselves, and then something else happens and they dash in to put *that* right –'

'You mean they kidnapped Barbara because she stumbled on something, then tried to tidy that up, and then Mrs Barnell . . . ? But they'd left Mrs Barnell alone until now.'

'I've an awful feeling I may have caused that,' he said in distress. 'When I first went to Parady I introduced myself to Grashenko and was driving the Mercedes. When I stole the parcel from the office, I was driving the Mercedes. I thought I saw someone staring after me as I drove away.'

'Oh. You mean whoever-it-was knew you'd taken the parcel?'

'Yes. But how?' he demanded, throwing out his hands in protest. 'The postman had just that minute delivered it. He actually thrust it at me. I don't see how it would be known that I'd taken anything. I left all the rest of the delivery there on the office desk.'

She thought about it. 'There's no way it had anything to do with that, then. Don't you think . . . Perhaps it was something that Mrs Barnell did. Miss Lessiter said she was a bit restive. She has this tremendous admiration for Barbara, almost like a groupie – and felt she was somehow involved in her disappearance. What if she decided to have another go at Shanigan's flat and . . . and . . . I don't know . . .'

Greg had followed her reasoning and, though not convinced, had a contribution to make. 'She may have disturbed his belongings. And he noticed it and called in the famous Mr Rivers.'

'If they began to suspect she put Barbara on to them, they might conclude she knew more than she actually did.'

'But, Liz, how would they know Barbara got helpful information from Mrs Barnell?'

Liz was in full flight by now. 'Oh, Barbara probably let it out, sort of by way of introduction. "A friend of mine mentioned Parady to me, a Mrs Barnell."'

'But journalists don't reveal their sources, Liz.'

'Well, perhaps not.' It gave her pause. 'But arriving at Parady out of the blue, in the middle of winter? She probably felt Mrs Barnell's name would mean nothing. And it meant nothing *much*, unless and until she meddled a second time.'

He looked fairly convinced. It relied more on feminine intuition than he liked, but Liz was often right. On the other hand . . . It came to him that if Barbara Rallenham arrived and introduced herself, they might have known her by reputation. 'Mr Rivers' was thought to be English, and perhaps read the *Clarion*. With good reason to be alarmed, they might have used effective persuasion to find out who had sent her there.

He decided to keep that thought to himself.

They parted outside the restaurant. Liz had work to do, Greg telephoned Mandy to ask if they could meet. She suggested he should drop in that evening at her Mayfair flat, which she shared with others. He counter-suggested they should meet at Claridge's for an early evening drink. She thought the idea of Claridge's was 'a hoot'.

'No, no, let's go to Zinka's.'

'Zinka's?'

'It's off Green Lanes. Great fun!'

It wasn't his idea of fun, he felt sure, and was confirmed in that belief when he got there. It was a Cypriot restaurant and bar, trying desperately to be different, decorated with fluorescent tubing and sunk into a welter of loud sixties music. Since it was early evening, the 'in' crowd hadn't yet arrived and it was possible to find a corner where the thunderous rendering of 'Love Me Tender' didn't quite engulf them.

She listened in silence to his account of Mrs Barnell's disappearance while drinking a cocktail of strange ingredients including ouzo. Whether she took it all in, or could even hear it distinctly, he was uncertain.

'So you say that was what you were on about last night?'

'Yes, it was.'

'This Mrs Barnell?'

'Yes.'

'Oh well . . . So the fuzz is getting a bit more involved?'
'Yes.'
'Well, that's good. So do I have to do anything?'
'Not that I can think of.'
'You're so sweet, Greg, taking all this trouble for little old me.'

He shook his head and made disclaiming murmurs. It seemed to him she was under the influence of something, less so than last night but still not firing on all cylinders. Her attention wandered to the tape now being played, at an even louder level than before.

'Ooh, that's The Animals!' she cooed. 'I do love them, don't you?'

He had never heard of The Animals, but looked approving. Someone came in and headed straight for their little table. 'Oho, Mandy! Got a rival, have I?' A tubby young man in open-necked blue shirt and green blazer. Greg now understood why he'd been asked here; Mandy was meeting friends before going on to something even more fun than Zinka's.

It was a good opportunity to take his leave. He went out with the lyrics of 'House of the Rising Sun' crashing about in his head.

He spent a couple of hours in second-hand bookshops around Camden Lock in search of operetta scores, without success. He got back to Liz's flat to find her involved in a telephone conversation with one of her clients. Changed from her business clothes into jeans and a sweater, she still looked gorgeous – by comparison with Mandy, positively angelic.

He dropped a kiss on top of her head. She raised a hand to pat his cheek then wave him on towards the kitchen. A loaf of bread and some sandwich ingredients were on display. Cooking was not one of Liz's strong points.

Sandwich in hand, he returned to the living room. Liz had organized her flat according to her own needs and without much regard for gracious living. Anything to do with her work was of first quality – drawing-board, chart drawers, cupboards holding sample garments and bolts of fabric had all been handmade to her specifications. The other furniture looked as if it had been picked up at car boot sales. But on the whole the place was friendly and comfortable.

He sank down in an armchair. 'I saw Mandy,' he reported, 'brought her up to date.'

'Did she burst into tears?'

'She remained emotionally stable.'

'She make any useful suggestions?'

'No, she was giving her attention to the loudspeakers, and then her boyfriend turned up.'

'Boyfriend?' Liz was all attention. But then the buzzer from the entrance door sounded, so she had to defer gossip. She went to the wall phone in the vestibule. 'Yes?'

'Ms Blair? This is Bob McVeigh of the *Walthamstow Herald*. Could I come up and speak to you for a few minutes?'

'Oh!' She leaned out so as to wag a hand for Greg's attention in the living room. He came to its door. 'Press,' she mouthed. He shook his head with vigour. 'I'm afraid I'm very busy, Mr McVeigh,' she said.

'Please, I only want a few minutes to—'

'I'm sorry, it's just not convenient—'

'Miss Lessiter said it might have something to do with Barbara Rallenham – she said I should see you—'

'Miss Lessiter!'

'I did a short interview with her earlier on. She gave me your address.'

'Just a minute.' She covered the mike with her hand so as to say to Greg, 'He's been talking to Miss Lessiter.'

He thought quickly. He shrugged. 'What of it? She's not directly concerned in—'

'She seems to have mentioned Barbara's name.'

'Oh,' he groaned. 'We'd better see him just to keep things calm.'

'OK.' She turned back to the wall phone. 'I can give you ten minutes.'

'Thank you,' said McVeigh.

She pressed the button to open the outer door. A moment later he arrived at the flat. Greg retreated to the kitchen with his sandwich, to set the coffee-maker going.

'Evening,' said McVeigh as he came in. 'Robert McVeigh, editor and chief reporter of the *Walthamstow Herald*.'

'How do you do. Please.' She nodded him to a chair. 'Can I get you a drink or anything?'

'That is nice of you but no thanks. I just want a word or two, I can tell you're just having supper.' For the smell of brewing coffee was in the air. 'It's about what Miss Lessiter told me.'

'How did you come to be speaking to her?'

'Well, of course, local resident goes missing, I have to take an interest in case it develops into something for the paper. The local police are good about keeping us in the know on local events.'

'I see. So how's Miss Lessiter? Getting over things?'

'To some extent, I suppose. But of course as she calms down she remembers little things, and she's worried over the fact that Mrs Barnell had "meddled" – that was her word – meddled with that Barbara Rallenham.' He grinned. 'Miss Lessiter despises the tabloids and their columnists.'

'So?'

'When I hear that the great Barbara Rallenham of the *Clarion* came slumming to talk to an old lady, I'm very interested, Ms Blair.'

'Slumming! I'd hardly call—'

'The more so as she dignified us with her attention a couple of years ago and promised to let me know what came of it, but never got in touch again.'

'Really?' exclaimed Liz, surprised.

And clearly so was Greg, because, having overheard all this from just beyond the kitchen door, he now reappeared. 'Barbara Rallenham had a story that interested her a couple of years ago?' he asked.

'Hello, who're you?'

'The name's Crowne, I'm a friend of Ms Blair –'

'She' – he pointed at Liz – 'came to see Mrs Barnell a while ago and came rushing back when she heard the old lady'd gone missing. You're interested in this Barnell thing too?'

'Ms Blair and I are—'

'You're not a reporter, are you?' demanded McVeigh, put out. Then he paused and studied Greg. 'Do I know you?'

'No, I'm just visiting Ms Blair for a day or two. I'm in the music business.'

'Uh-huh.' He turned back to Liz. 'Is that right, that you got to know Mrs Barnell because of her contact with Rallenham?'

'Well . . . you could say that.'

'So why's Rallenham back in Walthamstow chatting up old ladies? Last time, she spent a whole day picking my brains, and I had what I thought was a promise she'd tell me if she got a story out of it, but she weaselled on me. After I spoke to Miss Lessiter I tried ringing Rallenham's number, but the mobile seems to be dead. And her paper says she's not available.'

'You say she was researching a story with you?'

'Spent all day. That was in September just over two years ago.'

'She didn't tell you what she was after?' Liz said, as if wondering aloud.

'Well, to some extent.'

'Two years ago and you still remember?' Admiration in her tone.

McVeigh grinned. 'You think I'm a Homer Simpson? Of course I remember. She wanted to know what I could tell her about a local biggie who'd been given a swift exit from his job. It made the nationals, but only as a paragraph on an inside page. She must have got hold of something off her own bat, but she wanted more so she'd eventually accessed our website. Local paper, you see – local knowledge. That got her on the phone to me – had I met him personally, could I tell her more.'

'And you could.'

'Sure thing. He was important down Walthamstow way. Local boy made good, you know? Started from nothing, won scholarships to Cambridge, landed a good post in the Civil Service. He made some impact locally – opened bazaars, helped raise money for a children's clinic, that kind of thing. So of course I met him and his wife from time to time over the years.'

'So what happened? I mean, a goodie-goodie like that doesn't sound the sort of thing that would interest Barbara Rallenham.'

'How right you are! Ministerial strolls on Clapham Common, drugs in the guitars of a pop group, that's more her line.' He scowled. 'She led me on to think she'd let me in on the pay-off and she never did.'

'So what could have been her interest in this man?' Greg said in a seemingly casual intervention.

'Oh, he was got rid of in a bit of a dust-up. The whole thing was kept pretty quiet because it was an embarrassment to his department, but I gather he'd been caught taking bribes. And that figures, you know, because Waters had a very glossy life style. He'd moved out of Walthamstow, though he always kept his contacts there. I think it massaged his ego to have folk wanting to shake his hand, so even when he bought his house up by Waltham Forest he was still around at The Bell. Of course he dressed down for that,' McVeigh said sourly. 'When he was entertaining the nobs at his house, he would put on the Savile Row wardrobe. His wife wore clothes from the big fashion houses, at least so my missus told me.'

'So that was what was in the paper?' coaxed Liz. 'He'd got the sack for accepting bribes? And was taken to court?'

'No-o, no-o, girlie! He was hurried out by the back door and very soon he'd taken himself off to pastures new. I suppose the Crown Prosecution Service didn't have enough evidence to bring a case.'

Greg had begun to understand why McVeigh was editor of a small local paper instead of a national like the *Clarion*. He preferred to talk rather than listen. Whereas Barbara Rallenham had a reputation for playing her cards close to her chest, McVeigh seemed to like to lay them out face upwards on the table.

'So you think Ms Rallenham was looking for something more? And she felt you could help her?' he prompted.

'That's how it seemed. She wanted access to my notes, so I dug them out – the whole thing had happened about a year previously but I keep my notebooks and my recorded tapes on file for a bit. When the old girl told me today that she'd been back to Walthamstow I thought I might dig them out again, but really, unless something big's going to come of it, it's hardly worth the trouble. Waters resigned, he sold up and left. I heard his wife divorced him but I never checked the record on that because it was a dead letter. It all dwindled out.'

'What was the department he worked in?' Greg enquired.

'Some wing of the Board of Trade. Engineering stuff – that

was his speciality, took a degree in metallurgy at Cambridge, if I remember right.' He paused and seemed to remember that he was here to collect information. 'So why was Rallenham interviewing an old lady who lives on my patch?'

Greg gave Liz a glance, which she understood to be encouragement. She said: 'Barbara was following up a letter that Mrs Barnell wrote to her. You know she encourages her readers to get in touch if they have any tips about funny business. Mrs Barnell thought her upstairs tenant was up to something.'

'Who?' McVeigh scratched his head to encourage his thought processes. 'That'd be Tom Shanigan, right? Is it something about rigging the results at the dog tracks?'

Liz shrugged.

'Can't be that! Shanigan's quite well known for being a loser.' He considered. 'Although of course you can arrange for your dog to lose so that you can back the winner . . . Hmm . . . I've got a stringer who does sport for me, I'll get him to ask around at the tracks. Thanks for that.' He scribbled a few words in his notebook then offered his hand in farewell.

He bustled out ahead of Liz, who returned frowning after closing the door on him. 'That seemed a lot more than ten minutes,' she complained.

'But very rewarding.'

'What? For heaven's sake, how?'

'Didn't you hear it?' he countered, smiling with what she thought was triumph.

'Hear what?'

'Waters.'

'Beg pardon?'

'The man Barbara was interested in a couple of years ago was called Waters.'

'So what?'

'Waters,' said Greg. 'Rivers?'

Twelve

Liz blinked once or twice then rose and headed for the kitchen. 'I need strong black coffee,' she muttered.

Greg followed her there. She poured two mugs of coffee but one sip told her it was too hot. She got an ice cube from the freezer, dropped it in, then sat down to watch it melt.

'So you're saying that this guy let himself into Barbara's Maida Vale flat, was surprised when the cleaner asked who he was, and did some fast lateral thinking.' She gathered the ideas together. 'He couldn't say he was Coco the Peasant Potter from Parady, because he didn't want to let on where he'd come from. He couldn't say he was Mr Waters because . . . because . . . Why couldn't he say he was Mr Waters?'

'Because he'd shed that personality. Didn't you gather from McVeigh that Waters escaped prosecution on some kind of technicality? So he doesn't want to announce himself as Waters in case it rings any bells, and Rivers is the first thing that comes into his mind.'

She nodded. 'Could be. So does that help us?'

'Let's see. Barbara Rallenham was interested in Waters when he first got into trouble. A bit later she courted our poor friend McVeigh for background information but took it no further. Two years later Mrs Barnell writes to her about the good fortune of her tenant Mr Shanigan. Mr Shanigan seems to have come into money over the past – how long? Two years? Eighteen months?'

'Wait, wait,' she cried. She took a reviving swallow of coffee. 'I have a question, sir.'

'Go ahead.'

'You started with Mr Waters. Barbara's interested in him. She follows up Mrs Barnell's letter. But Mrs Barnell is writing about Tommy Shanigan, not about this guy Waters.'

'Oh. Yes. Hang on.' He pushed his coffee mug around on the kitchen table. 'Parady? She knew Waters had gone to Parady?'

'No, no, no.' She was shaking her head. 'She didn't find out about the parcel and the address until she went to see Mrs Barnell.'

'Mrs Barnell told her that in her letter.'

'I don't think so, *mon brave*. Unfortunately Mrs Barnell didn't keep a copy of the letter, but I think if she'd mentioned a foreign address in it she'd remember that. She tried to summarize what she'd written but it was along the lines of "feeling something funny was going on", that's all.'

'*Ach, wie lästig!* Are you sure of that?'

'Am I sure of anything? Will the universe contract or continue to expand? Greg, the poor old soul nattered on for ages about Barbara but I got the firm impression that she told her about the packet and the address when they were face to face. You don't read the *Clarion*, do you?'

His shrug admitted it.

'So you don't know what Barbara says at the end of her column. She invites hints and accusations but insists they have to be short. I imagine Celia Barnell obeyed those instructions.'

'Thank you,' he said. 'You've just sunk my gunboat.'

'Don't mention it.'

They sat sipping their drinks, a long silence enveloping them.

'So Barbara was interested in Waters,' he picked up with persistence. 'She tried to follow it up with McVeigh, that didn't work, she files it away until something in Mrs Barnell's letter puts her on track again and she takes off for Parady.'

'I agree with that.'

'So what was in Mrs Barnell's letter?'

Liz gave it consideration. 'I imagine it went something like this: *Dear Barbara, you ask for suspicions about anything illegal. My tenant Tommy Shanigan has come into a lot of money over the past months and I think he's up to something.*'

'That's no help,' he said with a sigh.

'Well, let's push on. I think you're right that Barbara had reason to follow up Mrs Barnell's letter whatever that reason was. Having met her, she pushes off at once for Parady.'

'And there she meets Mr Waters of the Board of Trade. Who isn't pleased and causes her to disappear.'

'That seems probable.'

'Why isn't he pleased? There he is earning an honest living by helping Grashenko with her pottery. There's no shock-horror for her in that.' She waited, eyebrows raised, for his answer.

'But Tommy Shanigan keeps sending him a packet every week.'

'And getting paid for it, we think. We do think that, do we?'

'It's quite a lot of money because he buys pedigree racing dogs and travels about to watch them compete and lose. But Grashenko can't make a fortune – we agreed on that before.'

'Yes we did. So if Mr Waters is paying Mr Shanigan, where does the money come from?'

'I wish I knew,' he said.

He got up to rescue his discarded sandwich from the worktop. He took a bite or two. He discarded it again, felt in his inside jacket pocket for his address book. 'Pollard, Pollard.'

'Are you going to ring a tree surgeon?'

'What?' He gave her a baffled look.

'Pollard is what you do to a tree.'

He rewarded her with a grin but was gone into the living room next moment. There he pressed buttons on her fixed phone to ring a mobile. After a moment a hearty male voice said, 'Pollard here.'

'That's you, Poll? This is Greg.'

'Ah, the artist formerly known as Prince.' The prince had heard this too often to find it funny any longer but he made an appreciative sound and Pollard continued. 'Did you go to the Singer of the World competition, Your Musicianship?'

'No, I couldn't fit it in, but I watched bits on television. You didn't either or you'd know I wasn't there.'

'Perfect logic. And logic also tells me you wouldn't be ringing unless you wanted something, and let me tell you if it's that tape of Janet Baker the answer's no.'

'Nothing like that. I want to pick your brains about something.'

'If any, you mean. Carry on.'

'Well, not on your mobile, Poll. Could we meet?'

'Oh, *sub rosa*, eh? Why not, it's months and months since we saw each other. When and where?'

'Where are you now? At home?'

'Dear chap, I'm about to engage in a contest of the cues!'

'I beg your pardon?'

'Billiards, Greg. I'm at my club.'

'Oh, in that case! Could I drop by for a chat?'

'What, now?'

'Well, in about half an hour.'

'Urgent, is it? Want to persuade me to back a loan to little old Hirtenstein?'

'Of course, for the further construction of banks and financial premises. Is it all right if I come?'

'Sure, old boy. I'll leave word with the porter.'

He went back to the kitchen to finish the sandwich. Liz said, 'Was that another of your Festival Hall friends?'

'He's a civil servant.'

'A mandarin?'

'Not as high up as that.'

'A satsuma, then.'

He laughed. 'He is rather like a satsuma. Round and fairly juicy. I'm going to ask him about Waters.'

'Aha. And leaving now, I take it?' she enquired, watching him gulp down the remains of the coffee and head out through the living room.

'Back in a couple of hours.'

'Right.'

He took a taxi from Archway to St James's. The hall porter nodded when he gave his name and directed him to the billiard room. He went up some shallow stairs, along a corridor whose walls were hung with portraits of former mandarins, then eased open the door bearing the ivory plate: 'Billiards Room'.

A fine old table took up the centre of the room. A special lighting system illuminated the cloth. Leather chairs were grouped in two or three settings for those who were resting from their labours. The air was redolent of good cigars and fine liquor. Wilson Pollard rose from one of the chairs to greet him.

'Good to see you, old man,' he said with a hearty handshake. 'Last time was the Met, wasn't it?'

'*Hänsel and Gretel*, don't remind me.'

'Yes, well, we all have our sorrows.'

'Have you played yet?'

'No, and it looks like it'll be a bit of a wait. So why don't we go in the bar and you can tell me what's on that tiny mind of yours.'

Pollard led the way, his tubby body trotting with unexpected lightness ahead of Greg. Without waiting to consult him he ordered brandy for himself and whisky for Greg. The bar had walls of dark-green silk and framed cartoons of political figures. Faint music offered a soothing background – Greg identified it as Satie.

'So . . . ?'

'I was wondering if you could tell me anything about a man called Waters, who was sacked from the Board of Trade about two years ago, more likely three.'

'Waters, Waters . . .' Pollard plucked at his double chin. 'I hear a faint tinkle.'

'Did you know him?'

'Ah . . . Well, you know, yes, I came across him from time to time. No direct contact at work but at conferences, get-togethers, that kind of thing. He wasn't a member of my club, if you get my meaning.'

'He got in some sort of trouble but was allowed to resign, I heard. '

'Mmm.' Pollard sipped.

'For taking bribes.'

'You seem to know all about it, dear boy.'

'No, that's the sum total. Come on, Poll, do you know what it was about?'

He wrinkled his nose at his guest. 'I'll tell you if you'll lend me your vinyl of Claudia Muzio so I can tape it.'

'Done.'

'Oho. It must be important if you'll go that far. All right then, the story as I heard it on the grapevine was this. You know Waters came from a humble background, do you? Yes? Well, it turned out he had some notions that weren't exactly blue chip.'

'You're not going to tell me he was a Communist sympathizer,' groaned the prince.

'No, not that. But the intelligence service suspected him of having connections with rogue states – I don't know which, because of course it was rather hush-hush, but let's say Libya, or perhaps North Korea.'

'Good Lord!'

Pollard was smiling at the consternation he'd caused. 'Nothing Your Serene Highness would want to be connected with, is it?'

'Absolutely not!' A great part of his life was spent in not being involved in politics. An ex-royal is sometimes courted by groups that would like to restore the monarchy, or some organization for the freedom of somewhere thinks it would be good publicity to kill a dauphin or a rajah. The policy of Greg's family was to steer absolutely clear of all that.

'Waters was selling illegal export permits to governments who were not in favour with ours. If it's any comfort to you, the general opinion was that he did it for the money, not out of idealism.'

'Permits for what?'

'Ah . . . Let me run that through the upper storey. I seem to recall it was for metals that could be used in weapons production.'

'Metals such as what?'

'My revered companion, how do I know? Money's my department, not sheet metal. Nor is it likely anyone could tell you exactly what got exported with his licences because, as they now say about tortillas, it was a wrap.' Delighted with this witticism, Pollard took a celebratory swallow.

Greg produced the sketch made by Liz – the original, now somewhat creased. It seemed to him he'd been carrying it around for decades. 'Is this Waters?' he asked, offering it.

Pollard inspected it. He pursed his lips. 'Not very lifelike, is it?' he parried.

'It was made from a description.'

'Identikit? Police work?'

'No, a friend did it. It's from the description of a stranger who let himself into someone's flat.'

'Oh, now that sounds just the sort of thing Waters would

get up to. A bit sneaky, if you know what I mean. Now, is this his portrait?' He pondered. 'It's like-ish. The Waters I was acquainted with had a gleam, a glint, that's not here. But then that was before he got his trousers dusted.'

'Dusted?' the prince echoed, baffled.

'Before he got his behind smacked. Before, to put it plainly, he had to resign.' Pollard grinned. 'One forgets, does one not, that although you had a princely upbringing in languages, mathematics, music, and all the other accomplishments required of royalty, your command of English isn't boundless, dear fellow.'

'My princely upbringing prompts me to suggest that you're getting a little too drunk to play billiards.'

'"Wine does more than Milton can, To justify bad play to man." I don't play well even when sober. And despite your unjust criticism, I'll do you a favour. Somewhere back at Château Pollard I've got snapshots of Waters—'

'What?'

'Oh yes, you know, those jolly do's – someone retires, we all assemble and give him a gold watch and a bottle of champers and there's a cameraman taking pix. Heaps of those at home. I'll look through 'em, sure to find Minnehaha Laughing Waters among 'em.'

'Thanks a million! You're a pal, Poll!' Greg rose.

'That's very true, very true, I'm a pal Poll, and you've just made me a very happy man. Goodnight, sweet prince.'

'And you won't forget the photos?'

'Never in a million years. I'll post 'em – what's your address at the moment?'

Greg got out one of his concert-arranger's cards and scribbled Liz's address on the back. He added 'Send pix of Waters' just in case Poll's memory failed him. He tucked it in the breast pocket of Poll's suit, they shook hands, and he turned to go.

'Don't forget the Muzio record,' grunted Pollard to his receding back. Greg waved a hand above his head as he went out.

The diplomatic and political greats of the past frowned down at him as he went. What a depressing place, he thought. If I spent much time here, I'd resort to brandy too.

When he got home, Liz was curled up in an armchair, half

asleep. It was well known that Liz was not an evening person, unless she had a piece of work to finish or was at a party. She roused at his entrance, tried to focus. 'How ... er ... how was the tangerine?'

'Pickled, to some extent. But he says he's got photos of Waters.'

'Oh, that'd be good. You hungry?'

'I could eat.'

'Well, let me just get something out of the freezer—'

'That's all right, you go back to sleep. I'll find something.' His head was full of thoughts and ideas. Unlike his beloved, he functioned best from about six in the evening. What he would ideally have liked to do was to find a piano and sit down to something strong and difficult – a Chopin polonaise, for instance.

Lacking a piano, he had to make do with the microwave. He found a pasta dish, heated it up, poured himself a glass of something that Liz was keeping cool in the fridge, then sat down at the kitchen table with a pen and the back of an envelope.

Things to do, he headed the list. *Assure myself that 'Rivers' is Waters. Consider Tommy Shanigan – was it* his *name that alerted Barbara's attention? Nothing else in Mrs Barnell's letter seems worth her attention. Does he have influence/ authority at Parady? Waters turns up at Mrs B.'s flat, query is that because of Shanigan or not? The last two items on the list were: Overalls in package – what does that* mean*? Conclusion: think a bit more about Tommy Shanigan.*

It took him some time to finish the pasta and the list, after which he put his crockery in the dishwasher and switched off the light. When he got into the living room, Liz was fast asleep. He picked her up gently. She said 'Mmm?' without entirely waking. He carried her to the bedroom, got her undressed while she made little sounds of protest at being disturbed, and slid her into bed. After quiet bedtime routines he got in beside her. She said, 'Ah, darling!' in her sleep and threw her arms around him. But she remained dead to the world.

However, in the morning, waking early as she always did, she didn't go running. She coaxed him awake for activities of a more enjoyable sort.

Thirteen

Breakfast was later than usual. But, 'After all, it's Saturday,' said Liz.

'Right. And my organist will be doing his stuff this afternoon so I must ring to wish him well. I'll do that first, because I don't think Poll will have surfaced yet.'

He had brought her up to date with the information Pollard had given and his offer of a photograph. It had raised her hopes. 'We'll take it to the cops,' she said. 'They'll have a name and a picture then, and they can transmit it by scanner to the Avignon station. And then the Avignon boys will . . . er . . . what will they do?'

'I hope they'll take it to Parady and compare it with the man you call the Peasant Potter.'

'And if it's him, what then?'

'They'll question him.'

'Uh-huh. And what will he say, darling?'

He sighed. 'He'll probably say, "Never heard of Barbara Rallenham." But if the *juge d'instruction* knows his stuff, there ought to be a result of some kind.'

'I don't know anything about the French system. Are you saying the case goes before a judge at once?'

'No, no, the *juge d'instruction* is the examining magistrate. He instructs the detectives, guides them you might say, and a lot would depend on whether he liked the look of the preliminary evidence. If he thinks it's a waste of time, the inquiry might not go any further.'

'Good grief, Barbara's missing! He's got to take on the case!'

'Oh yes, the police will go on looking for Barbara. But they might not look any closer at Waters – they might go off on some other track that they thought was more rewarding.'

'Well, if that happens we'll have to convince the Walthamstow police to keep at it.'

He didn't reply and she gave him a hard look. 'What now?'

'When we get the photograph, who's going to identify Waters as the man who took Mrs Barnell away?'

'Well . . . Mrs Dandry. She saw our Mr Rivers at Barbara's flat.'

'Yes, but *Barbara*'s case is being handled by the *Maida Vale* police. It's the British end of a French case.'

'That's not what I'm talking about, cloth-head! I'm talking about the guys going after him about Mrs Barnell.' He was shaking his head. 'Yes,' she insisted.

'No. The only witness is Miss Lessiter. Whose eyesight is very poor.'

Liz was stunned. She jumped up from the breakfast table to thrust her cereal dish into the sink with unnecessary violence. She ran water into it, swished it about, then set it on the draining board with a thump.

'I'm sorry,' he said to her back. 'I think the photograph will count on the French side of the affair. As to Mrs Barnell, I don't know.'

She turned back. There was a glint of tears in her eyes. 'Poor old darling,' she mourned. 'It's just awful to think . . . to think she may have come to harm.'

'I know, I know.' He went to her and put his arms around her. Her head fitted neatly under his chin. She sniffed a few times then released herself from his embrace.

'Telephone,' she commanded.

He obeyed. Lucius Kremer answered at once, delighted to hear from him and assuring him that all was well with his organist. 'He's over in the church practising now,' he reported, 'and M. Petiran will join him in about an hour to rehearse with the trumpet. All will go well, I assure you.'

'Give them my best wishes,' he said. 'I'll ring about five, after the first recital is over. M Kremer, you will make sure they have a meal and a rest before the evening event?'

'*Bien sûr, bien sûr,*' murmured M Kremer, who was quite accustomed to festival nerves. The church was often used for music performances.

It was now after ten thirty. Time now, perhaps, to ring Wilson Pollard. His wife answered.

'Ah, Lillian, how are you? This is Gregory Crowne.'

'Who – oh, Greg, how nice to hear you! Where are you? In London?'

'Yes, although I should be in Avignon where today's concert is happening.'

'Avignon – oh, I love Avignon. Though I prefer it in summer, you know.'

'Me too, if the truth be told. But you know, the Winter Festival is an opportunity for – Well, you don't want to hear all that. Lillian, may I speak to Will?' Poll's wife didn't like to hear him called Poll.

'He hasn't appeared yet, my dear,' she said with tolerant amusement. 'Got in at some ungodly hour this morning, I think it was about three, and stumbled about trying not to wake me. And when he does come down, you can bet he's going to have a monstrous hangover.'

'Oh dear.'

'I'm sorry. Was it anything I can help with? Mind you, if it's anything to do with his precious records and tapes, I'd rather not—'

'No, it's about a photograph. I had a chat with him last night and he promised to look it out.'

'You want a photograph of Will?' she asked in astonishment.

'No, no, it was of a colleague of his. Not in his own department and not of top-line importance, I think. He said he was pretty sure he had one, taken at some party or event or something.'

He heard a hesitation then Lillian said, 'I don't think so, Greg dear. That dunderhead! He should have remembered. We don't keep that kind of photo any more.'

'You don't?'

'No, well, you know how they mount up! And Will's been a civil servant for twenty years. If we kept everything, we'd need hired storage for them. No, we decided a while ago to keep only two sorts – family pix, which means weddings and christenings and twenty-firsts and so forth, and official ones, which means important occasions like conferences—'

'Yes, perhaps one taken at a conference—'

'And then only pix of Will with the bigwigs. In case he ever wants to write his autobiography, which God forbid.'

'Oh, Lillian,' he groaned.

'Is that a big let-down? I'm sorry, my dear.'

'You really don't have any of him with a few friends at an office party?'

'No, I really don't. I put everything non-essential out for recycling ages ago.'

'Well . . . Thank you, Lillian. I'm sorry to have bothered you.'

'Sorry not to be a help. I'll mention it to Will once the aspirin have taken effect but really I've kept nothing in the albums that shows minor colleagues. I look after the albums so I know I'm right'

'I understand.'

''Bye, Greg.'

Liz, passing through the living room on her way to dress for the day, saw the frustration on the angular features. 'No go?'

'His wife threw everything out.'

'Aw-w!' She sat down beside him on the sofa. 'What a shame!'

'*Malédiction!*' he muttered. 'What's the matter with the world? Every time I think we've got hold of something, it slithers away!'

'I know, darling, I know. It's rotten.'

'I want to get the police involved but it's no use going to them and saying, "We think Barbara was interested in this man Waters and that's why she came to Avignon, because the man's living at Parady now." They won't take my word for it – why should they? They went when I accused Grashenko and that was a fiasco so why should they take me seriously a second time?'

'And even if they did go, and questioned Coco the Potter, he'd say "Not me, guv."'

'He'd say what?'

'"Not me, guv." It's what British criminals are supposed to say when they're arrested.'

He smiled, put his hands on her shoulders, drew her close,

and kissed her. 'What would I do without you?' he asked.

'Flounder.'

'Now, that's a fish,' he said, and she was about to correct him when she saw he was teasing. Well,' he went on, 'I must now telephone Bredoux to let them know where I am. My grandmother is probably back home by now.'

'Oh, her,' muttered Liz as she went on to the bedroom.

The ex-Queen Mother was full of cheer. 'My *cabine d'amis* has been well received,' she boasted. 'I am invited to do another at his place on Mahe, which is one of the Seychelles—'

'Grossmutti, you're not thinking of going to the Seychelles!'

'No, no, of course not, you know how I hate a temperature higher than twenty-one degrees. But think, *mon enfant*, I can draw up little plans and collect samples of colours and materials, and send someone out to do the work at my instructions.'

It sounded very unlikely. What ex-Queen Mother Nicoletta enjoyed was the hands-on experience. But he said he thought it was a fine idea, reported to her about his series of musical events in Avignon and that he was now in London. She knew it meant he was with Liz, and said only 'Mmph' in her most disapproving tone.

'Papa is well?' he asked.

'Out at the moment, helping one of his pupils buy a new saddle. But he's well, and you are too, I hope.'

'Yes, fine, Grossmutti. I'll ring again soon.'

'Grego, you aren't doing anything . . . foolish?'

'Foolish? Me? Never.'

'I mean, nothing that will get you into the newspapers.' Meaning suddenly being persuaded to marry a nobody like Liz Blair.

'It is always my ambition to stay out of the newspapers, madame.'

'Keep it that way.'

When they had disconnected, the word 'newspapers' lingered on.

Newspapers illustrated their news with photographs. Mr McVeigh of the *Walthamstow Herald* had said that Mr Waters did newsworthy things. There should therefore be a file of photographs of Waters at the *Herald*.

He didn't have a telephone number for the *Herald*, and chided himself for that. But Enquiries furnished it, he pressed buttons and heard the ringing tone. It went on for quite a while.

'*Walthamstow Herald*, Marcia speaking, how can I help you?' announced a somewhat harried female voice.

'May I speak to Mr McVeigh, please?'

'Mr McVeigh is not available at present, I'm afraid.'

'Is he in the office? Please tell him it's Ms Blair's friend Greg calling.'

'He's not at the office, Greg. Today's Saturday. He's out covering our weekend programme of local events.'

'Oh!' Of course, he should have thought of that. 'Well, can you give me his mobile number?'

'No, that's against policy, I'm afraid.'

'Listen, Marcia, this is very important. Mr McVeigh and I had a conversation last night and I've got something more to say. Can you contact him and ask him to ring me?'

'Um, well, I could do that. Give me your number.' He dictated his mobile number. 'I'll pass that on to him but I'm afraid it may not be for a while. I'm on the advertisement desk, you see, and he may have switched off temporarily because he's in church reporting a wedding. But I'll pass it on.'

'Thank you.'

When he went into the bedroom he encountered Liz coming out of the shower in a pale blue bath robe and with her fair hair wet and clinging to her head. He picked her up and swung her round. '*Sesamo, apriti!*' he cried.

'Absolutely,' she agreed, laughing. 'What does it mean?'

'Sesame, open! I tried another door! For the photograph. McVeigh's paper should have photographs, no?'

'I would think so.'

'Let us celebrate,' he urged, pulling her towards the bed.

'Not until you've shaved, lover.'

So there was a delay.

And another delay in having a reply from McVeigh. Liz had gone off on household shopping and Greg was visiting book shops and music stores in Soho in search of operetta scores when at last his mobile buzzed.

McVeigh said: 'You called?'

'I did. I wanted to ask you something, Mr McVeigh. Do you have picture files at your newspaper?'

'Huh? Well . . . Mostly I do digital now so of course it's computer-stored. What's the subject?'

'Subject?'

'Of the photograph.'

'Oh – I wondered if you had a photograph of your local bigshot, Waters.'

'Oh, sure. Bound to. But not on computer. He'd be in the old-fashioned file cabinet. I only got into digital about two years ago.'

'Would you look him out for me? I'd appreciate it. I'd like a nice big clear photo, if you've got one.'

'Happy to oblige. I'll get to it in a day or two.'

'What?' cried His Highness, taken aback. 'Can't you do it today?'

'You're joking, mate. I'm not going back to the office until Monday—'

'But this is important—'

'So is this! Saturday and Sunday are big days for a local paper. I keep typing paragraphs and sending them in from my home, but I'll be too busy to get to the office until Monday morning.'

'But you don't understand—'

'Perhaps not, and that's because you're not explaining yourself. What's this about?'

He hesitated. He was tempted to tell McVeigh. But he heard the voice of his grandmother: 'Nothing that will get you into the newspapers.' Once he divulged the fact that he thought Waters was in some way connected with the disappearance of a Walthamstow citizen, McVeigh would get his teeth into it.

'I'm sorry, I can't explain,' he said with a sigh.

'OK then, I'll see if I can find a picture for you on Monday,' said the editor huffily. 'Are we clear on that?'

'Yes.'

'You'll be at Ms Blair's address?'

'Yes.'

'OK then—'

'Just a moment—'

'What?'

'One more thing. About Mr Shanigan.'

'What about him?'

'Did your sports writer find out anything about his winnings?'

'You're joking! My "sports writer" was at the local football derby last night and he's got a rugby match today. He might get to it tomorrow. It's not urgent, is it?'

'No, no, of course not—'

'Because the police are confident Shanigan isn't in any way involved with the Mrs Barnell thing. He was at work at the time.'

'Yes, so I understand.'

'Besides, Tommy Shanigan's a bit of a bonehead. No way is he going to be doing anything that needs any planning, such as kidnapping his landlady. She hasn't got any money and no one to ransom her, so even Tommy would see it as stupid. If that's what you're imagining.'

'But he has to plan sometimes – getting his dogs to the tracks where they're to race – seeing to their transport and—'

'Oh, his trainer does all that for him. Look, forget Tommy Shanigan as a suspect in the Barnell thing. He's been around in this neighbourhood all his life and, as far as I can learn, never amounted to a spoonful of cornflakes.'

'You speak as if you've known him a long time.'

'Well, I've been with the paper almost twelve years. Started as a junior and, just think, I've risen to the lofty rank of editor.' There was heavy irony in the tone. 'So I could say I've known Tommy to some extent for twelve years, but people I've worked with or talked to have known him a lot longer. People who went to school with him, for instance. He's always had this daft thing about greyhounds.'

'A local boy, in other words.'

'Absolutely.'

'And . . . er . . . the notorious Mr Waters. . . he was a local boy?'

There was a sudden pause in the quickfire response from McVeigh. After a moment he said: 'Hey . . . ?' It was a long, surprised question.

Greg remained silent.

'You're not suggesting there's any connection?' Then, with scorn, 'Nah! Dog racing? Waters was more into Ascot and seats at Wimbledon. And he was brainy – got himself into Cambridge. Whereas Tommy trundled through school without ever winning even an egg-and-spoon race, so far as I ever heard. And look where he ended up – working in a factory on the industrial estate.'

None of it sounded promising. Greg sighed inwardly. 'Perhaps he's done well at work. He's a manager?'

'No, not at all. I don't think he's even a foreman.'

'You've taken an interest in him?'

'Well, occasionally, because of the dog racing. But I never thought to ask about his position at the factory. Even if he's risen to foreman, he's not making any kind of a fortune at Bestadyne. You know, that really does make you wonder where he gets the money to look after those dogs.'

'Bestadyne? That's the firm he works for?'

'Yeah, makes metal containers or something, part of a bigger concern with one of those boring names – Elite Metal Tubes and Sheeting or some such.' He laughed. 'Their local PR boy comes to me from time to time trying to get favourable mentions in the paper but what can you say about metal tubes and sheeting, eh?'

'Not very glamorous.'

'You said it. Well, listen, Mr Crowne, I've got to get on, there's a diamond wedding party I've got to attend.'

'You won't forget to look for a photo of Mr Waters?'

'I've listed it on my notebook.'

'Many thanks.'

So should he now ring the police? Tell them that McVeigh could provide a picture of the man who might have abducted Mrs Barnell? Get them to call McVeigh from his weekend reporting to look for the photograph urgently? They would say, 'Who's going to look at the picture and identify him for us?' The answer was still, 'only Miss Lessiter.' Who had already said she couldn't give a description of the mysterious car driver.

The mere fact that the police were asking for a photograph would tell McVeigh that Greg was involved in the police investigation. McVeigh would wonder about that, perhaps make some enquiries, and learn his real identity. His Highness recalled how he'd looked at him last night and said, 'Do I know you?'

Would delay in getting a photograph make a difference to the police investigation? The answer was no. The culprit was back in Parady by now, beyond the reach of the British police.

And to tell the truth, Greg greatly doubted that anything they were trying to do would help Mrs Barnell. He had a desolate conviction that both Mrs Barnell and Barbara Rallenham were beyond help now.

He was passing a public library as this unhappy thought went through his mind. He paused. Bestadyne of the industrial estate near Walthamstow. He went in.

There were shelves of telephone directories and reference books. Examination of the directories and Yellow Pages yielded the information that the firm was a subsidiary of a larger concern called Renown Tubes and Sheeting. Yellow Pages had a box advertisement with a website address. Hiring a session on the Internet brought him the website and by clicking links he discovered that the Chief Executive Officer of Renown Tubes and Sheeting was Sir Rupert Modd. *Who's Who* gave him Sir Rupert's address, Halborough House in Berkshire. Directory Enquiries informed him that Sir Rupert's telephone number was ex-directory but that there was a number for the gatehouse.

The gatehouse! Very aristocratic. He rang the number, to be answered by a sergeant-major type of voice. He asked to speak to Sir Rupert.

'Who is calling, please?'

'My name is Gregory Crowne, but that won't mean anything. Would you tell him that Wilson Pollard of the Treasury will vouch for me.'

'Wilson Pollard of . . . ?'

'The Treasury. Mr Pollard is an advisor to the Chancellor of the Exchequer.' Which was true, although it had nothing to do with his call.

'Ahem . . . And this is in reference to what, sir?'

'I would like to ask for advice about a business matter – a factory I shall be taking over in my homeland, Switzerland.'

'I shall ask you to give me your number, sir. If Sir Rupert wishes to contact you, he will ring.'

'Thank you.'

Clearly there was a switchboard where a screening process went on. Quite understandable. The prince had gone out to the stone-floored entrance hall of the library, since there was a notice asking visitors not to uses mobiles among the books. He hung around reading notices on a big board: German lessons, guitar lessons, the University of the Third Age invited newcomers, a debate on ecology would take place the following Wednesday, a zither recital on Friday next. Zither recital? He read on. 'The Harry Lime theme . . . Hungarian gypsy melodies . . .'

His mobile buzzed. He picked it up, connected, and announced himself.

'Mr Crowne? Ah, yes. I had my secretary look you up in our personal directory. What can I do for you, sir?' No direct intrusion on his position of anonymity, but he was being told firstly that Sir Rupert had recognized the pseudonym and secondly that he was a very shrewd old crow. An elderly voice, dry and precise.

'Sir Rupert, is it convenient to speak to you now?'

'Not entirely, I regret to say. I have people here at the moment, and this evening my wife and I have a dinner engagement. You want advice on a business matter – would it take long?'

'Well, it might take a while.'

'Quite, quite. You are where? Not in Switzerland, I imagine.'

'No, sir, I'm in London for a few days.'

'Let me see, let me see. Tomorrow? Are you free tomorrow to have this conversation?'

'Yes, indeed. Tomorrow would be fine.'

'I play golf on a Sunday, Mr Crowne.' He gave a little sharp laugh. 'A cliché, of course, but I do enjoy it. And I would be unwilling to give it up, but on the other hand, if you would not mind coming out to the club, I could offer you lunch. The food at the Hither Downs Club is very good.'

'That's very kind, Sir Rupert. I should love to—' He broke off. What would Liz say to his taking himself off for most of Sunday?

'It isn't convenient?' asked Sir Rupert.

'Well, the fact is, I'm staying with a friend . . .'

'A friend.'

'A lady friend . . .'

'Ah, I see. Oh, my dear fellow, if she doesn't mind listening to us discuss business over lunch, she'd be very welcome. We do have lady members at the Club. And if she'd be bored by business, there are some nice walks round the outside of the course.'

'That's very good of you, sir. I'm sure she'd enjoy that.' He tried to imagine himself telling Liz she was to go for a walk while the menfolk had their discussion.

'Excellent. Well now, to get to the club, you take the M1 . . .' There followed some complicated directions which he scribbled down on the back of one of the notices grabbed from the notice-board. When they disconnected, he transferred these to a blank page in his address book and faithfully pinned the notice (about the zither recital) back on the board.

He now went to the rendezvous he'd arranged with Liz. They went in search of lunch but it was Saturday. Everywhere in Soho was full. They turned north, towards Marylebone, and ended up in a restaurant he knew of not because it was close to Madame Tussauds, although it was, but because it was near the Royal Academy of Music.

He recounted first his conversation with McVeigh, as they ate a very hearty soup with French bread. 'You got him on to Shanigan and kept him there,' she remarked approvingly.

'Yes, because it seemed possible that it was the name Shanigan in Mrs Barnell's letter that caught Barbara's interest.'

'And so now you know that Shanigan's been around in Walthamstow all his life and never got anywhere except into a factory on the industrial estate.'

'Yes.'

'Marvellous. Does it seem to you that you've wasted your time?'

'Perhaps. But two things seem to emerge. One is that Shanigan and Waters are both Walthamstow boys. You remember that when McVeigh was moaning about how Barbara dropped him, he told us that Waters kept up his contacts with his old neighbourhood. It seems possible – perhaps even probable – that Waters and Shanigan knew each other from a long way back.'

'Oh-h.' She looked dubious. 'That's one thing. What was the other?'

'The boiler suit.'

'Pardon me?'

'I looked in a shop window in Soho while I was book hunting. It sells occupational and industrial clothing, like chef's trousers and so forth. The complete overalls I saw in the packet should be called a boiler suit, I think. And who wears that kind of covering?'

'Who?'

'A factory worker.'

'Eh?'

'A factory worker in a factory that makes metal containers.'

'You mean a factory like United Piping and Fluting?'

'Renown Tubes and Sheeting.'

'Whatever. So what are you saying?'

'Mr Shanigan wears a boiler suit while he works in the metal factory – yes?'

'Probably. Go on.'

'I opened a packet sent to Parady and it contained a boiler suit.'

'Yes.'

'We asked ourselves why Mr Shanigan should send a boiler suit every week to Parady. We asked ourselves how much a boiler suit would cost every week.'

'So we did.'

'But what if Mr Shanigan is sending his own boiler suit to Parady every week.'

'Don't be daft, Greg! He'd have to keep buying a new one very week.'

'No, think about it. He sends a suit to Parady, he wears another suit at work for a week, then he gets the first suit back from Parady and wears that at work while the second suit goes in the mail to Parady. And so on.'

'Say that again.'

'He wears a boiler suit to work and at the weekend he sends it to Parady. He has another suit to wear next week. Meanwhile the first suit comes back in the post.'

'Yes. No. Wait.' She set her soup spoon down to think about it. 'Mrs Barnell never mentioned a word about Shanigan *receiving* a packet every week.'

'No. Because . . . he has an arrangement . . . what do you call it, *poste restante*?'

'Till called for. Or more likely a convenience address. Well, yes. He collects a packet from that, and sends another packet by post every weekend.'

'I think so.'

'You do?' She was shaking her head. 'Shanigan sends a packet of work clothes to Parady every week and gets one back? His own work clothes?'

'It seems possible.'

'But why? Why?'

'The only reason I can think of,' he said slowly, 'is that there's something in the clothes.'

'A letter? A key? A . . . a what?'

'I don't know.' He sat trying to picture the packet. He'd slit the sticky tape, drawn out a polythene bag containing dark-blue clothing which he now knew was a boiler suit. He had glimpsed nothing that might have been a letter. He had felt nothing that might be a key or anything hard. Squishy had been Mrs Barnell's word. The contents of the polythene bag were squishy.

Once he'd recovered from his disappointment that morning, he'd pushed the polythene bag back into the padded envelope. To do so he'd squeezed the contents. He closed his eyes and tried to remember. Nothing hard. Nothing white like a letter.

Something red?

Some slight touch of red in the upper folds of the clothing. He'd felt the yielding line of a zip, seen just the merest glint of the zip and somewhere in there. . . just a hint, perhaps piping along the edge of a pocket? Once in the padded envelope there was no sense of the zip. The whole thing was soft and pliable.

'Eat your soup, it's getting cold,' Liz rebuked him.

'*Oui, Maman*.' He obeyed. Then he said, 'If the boiler suit comes back to him, he has to launder it, doesn't he? Before he can wear it again.'

'I suppose so.'

'He has to have a clean boiler suit to go to work on Monday morning. So it must come back to allow for the laundering. How long does it take to wash and dry a set of overalls?'

'You're asking me?' she cried. 'Next you'll be asking me how to darn socks.'

'I'm sorry, I didn't mean to insult you. But how long, at a guess?'

'Well, not long if Shanigan has a washing machine and a tumble dryer.'

'But he's away a lot – his spare time is spent watching greyhounds race, and sometimes he goes on quite long trips to see his own dogs run.'

Liz allowed the waitress to remove her soup plate. Then she said with a shrug, 'He has more than two sets, probably. My mother used to say, "One to wear, one for spare, and one in the wash."'

'My grandmother says something like that about handkerchiefs.' His soup plate was taken. The waitress said, '"One for show, one for blow, and one in the back pocket."'

'Universal wisdom.' They all smiled at each other. The waitress went away to tell the kitchen staff they should take extra care with the order for table six because they were nice people.

'Now we've solved Tommy Shanigan's laundry problem, where has it got us?' Liz enquired.

'Nowhere.'

'Oh, that's encouraging. What are we going to discuss with the next course?'

'I think we'd better talk about our trip to Berkshire.'

'We're going to Berkshire?'

'To the golf club of Sir Rupert Modd.'

'Oh good. I do enjoy a jaunt to the country for some fresh air at the weekend.'

He looked guilty. 'I knew you wouldn't like it.'

'*Why* are we going to the golf club of Sir Rupert Mudd?'

'Modd. Because, dearest love, he's the Chief Executive Officer of the firm that owns Renown Tubes and Sheeting. It says in *Who's Who* he is an industrialist who has made his name in the production of special metal casings. He gives his hobbies as golf, reading, and the welfare of his employees.'

'And you're going to talk to him about Tommy Shanigan, who works in one of his factories and whom he's never heard of.'

'No, of course not.'

'Then what?'

'I want to find out why those confounded boiler suits are being sent back and forth across the Channel. Sir Rupert has spent his life in making things with metal and says he's devoted to the welfare of his employees. He ought to know why boiler suits are important.'

'So we're going to sit there over our roast beef and talk about boiler suits.'

'Yes, my love, we are.'

She frowned. 'Can we ask him if he has trouble with a name like Modd?'

'That would be tactless.'

'I was afraid you'd say that,' she sighed.

Fourteen

Liz had a problem next day. 'What do you wear to a posh golf club?'

'How about what you wore the other day?' suggested Greg. 'Those beige slacks – and wasn't it a brown jacket?'

'Umm,' she said.

When at last they set off, she was clad in a pleated grey skirt, a dark-green Barbour, and a cream silk blouse. For his part Greg sported charcoal slacks, grey flannel shirt, and a dark-red pullover. Good taste to the nth degree.

Liz was driving. Having read through the directions scribbled by Greg in his difficult continental hand, she'd transcribed them into large capitals. She had no problems except for getting through the Sunday traffic of London. Her bright little Nissan sped along the roads in what she felt was a very pleasing manner, but her satisfaction was greatly diminished when she had to park alongside a silver Lexus at the club. And the Lexus was by no means the only grandee in the car park.

The whole place breathed wealth, exclusivity. What had once been a substantial country house had been made into the club house, the grounds had been transformed by a master course-planner into a vista of rolling greenness. They went in at a handsome entrance flanked by bay trees in tubs. A uniformed attendant came forward at once to greet them.

'Mr Crowne? Sir Rupert is just changing after his game. May I show you to the bar, sir? And your jacket, madam – shall I show you where they are hung?' Thus tactfully steered to the ladies' room, Liz followed him, while Greg went into the bar.

When she joined him a few minutes later, the bar was busy with loud conversation and the clink of bottle against glass.

'If you hadn't missed that putt at the eleventh . . .' 'I *told* you that club was wrong for the uphill . . .' Among the sound mix she could hear a few feminine voices. She tracked them to a window seat, where four women were arguing and waving their hands about. She was glad to note that she'd guessed the correct style; they were wearing shirts or muted sweaters so far as she could see.

A waiter hurried up. Liz asked for a glass of white wine but Greg opted for Perrier water. She raised her eyebrows at him. 'Don't trust their wine cellar?'

'Quite the contrary. What do you bet Sir Rupert is going to show off his expertise with the wine list at lunch?'

'Oh, I never thought of that. Well, I won't drink much. I'm the driver, aren't I.'

They could look out of the window at the grounds. Winter trees looked as if they had been etched against a pale-grey sky. Men in brightly coloured jackets moved away into the distance. It was all a long way from the miseries of Mrs Barnell's house in Walthamstow.

After about ten minutes the uniformed man reappeared with another in his train – a stout gentleman of medium height, rectangular face and bushy brows, with his thinning hair brushed back and carefully styled to balance his heavy jowls. He was wearing casual clothes – well-creased slacks, a light-weight hound's tooth jacket and a pale-green shirt.

'Mr Crowne! Delighted to see you. No trouble finding us, I take it?'

'None at all, thank you. Liz, this is Sir Rupert. My friend Ms Blair.'

'How do you do! You've been looked after, have you, my dear?'

'Beautifully, thank you. What a lovely place this is.'

'Isn't it? Belonged to a country squire who gave it up after the First World War, couldn't afford it any longer. Sad in a way but it lives on.' They made conversation for a few minutes until Sir Rupert could tell they had either finished their drinks or had had as much as they wanted. 'Well, now, if you'll just follow me, I'm told our table is waiting.'

The dining room on the first floor was large – perhaps the ballroom of the squire's home. Expert hands had produced the effect of an Edwardian country house without sacrificing space and light. Their table was in a splendid spot with a view over another expanse of landscape.

Chairs were pulled out for them, menus were proffered. They gave their attention to the list of dishes, which seemed to lean towards traditional English – roast beef and Yorkshire pudding, steak and kidney pie. Both Liz and Greg chose to have avocado and then an omelette, whereupon Sir Rupert studied the wine list and decreed Beaujolais Blanc – 'And I'll decide later about what to have with dessert.'

As they ate they made polite conversation. Sir Rupert talked a little about golf with a transition to countryside affairs, then they discussed fitness regimes with a little compliment to Liz when Sir Rupert learned she was a morning runner, then the topic became London life and had they seen the latest production at the National?

As coffee was served they began to have gaps in the chat. Greg felt it was time to broach the subject of his supposed business venture in Switzerland. He'd given it some thought. His first idea was to say he was going into the production of watch parts, because after all Switzerland is famous for watches. But he had no idea what watch parts were made of, or whether those in the industry had to wear protective clothing.

His next thought was agricultural machinery. He knew a little about that because he saw it in action on the hillsides near Bredoux. But somehow that seemed dull, so he reviewed his circle of friends and decided to use information he'd got over the years from Claude Juvain. Claude was a motor racing fanatic. So Greg decided he was going to invest money in a mythical factory for the manufacture of racing car engines.

'I imagine you have plans for this afternoon, Sir Rupert, so perhaps I could mention my business project?' he ventured.

Sir Rupert flashed a glance at Liz, as if to say, 'Are you going to talk about serious matters in front of the lady?'

Liz chose to ignore this hint, while Greg forged straight on as if he hadn't seen it. He outlined his new enterprise, made it sound as if a group of enthusiastic young men were putting in the money, then ended by saying, 'I've undertaken to be the personnel and welfare manager, because I'm not mechanically minded. My chief role will be the care and safety of the employees. You understand that Swiss standards in that regard are very high . . . ?'

'Yes, indeed, very commendable. But even so you'll need to take special precautions. You'll be making high performance racing engines?'

'Exactly.'

'The problem with that sort of production is that specialized metals are needed. The heat generated by a racing engine must be formidable. Your specifications will include . . . let's say, zirconium?'

Greg was baffled. To his rescue came Liz. 'Zirconium, that's those lovely stones that look like diamonds, isn't it?'

Their host gave her a kindly, tolerant smile. 'Not quite, Ms Blair. The stones you mention are zircons. More correctly, square prismatic crystals of zirconium silicate, $ZrSiO_4$, very attractive of course and quite useful too in industry in some of its forms.'

'My word,' breathed Liz in admiration. 'How amazing that you can remember all those scientific terms!'

'That's part of my business, my dear. Not zirconium silicate but the element zirconium, which is number 40 in the atomic table, you know.'

'In the atomic table! That sounds scary—'

'No, no, it's just a list of atoms that includes substances such as oxygen and hydrogen, and metals of course, such as titanium, which is Atomic Number 22. You shouldn't worry your head about that, my dear. You concentrate on the element C, which in its crystallized form is a diamond – a girl's best friend, I hear.'

Greg was coming to the conclusion that Sir Rupert would be lucky to escape with his life from this encounter with Liz, so hurriedly intervened. 'To return to the question about specialized metals in the production process, you would recommend coveralls for the employees?'

'Certainly. And goggles and masks for the very fine milling. Inhaled dust can be a problem.'

'Should we give an allowance for the men to purchase their clothing?'

'Oh, well . . . It's much better if you supply it yourself,' chided Sir Rupert. 'You see, in that way, you can ensure that the dust is recovered from the overalls.'

'I beg your pardon?' Greg said in surprise.

Sir Rupert smiled. 'It's something that comes down to us from the days of the old gold strikes in Alaska and California. Laundry women became quite rich.'

'I don't understand.'

'They washed the miners' clothes for them. When they'd washed and rinsed out the shirts and trousers they saved the laundry water. Quite a lot of gold dust was sieved out of the wash tubs.' He sat back to enjoy their astonishment.

'Good heavens!'

'Barbers kept the hair from the heads and beards they trimmed. They washed the hair and collected the gold dust. The saloon owners would have their floors brushed very carefully because when men danced with the bar girls they shook gold dust from their clothes.' He undid a packet of brown sugar and nodded to himself as he emptied it into his coffee. 'Oh, I can tell you, a lot of minerals can be salvaged from work clothes, and that's why I recommend you to *supply* your workers with their protective gear. They hand it in once a week and it's laundered or put through a vacuuming process. Once cleaned, the clothes are put back into the issue system, but if for instance you're using a special alloy of zirconium, you've saved several grammes of dust from each suit.'

'And it's valuable?'

'Well, some metals are valuable in themselves, such as gold. But some are valuable in that they are used in very specialized production processes.'

'You know,' Liz put in, 'I believe I pass one of your factories when I drive out to Essex. Bestadyne, I think it's called – it's on an industrial estate—'

'Oh, that's rather a good logo, isn't it? Visible from the motorway – yes, that's a good example. We make specialized metal containers there, and yes, we run a recovery process from the overalls.'

Liz giggled. 'Are you recovering gold or diamond dust there, Sir Rupert?'

He gave a booming laugh. 'Only our friend zirconium, I'm

afraid. You couldn't make yourself any diamond bracelets from that.'

'But it's worth recovering?' Greg said. 'We should put in that sort of system in our factory?'

'That's my advice. The metal itself isn't expensive but its value lies in the restrictions surrounding its particular properties . . .'

'Such as?'

'Well, we use it in the production of our containers. But what our containers eventually contain, I'm afraid I mustn't tell you.'

'Oh, of course, in that case I mustn't ask,' said Greg. 'You've been more than kind already.' He began to wander off on other aspects of welfare – how much he and his co-investors should allot for accident insurance, whether it was better to have vending machines for drinks, should they have a nurse or merely trained first aiders. Sir Rupert answered every enquiry with the assurance of a thirty-year career.

'I'd like to thank you most sincerely for your patience and for sharing your vast knowledge,' said Greg at length. 'If there's anything I can ever do in return . . .'

'Not at all, not at all . . .' But Sir Rupert was considering. He lowered his voice. 'But you know, Your Highness, once you're past the start-up period you may feel the need of outside investment. I'd be interested to hear.'

'Of course. Once we get the thing going.'

'In whatever timescale you prefer.'

He escorted them to the hall, shook hands, the porter came hurrying up with Liz's jacket, and they went out to their car.

When they were in the car park and safe from any listening ear, Liz said, 'Wow!'

'Congratulations. I thought your performance was wonderful.'

'I was good, wasn't I? Kept my temper beautifully.'

'You played him like a violin. And I shall buy you a zircon ring as a reward.'

They got into the car. She drove out of the car park and along the country lane. As they approached the main road junction she paused, waiting for a traffic opening to emerge. 'Zirconium,' she pondered.

'In the work clothes.'

'That's what Shanigan's sending to Parady.'

'It seems likely.' He thought about it while Liz emerged into the country road. 'You know, I think what I saw on the boiler suit was a logo. Probably the one Sir Rupert was so proud of. They do that, don't they? Embroider a logo on the breast pocket.'

'That they do.'

They drove on in silence for while. 'Wait a minute,' Greg said. 'We're supposing Shanigan bought extra boiler suits so that he could send his factory-used set each week to Parady. But if that glimpse of red I saw was a logo, how could he buy an extra suit? The kind you buy in shops wouldn't have the logo.'

She was making a head-shaking motion. 'No problem, sweetie. All you have to do is to go to the area where the suits are made – probably in the Midlands, around Leicester perhaps, or Birmingham. I bet he'd find boiler suits on sale at street markets. Seconds, they're called.' This came from her long experience of the garment industry.

'With company logos?'

'Oh yes. That's one of the things that goes wrong in making clothes. The machine for embroidering a name or a pattern gets a hitch in it – the thread breaks, or the needle. The manufacturer can't put that out as perfect so he sells it off cheaply as a second to some market trader. It's quite common.'

'But how would Shanigan know where to find a market stall with his company's overalls?'

'All he'd have to do is look at the maker's tag in the suits issued by his factory. Then a few weekends strolling around the markets near the clothing manufacturer. If you're buying a set of overalls to wear while you paint your house, who cares if it says Bestadyne on the pocket? Oh yes, that kind of garment is available if you look for it. The difference is, at your place of work you get it for free. At the market it might cost you a couple of quid.'

Another period of silence and thought. Then Liz said, 'But Greg . . .'

'Yes?'

'How much zirconium dust could you get by vacuuming a set of overalls?'

'Hmm . . . Fifty grammes?'

'That's not much, is it?' She still thought in pounds and ounces.

'No, but fifty grammes a week for a whole year . . .' He did the arithmetic. 'That's about two-and-a-half kilos.'

'Is that a lot?'

'A kilo is . . . is . . .' He tried to envisage the things in her kitchen cupboards. 'You know that bag of sugar you have at home?'

'Yes, so?'

'That's a kilo. Two of those plus half of one of the bags.'

'Oh, well . . .'

More cogitation.

'What do they do with it at Parady?' she asked.

He leaned his head back to stare at the roof of the Nissan. 'I wish I knew,' he said.

It was late afternoon as they entered Reading. They passed a library. 'Stop,' he exclaimed.

'What?'

'Stop. Let me out. I want to go into the library.'

'What for?'

'To look up zirconium.'

'Right.' She drove on for a few yards until she came to a gap at the pavement. There she pulled in very neatly. It was a Sunday so there were no parking restrictions. She switched off, they got out and she locked the car. They walked back to the library, where a notice announced it was open until five p.m.

Inside he directed their steps to the shelves of reference books. A row of encyclopaedias took up one shelf and half of another. He hefted out the last volume. Liz had already found a seat at a long table scattered with newspapers and magazines. Bringing the book to the table, he sat alongside her.

The subject he wanted was, of course, near the end of the tome. 'Zirconium, symbol Zr, Atomic Number 40, atomic weight 91.22, a metallic element which occurs naturally as the silicate zircon. The metal is obtained by heating the fluoro-potassium compound . . . Super-conductive at low temperatures . . . Uses: Zirconium is highly resistant to corrosives and is therefore useful in containers for such chemicals as hydrochloric and sulphuric acids . . .'

Liz was leaning sideways, trying to see what he was reading. She heard him give a sharp intake of breath. 'What is it?' she asked. He pushed the encyclopaedia a little towards her and pointed.

She read: 'Zirconium is also used in the nuclear industry.'

Fifteen

As they went slowly out of the library, Greg said: 'Something to do with the nuclear industry. That *would* interest Barbara Rallenham.'

'You can say that again.'

'And if Mrs Barnell began to be a nuisance in something so important—'

'That would be a good reason to disappear her.'

When they reached the car, he said with great earnestness, 'We've got to go to the police at once. I should have gone yesterday, to tell them they could get a picture of Waters, but I thought it could wait until McVeigh actually produced it.'

'OK then. Which one – Walthamstow?'

He was shaking his head as he got in. 'No, that means bringing them up to date on the Rallenham side of things. Let's go to Maida Vale.'

Once they were en route, he got out his mobile to call Maida Vale and ask for Sergeant Orlan. It was Sergeant Orlan's day off. He urged the detective who answered the call to get in touch. 'I'd rather not, sir. He's probably at an amusement park with his kids.'

'Please, it's very important. Ring him, at least. Tell him it's Mr Crowne, say it has security implications.'

After a few more exchanges he got a promise that the message would be passed on. It took them some time to reach the station because the Sunday traffic in north London was as thick as sodden cornflakes. In days gone by, the streets of Britain were deserted as the population stayed away from church. Now it seemed they were congested with the population heading to or from shopping malls.

Sergeant Orlan hadn't yet arrived at Maida Vale. He was on his way, they were assured. They were shown into the semi-comfortable visitors' room and brought tea and biscuits.

Greg used the interval to ring Lucius Kremer in Avignon, to ask how the afternoon organ recital had gone. Not bad, he was told. There was a slight problem, however. The trumpeter, a local man, had refused Greg's cheque and asked to be paid in cash. The regular organist at the church had paid him but was firm in his assumption that Mr Crowne would refund the money *instantly*.

'Of course. As soon as—'

'By tomorrow, monsieur,' insisted Kremer. 'I had to take the money out of my wife's housekeeping allowance.'

'That was enterprising of you, M Kremer. Of course you shall have it refunded.' He broke the connection before Kremer could ask for time and place. He by no means wanted him to realize that he was far away in London.

Sergeant Orlan arrived wearing a sweatshirt and jeans, frigidly polite and clearly in a dreadful mood. 'I hear you have something of international significance to tell me,' he began.

'Yes, I have,' said Greg. 'First I want to apologize for dragging you in on your day off but we really think it's very important. It's to do with the nuclear industry.'

'What?' The sergeant sat up straight in his chair, all attention.

Greg went through the conversation with Sir Rupert Modd, prompted now and then by Liz. The sergeant listened in complete silence. At the end he said, 'Zirconium?'

'Yes. We looked it up. It has nuclear applications.'

The sergeant frowned, pondering. 'And the dust is being sent in these overalls to this artists' commune?'

'Yes.'

'And you think that's why Ms Rallenham was interested, because there was a nuclear aspect to the story?'

'Yes. And they didn't want her poking her nose in,' Liz supplied, 'and got her out of the way.'

The sergeant was clearly sceptical. He had a file with him. From it he produced the photocopy of her sketch. 'And you think this is the man who did it.'

'Yes. And listen, Sergeant, I should tell you – there's a proper photograph of him in the files of the *Walthamstow Herald*—'

'There is? How do you know that?'

'Well. . . I asked,' Greg confessed, looking apologetic. He went into an explanation of McVeigh's part in the matter, which led into a discussion of Mrs Barnell's disappearance, and so on and so on until Sergeant Orlan was looking not only sceptical but confused – and angry again.

'So there's this case at Walthamstow that you're saying is linked to Ms Rallenham's?'

'Yes, because you remember Mrs Barnell was the person who first got Barbara interested.'

The sergeant rose. 'I'm going to check with Walthamstow,' he said in a clipped manner, 'and get them to have that picture out of the *Herald*'s files on the double. I'll also do a bit of research on this nuclear tie-up. In the meantime a constable will come and take notes of what you're saying now.'

He went out, closing the door with unnecessary firmness.

'Oh, golly,' muttered Liz.

'He is *not* pleased.'

'Well, I admit that when I was with the Walthamstow lads I should have told them there was a tie-up with Barbara's disappearance. But you know . . . at the time . . . I was worried about Miss Lessiter.'

'Yes, but I should have told them that there was a photograph of Waters in the newspaper files. I should have done that yesterday. The French police could have had it by now, they might have gone straight to Parady and arrested him.'

'Well, we're a pair of no-goodniks, that's the long and short of it.' Though she tried for lightness, there was distress in her tone.

'The only thing I can say by way of justification is that Waters has no idea we know his true identity. He's probably at Parady now having a comfortable pre-dinner aperitif.'

She held out her hand, and he took it. It was at least some comfort. They were feeling guilty, and with good reason.

The constable came in, a fresh-faced young man who looked as if he'd just left training college. And probably that was the case, because after all who would be on duty on a quiet Sunday afternoon in January?

Once again they went through their story. This time they started earlier and told it in chronological order. The constable wrote quickly, in some sort of short hand. He looked up from time to time, interjecting a query and seeming somewhat at a loss. It took a long time. He ended by closing his notebook and saying, 'Well, sir and miss, if this goes further up the line, I'd think they'd want it as an official statement and perhaps a taped interview.'

'Of course.'

'Would you like more tea?'

'No thank you.'

Off he went. More time passed. It was now after six in the evening. The door opened to admit Sergeant Orlan. His mood had improved.

'Now, sir, I've followed up on everything and as far as I can I've got results. Mr McVeigh is coming into his office to get a photograph and transmit it to us – that will be later this evening. We will then transmit it to Avignon. I've been in touch there, through an interpreter because my French is mostly guidebook stuff. They say they'll have a look at Parady as soon as they can.'

'Excellent.'

'Next, then . . .' The sergeant seemed to be suppressing a smile. 'About the zirconium.'

They waited, looking at him in some suspense.

'I got in touch with one of our forensic guys. You know we have specialists on call, they don't only brush dust on fingerprints like you see on TV. This chap is Russell Fromley, an expert on metals.'

'And?' urged Greg.

'I'm sorry to poke holes in your big theory, sir, but zirconium is used in making pottery.'

Utter silence.

Twice in one week, thought Greg to himself. Twice in one week, I've made a complete fool of myself. First with the theft of the padded envelope, and now with the drama about nuclear weapons.

Since no one was saying anything, Sergeant Orlan took it up again. 'They're called opacifiers. Fromley tells me there's quite a group of them. Tin oxide is one, and . . . let me see . . .' He consulted scribbled notes, clearly taken during a telephone conversation. 'Titanium dioxide – that's used in ordinary paints too – and dolomite, which I've heard of because my dad takes that as some sort of vitamin supplement.'

'And zirconium is one of these?' Greg asked, having found his voice.

'Fromley says it's used for glazing earthenware. It gives . . . which one does it give . . . ? It gives a white effect to the glaze. The others give different effects, cream and sometimes a cracked effect . . . I'm not into pottery, so I don't know if I got it right, but Fromley assured me that zirconium is used quite a lot.'

'Well, I'm not into pottery either, Sergeant, as I think I've just proved.'

'That's all right, sir, we can't be experts on everything, now can we? But it's a bit of a relief to me because if you'd been right, I'd have had to call in Special Branch, and you've no idea what a hassle that can be.'

The prince didn't say that he did indeed know what a hassle it could be, from a previous experience with the CIA. He nodded, accepting that he'd made a stupid mistake.

The sergeant had a satisfied look, like a cat that has licked cream. Greg imagined that he was feeling justified, having categorized him as another inbred royal twit, with a knowledge of the nuclear industry on a par with Homer Simpson's.

'But, of course, as to the photograph and the possible identification of the man seen at the alleged crime scenes, we'll be going ahead with that. Mr McVeigh had to get back from some big charity fair, antiques and an auction, that sort of thing. However, I'm assured we'll have the photograph as soon as he can dig it out, and certainly some time this evening.'

'And then you'll transmit it at once to Avignon.'

'Of course.'

It occurred to Greg that probably in Avignon the police station was in low-maintenance mode. The photograph might sit waiting to be downloaded until the morning. But there was nothing he could do about it now. He'd made such a fool of himself that his standing as a reliable individual was in tatters.

He and Liz said their goodbyes. Outside it was dark and cold. Greg got out his mobile. 'What are you doing?' Liz enquired.

'Booking a seat to Nice.'

'For the morning?'

'No, I'm going tonight if I can get a flight.'

'But, Greg . . .'

He was connected to the booking clerk and turned away so as to have the conversation on the side away from traffic. She could see him nodding in satisfaction.

'Eight thirty,' he told her.

She was affronted. 'Why didn't you ask me? I want to come too!' Then she caught herself up. 'Oh no, I can't. I've got to be in Birmingham tomorrow. Oh, what a nuisance!'

'Never mind, you can—'

'Just a minute.' She was trying to reorientate herself. 'What's the urgency, anyhow?'

'In the first place, I want to be there once the police have that picture of Waters. It's not that I don't have confidence in them, but I'd like to make sure they go straight out to Parady and compare it with *mon cher* Coco. And in the second place, someone has had to pay my trumpeter in cash. He needs the money back so his wife can do the household shopping.'

She began to giggle. 'Oh, Greg . . .We're not exactly being brilliant, are we?'

'No, this is not our finest hour.' He gave her a hug. 'Now, can you ferry me to the airport or should I call a cab?'

'I'll take you. Do you need to go back to the flat for your passport or anything?'

'No, it's here.' He felt in his inside pocket to make sure. He almost always carried it when he left Switzerland. 'I don't need the things in my travel bag, I've got clothes in my room at the Glaneur. . .'

'Right. We can have dinner while we wait for the plane. And I'll tell you what – as soon as I've finished with the department store in Birmingham, I'll come and join you. I ought to be able to fly direct from there, on Easyjet or something.'

'Don't push yourself hard, darling, it turns out not to be as urgent as we thought it was.'

'No, but I *want* to come.' She did indeed. She wanted to be with him, to cosset and protect him. His pride had taken a hard knock.

But common sense told her that she must be in Birmingham tomorrow or lose a lucrative opening. And while she wasn't unduly mercenary, her income would take a knock if she let this opportunity slip.

She let him go unwillingly at departure time. He for his part was glad to be alone. He was still trying to come to terms with the fact that he'd been an idiot, not once but twice.

At Nice-Côte d'Azur he got euros from a cash machine. He took an expensive taxi into Avignon. At the Hotel Glaneur he got an envelope from the supply in his room, wrote the name Lucius Kremer on it and, at the foot, *With the compliments of G. Couronne*. He walked through the quiet city to the house of the organist and slipped the envelope through the letterbox.

There. Mme Kremer could buy tomorrow's groceries.

Hands in pockets to shield them from the unexpected chill of the night, he started to walk back to the hotel. In his pocket he found the key to the rehearsal studio where he had worked with Robert Jäger on his recital of Swiss songs. He didn't have exclusive use, but at this time of night there would be no one there.

He let himself in. He needed only one light to find his way to the Steinway. He opened the lid, adjusted the piano seat, sat down and touched the keys.

Something gentle. Something soothing. Something to help him recover his equilibrium. After a moment he found he was playing the rippling accompaniment to Schubert's 'To be Sung on the Water'. He played on for a while then began to invent variations. Not that he could ever improve on the magical evocation of a river flowing under a boat – no, just to give himself something to *think* about.

By and by he found he was playing Chopin, which was odd, because he wasn't much of a Chopin fan. From there he moved on to Beethoven . . . the Moonlight Sonata . . . what a cliché, sitting in a darkened room playing music with a title to do with night-time. Still, the chords were so rich, so healing . . .

It was almost three when he stopped. Did he feel better? Perhaps he did. Outside there was absolute silence. He noticed with the active part of his mind that it was really cold, colder than when he'd left Avignon. Perhaps the mistral was coming.

Before getting ready for bed he set the radio alarm in his room to wake him at six thirty. He wanted to be at the police station before eight. He telephoned the night sergeant to give him advance notice of this visit. The night sergeant said blankly, 'Very good, sir, I'll tell the sergeant.'

The hotel wasn't really geared for early morning activity. The breakfast room wasn't even lit up. He went out, bought coffee and a baguette at a stall catering for the market traffic. He was glad of his lined car coat, for it was still dark and still cold. Never mind, the temperature would probably rise when daylight came.

Sergeant Aristide Cuzor was awaiting him when he went in. 'Good morning, sir. I got your message and also I have to tell you that the picture arrived last night and Detective Inspector Yverre will be with you in a moment. This way, please.'

He led Greg to a small room in which the heating system was doing its best against the influence of draughts from under the door. The carpet was a serviceable grey, the walls were painted a neutral beige. The sergeant ushered him to a seat, and pointed to a vacuum jug and beakers on a pine table. 'Coffee if you'd like it, sir. I'll tell Inspector Yverre you're here.'

An inspector. He'd been told last time he was here that the matter of Barbara's disappearance would be referred higher. Perhaps this was the senior officer who'd been given the case.

He poured coffee and sipped. Better than the market stall. He was feeling quite pleased with himself. Here he was, at an hour when he was usually just rolling out of bed, wide awake and thinking useful thoughts.

Inspector Yverre came in. He was a big man, in his late forties, with a greying head of hair and a tidy moustache. They shook hands. The inspector sat down. 'Well, sir, let me just get out the photo.' He opened a red plastic folder to produce a twenty by twenty-five centimetre colour picture of a man surrounded by a group of five or six other people in evening dress.

From his inside pocket Greg produced the sketch made by Liz. His glance went from one to the other. The sketch was like yet unlike. The outer edges of the face were similar in size and shape. The dark hair was the same but it had a gloss in the picture that was lacking from the sketch.

'You recognize him, sir?'

Greg shook his head. 'I've never actually seen him, Inspector. He fits the description of a man who entered Mlle Rallenham's flat a few days after she allegedly paid her bill at the auberge and left with her luggage. My assumption – the assumption of myself and a friend and the sister of Mlle Rallenham – is that this man might know where she is now.'

'By what means were you led to favour him as a suspect?'

'His name. He called himself Mr Rivers when he was challenged at the flat. Later we became aware that a man called Waters had a connection with the events.'

'Ah . . . Rivers . . . Waters . . .' He had trouble with the pronunciation of Waters, but understood the terms. 'I see.' Greg could almost hear the cogs going round as he accepted the imaginative leap. 'And I gather that the cleaning woman in the flat at the time gave the description for the sketch.'

'Exactly. Has she seen the photograph?'

'I hear from my London colleagues that she has. She was shown a selection of about half a dozen and asked if any of them looked like the intruder. She chose this one and one other, but he in fact was an officer at the police station. My colleagues are satisfied that this is the man she saw.'

'And this man is called Waters. Did you make enquiries about flights taken to London under that name, around the time that Mrs Dandry saw him?'

'Indeed we did. We enquired for Mr Waters and also for someone perhaps travelling as his wife. But no.' He shook his head with regret.

'Oh, *merde*,' muttered Greg. He was turning over the photograph to read the caption slip glued to the back. 'Colin Waters, known to his friends as Coco, celebrates the opening of a pet project, the Forest Arts Studio. With him are his wife Amy and friends.'

His sudden indrawn breath drew the inspector's attention at once, 'Something of importance?'

'Coco. That was the name of the employee who vouched for Mlle Grashenko's presence at Parady.'

The inspector consulted the papers in his file. After a moment he said, 'So it was.'

Greg had turned back to the picture. Mrs Waters was clearly the lady whose arm was linked through that of Waters – a pretty, plump thirty-five. There were two people on his left, one on Mrs Waters right, and behind three or four others.

He was staring at one of them. A tall serious-looking woman with big dark intelligent eyes, and very dark, almost black hair, worn very short, and long filigree earrings bearing a baroque pearl at the pointed end. Little more of her was visible. But in his head he heard the echo of Mrs Dandry's voice: 'Long dangly earrings . . .'

Give this figure the gypsy tresses he'd seen on the woman glazing the vase at Parady, and it could be Estelle Grashenko.

The inspector allowed himself a smile when he heard what Greg had to say. 'We had thoughts of this kind too, concerning that lady,' he said. 'And so we are organizing a little visit to the pottery, to interview her and – now that we have the picture – to inspect the male division of the community.'

'I'd like to go with you, Inspector.'

'Oh no, monsieur, that's not possible—'

'But I could be of use! I could suggest questions that might not otherwise occur to you.'

'Questions . . . ?'

'Bear in mind that I know Barbara Rallenham.'

'Alas, friendship is not enough to allow your participation.'

'I'm not a friend, simply an acquaintance. But I was brought into the matter because her sister came to me in tears. I've been close to the investigation ever since and so I feel there are points I could suggest . . .'

The inspector was studying him with steady blue eyes. He was thinking, and after a moment the neat moustache twitched as a smile formed on the lips underneath. 'Monsieur Couronne,' he said, 'in about twenty minutes I and my associates will leave for Parady. You are an honoured guest in our city, a respected participant in its festival. Should you wish to visit one of our rural sites, I certainly have no power to prevent you.'

'Twenty minutes?'

'Not more.'

Greg got up, shook hands, and hurried out. He ran through the streets to the hotel, thinking that Liz would be proud of him – an early morning runner at last, although lacking the trendy tracksuit and trainers.

His trusty Mercedes was in the hotel car park. When he put the key in the ignition he was saying a prayer because he'd left her here unused for several days. But the dear old lady sparked into life at once.

The drive back to the police station was hampered by market traffic. Nevertheless, he was in good time to see the unmarked police car leave, a woman officer and three plain clothes men in it, one of them being Inspector Yverre.

He stayed about a hundred yards behind them. There was no problem in following them since *they* knew he was there and *he* knew where they were going. Once as far on their way as Fontaine de Vaucluse, traffic became no problem. A rising wind buffeted his car. He could see the tips of the pine trees swaying as if in a painting by Van Gogh.

He let the police car get well up the lane posted as leading to Groupe Locke Daniels, then turned into it through the open gateway. He parked alongside the police car, in which the driver was still sitting. No sign of activity in either the office or the restaurant; a Closed sign hung in the door of each.

A nod from the driver directed him to the pedestrian path. He made his way along it. As the bends in the track gave him a view, he could see the detectives gathered at the entrance to the workshop of Estelle Grashenko. Lights within suggested that someone was already at work there, had been there before the coming of daylight.

Inspector Yverre acknowledged his arrival with a slight inclination of the head. Greg stayed a few yards behind the group. Yverre raised his hand as if in some impatience and struck the door of the workshop. A faint voice from within could be heard in response. 'Perhaps she's in the middle of something she can't leave,' Greg murmured.

The inspector nodded at one of his men as if to command him to knock even harder. But at that moment the door opened and Estelle Grashenko appeared, holding the doorknob with a moist rag.

She took a step back at the sight of the crew outside. Alarm flooded into her eyes, eyes so dark it was difficult to see the pupils in the buffalo-brown of the iris. She was wearing a denim smock over trousers tucked into thick grey socks. Her abundant hair was bound up in a checked woollen scarf.

'What . . . ?' she gasped.

'Mlle Grashenko?' said Yverre. 'May we have a word?'

'What about?' she said, trying to stand her ground. But the steady forward movement of the newcomers forced her back, and they went in, Yverre, the woman detective, a detective constable, and Greg.

The interior of the building was cold. The back door was standing open so that the cold breeze blew right through. Outside the back door a couple of pallets could be distinguished, one on top of the other and stacked with something protected in a kind of wrapping.

Mlle Grashenko led them into the room Greg had seen before, where the electric kilns stood. None of them seemed to be in action, no red indicators were alight. She retreated to a spot between the kilns. Yverre came in next, to confront her almost face to face. The woman officer stood at his shoulder. Greg and the constable had to be content with places in the doorway.

Yverre introduced himself and his colleagues. For the first time her eyes went beyond him and took in the sight of the man who had not been introduced. She frowned, wiped her hands roughly with the damp cloth, and threw it almost petulantly on top of a kiln.

At a nod from Yverre, Greg gave his name. 'I was here before, you remember?' he said. 'M Couronne, enquiring about Mlle Rallenham.'

Her lips came together in a grimace of annoyance. 'I remember. What is all this nonsense about a Mlle Rallenham? I never heard of her.'

'She came here, mademoiselle. It would be about a month ago now.'

'People come here,' she said with a shrug. 'That doesn't mean that I see them.'

The inspector took the photograph from the briefcase he was carrying. 'Do you know this man, mademoiselle?'

She took it, looked at it. It was clearly a big shock. Her

eyes went wide. She gave a sideways glance as if looking for escape. Then her chin went up and she said, 'You mean the man in the centre, I suppose? I don't know him.'

'Colin Waters,' said Yverre, pronouncing the surname 'Vatterre.'

'No.'

'Where is your assistant, mademoiselle?' Greg enquired. 'The man you called Coco.'

She smiled. 'Oh, wandered off, you know. A transient. I employed him by the day and he just left when he'd earned enough for a good tipple.'

'Where has he gone?' Yverre demanded, his tone becoming harder.

'Who knows? To one of the farms, perhaps.' She threw out her hands in a gesture to show how far Coco might have wandered. 'And now if you'll excuse me, Inspector, I have some clay on the wheel – I must go back to it—'

'Not so fast. Mademoiselle, tell me about these packets that you receive each week in the post. What is their merit to you?'

'What?'

Once again she was shaken. Her brows came together in perplexity and alarm. Greg could tell she was wondering how they knew about them.

'Packets?' she faltered. She clasped her arms about herself as if stricken by a shiver, and indeed the breeze from the open back door was extremely chill.

'Packets posted to this address each week by a man called . . .' He looked towards Greg for pronunciation of the barbaric foreign name.

'Tommy Shanigan,' Greg supplied.

Mlle Grashenko shook her head so vigorously that the woollen scarf was dislodged and fell to the floor. 'The name means nothing to me.'

'Nothing? According to our information the package has been sent every week for over a year.'

'You have been interfering with our postal service? Is that legal, Inspector?'

'There has been no interference. We received information, and we rely on it. Explain it to me, mademoiselle. A packet from London to Parady each week . . .'

‘To Parady, why not?’ she interrupted, with an upward lift of her head. ‘Why do you come here, pestering me? Parady has at least eleven tenants. Have you knocked at the door of all of them?’

Yverre maintained a poker face, but Greg could see the jab had gone home. ‘You are our prime suspect, mademoiselle,’ he returned calmly.

‘Suspect? Suspected of what? This is harassment, and simply because we have our community and prefer our simple way of life—’

‘Why did you go to the Auberge Mignard and pay Mlle Rallenham’s bill for her?’ Greg struck in with strong accusation in his voice.

‘Pay her bill? Why should I pay the bill of a woman I don’t know?’

‘You were wearing her jacket and used her credit card—’

‘I did not! I deny it absolutely!’

‘Why are the packets sent?’ he went on, imposing his questions above her denials. ‘The work clothes inside are certainly not important in themselves.’

‘What?’

‘It must be for the zirconium. Explain about the zirconium, mademoiselle.’

For a moment everything about her seemed to be on the verge of collapse. There was a wildness in her, like an animal seeking escape. But she made a huge effort. She returned to calm indignation almost at once.

‘Zirconium? Why are you asking about zirconium? I use it in my glazes. Many potters do. I have no idea why you should be interested but if you like I can take you into my glazing room and show you how it’s done.’

‘We will examine your glazing room, Mlle Grashenko, and anything else that we think is relevant,’ grunted Yverre.

‘You will? You have a warrant? On what grounds did the *juge* issue a warrant?’

‘All in good time, mademoiselle, all in good time—’

The inspector broke off as voices were heard at the main entrance. Footsteps came along the passage. A man called, ‘Estelle, you there?’ in English.

They all turned. A young woman in a poncho stopped at

the threshold, astonished at the crowd in the kiln room. The man following her almost bumped into her. He was clad in a thick Breton sweater and jeans. He had the young woman by the elbow, as if guiding her. She came in, everybody moving to allow her entrance. The man stopped in the doorway with his mouth half open.

It was clearly the man in the photograph.

He stood transfixed. Then he half turned. But he changed his mind and came back to face the others. 'What's going on?' he asked in French.

Inspector Yverre had recovered from his amazement in the same instant. 'M Vatterre?' he enquired.

Waters hesitated, then shook his head. Before he could reply the young woman said, 'Vatterre? Isn't this M Daniels, who owns the complex?'

Greg was seized with a desire to thump himself on the brow. He glanced at Yverre, who was taking a fraction of a moment to recover.

'M Daniels?' he said. 'M Locke Daniels?' Like all those in the neighbourhood, he pronounced it 'Lo Danièle'.

'Y-yes,' he agreed, since there seemed no alternative.

'And you are?' the inspector said to the young woman.

'I'm Mme Vidoglio. My husband and I are thinking of renting a workshop. Who are you?'

The inspector introduced himself. Mme Vidoglio looked vexed. 'What is all this?' she cried. 'Don't tell me this is another place where you're on the verge of bankruptcy!'

'Not at all, not at all,' soothed Daniels. 'Look, madame, if you'll just go to the café – it should be open soon – I'll catch up with you as soon as I can.'

She turned to go. The woman detective moved as if to prevent her but Yverre shook his head then nodded that she should escort her. Mme Vidoglio went out, and if Greg was any judge she'd changed her mind about renting any premises.

There was a general shifting of position as the two women went out. Yverre murmured to the constable, who then moved out of the room to a post of surveillance in the passage. That put him behind Daniels, who remained by the doorway. The inspector was facing him now, with Greg at his side and Mlle Grashenko by the kilns.

'Mr Daniels,' he began with a polite little bow. 'You own the site?'

'Yes, I do. What's this about?'

'In a moment, monsieur, in a moment. Is that your office by the car park?'

'Yes.'

'The mail delivery is made to your office?'

'Yes.'

'Each week a packet arrives from London. It is addressed to . . .' He sought among his papers. 'To Locke Daniels, Parady, near Fontaine de Vaucluse.'

'So?'

'To whom do you allot that packet, monsieur?'

'What do you mean?'

'Is the packet for you yourself? Or do you give it to Mlle Grashenko? Or to someone else?'

Daniels let his gaze go past the inspector to Estelle Grashenko. Some message must have been conveyed because he said with almost no hesitation, 'The packet is for me.'

'Indeed. What does it contain?'

'That's none of your business!' declared Daniels with annoyance. 'What right have you to come here and ask questions about my private affairs?'

The inspector held out the photograph. 'Is this you in this photograph, monsieur?'

The photograph caused him consternation. He gaped at it. He tried to look at Estelle Grashenko but the inspector moved to block his view.

When in doubt, back out. 'I . . . er . . . it may be. I've been at parties where they've taken pictures.'

'Parties in London?' asked the inspector.

'No, I'm seldom in London.'

'Then why does it have your name on the back?' enquired Greg.

'It doesn't!'

'But it does. And that's your wife holding your arm, and that's Mlle Grashenko at the back.'

The inspector was turning the photo to read the names off the caption. Daniels made a move as if to snatch it from him.

'No, Coco!' cried Estelle Grashenko in warning.

Then she clapped a hand over her mouth, horror stricken.

Daniels turned, dashed out of the kiln room, hit the constable a hard blow in the chest with his elbow, and turned away from the main entrance to the back door. The constable staggered but made after him within a second. The others rushed out of the door, a momentary log jam in the passage. Daniels was outside, running past the pallets with the wrapped goods. He darted off to the left, and was lost to view by those in pursuit.

Inspector Yverre ran outside speaking urgently into a radio. Greg was about to follow him when he was shoved hard as Estelle Grashenko turned past him towards the front entrance.

Recovering, he ran after her. She ran along the path but not towards the car park. She was heading for the spot where the alley went up the side of the administration office. That would take her up into the living accommodation. He went after her, towards an astonished young man hanging trusses of basket-weaving twigs and willow wreaths outside his shop.

Grashenko was making good time. Presumably there was transport of some kind at the living quarters. She was going to get away.

In desperation Greg seized a willow wreath from the shopkeeper. He skimmed it towards Grashenko at about knee level. The winter wind helped it along. The wreath caught at a leg of her jeans She stumbled, yelled in anger and frustration, and went headlong.

When Inspector Yverre got back from the chase, he found his woman officer holding Mlle Grashenko with her arms behind her back. She had grazes on her cheek and nose. Greg was standing by looking embarrassed. It went against his upbringing to cause physical harm to a woman.

At a nod, Grashenko was led off towards the police car in the car park.

'Daniels?'

A shrug. 'Got away. But only for the moment.' The inspector looked angry with himself. 'And *she*'ll tell us what this is all about.'

Sixteen

Not so, however.

Mlle Grashenko was reported as making stubborn, uncomprehending denials. She knew nothing about Mlle Rallenham, she knew nothing about Tommy Shanigan, she knew nothing about any packages he might have sent to Parady.

Over a beer at a bistro not far from the police station, Inspector Yverre admitted he had a problem. It was about two in the afternoon. The lunch crowd was leaving, the clientele in the bar was scant. The conversation was being conducted with discretion, partly in French, partly in English.

'The *juge* is keeping a strict eye on my interrogation. Mlle Grashenko isn't unknown in these parts, you know. Her work is well thought of.'

'Her work as a potter.'

'Yes.' The word brought something back into his memory. 'That was remarkable, wasn't it? How shocked she was when you mentioned this material that she uses in her pottery.'

'Zirconium.'

'What made you bring that up?'

'Well, you see, when I told the detective sergeant at Maida Vale about it, he called in an expert. I'd had this conversation with an industrialist about overalls—'

'Overalls, yes. The packet that comes from London is said to contain *des bleus*.'

'Exactly, what in English is called a "boiler suit".'

'Boiler suit? What does it boil?'

'As to that . . . I think it is clothing for the man who looks after the central heating. Which, I believe, is called a "boiler" in English. I may be wrong.'

'Well, well, this "boiler suit" is important because it is sent across the Channel regularly by M. Shanigan. Yes?'

Greg nodded agreement. 'I was told that, at the factory where M Shanigan is employed, the suits are collected and laundered by the firm. This is so as to extract the metal dust, which has a value. The metal dust from M Shanigan's suit would be zirconium.'

'And the expert said what?'

'That zirconium is quite commonly used in pottery. To make the glaze, you understand, *le vernis*. Now, I accepted that, because he is an expert. But two women have disappeared – Mlle Rallenham here in Provence and Mme Barnell in London. And so I wondered what the devil this *zirconium* meant to the people at Parady, and therefore I asked the question.'

The inspector took a pull at his beer. He looked rather worn. Already it seemed to him that it had been a long day. He'd had only a sandwich for lunch, at his desk and with reports coming in while he ate, reports from his men conducting a search at Parady. It wasn't the routine to which he was accustomed. Moreover, the weather was dismal, cold and windy. And to add to the gloom there was the shadow of M Quenellier, the *juge d'instruction*, for whom the English term 'nit-picker' seemed very apt.

'It is certainly true that she was very upset by your question,' he recalled. 'While I was interrogating her I took it further. But she maintains that it is merely an ingredient in glazing. And as to the photograph, she insists that the resemblance between the M Waters named on the back and M Locke Daniels is a coincidence. She says she is not the woman in the photograph, that she doesn't know your M Waters.'

'But his sobriquet is there on the back. She called him by it, she cried it out: 'No, Coco!''

She denies that. She says she exclaimed 'No, no, no!'

'What a fairy tale! We all heard her.'

Yverre shrugged and spread his hands in acknowledgement. 'Her story is that M Locke Daniels and M Waters are two different persons. She says that she has not been to London for many months – she went for some exhibition at a museum but it was some time ago. However, we have now ascertained that a M Locke Daniels and his wife travelled to London early this month.'

'Ah!' said Greg.

'When challenged with that, Mlle Grashenko shrugged and said she was not responsible for what M Daniels and his wife did. In other words, she denies that she is his wife.'

'And what do the other people at Parady have to say to that?'

'They look bemused. They know her as Estelle Grashenko.'

Greg was silent a moment, studying the inspector. Then he said, 'What does your policeman's instinct tell you?'

Yverre sighed. '*C'est une dame redoutable!* I think she is a very strong, capable woman. I think she travelled to London with a passport that said 'Mrs Locke Daniels' but I'd take a bet that it's forged. And so is his. I think he is Mr Colin Waters, and my colleagues in London tell me that Colin Waters was under a very black cloud because of taking bribes. But there is nothing against him in police records.'

'He was allowed to resign,' Greg explained. 'The evidence against him wasn't sufficient to make a good case in court. So it seems he moved to France, bought this place at Parady, and set up an artists' community. With Grashenko, whom he already knew.'

'*C'est ça.*'

'You know, Inspector,' he added thoughtfully, 'when he resigned, it was over granting illegal permits for the export of metals.'

'Metals. Zirconium is a metal, no?'

'Yes, it is. Inspector Yverre, when I mentioned it to the detective in Maida Vale, it was brushed aside. But I went to them because I thought zirconium was used in the nuclear industry.'

The inspector's eyes went wide with alarm. '*Dans une centrale nucléaire?*' He began the question in a voice loud with fear, but muffled it almost at once. He glanced about to see if anyone had noticed.

'I thought it possible, 'said Greg. 'Of course I know nothing about metallurgy. I looked it up in an encyclopaedia.'

'But why? What made you suspect something to do with nuclear affairs?'

'I didn't suspect any such thing. It all came about because I got an introduction to the industrialist who employs Tommy Shanigan back in London. When he was telling me about how the dust was reclaimed, he mentioned that his factory uses zirconium. And as I knew nothing about it, I looked it up.'

'Is he in the nuclear industry, this industrialist?'

'No, he makes metal containers.'

Yverre drew in a breath of relief then blew it out. 'You gave me a scare, M Couronne.'

Greg nodded. 'For a moment you looked as scared as Estelle Grashenko when I mentioned zirconium.'

The words had overtones and undertones. Yverre thought about them. 'Are you saying, my friend, that . . . that . . .'

'I don't know. But it all seems so strange. If zirconium is regularly used in pottery, why not buy it on the open market? Why go through this method of sending it in small amounts and in secret?'

'It seems to imply that there is something special about the metal from the factory,' mused Yverre.

'It may be a special alloy.'

The inspector glanced at his watch. 'I must go back,' he said. 'My people are carrying out searches at Parady, so there will be more news on my desk. And I must put it all together for a report to M Quenellier this evening.'

'May I ring you tomorrow to see how things are going?'

'Of course, but you understand this is completely unofficial.'

'I understand.'

They shook hands, Yverre hurried out while Greg remained to pay the bill. Back at the hotel he made some phone calls, one to Bredoux to report that he was back in Avignon, one to the leader of the vocal quartet who would be coming on Thursday to perform in the festival, one to Liz. But Liz was unavailable, both on her mobile and at her flat.

Later he set out for Nice. Liz would probably take a flight as soon as she finished work in Birmingham, so she could be expected at Nice-Côte-d'Azur about mid-evening. Meanwhile he would continue his search for operetta scores in bookshops in the old quarter of the city, have a meal, and be in good time at the airport.

He had some luck in one of the bookshops. He found a beautiful old bound copy of the score of *Véronique* by André Messager, which he browsed through as he ate a felafel. It was full of great melodies, one of which was 'Swing High, Swing Low', a waltz taken at a rather fast tempo and ideally suited for the young and vibrant voice of Robert Jäger.

He was on his way to the airport when as expected his mobile rang. It was Liz. 'Greg? I'll be on the flight arriving at eight thirty. Darling, I'm bringing Mandy with me.'

'*What?*'

'I don't have time to explain now, we're just going to board. It's a long story.'

'What's happened?'

'Greg, I'll miss the flight! See you!'

'I'll be there to meet you!'

Half the pleasure of expecting Liz was blotted out by the thought of Mandy. All the same, as he considered the fact of her coming, it struck him that something important must have occurred. Mandy was a habituée of the weekend party circuit. She would recover only slowly from these jaunts. For her to be travelling on a Monday meant some calamity.

He remembered how he'd first seen her, also on a Monday, tears washing away her mascara, her hair like a maenad, accusing him of having done something evil to her sister.

He waited on tenterhooks. When they came through the arrivals exit he heaved an audible sigh. Liz came first, apology in the smile she gave him, but bright and smart in a business suit and a pale-yellow blouse. Behind her Mandy was almost subdued: green bootleg trousers and a knitted jacket buttoned up to the throat. Even her hair was restrained, in a wide headband of dark-red velvet.

Liz threw herself into his arms. 'Darling,' she said in his ear, 'bad things have happened.'

Mandy joined them, holding out her hand for a formal greeting. 'Greg,' she said with a slight nod. No ebullience, no effusion. This was not the Mandy he knew and disliked.

'What shall we do?' he asked. 'Are we going straight to Avignon or would you like to stop for a drink before we go?'

'It's quite a long drive and you've already come all the way out here,' Liz pointed out. 'Let's find a quiet bistro, shall we?'

He got the message. He drove along the coast road with the two women in the back seat, Mandy unexpectedly silent.

Somewhere near Cros-de-Cagnes he found a restaurant with a glassed-in terrace glowing with a warm light. They went in, ordered wine and coffee, and then there was no more putting it off.

'Mrs Barnell has been found,' Liz said.

'Oh, that's—' He broke off. He'd been about to say 'That's good,' but one look at her face was enough to tell him it was not at all good.

'She was found in the Thames down by Woolwich early this morning,' Liz said.

He was too appalled to say anything. He'd felt in his bones that Mrs Barnell was no longer in the land of the living, but this . . .

Mandy unexpectedly took his silence for some kind of censure. 'You don't have to tell me it's my fault!' she cried, grasping at her hair with both hands. 'I see now I shouldn't have gone to her house.'

'You went there?'

'Yes, after you rang me and I couldn't remember who she was, you know. I remembered her afterwards, Mrs Barnell, the woman Barbara went to see. And I felt a bit bad about it, so I went to have a chat, but it was in the afternoon and she was out, probably shopping, you know. So I was standing there, and this man came up the path and had a key so I knew he lived there. So I left a message with him to let Mrs Barnell know I'd dropped by.'

Greg said nothing. Liz met his eyes. She'd clearly heard all this already and understood its significance.

'This man was Tommy Shanigan?' he prompted.

'Yes, Shanigan, that's what he said.'

'And you asked him to let Mrs Barnell know you'd been there.'

'Yes, he was quite nice about it, I didn't see anything wrong, after all, he was quite amiable, though not my type at all, if you know what I mean. So I said would he tell Mrs Barnell I'd been there, and that I'd come back another time, to have a chat about all the help she'd given to Barbara.'

'And you gave him your name.'

'Of course. Mandy Rallenham.'

He couldn't think of anything to say. He blamed himself.

He should have kept her more in the picture about what they were finding out.

Desperate to re-tell her story and thereby exonerate herself from blame, she swept on. 'So then on Friday I thought I'd better follow up on that, so I got her telephone number from the phone book and rang her, and a *policeman* answered the telephone.' She shuddered. 'He asked me what I wanted and I explained and he took my number and asked me to ring off and wait by the phone. And then some chap at Walthamstow rang and asked me questions like when had I last seen Mrs Barnell, and stuff like that. I was terribly spooked by it, I can tell you. So then I discovered that she'd gone missing. Just like *Barbara*!'

She stared at him with entreaty, as if he could somehow lift the burden from her. She swallowed some wine, then hung her head a little. 'I admit that when I heard that I went straight down the rabbit-hole. But I got home on Sunday evening and sort of got myself together, and thought about it, and rang Walthamstow and they said there was no news, so I rang Liz, and she said you'd gone back to Avignon, and then this morning . . . this morning . . .' Her voice cracked. She fell silent.

Liz took it up. 'This morning the police let her know Mrs Barnell had been found drowned.' She was pale, and he knew she'd had a terrible day. 'She rang me and I dashed back from Birmingham—'

'You did?' He wouldn't have thought she'd rush to the aid of Mandy. But she immediately cleared it up.

'I was worried about Miss Lessiter. She's really a very old lady, and you know, whatever they might say about each other, on some level they were close.'

'How is Miss Lessiter?' he asked, knowing it couldn't be a happy response.

'Shattered. She's got no one to turn to, you see. She says she's outlived everyone she was friends with, and puts on a very independent "I-don't-need-any-help" attitude. But I got the Social Services to come and as a temporary measure they moved her to a nursing home. She was glad to go, although she'd never admit it. She needed some TLC.'

'Well . . .' He didn't know what to say. He'd have liked to give her a hug but with Mandy sitting there looking like the mask of Tragedy, it seemed inappropriate.

Mandy was dying to get back to her own story. 'I asked the police what had happened to Mrs Barnell. They said she'd drowned. Just drowned, that's all. This Miss Lessiter says Mrs Barnell couldn't swim. It's just so awful. I wish I'd hung around and spoken to her – I hear she lives just across the road from Mrs Barnell. But I didn't because I'd left a message with that chap I saw.' She shook her head in perplexity. 'And that's the very chap the police have arrested.'

'He's not arrested, Mandy. He's helping the police with their enquiries.'

'But you know that means the same thing, Liz!'

'But they *can't* arrest him, ducky. They're treating Mrs Barnell's death as an accident.' She turned to Greg and said indignantly: 'An accident. She was supposed to be going to Victoria for the train to Brighton. What was she doing by the Thames? And without a coat on a cold January day?'

Greg sipped his coffee, which was now tepid. Mandy was knocking back too much red wine. Liz sat alongside her, turning her wine-glass between her fingers, sad, weary, and longing to be alone with him.

'What happened to her luggage?' he asked, thinking back. 'She'd packed a travel bag.'

'No sign of it.'

He felt fairly sure the travel bag was either at the bottom of the Thames weighted with several large stones, or on a rubbish tip somewhere.

'And if Mrs Barnell's ended up like that,' lamented Mandy, 'what's happened to Barbara? Oh, Babs, Babsie, it's so dreadful, where *are* you, why did you ever go off like that on your own?'

'Now, now,' soothed Liz, putting an arm round her shoulders.

'But you were always so sure of yourself, weren't you? And now it's weeks and weeks since you went, and it all seems so . . . so . . .' She hid her face against Liz's breast. The waiter was politely turned away and in conversation with another customer at the bar counter. Greg gazed at Liz over Mandy's tousled head and wished he could go back to the beginning of this cold, harsh January and do things differently.

By and by Mandy recovered and stared in accusation at

Greg. 'Liz tells me you came back here because you thought you could do more good here. Something about a photograph.'

'Of Mr Waters, yes. I wanted to be here when the local police went to Parady with it.'

'Did you go?' Liz asked before Mandy could begin a lament that her sister had ever heard of Parady.

He nodded. 'Mr Waters is identified as Mr Locke Daniels, owner of the Parady site. Estelle Grashenko may or not be Mrs Daniels. Those are perhaps false identities but they have passports in those names according to police information. And it's pretty certain that the two of them were in London earlier when Mrs Dandry saw them at Barbara's flat.'

'So they've been arrested!' This was Mandy, in something like exultation.

'Grashenko is being questioned. Locke Daniels did a bunk.' Greg allowed himself the little luxury of being pleased at knowing this English idiom. There was certainly little else to be pleased with at that moment.

'Did a bunk! How could that happen? Good grief, even when the police begin to take it seriously they can't do anything right!' Mandy had gone from grief to outrage. 'I'm going to the British ambassador! It's time I got some consideration from somebody! As soon as we get to Avignon I'm going to go to the ambassador and tell him—'

'Now, now,' Liz said again in her soothing tone.

'It'd be a consul, Mandy. And I think the nearest one is in Marseilles, Avenue Prado,' said Greg. 'But don't you think we ought to get to the hotel and get a night's rest before we decide what to do?'

'Oh yes – I'm beat! And I bet you are too, ducky.' This to Mandy, still soothing.

'Are you hungry? Let's get a bite to eat,' he suggested, 'and then we can head for Avignon.'

In a day of commotion and activity, meals had been snacks taken as the opportunity afforded. The refreshment on the plane seemed a long time ago to the two newcomers. They decided to eat, and then made the trip to the hotel in a night of rushing cloud and stormy wind.

They agreed to get up when they had had enough sleep, and then to meet and decide on a course of action. It was after ten when they sat down together in the hall of the Glaneur to plan the day. Mandy was firm in her decision to go to the consulate and Greg couldn't think of a reason to stop her. On the whole he had a poor opinion of diplomats, due to scandalous tales from his grandmother's past and occasional unenthusiastic comments from his father.

'Before you go, shouldn't we find out what the police have been doing?' he suggested.

'If you think that's best.'

He rang the station on his mobile. He was put through to Inspector Yverre without delay. 'Good morning, *mon ami.*' The inspector didn't sound in good spirits.

'The sister of Mlle Rallenham has come to Avignon,' Greg said. 'I wondered if you had any news for her this morning?'

'News? My friend, there will be no news from now on. From now on everything is *sous couvert.*'

'Under cover? What on earth do you mean, Yverre?'

'The whole case has been taken over by the DGSE,' he groaned.

Direction Générale de Sécurité Extérieure. The equivalent of MI6.

Seventeen

Greg had gone to the phone booth in the hall to make the call because he didn't want to use his mobile while with companions – he thought that impolite. He was glad, because the DGSE could only mean trouble, of which they had enough already.

'Is this because of the nuclear thing?' he asked.

'I'm not allowed to say.'

'When did this happen?'

'I'm not allowed to tell you – but my *juge* passed on my report to them because he got cold feet on reading the fateful words "used in the nuclear industry". They arrived in the middle of the night, dragged me out of bed, and closed off Parady like a prison camp.'

'*Oh weh*,' sighed His Highness.

'It's all right, I played down your part in it. They know who you are, of course, but they regard you as a mere innocent who wandered in on the situation.'

'Which I am.'

'Yes, which you are. And keep it that way, *mon brave*, because I'm in enough trouble as it is.'

'I'm sorry—'

'Not at all, not at all – your intervention caused the interesting M Locke Daniels to take off like a criminal in a panic, which made the case important. And if it *is* connected with you-know-what, it's good that it's been brought to light.'

'So are they questioning Mlle Grashenko and all the people at Parady?'

'I'm not allowed to say. But yes, they are.'

'And doing a link-up with the British authorities over Mlle Rallenham's disappearance?'

'So one conjectures.'

'Her sister is here, Inspector.'

'*Les messieurs* may want to speak to her.'

Good luck to them, he thought. Not even the DGSE would get much sense out of Mandy. 'May I ring you on some future occasion?' he enquired.

'*A-ah . . . non . . . je ne le pense pas.* At least, not until *les magiciens* have done one or two of their tricks.'

'I understand. In that case, good luck, my friend, and until another time.' He sympathized with the inspector's jaundiced view of the agents from the security force. Such people always seemed to get more of the government's money than mere law-keepers. Moreover, it must be galling to have the case whipped away from under his nose just as it began to have some substance.

He went to rejoin his companions. He explained that there was no news from the Avignon police, saying nothing about national security. However, he now judged it a good idea for Mandy to see the consul. The DGSE would have been in touch with British colleagues, who in turn would have alerted the British consul. If anyone were to break the news of their appearance on the scene, let it be the British consul.

So he drove them all to Marseilles, dropping Mandy off in Avenue Prado. They were all to meet at the *Centre Bourse* shopping centre on the Canebière at two o'clock for a late lunch; there was sure to be a café there that would cater for latecomers, and moreover it was a splendid place for Liz to go on a fashion shop tour. Greg for his part took himself off to Place Carli, where the antiquarian books and old records would be on sale until early evening.

The piles of dusty books on the stalls were being agitated by the cold wind. He moved a great many from one pile to another, but found no operetta scores. However, among the aged long-play collections he found a complete recording of *The Dollar Princess,* a work he'd never heard of by one Leo Fall whom he'd also never heard of. Yet the singers were famous – the soprano was Rita Bartos, who in her time had sung Wagner, the tenor was unknown to him, and the baritone was Willy Hofman, well known for his performances in what Robert Jäger called 'The dreaded *Fledermaus*'.

Another vinyl treasure to be coveted by and perhaps shared with his old friend Poll, he thought to himself.

Having parked at the *Centre Bourse*, he returned there on foot, pushed by the north wind and buffeted at every corner by angry lateral tempests. The white caps on the *Vieux Port* were evidence of continuous bad weather; he'd never seen it in such a turmoil. He bethought himself that it had been blowing like this for two or three days now, and turned up the collar of his car coat for greater protection.

Liz and Mandy were already there. They had found a quiet bistro where the dish of the day was of course *bouillabaisse* but where the prices were low and the wine list encouraging.

Once seated, Mandy was eager to report on her interview at the consulate.

'I was shown into an office and, do you know, she was expecting me!'

'It's a woman?'

'Oh yes, very nice, gave me coffee, answered all my questions. *Do you know*' – she lowered her voice significantly – 'a special team has been brought in to take charge of the investigation!'

'Really?' said Liz.

'Yes, it's because they've been in touch about Mrs Barnell and all that – I mean, the London police have been in touch with the bunch at Avignon about it. It seems they've definitely linked it all up. Ms Portmann couldn't tell me much as yet because the special team have only just taken over, but she says they'll be giving it their undivided attention. She's really nice, and seems tremendously efficient, and it's such a relief to talk to someone who speaks English and so you don't have to have someone translate all the time, although of course I don't mean anything against you, Greg, because you're always so kind and helpful with everything.'

'Yes, he is, isn't he? With everything,' teased Liz. She gave Greg a glance that made him smother a grin.

'So what follows?' he asked. 'Is she going to keep you in touch with results?'

'I . . . er . . . I suppose so. I didn't actually ask about that. But I've got her phone number and she says feel free to ring her, and I will. And, in fact, I feel that perhaps I might as well go home, because I can ring just as well from there, and, you know, it's so *cold* here!'

That was true. Each time someone came into the restaurant, a wave of cold air came too, and the café curtains at the windows were moving from the tiny draughts where the frame didn't quite meet the glass.

'*Le vent sacré,*' sighed Greg.

'*Le* what?'

'The accursed wind – the mistral.'

'Oh, yes,' Liz said scornfully, 'this is the one that coats the palm trees with snow, isn't it?'

'Well, it sometimes does.'

'Don't *say* that,' cried Mandy. 'I hate the cold. And I haven't got anything thicker than this jacket with me.' The jacket was a bulky knit garment, no doubt warm enough, except in a high wind, which could penetrate the space in every stitch.

They finished their fish soup, then had almond cake and coffee. Afterwards Mandy thought she might buy a windproof jacket, so they sauntered round the shopping centre. Greg was dreading the thought of being asked to interpret while she bought something in one of the shops, but luckily the sales girls needed no interpreter. So it seemed that Mandy, thus protected, would change her mind about going home.

But nothing of the kind. Wednesday morning she was heavy eyed and cross. 'I could hardly sleep all night,' she cried. 'That wind kept moaning and whining at the window, and those rotten shutters kept coming undone, it was dreadful.'

So she rang the consulate to say she was going back to London but would keep in touch from there. They took her to Nice-Côte-d'Azur and waved her goodbye. 'If I have to drive up and down on this road one more time,' Greg said wearily as they made their way back to Avignon, 'I'll probably fall asleep at the wheel.'

'Poor darling. And diddums get kept awake all night by the nasty wind?'

'No, that wasn't what kept me awake.'

She smiled, and put a hand on his arm as he drove. Her intention in returning to Provence had been to be supportive, in view of the anxiety caused by the disappearance of Mrs

Barnell. Monday's news of her death had made the trip all the more necessary. He needed someone to talk to, someone with whom he could relax – in short and in the jargon she generally used, he needed TLC and she was going to supply it in every way.

When they got to the hotel, she put her plan into action. 'Let's snuggle down,' she murmured. 'We need some rest, don't we, lovey?'

So they went to bed to get some rest as she suggested, and then later on they found something else to do that was more entertaining, and after that they showered and dressed and watched some television, and then they were hungry and went out to have supper.

Next morning, when they woke, a pale-blue dawn was edging into the sky. The sun rose, a disc of soft gold. As they wandered down to the breakfast room Liz was pleased to see that Greg looked at ease with himself.

'What are we going to do today?' she enquired as she dripped honey on a brioche.

'You choose. You got dragged into accompanying Mandy on the flight here, and dragged around while she did stuff with the consul, and then dragged back to Nice to see her off yesterday. It's time you had your say.'

'Haven't you got some musical types arriving today?'

'Yes, *Les Chanteuses Médoc.* But not until evening.'

'Poor love. Another trip to Nice?'

'No, thank heavens. They're coming by train.'

'Mmm.' She thought about it. 'So we've got most of the day, have we? You know, I've never seen this place, Parady. Might be nice to drive out there and take a look.'

'Oh, I think that's out of the question. I gather it's been more or less locked down while the investigation goes on.'

'Dear me. Well, I didn't mean actually go in, you know, if that's *verboten.* I just thought we'd take a drive and look at the countryside and that sort of thing.'

He knew very well she hadn't been thinking any such thing. She was interested in Parady because it was the scene of his dramatic confrontation with Colin Waters on Monday. And to tell the truth, he himself would be happy to see what the security men had achieved.

'I'll ring Yverre when we finish breakfast,' he said. 'No harm in asking, because things may have moved on a bit since he warned us off.'

While she was putting on coat, scarf and woolly hat upstairs, he rang the inspector on the land line. They exchanged greetings and asked after each other's welfare. That done, Greg said: 'My friend Mlle Blair and I thought of going out to Parady this morning. But I suppose the DGSE would turn us away?'

'Oh, my friend, good news! The clever boys have withdrawn from the affair—'

'What?'

'Yes, would you believe it? They released Grashenko yesterday and—'

'Released her?'

'Yes, because, after all, *mon vieux*, there's no case against her here in France. What has she done? She went to London as Mrs Locke Daniels, that we know almost certainly and could probably prove. From what we hear from our colleagues over there, she stood outside the apartment of Mlle Rallenham. That's no crime. Here in Provence, she runs a pottery, she rents accommodation from M Daniels, and it's almost certain she knows things about him we would be glad to hear. But she admits nothing.'

'And the DGSE have closed the case?'

He could picture the inspector's shrug. 'Well, they confiscated a lot of stuff at Parady, so I suppose they hope to learn more from that. But otherwise they seem to have put it on a back shelf. They've taken the guards off the site, and allowed everyone back to carry on their business, such as it is.'

'So it would be OK for us to make a trip there?'

'Why not? You *might* encounter Grashenko, but she's probably left for Lyon. She had to leave an address and telephone number where she could be reached, and that's where she said she was going, to friends in Lyon.'

'Well, in that case . . .'

'If you go there, take a look around, M. Couronne. We still have to find Mlle Rallenham. Anything that strikes you as helpful to the inquiry . . . ?'

'Of course.'

*   *   *

Liz was pleased at being given an all-clear. They had to wipe frost off the windscreen before they could set out, and Liz wound her scarf more closely around her neck. With her grey woollen hat pulled down over her ears and the folds of scarf round her neck, Greg thought she looked like a turtle. But he had too much sense to say so.

A grey cloud was moving into the pale sky. As they drove, a flake or two of snow drifted past. 'There you are! I told you it could snow in Provence!'

'Huh! Very impressive. I've counted five flakes so far.'

'Well, you've been warned.' But he knew there would only be a flurry or two because the cloud was high and being swept along by the strength of the mistral, racing south to reach the Mediterranean. Perhaps by the time it got there, snow would have gathered in the clouds with enough weight to coat the palms on La Croisette.

At Parady the gate was open in the usual way. They drove in. The visitors' car park was empty. The restaurant and the office were closed. From somewhere within the confines of the settlement there drifted intermittent wisps of music from a radio.

They got out and made their way along the pedestrian path. The wind was now turbulent, catching the ends of the woollen scarf Liz was wearing, causing the cypress trees to lash about, sending dust and pebbles swirling into the air.

The music was coming from one of the workshops. 'Liszt's Hungarian Rhapsody Number 4,' murmured Greg. Liz took his arm and hugged it in amusement at his immediate response to the sound. The shopkeeper came out to pick up a tub of oleander and lug it inside for safety.

There were more people at work than on his previous visits. The coming of the mistral had brought them to their holdings to make sure everything was firmly locked, tied down or shielded. There were no willow twigs hanging outside the basket-maker, no landscapes lined up outside the painter. A miniature cleaning tractor had been left unattended on a forecourt.

'It's not a very inviting place, is it?' mused Liz, cupping her hands against her cheeks to warm them.

'We're seeing it at its worst. I'm sure it's very attractive in summer.'

'They must be very devoted to their craft to stay on in the winter. There seem to be no customers at all.'

'Well, it's still quite early. The restaurant menu is pretty good. They probably get a fair crowd coming for lunch – people in this district will drive long distances for a good meal, you know.'

She nodded. They walked on around the pathway. A few yards off, Greg gave a little gesture at the building belonging to Estelle Grashenko. 'That's the pottery.'

'It's bigger than I expected.'

'Oh yes, two electric kilns inside and that old brick affair off to the right is a kiln, I think. She does quite big pieces, more sculpture than pottery, I was told.'

The place seemed deserted. One or two plastic bags were gyrating in the gale over ornamental shrubs planted either side of the path. A pair of clippers lay discarded, as if the groundsman had given up on his chores and gone for shelter. One or two wilting twigs had caught in the shorn greenery. It was a depressing scene.

The door had a Closed sign hanging. 'Gone to Lyon, I was told,' said Greg.

And even as he spoke the door burst open and Estelle Grashenko flew out, hands outstretched like claws to rake his face.

'You!' she screamed. 'You! I'll kill you!'

He stepped back. He threw up an arm as a shield. It was against his nature to hit a woman.

Liz had no such inhibition. She picked up the hedge clippers and threw them. They hit Grashenko in the chest.

Luckily, handle first.

Greg's assailant gave a shriek and staggered backwards. She fetched up against the wall near the door of the studio. She put both hands to her chest, bending over, moaning.

'Oh, God!' Greg cried. 'Liz, what have you done?'

'Socked her a good one,' she said.

They went to the injured woman, helped her up, and led her inside. In the vestibule they stopped, uncertain. 'A chair,' Liz suggested.

He recalled seeing a chair in the glazing room. He dashed there, grabbed it, and hurried back. Mlle Grashenko sank on to it, her breathing broken up with sobs. 'Oh, that hurts, that hurts,' she gasped.

'Liz, run back to the—'

'I'm not leaving you here with this maniac!' she said. 'She's shamming – she's not going to die of a shove in the chest—'

'Liz!'

'She was going to scratch your eyes out!' She stooped over her. 'How're you doing? Getting your breath back?'

Grashenko raised her head to glare at her. Her black eyes were like coals lit with invisible fires. 'I'll make you pay for this,' she spat out. 'You and *him*!'

'Feeling better, are you?' Liz enquired caustically. 'Ready for round two?

'I'll sue the pair of you! Assault and bodily harm!' Her voice grew stronger as her breathing improved. She stared past Liz to Greg. 'This is the second time you've attacked me! I'll make you pay!'

'You see?' Liz said. 'She's not really hurt.'

'Can we get you anything?' Greg asked. He was still in shock. Not from her attack, but from the reaction of Liz. This was a side of her he had never seen before. 'A brandy from the restaurant—'

'All I want from you is your departure! Get out! Get out! Why are you tormenting me?'

'Tormenting you? I like that!' Liz said, throwing up a clenched fist in anger. 'You're the one who ran at us—'

'I don't want you on my property. Get out!' She rose from the chair, perhaps not with energy but with enough strength to show that Liz was right – she was comparatively unharmed despite the blow on the chest.

Greg thought it wise to withdraw. He took Liz by the elbow to urge her out. The riotous wind had slammed the door shut, so he opened it then stood so as to keep it open while Liz stepped through. Estelle Grashenko came hard on her heels, glancing about as if for a weapon for a farewell blow. Finding nothing, she came out on to the path, making sure that they would leave.

'Don't come back,' she said, 'or I'll call the police.'

'Ha! They'd probably arrest you again—'

'I was *not* arrested. There is no charge against me—'

'Well, there should be!' cried Liz. 'What happened to Barbara Rallenham? Tell me that!'

'Liz,' cautioned Greg.

'Barbara Rallenham, Barbara Rallenham! I know nothing about her!'

'And Colin Waters?' Greg asked, seeing that she wasn't a war casualty.

'I never heard of him.'

'But you're there with him in the photograph.'

'Nothing of the kind.'

'He was standing there in your workshop.'

'That was *not* Colin.'

'So why did he run?'

'Because he—' She broke off. 'I don't know what you mean.' She put up her hands to clear her hair from her face. The wind was blowing it across like a veil. They could all feel it, attacking them from the alleys between the outbuildings, coming from the north, strong and fierce.

'You went to Barbara Rallenham's flat. You were seen there—'

'I did not! I tell you I never heard of her!'

Something skittered along the path and ended up tangled in the roots of the ornamental shrubs. It drew their attention, they all glanced at it. Estelle Grashenko turned away as if to re-enter her studio.

But Greg stared at what lay there. It was a beige handbag.

He walked over to the shrubs, leaned down, and hooked a finger through the handle. He brought it back to Liz, holding it up for her inspection.

She stared at it. 'Vuitton,' she whispered.

It was a beige leather handbag by Vuitton. Exactly as they'd heard described, belonging to Barbara Rallenham.

'Anything that strikes you as helpful to the inquiry . . .'

Eighteen

Mlle Grashenko had reached the studio door, but half turned at the activity behind her. When she saw what Greg was holding, her face changed. She fumbled at the door-knob.

Greg threw the handbag in among the roots again. In two strides he reached her. She was throwing herself through into the passage. He grabbed the back of her *blouson*. She staggered back against him. He staggered too, but clamped his arms around her.

At once she began to struggle like a wildcat. 'Let me go! Let me go!'

Liz rushed to his aid. 'Mobile,' he gasped.

'Where?'

'Inside pocket.'

Impossible to reach it while Estelle Grashenko was kicking and writhing in his arms. Never at a loss, Liz took off her long scarf, looped it around Grashenko as far as she could, and heaved. The prisoner's head jerked forward, she screamed. Not troubling to be gentle, Liz heaved again.

Tethered by the scarf, Grashenko jerked forward as Greg loosened his grasp. He held her with one hand while he got out the mobile with the other. He tossed it to Liz. She let her captive go, and caught the mobile.

'Speed dial – Number 8.' He grabbed at Mlle Grashenko again, but this time she had turned towards him. He captured her flailing hands just before they reached his face. She tried to wrench herself away.

But a pianist has strong hands, and the ex-Crown Prince had wanted to be a concert pianist. He got both her wrists together in one grip, pulled the scarf from around her shoulders with the other, and wrapped it round and round her forearms to hold her securely. She kicked at him. He sidestepped. It was like dancing the tango with a timber wolf.

It seemed her energy was limitless. He wondered how long he could keep her under control. Perhaps he should hit her? No, no, one didn't hit women. Liz was speaking urgently into the phone. He couldn't make out what she was saying because of the screams from the termagant he was holding.

Liz finished the call. 'As fast as they can,' she said.

How fast could that be? The nearest post must be Fontaine de Vaucluse. Liz, understanding the dilemma, looked about for something to tie her with. Seeing nothing, she made for the door of the studio.

A faint purring sound became noticeable. Or, on the contrary, it must have been quite loud, because it was audible above the screams and imprecations of the enraged Estelle. From the slope beyond the low fence that encircled the site, a little motorized bike came buzzing. The rider was a young man in a dark-grey windcheater. He jumped off without bothering to put on the brakes, leaped over the fence, and arrived on the path beside them.

'Having fun?' he asked.

Greg stared at him. Liz was astounded Even the prisoner was silent. Slipping a hand inside his jacket, he brought out a wallet. 'Agent Nerincourt,' he announced.

Liz looked at him and then at the mobile phone. 'That was *fast*!' she said.

He shook his head. 'I was up on the knoll, with field glasses.'

'Ah,' said Greg. He understood. The DGSE had by no means quit the field; that had been a ruse. They had let Mlle Grashenko free so as to watch her next actions. Perhaps they had hoped she would lead them to Locke Daniels.

Agent Nerincourt produced handcuffs. 'I presume we have a reason for tethering her?' he enquired.

'The handbag,' Greg said, then remembering that Liz couldn't understand what was being said, repeated it in English.

'The handbag,' she echoed. She went to it, stooped to pick it up.

'Liz, don't!' Greg exclaimed. 'Fingerprints.'

'O-oh. Sorry, sorry.'

'What about the handbag?' asked the intelligence officer.

He pushed the scarf aside and substituted handcuffs before unwinding it. The captive seemed too dazed to do anything.

'It belonged to Mlle Rallenham, the Englishwoman who is missing,'

'Excellent. It's not quite what we were expecting – we thought either she'd take off after her partner, or he'd come to her. But we're grateful for anything we can get.'

'That's my handbag,' said Estelle Grashenko, recovering.

Greg almost laughed. Unquenchable! He had been able to step away from her, which was the most enjoyable thing that had happened in the last ten minutes or so.

'It belongs to Barbara Rallenham, and well you know it.' To Nerincourt he said, 'I'm sure if you examine it thoroughly you'll find Barbara's fingerprints on it.'

'Delightful. Now, I think I'll make a call to my boss to say that we need some transport—'

'You can't force me from my home!' cried the prisoner. 'You can't arrest me! You've no grounds—'

'No grounds? You attacked this gentleman. I witnessed the whole thing through my glasses.'

'You're a liar!—'

'Mademoiselle,' he said with a sudden change of tone, 'shut up. I want to make a phone call.'

Once that was done, Nerincourt asked Greg to retrieve his bike, which was still whining and curveting uselessly on the grass outside the perimeter. This done, he was asked to pick up the handbag and place it in a plastic bag which Nerincourt produced from the saddlebag of his bike. They went into the workshop building, out of the bitter wind.

Greg closed the front door behind them, led the way to the kiln room, left them there while he closed the back door through which the wind was howling. Liz meanwhile brought the chair on which the supposedly injured Grashenko had collapsed. There was one other chair. The two woman sat, the two men stood guard.

By and by Nerincourt's phone buzzed. He listened, nodded, then said, 'They're just coming in at the gate. They'll send someone to escort us to it.'

So the DGSE local command post was closer than Fontaine de Vaucluse.

The wait was short. Another man in a grey windcheater appeared in the passage then stood aside as they came out. They made their way towards the entrance of the site. Shopkeepers came out to stare, and one or two accompanied them to the parking area, wondering if they should protest. They seemed astonished, uneasy, but were restrained by the sight of the handcuffs. And perhaps even more so by the significant bulge on the hip that meant the men were armed.

An unassuming white van stood in the parking lot. The driver remained at the wheel. Nerincourt took Mlle Grashenko to the back, where the doors were opened from inside. She was helped in, the doors closed behind her. The onlookers gave a general sigh.

The driver revved up. 'You're going?' Greg said to Nerincourt in surprise.

'Why not?'

'But I told you, we phoned for the police.'

'So you did. Perhaps you'd be so good as to tell them, when they turn up, that everything's taken care of.'

'But they'll want to know – aren't you going to take her to Avignon—'

'Don't worry about it, sir. We'll let them know what's happening.'

That's very good of you, thought Greg. But he didn't say it aloud.

The van drove off. Nerincourt went back to his *motocyclette* and a moment later buzzed past them with a wave, zoomed out through the gate, and away.

'Have we been abandoned?' Liz asked.

'Seems so.'

'Let's get in the car and keep warm.'

He went towards his Mercedes. Liz was hugging herself with her arms, trying to feel a little warmth. One of the bystanders said: 'If you'd like to come in and wait, mademoiselle, the café can provide something hot.'

They agreed to that. Despite the excitement of the last hour, they were chilled to the bone. No doubt the café proprietor hoped for some gossip while they drank the hot chocolate he made, but he was disappointed. The conversation was not only desultory, but also in English.

'What do you think?' murmured Liz. 'About Barbara?'

He shook his head. His meaning was clear.

After a pause he said: 'Inspector Yverre said the security people had taken away a lot of stuff from here. How did they miss that handbag?'

She shrugged. 'I suppose she hid it.'

'But why keep it?'

'Oh, that's easy,' she said, smiling. 'It's a Vuitton. She couldn't bear to part with it.'

'What?'

'Oh yes. It's a beautiful thing. And something she wouldn't normally look at.'

'No, that's why I can't understand—'

'She's into this ethnic style, peasant shawls, Indian earrings. But then she sees that high-fashion thing and she recognizes it as perfect in its own way, so she covets it.'

He sighed and shook his head. 'I wonder if they can establish that it belonged to Barbara . . .'

'Didn't you say "fingerprints"?'

'But it's been a month. And perhaps she's wiped it or cleaned it in some way. Do women polish their handbags?'

'Not likely! Life's too short for stuff like that.'

The brevity of life – Barbara's life – was what had brought them here in the first place. They fell silent.

A police patrol car came rushing into the car park, lights flashing. The driver door opened. As Liz and Greg came out of the café they could hear the car's radio going. A uniformed man got out.

'Monsieur Couronne?'

'Yes.'

'In response to your call, sir. A radio message en route informed us that it was no longer urgent. Is that so?'

'Quite right.'

'The emergency has been taken care of?'

'Indeed it has.'

The policeman looked vexed. He muttered something under his breath which sounded like 'High-handed prima donnas!'

'Are you or the lady in need of help?' he enquired. 'First aid?'

'No, thank you, we're fine.'

He grunted and shrugged. 'In that case, sir, you're free to go.'

'Thank you.' They got into the Mercedes, expecting the police car to turn and go ahead of them. Instead the driver turned off his engine. His companion got in beside him. They sat inactive.

'Waiting for reinforcements,' muttered Greg. 'I suppose they'll tape the place off again until they've sorted out how they came to miss that handbag.'

'D'you think they'll tell us?'

'Unlikely.'

'But *something's* got to come of all this!'

'We'll see.'

They drove back to Avignon in comparative silence. Once there, Greg felt they ought to drop in at the police station to see Inspector Yverre. Yverre received them in his office, but shook his head when they attempted to give him an account of the morning's events.

'One has heard a report on the handbag,' he said, speaking English for the benefit of Liz. Greg could detect some hidden glee at the thought of DGSE being handed evidence they had missed. 'Everything is being taken care of.'

'What does that mean?'

'Who knows? We have to wait and see.'

'And in the meantime?'

'In the meantime we say nothing, we know nothing, and we behave ourselves.'

'Behave ourselves? For instance?'

'We do not contact the troublesome sister to let her know what has occurred,' said the inspector very seriously.

'But that's inhuman!' cried Liz.

'It is politics, mademoiselle.'

'Come on, Yverre,' Greg urged. 'That poor woman has been back and forth to Avignon trying to—'

'She is emotional, my good friend. And I think she indulges in mood enhancers, no? What is the expression . . . This has to be kept under wraps. Those are my instructions. And I would advise you to give them regard also.'

There was nothing to be done. They left. It was by now time for lunch but neither of them felt hungry. They went to a quiet bistro by the river where they had coffee and made phone calls – Greg to his family in Bredoux, Liz to business contacts in London.

That evening they went together to meet Greg's singers off the train from Bordeaux. They turned out to be a quartet of women, which was a considerable surprise to Liz – the more so since one of them turned out to be extremely pretty.

She was therefore quite happy to spend the rest of the evening with them, so that she could keep an eye on proceedings. She helped settle them at their hotel and accompanied them to dinner.

Next day, Friday, she even attended the practice sessions in the rehearsal studio. It wasn't her kind of music, but she stuck it out just to make sure there was no passionate operatic stuff that might rouse a romantic response. Not at all – the ladies were singing hymns composed by Hildegarde of Bingen, a medieval nun. Unaccompanied, at that.

Saturday morning they were to rehearse in the recital hall. She didn't think she could stand two more hours of hymns. She excused herself and found on enquiry that there was a bus trip to Arles, for the benefit of market-goers. There she was rewarded by the sight of the bustling street market. She spent the morning sampling delicious snacks from the stalls to protect herself against the intense cold, and then waited outside the doors of the Fondation Vincent Van Gogh to go in as soon as it opened at two o'clock. It contained works by contemporary artists, among whom she recognized one or two former schoolmates from her days at art college.

Next she gravitated to the Place du Forum, to spend the remains of the afternoon wandering around trying to recognize the places painted by Van Gogh. But the clouds were heavy and it was soon growing dark. She took the bus back to Avignon, glad that it was crowded, because the passengers generated a comforting heat.

Snow actually fell during the night. In the morning the city looked totally transformed under a white garment about five centimetres thick. She was delighted, although she didn't have shoes fit for walking in such conditions. However, the shops opened as usual in the afternoon so she bought a pair of elegant boots. She was happy, and Greg was happy that she was happy. Moreover, his singers last night had been rewarded with a full hall, Hildegarde of Bingen being an icon among the feminists of Europe.

Their second and final recital on Sunday night was a sell-out despite the snow. *Les Chanteuses Médoc* held a muted kind of party afterwards and were escorted to their late-night train by both Greg and Liz, the latter standing by with great tolerance while the four ladies embraced him in farewell.

Monday morning was the first Monday in February. Liz thought the city less attractive. The snow had melted as the mistral relented so now there were puddles of melting slush outdoors. She began to think she should go home, for there was work awaiting her there.

'I think I'll ring the airport to ask about flights, Greg. The police won't mind if I go home, will they?'

'They didn't say "Don't leave town" – no, no, I don't think there's any embargo.'

'It's just that nothing seems to be happening . . .'

But she was wrong, because Inspector Yverre walked into the breakfast room at that moment. He looked somewhat nettled. 'Good morning,' he said. 'I rang to check that you were still in the hotel. You don't mind if I interrupt your breakfast?'

'Not at all. Sit down, Inspector. Coffee?'

'No, thank you, I come merely as the bearer of a message.' His tone was chill but his expression let them know they weren't to blame. 'You are free this morning?'

'Well, yes. Why do you ask?'

He drew in a breath, as if to inhale composure. 'A car will call for you at ten thirty. Our friends the magicians would like to have a discussion with you.'

'Magicians?' queried Liz.

'He means the intelligence people,' Greg explained.

'Oh, does that mean they're actually going to tell us something about Barbara?'

'Who knows what they are going to say, mademoiselle. I am merely the messenger. I was asked to pass on this invitation because it is known that monsieur and I are acquainted. The DGSE thought that a direct approach from them might seem alarming.'

'Very considerate.'

'Shall I let them know you agree with this arrangement?'

Greg exchanged a glance with Liz. 'Yes, we agree.'

'In that case an agent will come into the hotel foyer for you.'

'How shall we know him?' Liz enquired. 'Will he wear a red rose in his buttonhole?'

Yverre allowed himself a little smile at the mockery. 'I believe you have already met him, mademoiselle. Agent Nerincourt?'

'Oh yes.'

Yverre bowed and said goodbye. Even his back view expressed mortification. 'He's hopping mad,' said Greg.

'No wonder. They could have sent that chap Nerincourt to say all that.'

'Interdepartmental politics . . .'

They finished their breakfast in comparative silence. Then Liz rose. 'I must go up and change,' she said.

'Change?' His eyebrows went up. 'What's wrong with what you're wearing, *Liebling*?'

'This?' she said, holding out from her waist the comfortable dark blue sweater. 'If I'm going to be grilled by the security police, I want to look my best!'

Nineteen

When she came downstairs Nerincourt had arrived and was standing expectantly with Greg. His admiring gaze told her that if he were in charge of the grilling she'd be let off lightly. He led the way out at once.

A new-looking Citroën Picasso was waiting. He opened the back door for them, they got in, he closed the door and took his place in the driving seat. The car slid smoothly away.

'Where are we going?' Greg enquired.

'Not far, sir. It's just tricky to find, that's all.'

They crossed the Pont du Royaume and turned right. After skirting sixteenth- and seventeenth-century buildings of some splendour, they headed out of Villeneuve-les-Avignon along the Rhône. Here there was wintry woodland among which modern buildings could be glimpsed. They went along a country road then turned down an unexpected track. Tricky was the word for it.

Nerincourt pulled up in front of a villa with an intricately paved courtyard. He got out and ushered them in through a door of reeded glass. 'Would you like to leave your coats?'

Greg gave him his car coat. Liz had put on her 'business' outfit: beige slacks, silk blouse, tailored brown jacket. She preferred to keep the jacket. Nerincourt led them to the back of the tiled hall, tapped on a door, then announced them.

They went in. No sign of office equipment. The room had an ivory carpet, easy chairs upholstered in pale-blue linen, contemporary low tables of glass and pale wood. This was clearly someone's holiday home, rented for a short winter stay.

Two men were sitting by windows which looked out on a distant view of the Rhône. They rose. One was wearing a suit that, if not a real Cardin, was a very good copy. His cologne was *Acqua di Giò*. He was tall and thin with rimless narrow glasses that gave him the look of an intellectual. The other man was more the Aquascutum type, ruddy complexioned, less tall but more thickly muscled than his colleague. Greying hair cut close to his head was reminiscent of the style favoured by the American marines. A bluff, country-gentleman look.

Greg began to think that Liz had been right to run upstairs and change. Compared with her and the two strangers, he felt considerably outclassed in his jersey and jeans.

'Good morning,' said the tall thin man. 'I am *Commandant* Traumont of the *Direction Général de Sécurité Extérieure*. This is Major Whittley of the British Security Service.'

They all shook hands. Traumont gestured to armchairs that more or less faced those in which they had been sitting.

'Refreshments? Coffee? Something stronger?'

'No, thank you.'

'Later, perhaps,' said Whittley, speaking for the first time. He had a rich, almost operatic voice.

Liz realized that the conversation was to be in English in deference to her lack of ability in French. She settled herself in an armchair, grateful she was wearing slacks, because she slid back so far in the chair her legs would have been exposed almost indecently in a skirt. Greg and Traumont sat down. Whittley remained standing.

'We thought we ought to have a little conference,' Whittley began. 'But before we can have our talk, I must ask you to sign an agreement of confidentiality.'

'Sign?' Liz exclaimed, astonished.

'I could say it's a mere formality. But that wouldn't be true in this case. My colleague and I want to talk to you for a reason that will become clear, but nothing that's said in this room must be repeated outside.'

Liz was shaking her head. Whittley stepped to a table to pick up a folder. He took out two sheets of paper which he handed to Greg, and another two which he gave to Liz.

One was in French, the other in English. She read the English document. It had an official heading and numbered paragraphs requiring an initial after each. There were lines at the end for signature and witness.

She looked at Greg. He had finished reading the French

version. He nodded at her, to let her know she was committing herself merely to be silent.

'All right,' she said. She struggled up in her chair, accepted the folder from Whittley so as to write, then handed both documents and the folder back to him. As he turned away she got to her feet, walked across the room, and fielded two cushions from a sofa to prop herself up comfortably in the armchair.

Traumont, watching her, smiled in admiration at this defiant initiative. Whittley signed the two documents as witness before returning them to the folder.

'Now,' he said, 'if you'll bear with me, we have to go back a little in time. A little over two years ago, an official of the Board of Trade was allowed to resign without fuss. His name was Colin Waters.' He waited for their nod of recognition. 'A journalist called Barbara Rallenham got word of it and did some investigation around his home neighbourhood. She learned a few things that were common knowledge to the local gossips – that Waters wasn't averse to making money on the side, that he was unfaithful to his wife, that he kept on good terms with some of the lads he'd grown up with – the common touch, you understand. One of the lads was his cousin, Thomas Shanigan.'

Liz made a sound of recognition. Greg said: 'Shanigan is his cousin?'

'Yes, we've verified it.'

'How do you know that she found this out?'

'We have had her computer examined by our experts. The information about Waters was stored in an old file.'

'I see,' Greg said, vexed.

He realized now that they had ignored Barbara's computer after the discovery of her recent notes. But if the truth were acknowledged, he'd felt the important aspect was the situation at Parady.

Whittley continued. 'Waters disappeared from public view. Ms Rallenham did nothing then with her information because it didn't seem to lead to anything much. But a few weeks ago a lady called Mrs Barnell wrote to her in the usual run-of-the-mill nosy-parkering that Ms Rallenham invited. She said her tenant Mr Shanigan was sending a mysterious package to an address in Provence every week.'

'And Barbara recognized the name Shanigan from her previous notes,' Liz said.

'Exactly. She thought it likely it had something to do with Waters and his enforced but low-key resignation. She was hoping for a big scandal to use in her column and came to Provence to look into it.'

'And vanished from the daily round within three days,' Traumont added. 'Thanks to Mlle Grashenko, we now know what happened to her.'

He paused. Whittley said nothing. Liz said, in a faltering voice, 'Is she . . . Is she dead?'

'I regret, mademoiselle, but that is the case.' He took off his glasses, to let a beat of time go by, then as he began to polish them with a silk handkerchief he said, 'She made a call to her sister, as she frequently did, just to keep contact. It seems she appeared at Parady on the afternoon of the same day. She recognized M Waters the moment she saw him, in Mlle Grashenko's workshop.'

'And Grashenko went for her with her claws,' muttered Liz.

'No,' Traumont said with a faint smile. 'According to Grashenko, it was Mr Waters who "went for her". He got angry and afraid when she said she was going to find out what he was up to now. So he seized a pointed metal tool and stabbed her. Such a tool might be used to make a horizontal groove in a pot while it is turning on the wheel, or so our experts tell us. It was lying nearby on a bench, but we did not find it, or anything that could be used in evidence.'

'Have you found the body?' Greg asked in a low voice.

There was a long pause, which neither of the intelligence men seemed to want to break. At last Whittley said with grim concision, 'They burned the body.'

The winter sun sent a slanting sunbeam into the room. Outside the great river glided by. Liz sat with her head bent to hide the tears that rimmed her eyes. She had never even met Barbara Rallenham, yet her death struck a keen blow to her.

Greg got up to sit on the arm of her chair and put an arm around her shoulders. She looked up at him. She saw that he wasn't surprised by the news. She reached up a hand and he took it.

‘Perhaps you would like some brandy,’ suggested Traumont.

‘No. No, thank you. Please go on.’

Traumont hooked his glasses back behind his ears and looked at her seriously through the narrow lenses. ‘The body was disposed of in that big kiln you might have seen in the open at the side of the workshop. We understand that it is called a tunnel kiln, and must be fed with actual fuel such as wood, oil or gas. Grashenko used it for large pieces which she made as artwork. I don’t know if you’re aware that she has quite a reputation as an adventurous potter.’

‘Yes, I was told she’d had one-man exhibitions in the Riviera towns.’

‘The kiln must have suggested itself as an excellent method of getting rid of the body.’

‘But surely there was a risk that some of the other residents would find out?’

‘No, monsieur, they used it during the night when the shopkeepers had gone home – the workshops close early in the off-season, and the dwellings are some distance away. Moreover there are few occupants at the moment because the tourist season doesn’t really start until the summer.’

Greg sighed. ‘Bad luck for her. If she’d gone investigating in August there would have been too many witnesses to carry out a scheme like that.’

Traumont nodded agreement. ‘They kept the belongings of Mlle Rallenham for a few days. Grashenko wore Mlle Rallenham’s coat to go to the auberge to pay the bill and retrieve her luggage.’

‘And then they burned the coat too?’ Greg asked. ‘And her credit cards, her notebooks?’

‘They burned what was combustible. There was a little jewellery – a watch, some pearls. There was a laptop. These they included in a shipment of crockery going out to their clients.’

‘To their clients?’ cried Liz. ‘Wouldn’t the clients find that odd?’

Greg was nodding his head in understanding. ‘Their clients! They’re the reason for the whole set-up, aren’t they! Do you know who they are?’

Whittley gave a short angry laugh. ‘That’s what we are

now trying to find out. Grashenko says she only knows the address to which the consignment goes in Marseilles. From there it travels on by ship, but we're still trying to learn the destination. But even when we get that, it will only be a trans-shipping depot.'

'*But what are they shipping?*' demanded Greg.

Once again there was a break in the narrative. The two intelligence officers were thinking how to explain what came next.

'Do you know how a nuclear reactor works?' asked Whittley.

Greg shook his head. Liz didn't even bother. Nuclear reactors! They'd be asking about black holes next, she said to herself, taking courage from her own irritation.

'A nuclear reactor turns nuclear energy into thermal energy. Uranium is used to produce controlled fission, which makes heat. The uranium is suspended in the water reactor in containers made of an alloy called zircaloy—'

'Ah!' The crown prince had been half expecting it. 'We did mention this to the detective—'

'Yes, sir, I know you did, and got a brush-off. Luckily the *juge d'instruction* for this district is a nervous type and called in my colleague here.'

'But wait!' cried Greg. 'You can't tell me that the amount of zirconium alloy that Shanigan could supply is enough to be important in the nuclear industry!'

Major Whittley sighed and ran his hand over his bullet head.

'No, that's not what we're telling you.' Traumont took it up. 'Let us expand our field of thought. We have to move into the field of politics. You know, perhaps, that there are nations that are thought of as "rogue states"?'

'Of course, one hears about them on documentary programmes.'

'These nations have ambitions to become nuclear powers. But they know that if they make waves by buying equipment too openly the fact will be noticed. There's an international organization that monitors such things.'

'So they collect the necessary materials by a back-door method.' Whittley interjected. 'Uranium isn't difficult to acquire, as you perhaps know, sir, in this unstable world. The states of the former Soviet Union seem to be awash with it. Recently in Iraq the local population was carrying it away from industrial sites.'

'But that was low grade.'

'Quite true, but believe me there's a lot of reactor grade stuff that goes missing. There's a well-established black market in industrial grade uranium.'

'But if I understand the matter, that's only suitable for fuel rods in a nuclear generator—'

'Exactly. The government wanting to get into the nuclear weapons arena would begin by pretending it merely wants a power-generating plant for electricity. There are certain materials that act as red flags. If a rogue state starts acquiring zircaloy, the international agency for atomic energy control gets anxious. If it starts acquiring zircaloy through covert routes, the anxiety level rises fast. The monitoring agency would set up objections. "You don't need nuclear power, yes we do, no you don't" – you know the kind of thing, it can go on for years.'

'Yes, it can.'

'Four or five years down the line, while negotiations are still going on, the rogue government would have everything for a nuclear-powered reactor, supposedly for electricity. The monitor agency would never be able to get it closed down no matter how much they negotiate. And *then* uranium from the reactor is reprocessed and turned into weapons grade material.'

No one spoke.

'It's well known that North Korea has already done this,' said Traumont. 'Iraq was probably trying to do it. There is no doubt other countries are on that road.'

'Our task is to put as many obstacles in the way as we can,' Whittley explained. 'When we hear that zircaloy is being secretly collected and shipped out, we know that someone wants it for dishonourable reasons.'

'And enough could be obtained by the methods Colin Waters was using?'

'We think so. You don't need much, the fuel rods are narrow cylinders of uranium pellets.'

'So the dust from Shanigan's work clothes . . . is extracted how?'

'We found a mini vacuum cleaner in the workshop of Mlle Grashenko. We were able to test it out because one of the weekly packets happened to arrive from London. It must have been in the post about the time we began following up the case. We used the little vacuum and extracted measurable quantities.'

'But dust – a mere handful of dust – what do you do with it then?'

'You ship it to your customer, who is at the end of some kind of transport chain. Bear in mind that Waters might not be the only contributor to this collection system. The customer has the facilities to process the dust and roll it into sheet metal. There's no problem making the sheet metal into a container – that is what M Shanigan does at his factory, the factory owned by Sir Rupert Modd.'

'Right,' said Greg regretfully. 'I was told he worked in a factory that made special containers but it didn't sink in.' He thought it over. 'So the zircaloy dust goes to a factory somewhere and containers are made and filled with uranium, and then a power station goes on line. And then what?'

'There's some international disquiet, some protests from the big powers . . .'

'Sanctions may be invoked against the rogue state . . .'

'And much good that will do,' Whittley ended. 'They could take years, perhaps as long as a decade, to have any effect. Meanwhile more uranium 235 is being bought, the power plant produces spent nuclear fuel, it's reprocessed into weapons grade, and perhaps missiles are manufactured. And such nations are quite willing to support terrorist groups.'

Liz was clutching Greg's hand so hard she could feel every distinct bone. 'It's a frightening prospect,' she muttered.

'Indeed it is. We need to find out where the export journey ends. This is one of the reasons we had to ask for your pledge of secrecy, because we don't want to attract any attention.'

'How does it travel on, the dust?' Greg asked. 'Surely it wouldn't be hard to keep track of a packet through the postal system? You could put a homing device or—'

Whittley gave a snort. 'If only it were that simple. It doesn't go on in the form received at Parady.'

'No?'

'No, the conspirators want it to be unnoticed, innocuous. So it's baked into rather handsome earthenware plates that Grashenko produces for use in whole-food restaurants throughout the world. Some of her customers are perfectly innocent, as far as we can tell, and receive perfectly ordinary plates. But one of them at the end of the secret chain is an organization that wants to do harm.'

'Baked into plates?' Greg said in protest and shaking his head. 'But that would melt the zirconium into the plate, surely?'

'No, that's the extraordinary thing,' said Whittley. 'Earthenware is fired at about 1300°C, or so our experts tell us. The melting point of zirconium is over 1800°C. So Grashenko mixes the zirconium dust into the clay, as what is called a "grog". That's a name for an ingredient that alters the texture of the clay before it's fired, it seems. Generally it's something cheap, like ground-down old pottery.'

'We have had to take a quick course in the production of pottery,' Traumont put in with grim amusement. 'It's a subject I never thought would interest me.'

'Nor me. But it's proved very enlightening,' Whittley went on. 'In the case of Grashenko's plates, the zirconium dust blends in and remains unmelted as a sort of silvery mottle in the finished article. When the pottery is received at the other end, it must be ground down and the metal extracted – perhaps by some method like panning for gold.' He smiled. 'I only know all this because Grashenko explained it to me. She's quite proud of it – even showed me some of the plates.'

'Proud of it! She's an accessory to murder!' cried Liz. 'You sound as if you're getting quite friendly with her! She's not going to get off, is she?'

'Not at all, not at all,' soothed Whittley.

'No, mademoiselle, I assure you. France does not allow criminals to escape justice, nor does it allow the free existence of those who might wish to help Al Qaeda and the like. In time she will go to trial, when she has told us all she knows.'

'But has she told you how to catch Colin Waters?'

Both men looked mortified. 'She says she doesn't know where he's gone,' Whittley said. 'And we begin to think we won't catch him, because he's a very useful man to those who are able to pay him. He's a metallurgist, he's on the network of underground movements. I think he's long gone, Ms Blair, long gone . . .'

Commandant Traumont was not going to allow any pessimism. 'We hope by careful surveillance and investigation to find out where the shipment of plates goes—'

'So that's the reason you ask us to keep matters confidential?'

'A good guess,' said Traumont. 'And of course it is partly that. But in fact there is a very simple thing that we need your help for.'

Liz was immediately sceptical. When anyone in business mentioned 'a very simple thing' it usually meant complications. 'Well, what?'

'It's Mlle Rallenham.'

'But she's—'

'The other Mlle Rallenham, Mlle Mandy.'

'Mandy?'

Traumont was very careful in his choice of words. 'We have gathered from our colleagues at Maida Vale police station that Mlle Mandy is a very temperamental young woman. That she is volatile, talkative, and takes perhaps more than a little something when she goes to a weekend rave.' He raised his eyebrows enquiringly at her.

'Ah . . . yes . . . I think that's true.'

'When we ascertained from Grashenko that the elder sister was dead,' said Whittley, 'we knew we had to tell Mandy. But if we let her know all the circumstances she might . . . well, she might blab.'

An unattractive word. But it was perhaps accurate.

'And that we cannot allow,' said Traumont. 'If we are to follow the trail that starts with Shanigan in London, we must have absolute discretion.'

Discretion was not a thing that Greg could associate with Mandy Rallenham. He understood their problem. 'Somehow I get the idea that you've got Mandy under wraps. I'd have expected . . . I'd have thought she'd have been in touch with us as soon as she was told her sister was dead.'

Traumont looked embarrassed. 'Mlle Mandy is not a lady

one can leave unsupervised in a situation such as this, monsieur. You can see that, I am sure.'

'Are you saying that she can't even ring her friends without your consent?'

'We . . . er . . . preferred that you should be fully briefed before there was any contact between you.'

Liz jumped to her feet. Her colour was high. 'Who gave you the right to have "preferences" in the way Mandy behaves? Who do you think you are?'

It was Whittley who responded. He too couldn't conceal his mortification. 'Well, it's this way, Ms Blaire. We suddenly found ourselves facing an entirely new threat from an entirely new direction. We had to sort of batten down the hatches, at every level, if you know what I mean.'

'And that included denying her access to a telephone?'

'Yes, at first. We . . . we relaxed things a bit after a while, though we're still keeping an eye on her.'

'How very kind.'

Greg rose to put an arm round her shoulders. 'Come on, Liz, calm down. I'm sure they acted for the best.' Tales told by his grandmother had brought him to the knowledge that affairs of state would always take precedence over individual needs. He turned to the others. 'So what did you do? What have you told her?'

'First of all, we arranged for a bereavement counsellor to be on hand. Then one of our women officers told Mlle Mandy that her sister met her end in a fire.'

Liz looked at Greg, who frowned. 'But that's—'

'*In a fire*. It is true. Is it not?' challenged Traumont.

'Well . . . yes . . .'

'Our colleague gently conveyed to Ms Rallenham that the body was unrecognizable.' Traumont waited for protest but none came. He gave a tiny motion of the head as if to say, "That's true also." He went on, 'We arranged for a death certificate to be given to her. She was greatly, *greatly* distressed but the counsellor helped her through it.'

'You mean she accepts this story?'

'She does. She isn't coping very well,' Whittley informed them, 'but she's making an effort. She's let the editor of Barbara Rallenham's paper have the news, and she's been sending out letters to her sister's friends. At one point she asked if she could have Barbara's ashes to scatter in the churchyard back home – the family come from Hampshire – but we had to explain that it was really impossible.' He gave a great sigh. 'In fact, we did find some dust that seemed to consist of calcified human bone near the big tunnel kiln, but the mistral has blown almost every atom of it away.'

'The mistral,' murmured Liz. 'It was the mistral that blew the handbag up to our feet outside the workshop.'

'Ah yes,' Traumont said with some hidden mockery. 'She kept that because she fell in love with it. And she hid it in a narrow space between the two gas containers which fuel her outdoor kiln. I suppose she intended to bring it into use after all the fuss had died down. If the fuss had continued for long, she might have destroyed it. If the mistral had not teased it out, it might never have been found.'

Traumont didn't say that it was thanks to His Serene Highness that the fuss had continued at all. Liz felt that Greg's contribution was going to go unrecognized, and would have liked to demand some gratitude. But Greg was looking very sombre. She thought it better to hold her tongue about gratitude and instead asked, 'Did you find fingerprints?'

'A few partials that *might* be Ms Rallenham's,' Whittley acknowledged. 'But better than that, trapped in the kidskin lining we found a light-brown hair. Our scientists compared it by microscope with hairs taken from Barbara Rallenham's hairbrush, which was in her flat. We were hoping for DNA corroboration but there aren't any follicles, which perhaps you know are needed for a DNA sample. But the forensic scientists are satisfied that the handbag was in the possession of Barbara Rallenham originally, and Grashenko doesn't deny it.'

'It was the handbag that caused Mlle Grashenko to collaborate in our investigation. We may not have a body but we have Grashenko's statements.'

'She's singing like a lark,' the major agreed with satisfaction. 'Partly because Waters ran off and left her in the lurch.'

'But, monsieur, we cannot tell any of this to Mlle Mandy,' the *commandant* declared.

'So she's to be told a partial truth,' Greg said to him. 'And the murder of her sister is in fact to go unpunished.'

Traumont was not pleased at this point-blank assertion. He bridled and looked as if he might rebuke His Highness, but thought better of it. Whittley intervened.

'Things could change, sir,' he said. 'We might catch up with Waters. We'd charge him, you can be sure of that.'

The prince might have reminded him of an English proverb that mentioned the flying of pigs, but changed tack. 'And Mrs Barnell?' he enquired.

The intelligence officers exchanged wearied glances. 'There is nothing we can do about Mrs Barnell,' said Whittley.

'But we were told the police arrested Shanigan—'

'And had to let him go. Shanigan is an innocent, sir. We sat in on his interviews with the Walthamstow police and the fact is he's done nothing really wrong—'

'But he sent the packages!'

'The way he saw it, he was doing a favour for his cousin Coco. He admires and respects Coco. He himself was a bit of a dunce at school but Coco did great things, made money, had a high old time with attractive women, and so on. When Coco went abroad to set up this community-living thing, he told Tommy he needed this special metal dust for use in the pottery. All Tommy had to do was buy some extra sets of overalls so he could send the gritty pair abroad without being noticed. The factory was deprived of a few grammes of zirconium each week. Over a year or eighteen months it amounted to a lot more, but the management show no desire to bring a prosecution.'

Liz threw up her hands in protest. 'Celia Barnell *died*!'

Whittley could make no defence to the charge. He looked unhappy, fidgeting in his chair and gazing at the carpet. Traumont seemed unwilling to intervene in what he probably regarded as a purely British side of the case. A silence ensued, during which Liz glared at them in justifiable anger.

'Believe me, Ms Blair, if there was anything to be done, we'd do it. But Shanigan seems to have absolutely no knowledge about the death of his landlady. He freely admits that in one of his regular telephone conversations with his cousin he mentioned that Mandy Rallenham had been to the house asking for Mrs Barnell. But he sees no connection between that and Mrs Barnell "throwing herself in the Thames".'

'Oh, come on!'

'No, really. You must remember that Shanigan *doesn't know* Barbara Rallenham came to see Mrs Barnell. He *didn't know* Barbara had disappeared. Her name means nothing to him because he doesn't read the *Clarion*. In fact I don't think he reads anything except specialist publications about greyhounds. He's a thickie.'

'Mrs Barnell actually went into his apartment,' Greg said. 'Didn't he notice that?'

'Seems not. When Mrs Barnell disappeared with an unknown man a couple of days later he had no reason to connect it with anything that happened around him. He has absolutely nothing against Mrs Barnell, whom he describes as a decent landlady though a bit nosy.'

'Yet his cousin Colin Waters killed her,' insisted Liz.

'We can't prove it,' he returned, shaking his head. 'Grashenko agrees that Waters went to London at or about the time that Mrs Barnell vanished. But she says she knows nothing more than that.'

'And you believe her?'

There was a silence while they considered that. Traumont said, 'Speaking for myself, I do not believe her. It is a good act, but it doesn't quite convince. She is trying to limit her involvement with Waters, saying that she acted out of idealistic motives in the fight against Western imperialism. Her story is that she is a visionary, caught up in violent actions against her will, and that Waters is to blame. She says she knows nothing about getting rid of Mrs Barnell.'

'But it *was* Waters who came and drove her away—'

'There's no evidence to support that, mademoiselle. Mrs Barnell was a fan of the bingo. She had friends among the players, both male and female. It could easily have been a male friend who offered transport. Naturally, seeing the consequence, that is to say the death of Mrs Barnell, he is not going to come forward. Mrs Barnell's death is being regarded as accident or suicide. That has to be the official view.'

She was so depressed by this conclusion that she fell into silence. Greg too seemed at a loss for some moments. But then he said, 'You seem to think that Mandy can be manipulated into thinking her sister died in an accident. But the death of Mrs Barnell? Mandy blamed herself for that.'

'Our bereavement counsellor has talked her through all that. She has come to believe – she *wants* to believe – that Mrs Barnell's death had nothing to do with her visit to the house. She has enough to cope with already, sir. I think you'll agree to that.'

'But the man who came to Barbara's flat? The woman who waited outside?' Liz cried. 'I sketched them. Mrs Dandry gave me a description. You can't just wave that away! Mandy actually has copies of the sketches.'

'Well, as to that . . . She agrees now that the man who came to the flat was some colleague of Barbara's who had to get some information from the computer and somehow crashed it. The woman outside . . . well, Ms Blair, you made a sketch but Mrs Dandry never thought it was a very good likeness.'

'What?' Liz gasped, offended.

'Mrs Dandry is anxious not to make trouble,' Whittley said in a cool tone. 'She hasn't been declaring her earnings to the income tax authorities, so she goes along with what she thinks is best.'

'Mlle Mandy has enough problems of her own,' Traumont pointed out. 'She feels the loss of her sister very deeply, because the sister was to some extent in place of the mother who is long dead. She also feels guilt, because she in some ways resented her sister. More successful, regarded with respect by her readers, coping better with her life . . . some part of Mlle Mandy is glad that Barbara is gone. Or so at least our psychiatrist tells us. So she is trying to lose herself in these easily obtained medicines that she takes, and reality becomes blurred.'

Greg, who had been standing like a barrister in a courtroom, walked to the window where he stared out at the view. He was angry at what he was hearing.

Traumont looked at his watch. 'I think this would be a good time to have a break,' he suggested. 'Whittley and I have been up since the early hours, and, speaking for myself, a drink would be pleasant.'

'Right, old man,' agreed Whittley.

Greg listened to them without turning. They were a clever pair, needing the cooperation of himself and Liz. They had spun a tale that he regarded as reasonably accurate, but they knew they had brought about a temporary overload on their listeners. Now they were allowing them a chance to recover.

Liz had said neither yes or no to the suggestion. Taking silence for consent, Traumont went out to order refreshments. Liz got out of her armchair so as to join Greg at the window. She leaned against him. 'What do you think?' she murmured.

He sighed. 'I hate it all. But they've got some justification for their attitude. They want to trace the destination of Grashenko's pottery, and the only way to do that is to keep everything quiet.'

'But why do they have to call us in and tell us all this?'

'Because there's a loose end. Getting Mandy to sign secrecy agreements would be a waste of time. Nothing would stop her from chattering.'

This was only too true. 'They were hinting at something like that, weren't they?'

'Yes, and they want to get back to it. Hence the interval, so that the musicians can retune their instruments.'

'And what kind of tune will they play when they start up again?'

'Oh, hearts and flowers. "This is best for Mandy." Trouble is, I think they're right.'

'Mmm.'

Traumont returned, and shortly after came a minion pushing a little waiter's cart. On it there were several bottles of beer and mineral water with appropriate glasses, a coffee pot with faience beakers, cream, sugar, and on a plate little pieces of sugared *sablé*.

The two intelligence officers chose to have beer. Greg thought this was to show that they regarded themselves as off duty, that the meeting was totally informal. Liz asked for mineral water, which the subordinate poured for her, but shook her head at the shortbread. Greg filled a beaker with black coffee.

He waited to see how they would introduce the subject. It was Whittley who took the lead. 'We got a bit sidetracked, sir, if you recall. We were speaking of Ms Mandy Rallenham.'

'I remember.'

'Our difficulty is that our psychiatrist—'

'Psychiatrist? Is that the lady you introduced at first as a 'bereavement counsellor'?'

'Well . . . As a matter of fact . . .' Whittley looked rather sheepish. 'We were thinking of Ms Mandy's best interest, sir. She *is* a very erratic character.'

'I won't argue with that.'

'I know she's a friend of yours, but—'

'She's not a friend,' Greg corrected. 'She came to me because she thought I had something to do with her sister getting out of touch.'

'But you've got to know her to some extent.'

'I want to dispel any illusion you might have on that score, Major. I've spent quite a lot of effort trying to avoid Mandy.'

'Oh.' Whittley looked despondently into his beer glass.

'Monsieur,' said Traumont, 'I hear what you say. Yet Mlle Rallenham has feelings for you, no?'

Greg said nothing. He was remembering the embarrassing occasion when Mandy had draped herself on the coverlet of his hotel bed.

Liz said rather coolly, 'Mandy is the kind of woman who has to have a man around. It's part of her view of herself – fun-loving, stylish, in the know about all the latest clubs and discos and with a man at her elbow to admire her savvy. Greg isn't really her type.'

'But from what we could gather, she's been relying on him, mademoiselle. She regards him as someone she can trust.'

She had to admit that point. She nodded. Greg said, 'If this is leading up to some idea that I can act as father figure or something, forget it. In the first place, I'm not qualified for it. In the second, I have to be in Vienna next week.'

'If we could have just a few days of your time, sir?'

'To do what?'

Whittley cleared his throat. 'Er . . . Ms Rallenham is going to come into quite a lot of money. Her sister knew how to handle her finances. In the course of conversations with the bereavement counsellor she's mentioned the idea of using the money to set up business in Marbella.'

'No.' This was Liz. She could see what was coming. No way was she going to allow Greg to accompany Mandy to Marbella.

'I have to agree with Ms Blair,' said Greg. 'If you're asking me to help set up Mandy in a shop in Marbella, the answer is no.'

'Er . . . You see . . .'

'It would be very useful to us if Mlle Rallenham were to be totally distracted from her thoughts about Mlle Barbara,' Traumont intervened. 'At the moment she is divided between lamenting that there is nothing to memorialize her sister – no headstone, no plaque – and the feeling that she herself must get over it, start again. Our psychiatrist says that if she could be encouraged in the idea of going abroad, to a new life, it would be advantageous to her.'

'And to you.'

'Certainly. I don't deny it, monsieur.'

'I can't,' groaned Greg. 'I really can't.'

'She needs someone to go with her, to be a support, to translate for her. You speak Spanish, do you not, monsieur?'

'Well, yes . . . but . . .'

'You would be the ideal candidate. It might be for a week, perhaps two.'

'No, it's impossible. Besides, I don't know anything about opening a shop.'

Liz suppressed a smile. She could just imagine the kind of place Mandy would like, a salon with lots of shiny equipment and bright colours, the latest hard-house music belting out from big speakers, and customers as flaky as herself.

'More coffee?' Whittley enquired, picking up the pot.

Greg offered his beaker. Whittley poured. Liz sat in thought.

'Sweetie,' she said, 'you have friends everywhere among your musical mafia.'

'Well . . .'

'Surely you have friends in Spain.'

'Not in Marbella,' he objected.

'No, at the opera house in Madrid, I suppose. But couldn't you find someone?'

'No, really, Liz . . .'

'The kind of man Mandy needs,' she went on, 'would be connected with the party scene, clued up about money, free to travel and willing to go to Spain.'

'Do you imagine that describes anyone I know, my angel?'

She looked pensive. Major Whittley regarded her with interest but said nothing.

Desultory conversation took them through the remains of their drinks. As they took their leave, Traumont tactfully reminded them that everything they had learned today must remain classified. 'We still have much work to do,' he said. 'M Whittley and I rely on your discretion.'

'Of course.'

'You will be contacting Mlle Mandy?'

'Oh, of course – to offer condolences.'

'She's staying at her sister's flat in Maida Vale. There is some talk of selling, so she is getting rid of her sister's clothes and so forth. You should contact her there.'

Greg said, 'Politeness obliges us to ring her, to say how sorry we are. But that's as far as it will go.'

'You'll say nothing to counteract the way we've been handling things, however?'

'We won't meddle, if that's what you mean.'

They were conducted to the door. Unperturbed by the acerbity of the responses from the crown prince, Traumont went on, 'Nerincourt will take you anywhere you wish to go – back to Avignon, or to some other destination. The major and I thank you for your cooperation.'

They shook hands all round with great civility. Whittley looked at Liz with a slight frown, retaining her hand a moment longer than seemed necessary. But he made no move to put his thought into words. She gave no sign that she had understood.

But she had something in mind.

Twenty

They asked Agent Nerincourt to set them down in Villeneuve-les-Avignon.

They walked along the Avenue Peri, she with her arm round his waist and he hugging her by the shoulders. The weather was now back to mild and bright yet in her thin jacket Liz felt cold. She burrowed against the warmth of Greg's car coat.

'You think I'm hard hearted because I don't want to help Mandy with this Marbella thing,' he murmured.

'Not at all.'

'A couple of hours with her is enough to make me want to strangle her. And as to trying to guide her through a business matter . . .'

'I know what you mean. All the same,' she remarked, 'we ought to look in on her. She does sound as if she needs a shoulder to cry on.'

'We could just send her some flowers.' He was accustomed to sending flowers in congratulation after a good performance, and sometimes in commiseration after a disaster.

Her conscience was bothering Liz. She'd had some very unsympathetic thoughts about Mandy. 'I'll do it on my own, Greg. I have to get back to London anyway. I could go and see her tomorrow.'

'Oh, Liz . . .' It was a sigh produced by guilt. His sense of duty told him he ought not to leave Liz on her own to cope with the grieving sister.

'We'll go together,' he said. 'But I really do have to be in Vienna next week, and before then I've got to get home to Geneva. I've got to speak to Robert Jäger and give him those operetta scores. So I truly can't spend long in London.'

'Darling, it's all right. Just a couple of days, that's all. I want to see what this so-called bereavement counsellor is achieving.'

'Well . . .' he said. 'That's a thought.'

He'd had a feeling when the bereavement counsellor was mentioned that she was some kind of lookout, put in place to make sure Mandy didn't rock the boat. Perhaps they had an obligation to see that all was well.

They walked until they felt they'd shaken off some of the depression brought on by their interview with the intelligence officers. They had to reconcile themselves to the idea that Waters, responsible for the death of two people, was probably never going to be caught.

'I can't bear it that he's going to go free,' she mourned

'Free?' He considered the word. 'It's not my idea of freedom. He's going to have to hide from now on. He's probably going to rely for his safety on men who despise him. They know he's only in it for the money—'

'Whereas you think the rest of them are idealists?' she broke in with scorn. 'Huh! Grashenko isn't much of an idealist, is she? Talking her head off, in retaliation for the fact that he's ditched her.'

'Well, some terrorists . . . they *do* have their own version of high ideals. But of course it would be naïve to think everyone on their network is devoted to "the cause",' he mused. 'No. Perhaps, since Waters is only in it for the money, someone in the network will sell him out for the same reason.'

'Well, perhaps.' She shook her head. 'But let's not hold our breath in expectation.'

They caught a bus to Avignon railway station, where they parted. Greg had business to clear up. To his great satisfaction he'd done more than break even with the events he'd put on for January in the Winter Festival: the young and handsome Robert Jäger's two recitals had made a profit, but even more pleasing was the fact that Hildegarde of Bingen – dead for centuries – had brought in a full house. Now he had to pay the bill for the rehearsal studio, for the hire of the Salle Dubois, for the printing of recital programmes – a tidying up process.

Liz went straight to the hotel. Once she had packed for him, she sat down at the telephone. She booked seats on the early evening flight, then she rang Mandy to let her know they were coming.

'Oh . . . it's you . . . how marvellous to hear from you,' Mandy cried. And then, off the phone to someone nearby, 'It's Liz Blair – I told you about her, you know?'

Liz heard an indistinct response. Mandy went on, 'That's Frances – she came for lunch, we're going through some stuff together.'

'One of your friends from the Mayfair flat?'

'No, no, she's with the special investigating team – well, at least, she's not exactly with them, they introduced her to me – I don't know what I'd have done without her.' A giggle, as if she were alerting the helpful Frances to these words of praise. Frances said something that sounded like, 'It's been a pleasure.'

Well, good. Mandy wasn't going to pieces. Liz said, 'Greg and I are flying over this evening. We thought we'd drop by – perhaps tomorrow?'

'Oh, yes – how lovely – just a minute.' A little pause while a conversation took place. She's asking Frances if it's OK, thought Liz, and wondered whether that was good or bad. Did Frances have total control? What sort of a person might she be? 'Yes, that'll be fine, Liz. Frances will be here. I'd like you to meet her.'

'Some time after ten tomorrow morning?'

'Great. Yes, lovely. Love to Greg. See you.'

She sat for a few minutes thinking it over. Frances was a trained psychiatrist, she'd been told. So her attendance on Mandy had to be for the good. All the same, Frances couldn't be there for ever. Shipping Mandy off to Marbella might be one way to solve the security problem but surely she ought to have other options? It wasn't enough to tidy her away like an old case file. Liz thought about it, trying to look at Mandy as if she were some clueless teenager in need of career guidance. Which, despite her more than thirty years, was how she appeared to Liz.

At last, nodding to herself in approval, she called a London fashion shop. Its owner greeted her with pleasure, and there followed the obligatory recollections of clothes that had been a success and mourning over the failures. 'Now I want to ask you something, Oscar,' she said when the moment was right. 'Are you still thinking about your project?'

A long dissertation on his plans followed. She made encouraging sounds then she in her turn talked for some time. He listened with surprise and appreciation as she set some ideas before him.

Greg came in as she put down the receiver. She told him their flight was booked. 'Then I've just got to pay the hotel bill and we can be off,' he said.

They glanced about at the room they had shared during these hectic days. He thought to himself that Liz was so tolerant of him and his strange life: moving about the world putting on performances of music that meant nothing to her, always under the critical eye of gossip columnists who longed to catch him out doing something un-royal, often rather pressed for money because though gossip columnists hinted at crown jewels salted away, that wasn't the case. And she knew moreover that the ex-Queen Mother Nicoletta disapproved of her entirely.

Yet she loved him. And he loved her. It was strange. Thank God for it, he said to himself.

They drove to Nice-Côte-d'Azur where he put the Mercedes in the long-term car park. They caught the next flight to London.

At Heathrow they took the Tube to her flat. It wasn't very late but they were exhausted. They'd had the kind of day that took a harsh toll on the spirits, on the inner strength of the heart. They had a quick meal in a nearby café and went to bed to find comfort in each other.

When Greg awoke next morning, Liz was absent from her side of the bed. Gone jogging, he groaned to himself, and nearly went back to sleep. But then he recalled they were going to visit Mandy. He rolled out and dragged himself into the shower. As he was shaving he heard Liz return. 'Good morning!' she called cheerily. It was her one fault, he told himself. She insisted on being bright first thing in the morning.

Mandy greeted them with a drooping head. She had gone into mourning, her clothes in total contrast to anything else Liz had seen her wear. Black miniskirt, dark-grey sweater, plain black tights, flat-heeled black shoes. Even her hair was subdued in a plain pony-tail. She wore no make-up.

'I've missed you so much,' she cried, casting herself on the breast of the crown prince.

'Mandy, my dear, how have you been getting on?' he asked. Over her head he saw Liz looking askance, and tried to disengage himself.

'Oh, it's all so awful,' she sobbed. 'If it weren't for Frances, I'd lose my mind.'

A young-middle-aged woman came from the living room into the hall. 'How do you do?' she said. 'I'm Mrs Gibbs.' Her glance told them that she knew who they were, that she'd been clued up by her chief, Major Whittley. 'I'm just helping out while Mandy feels she needs me.'

They shook hands. Liz noticed that it was Frances who made the hostess gesture, inviting them into the living room, where cups were set out on a low table. 'I'll just fetch the coffee.' She disappeared towards the kitchen. Clearly she'd spent enough time there to be totally familiar with her surroundings.

Greg studied Mandy. She'd dried her tears but she had a lost look, and there was something about her that suggested a recent indulgence in tranquillizers. No matter how competent Mrs Gibbs might be, she had no power to stop Mandy from acquiring and taking something to form a barrier against harsh reality.

Mandy gestured them to seats then launched into a long and rather muddled account of her meetings with what she called 'the special team of investigators'. 'They were really awfully nice,' she insisted. 'You know that French detective – M Traumont – he came over specially to speak to me in person. He spoke perfect English so I didn't need you here to translate, Greg, but I really have missed you so much. You're such a *reliable* person.'

'We met M Traumont. We had quite a long talk, quite a serious talk.'

'Yes, well, I'm going to put all that behind me,' she said, in tearful determination. 'I'm going to make a fresh start. Aren't I, Frances.'

Frances had come in with the coffee. 'Yes, Mandy, a new beginning. When you feel up to it.' The prince noted her beautiful contralto voice, guaranteed to soothe anyone in trouble. She was clad in a trim dress of grey flannel with trimmings of white piqué. To the experienced eye of Liz, it looked as if she had inherited it from her mother – or she was into 1955 retro. Or perhaps Mr Gibbs liked her in that sort of thing – if there was a Mr Gibbs.

Whatever the provenance, her dress gave her an air of utter integrity and efficiency. Like an old-fashioned secretary, perhaps. But the watchful eyes had authority hidden behind them. She had a job to do, and she was doing it little by little.

'Oh, I'm feeling better all the time, aren't I?' Mandy turned to Greg and said with pride, 'You'd hardly recognize me these days. There's a lot to do here but I'm dealing with it bit by bit. The worst is Barbara's clothes . . .' She paused a moment, and despite her claim of improvement, tears glimmered again. 'Poor love,' she said, 'she was clued up about newspaper work and all that but really . . . her clothes sense . . . All good labels, of course, but she simply didn't know how to choose well from the fashion viewpoint. So I'm boxing everything up and I'm going to give it to the Sally Ann – aren't I, Frances?'

'And then we'll put the flat up for sale, dear.'

'Yes, that's next, and do you know' – Mandy turned in pleased expectation to her guests – 'I'm told it's worth *hundreds of thousands*. ' She spoke in the tones of one who had never had much in her bank account. Greg guessed that she probably lived to the limit of what she earned as a cosmetics consultant, and perhaps beyond it.

'You haven't thought of moving in here permanently?' Liz suggested.

Greg gave her a glance of reproof. He didn't want the conversation to turn to matters like that, or the next thing would be the move to Marbella and Mandy would be begging him to go with her as interpreter.

And it seemed he was right, because Mandy swept on, 'Oh, I couldn't live *here*! It's too . . . lofty . . .' She glanced up at the high ceiling of the living room. 'And plain . . . minimalist . . . Of course I could redecorate. I had some of the girls here from my flat – you know, where I've been sharing – and they said it could be livened up. Some neon, like perhaps bar signs, and perhaps a bit of paint. But . . . I've been thinking – I love the sunshine, you know, and I've been wondering if I couldn't start somewhere new. Where it doesn't get dark and gloomy like it does here. One of the resort towns, sort of. In Spain, or somewhere.'

Frances was nodding approval. Greg kept carefully silent. To his surprise Liz took up the opening at once. 'But do you speak Spanish, Mandy?'

'Me? Goodness, no. I absolutely failed every language exam at school, and that was only French. Never took Spanish. I'm just not cut out for that sort of thing. Not academic, me.'

'Oh, I sympathize,' Liz laughed. To the ears of her lover, it sounded insincere. But then he didn't understand what she was up to. 'I'm in the same boat,' she swept on. 'That's why if I were going to settle abroad, I'd go where everybody spoke English—'

'Well, everybody in the Spanish resorts speaks English.'

'No, I meant, as their own language. You know, somewhere like Sydney, or perhaps California.'

'California!' breathed Mandy. California, the land of the Beautiful People, of the rich and famous, of Rodeo Drive, high style and night-life and never-ending parties.

Greg looked sharply at Liz. Liz was smiling at Mandy in encouragement. Frances Gibbs seemed rather taken aback but not prepared to intervene. Mandy said, 'I'd love to go there, of course but . . . you know . . . that's a really *big* step.'

'It's something to think about,' Frances murmured. She was eyeing Liz with speculation. Her bosses had suggested that Liz and Greg would help in the matter of getting Mandy safely out of circulation in London, where she might chatter to her friends about recent events. But California? Liz, however, seemed quite easy in her manner. So Frances gave her a faint frown and a nod, meaning, 'Let's see where you go with this.'

They were finishing their coffee. Mandy rose. 'Come and look at the stuff I've sorted out for the charity shops,' she said to Liz. 'There are one or two things you might like – you're more into outdoor clothes than me.'

Frances began to rise as if to accompany them. Liz blocked her from doing so by walking right in front of her. She and Mandy went out. Greg sat still, knowing from instinct that Liz wanted to take over.

In Barbara Rallenham's bedroom, clothes were draped everywhere – on hangers hanging from the picture rail, over the backs of chairs, hooked over the edge of the dressing-table mirror, and heaped on the bed. Mandy picked up a cloth coat, held it against herself, and surveyed the result in the mirror.

'Awful, isn't it? Who'd wear anything this colour?' The coat was a muted blue and grey check. Beautifully made, first-class material, but completely out of keeping with the colour tones that Mandy loved.

'Well, come to that, who'd have thought you'd be wearing blacks and browns?' Liz countered.

'Oh . . . well . . . that seemed only. . . you know, sort of respectful. You couldn't wear anything glitzy *here*.' She glanced around and sighed. 'Tell the truth, I feel different about clothes now. I mean, before . . . before it all happened . . . I think I was a bit show-offy . . .'

Liz didn't contradict it. Instead she paused a moment then said, 'You and Frances were chatting about making a fresh start. Don't you think you need some new clothes to help that along, Mandy?'

At once she brightened. 'That *would* be rather nice . . . But you know . . . Frances . . . she's not into that sort of thing.'

'But she's not with you all the time, surely? She just helps you handle stuff like getting the flat cleared up for sale. You could take a break and go out shopping.'

'I could, I suppose. Yes, I could, but you know . . . It's funny . . . I just don't feel like going on my own . . .'

'I'll go with you,' Liz said.

'You? Why, that's awfully nice of you! Because, I mean, your look is – well, it's quite *today*, isn't it?' Then a doubt entered her mind. 'But I don't know if it's me, exactly.'

'Don't let that bother you, Mandy. I've got a friend in the fashion business who might be quite good for you.'

'A designer?'

'No, he's a stylist. At the moment he and his wife are running a shop for the tweenies – it's called Cheep-Cheep—'

'Oh, I think I've heard of it. But I don't want to dress like a thirteen-year-old, Liz—'

'No, no, Oscar runs the shop as a money-making venture,

he doesn't necessarily give high marks to what's on sale there. But he and his wife know their stuff, and they want to move on by and by. So I thought if you met him and let him guide you a bit over what you want to buy, he could show you a look that might suit you. I mean, a special *you*.'

There's a charm in being told that there is a special *you*, a persona that needs a special guru for its care and development. Mandy put aside the pallid checked grey coat so as to study her reflection again. The brilliant butterfly of the past had been changed by sorrow into this dull moth. Might a sorcerer bring about yet another change, into something that might help her to live with her future?

'It would be nice to get out and do something sort of cheerful,' she murmured. 'Frances is great, you know, but we've been dealing with solicitors and registrars of death and estate agents and it's kind of . . . Well, I don't think she knows anything about the high-fashion roadshow. She doesn't even know what a caramel cappuccino is.'

Mandy's face was brightening. 'It *would* be nice,' she breathed.

'OK then, put on some make-up and I'll tell the others we're going.'

Mandy found her handbag under the piles of clothes on the bed. She opened it and tipped out its contents. 'I don't seem to have my cosmetics bag . . .' When she left her Mayfair flat for Maida Vale, the last thing on her mind had been make-up.

'Never mind,' said Liz. 'I've got some.' She supplied Estée Lauder lipstick and foundation.

Mandy accepted them but said, 'No mascara?'

'Have a look among Barbara's things.'

'Oh, Barbara's things,' Mandy said with a shrug, but looked in the dressing-table drawer. She sat down to experiment with what she found. Liz knew she'd spend some time trying out the items; after all, she'd built her career on cosmetics.

Among the stuff spilled out on the bed from the handbag were a couple of creased sheets of paper, worn at the folds. Liz recognized them for what they were; silently picking them up, she turned to go.

She went back to the living room, where Frances was just ending an explanation of her progress so far. '. . . So although a couple of her friends from the Mayfair flat have been here, I've managed to steer the conversation quite safely—' She broke off as Liz came in.

'We're going out,' Liz announced. 'We're going to buy some clothes.'

Greg started up. 'Liz, what are you doing?' he asked with some anxiety. 'You're not going to let her get back on that shaky roundabout? I met one of her friends, he wasn't what I'd call reliable—'

'No, wait, sir, it might be a good idea,' said Frances Gibbs. 'I've coaxed her along so far, but I don't think I'm the right person to help her back into the real world. My husband and I are academics, really, I just don't know the kind of world she's used to.'

'I'm trying something that may help,' Liz explained. ' I'm going to introduce her to a hard-working and hard-headed couple I know. You remember I spoke about them, Greg? Remember Cheep-Cheep?'

'What?'

'Cheep-Cheep. The dress shop I told you about, recently opened in town, T-shirts, khakis and cams for the goldilocks crowd.'

'I . . . er . . . it does seem to ring a bell.' He looked puzzled. 'What are cams?'

'Camouflage clothes. It was quite the rage for a while at the end of last year. Not real camouflage, you understand – stripes and wiggles in shades of blue or purple – but it's died off now, I think.'

'You amaze me.'

'And always will,' she assured him. 'So, anyhow, Oscar and his wife run the shop, but they long to go out and make a fortune in Santa Barbara. Oscar's been out there on business and feels it's his ideal home. The only thing that's preventing him is money.'

'Cheep-Cheep isn't doing well?'

'Oh, well enough, I think, but the margins are small because though his teenage customers are well-heeled, they expect that sort of stuff at street market prices. Given time, the shop will do well. But Oscar's dream is California.'

'He wants to go to California to sell street market clothes?'

'Don't be daft, darling. He wants to go there so he can raise his sights. But he needs help with the finance. The right premises might be a bit pricey. This is the world of the really *rich* rich. So my plan is to put him together with Mandy, while Frances is still here to keep an eye on things. If she approves, something might come of it. Oscar has talent, Mandy now has money, and Mrs Oscar has a level head. It could work.'

Greg didn't have the basic information to assess whether this was good or bad. Frances, however, looked encouraged. 'California. That might be good. But . . . there's something of a drug scene out there, Ms Blair.'

'Don't let that bother you too much. Gina – that's Mrs Oscar – she's dead against that sort of thing. If anyone can get Mandy on to the straight and narrow, it's Gina. And in many ways, it would be a sweetheart set-up. Oscar wants to offer the complete package to his clients – clothes, make-up, hair care. He'd do the clothes, Mandy could do the cosmetics, they could bring in somebody to do the hair, and Gina would look after the money.'

'But is Mandy in a fit state to make a decision as big as that?' Greg countered.

'It's not going to happen overnight, Greg. I'm taking her to meet Oscar. I already talked it over a bit with him, on the phone. We'll see what develops. And while it develops, it'll keep Mandy happy and stop her from thinking about this.'

She lifted her hand, opened it, and let the folded papers fall on the coffee table.

Frances opened them out. They were photocopies of the sketches Liz had made, of Colin Waters and Estelle Grashenko, according to the description supplied by Mrs Dandry.

'Oh, marvellous!' cried Mrs Gibbs. 'There are copies of those in the files, but I'd no idea she had any!'

'Better if she didn't have them. They can only remind her of things she's better forgetting.'

'Thank you,' she said. 'I'll take them, if I may.'

'Sure thing. Mandy and I are going in a minute. What will you do, Mrs Gibbs? Do you want to come?'

'By no means! I'll go out with you but I'll head for the office to catch up on some paperwork.'

'You won't want to come,' Liz told Greg. 'You have less affinity for fashion than a lawn-mower.'

'Right as always, my dearest,' he agreed.

Mandy came in. There was a noticeable difference in her appearance. Partly it was due to the skilled application of a little make-up, partly it was because she had something cheerful to look forward to. 'I'm ready,' she said.

'OK, so are we,' said Liz. They all began to move towards the hallway for coats and briefcases.

Greg got close enough to Liz to give her a hug. She was going out to spend probably a whole afternoon in the company of someone she didn't really like, and all out of the goodness of her heart.

'Shall I see you back at the flat?' he whispered in her ear.

'Yes, we'll go out for an evening meal, shall we? I don't want to bother with food shopping, because after I've got Mandy together with Oscar I want to go out to Walthamstow. There's an old lady I'd like to look in on.' She meant Miss Lessiter but didn't mention the name for fear Mandy caught it and had unhappy thoughts.

'Right you are then,' Greg said. 'I've got a thing or two to do. See you later.'

They all parted outside. Greg went back to the flat, to collect the record album of the old operetta. He felt he owed his fellow music lover at least a glimpse of it.

Wilson Pollard wasn't too enamoured of it. 'Bartos,' he muttered when they met over a glass of wine in a Westminster watering hole. 'Do I want to bother transferring her to CD?'

'She sang a great Kundry in *Parsifal.*'

'Yes, but here she's singing some nonsense called *The Dollar Princess*.'

'Oh, well, if you're not interested, I'll just take it with me when I fly back tomorrow,' said the prince.

'Wait, wait, I didn't say I wasn't interested . . .' He closed the cover on the four long-play records. 'And I still get the Claudia Muzio record to copy?'

'Absolutely, Poll. I'll post it to you when I get home.' Greg felt he owed Poll for the information about Colin Waters and his granting of permits for the export of special metals. This had led on to Sir Rupert Modd, the industrialist. Without the information Sir Rupert had supplied, Colin Waters' machinations would never have been uncovered.

Poll toasted him with his wine glass. 'You're a good chap, Grego, even if you are a royal. I'm your friend for life.'

'Then tell me a good place to go to do some shopping,' said the prince. 'I want to buy someone a little present.'

He was reunited with Liz at mid-evening. She reported success with the introduction of Mandy to Oscar and Gina. 'I think something may come of it,' she mused. 'Gina adopted what you might call a maternal attitude to her, although they're more or less the same age. It's just the kind of touch that Mandy seems to need at the moment – someone who sort of takes the place of her sister.'

'And you went to see Miss Lessiter, didn't you?'

'Yes.' She sighed. 'She's decided to go into sheltered housing. All that business with Mrs Barnell really shook her up. She says she can't go on living there, because of the memories. Even though everything there is going to change, mind you. It looks as if Tommy Shanigan is going to have to move out. The house has been inherited by some distant relation in Stockport or somewhere, and they're selling it to a property firm. Tommy couldn't afford the sort of rent they're likely to ask.'

'The more so as his off-the-record pay cheque from Parady has been cancelled.'

'Exactly.'

'In a way, I'm sorry for him,' Greg said. 'He just got caught in the wheels of the juggernaut.'

'Yes, so many people did.' She sighed 'And all for just a handful of dust.'

'Come on, sweetheart,' he coaxed 'Don't let's be unhappy. I have to fly back to Avignon tomorrow to collect my car. And then it's home to tidy up a few things before I set off for Vienna.'

'Oh, Greg . . .' She couldn't help but feel mournful. 'It might be weeks before we can arrange to meet again . . .'

They went out to dinner in a nearby bistro. When they got to the dessert and coffee stage, the crown prince produced a little envelope with something rather bulky inside it. 'A gift to remind you of me when we're apart.'

She opened the envelope to find a little box. Inside was a

ring, an Art Deco setting in some silvery metal, a small shining stone gleaming up at her.

'I promised you should have a zircon ring, remember?' he reminded her.

'Oh, *darling*!' She slipped it on. It was a little loose but looked charming. Nothing too ostentatious and glittery, just the kind of thing that could be worn with almost any kind of outfit. Not new, but the work of some artist of the twenties or thirties.

Greg had found it by the recommendation of Pollard Wilson, who had rung his wife to ask for counsel about buying a love token. She had suggested Camden Passage. There, quietly persistent, he'd found something he thought Liz would approve of and that he could afford.

'Do you like it?' he asked.

'I adore it!'

She kept it on. That night when they were making love he could feel it against the muscles of his back while she strained him closer and closer yet.

Next day at the Nice airport, he redeemed his car and made ready for the long drive back to Geneva, some three hundred kilometres on a cool dull day. He switched on the heater. The rush of air brought the very faintest remembrance of her perfume, L'Air du Temps. He breathed it in, thinking about her. He wondered if she would ever work out that the stone wasn't a zircon, but a diamond set in white gold.

But as he pictured her with her hand held out, inspecting the ring on her slim finger, he felt it wouldn't be a mystery to her for long. Knowing Liz, he thought she'd probably have taken the ring to have it valued before the day was out.

When he rang her tonight, he'd ask her.

HALIW MYST
BARCL